DEATH OF A MONK

Alon Hilu

Death of a Monk

TRANSLATED
FROM THE HEBREW
BY

Evan Fallenberg

Harvill *Secker*
LONDON

Published by Harvill Secker, 2006

2 4 6 8 10 9 7 5 3

© Alon Hilu and Xargol Books, 2004
English translation © Evan Fallenberg, 2006

Alon Hilu has asserted his right under the Copyright,
Designs and Patents Act 1988 to be identified as the author of this work

First published with the title Mot Ha-Nazir
by Xargol Books, Israel

First published in Great Britain in 2006 by
HARVILL SECKER
Random House
20 Vauxhall Bridge Road
London SW1V 2SA

Random House Australia (Pty) Limited
20 Alfred Street, Milsons Point, Sydney,
New South Wales 2061, Australia

Random House New Zealand Limited
18 Poland Road, Glenfield,
Auckland 10, New Zealand

Random House South Africa (Pty) Limited
Isle of Houghton, Corner of Boundary Road & Carse O'Gowrie,
Houghton 2198, South Africa

The Random House Group Limited Reg. No. 954009
www.randomhouse.co.uk

A CIP catalogue record for this book is available from the British Library

This book was published with the financial assistance of the
Institute for the Translation of Hebrew Literature

ISBN 1843432765
ISBN 9781843432760 (from Jan. 07)

Papers used by Random House are natural, recyclable products made
from wood grown in sustainable forests; the manufacturing processes conform to the
environmental regulations of the country of origin

Typeset in Adobe Jenson
by SX Composing DTP, Rayleigh, Essex
Printed and bound in Great Britain by
Clays Ltd, St Ives PLC

Then along came this affair and it dawned upon me for the first time that I belong to an unfortunate, slandered, despised and dispersed people that has nonetheless been spared annihilation.

Moses Hess, *Rome and Jerusalem*, 1862

PART ONE
TOMASO

1

I had no love for Father and Father had no love for me and the two of us had no love for one another, or any other way there is of restating and reshaping the sentence of our non-love.

He had, Father, a pair of large, pendulous testicles and a holy staff that gave off a pleasant fragrance, and when the maids bathed him in our home these would be exposed together as a couple, dripping a thousand drops of water.

He had swarthy, expressive feet which he would cross, one over the other, on the small stool in the *alkhosh*, the courtyard of our spacious home, and occasionally he would root about between the toes and sniff with pleasure the bit of scum that clung to them.

I almost never saw Father during the day; it was his custom to rise early, pass quickly through the avenue of fruit orchards on the grounds of our home, which would cause him to grumble about the delay involved in walking its length, and attend to his thriving business concerns: lending with interest to peasants, releasing from customs goods that arrived from the far-off countries of Europe and taking care of his interests as far as his eye, which was never satisfied, would counsel and lead him.

Only at eventide, when the maids opened before him the carved wooden doors, would he return home, his presence filling the rooms at once like the blast of a ram's horn at the conclusion of a fast day. Straight away the members of the household would encircle him, excitedly dancing attendance on him, *Allah yatik ela'afia*, May God grant you health, and hastening to recount for him the day's news, starting with all manner of tales to vilify me.

Maman, Father's statuesque, long-haired, amply bosomed wife, bedecked with golden rings and chains, who throughout the day pretended to be my good friend and dress me up in silk clothing in which to prance about her room, would lecture him about things I had said to my cross-eyed sister, Rachel, for example that I had teased her about her deformed eye and her grating voice, and my whingeing sister of the blue eyes and pure white skin would affirm it all, teary-voiced, adding her own evidence, blasphemous notes that I had supposedly sent her and blessings I had bestowed upon her wishing a slow recovery for that malformed eye and, at the apex of her account, her pupils rolling like buttons fallen from tattered clothing, she would add that I had teased her with the words *Imek muvhama alleh eljamous*, that while pregnant with her my mother had gazed upon a water buffalo, which explained her perpetually angry countenance.

And while Maman and Rachel embraced and consoled themselves in one another's arms, my younger brother Meir would recount, each evening, each time in a different manner, how Aslan had confiscated his playthings, how Aslan had taken his garments and how this Aslan had a finger in every pie of mischief, and lo, I can picture Father's eyebrows contracting, the hairs protruding and erect, as he loosens his belt, the siblings grabbing hold of me in my tunic, which was always clean and pleasant as were all the garments I loved, and they convey me to wrathful Father, to his belt that is lashing my tiny feet, stroke after stroke, to the accompaniment of a long and vociferous string of curses, from the mild Stupid! to blessings of May God

4

take your soul, *Allah yela'anek*, or *Allah yah'dek*, after which I would not cry, nor shed a tear, but would walk, snivelling to my room, shoulders stooped and head bent, leaning for support on the arms of one of the servants.

My happy friend, while I impart these words to you, and as you record them with your industrious fingers and with expression in your large brown eyes, I would ask your indulgence in reviving for a few moments the former, innocent image of Aslan, the image of a hollow-cheeked youth whose days were as roses, plagued by persecution at the hands of members of his household; still, it is incumbent upon you to recall that his excessive wickedness is yet to come, and that you must not be bound to him by bonds of love, and further, you must establish no hard and fast hatred for his enemies, rather, take extreme caution to avoid his infectious, burgeoning evil.

Let us return to my father, seen through the eyes of young Aslan, who is steeped in senseless hatred. Indeed, when Father's thunderous voice rose from one of the rooms during one of his frequent disputes with Maman – the two would quarrel nearly every evening, after I had been given my lashing, about matters of great importance, such as why it was that his turban was once again stained and dirty, and why there was insufficient water in his narghile, and why once again the cesspit at the edge of the fruit orchards was filling the air with a putrid odour – when their voices rose and overwhelmed me, I would return to the date palms with their succulent fruits, a pure and cloudless desert day, and the sound of hooves reaches my ears and I am riding a wild stallion, tall leather boots on my feet and a sickle-shaped sword brandished in my hand, my arms no longer thin and spotted but thick, firm, hardened, and my legs are no longer blighted and evil, they sport the light calves of an experienced rider, and they push into the ribs of the horse and cause him to gallop and increase his speed, and my eyes do not covetously drink in all the beauty and grandeur of the world; instead they are generous and pure and appreciative, and I ride there, bare-chested and bronzed, exposed to the sun, my trusted ally.

I would bathe alone, never at the *hammam* in Kharet Elyahud, the Jewish Quarter, with the other men, but with a bucket of hot water in the room at the edge of the fruit orchards, so that no unfamiliar eye could catch sight of me, and I could gaze in wonder at my feeble body: the pale and bloated belly, which had not seen a ray of sunlight for some time and was always hidden under thick clothing; the toes, as separate and distant from one another as a band of brothers in hot dispute; the brittle fingers, unfit for labour, mottled pink and red; the shoulders, made like two marbles that roll and sway in every direction. And in summertime, when a tardy sunbeam flickered suddenly through the window and lit up the small room, tiny pores that covered my skin in flocks would reveal themselves and I would regard them without comprehending their meaning.

The long days and weeks when Father was absent from the city, travelling to Aleppo or Sidon and from there by ship across the sea, were my moments of happiness and pleasure; upon returning from the Talmud Torah school, when my evil and angry sister had turned her blue eyes to her games and my little brother was preoccupied with matters in his room, I would circle the large apricot tree that stood in the centre of the *alkhosh*, tossing crumbs of bread to the goldfish sailing the fish pond at the foot of the tree, and then with hesitation tinged with anticipation I would ask one of the servants to request an audience for me with Maman, and when the response came – that she awaited me in her room – I would walk slowly to her, close the door behind me, and give myself over to her cursory kisses and sugary hugs.

Then we would spread about the costly bolts of fabric she had had sent by special delivery from shops in Europe, and alongside them garments and dresses she had obtained from sharp-eyed local traders or from the travelling merchants who sometimes visited our estate. There were long-sleeved dresses adorned with feathers, and dresses ornamented with shiny beads and shells, and I would draw the choice cloths to my chest and inhale their fragrance, and when Maman was certain that no evil eyes were watching us, waiting to tell Father about our forbidden acts, she would remove the brooch pinning up her tresses in one swift motion, freeing her hair to flow to her waist, and then she would remove my tunic, momentarily fearful of my naked body dotted with the mysterious pores, and she would wrap me in an evening gown of her own choosing, a gown that covered my legs all the way to the toes and twisted around my arms and, in order to enhance the excitement, she would slip a pair of black, patent-leather shoes over my small feet with the disputatious toes, commanding me to sit upon her bed while she passed a variety of powders and coloured lotions over my face, after which I would stand before her glowing visage.

Not a soul knew of the garments I would don from time to time, not even the servants toiling in our home. Once, only once, while we were under the mistaken impression that he was off somewhere tending to one of his numerous business concerns, Father returned home early. His shoes hammered the marble floor as he rounded the fish pond, while Maman rushed frantically to strip me of my gown and remove the spots of make-up, almost ripping the expensive fabrics from my body so that Father would not catch us in our misconduct, and when he entered and found me in the room, sitting upon his bed, he grabbed hold of me at once by the forearm and faced us, awaiting our explanation.

She would not grant me the wink of an eye confirming our complicit secret, not even the quickest flash of mischief between conspirators: Maman rushed to inform him of my conduct during his absence, how I had come to her and bothered her and recited coarse poetry to her learned from the boys at the Talmud Torah, how I was uncouth and uncultured, more evil even than the wild Bedouin who plundered our caravans, and that my place was not in the pampering bedroom of my childhood, but in the prison dungeon beneath the Saraya fortress, seat of the governor of Damascus, where the cries of tortured prisoners could be heard each night. And when Father heard all this, his eyebrows became enraged once again, and he said I was worse even than the Harari brothers, may their name and memory be blotted from the earth, and he pushed me outside the room, towards the marble fountain standing in the shade of the apricot tree, and shoved my head into the small fish pond, the permanent residence of the goldfish, and pressed upon my neck until I choked and retched and did not know what was to become of me, and she called to him from behind, her breasts ample, protruding: Harder, deeper, teach him a good and bitter lesson.

I fared no better at the Talmud Torah, in spite of the good name of my family. Father and all the uncles were important personages, pillars of the community, and our family name – Farhi – stirred up envious whispers, though the exception was and always would be Aslan.

Farhi – yes, these were the sons of wealth, of roses, of merry days, but as far as Aslan was concerned: no, and again, no. Of Lazy Aslan it was said *Alvaga varda valtiz farda*, His face was as a rose, his arse like a pillow; Aslan was weak of character and prone

8

to tears, Aslan had a strange way of walking, prancing about and wiggling his bottom, Aslan was thin and fragile and quick to fall, Come, let us push Aslan, let us prod his ribs with dark objects, let us press upon his eye sockets and break his teeth.

My only friend throughout all my years in the Talmud Torah was Moussa. He, too, was narrow-boned, dreamy, his eyes blue and his hair fine and light unlike that of the Jews; he, too, was despised by many pupils and together we would remove ourselves to the corner of the room during break, and while the other children were tugging on one another's sleeves and teasing each other and stirring up quarrels and strife, Moussa would gaze into my eyes and I into his and we would recite poems that we loved, old, forgotten poems, poems that would never pass the lips of a soul in the Jewish Quarter, lovers' poems telling of succulent fruits in the orchards and the sweetness of nectared flowers in full bloom and sometimes, when no one was about to see or hear, Moussa would begin to hum, and his humming voice would rise to song, and in a clear and tender voice he would sing to a distant lover who had passed beyond the hills and mountains, never to return:

Min badak ahgor khali
Ya a'aeb an aynya

To you I will depart from myself
You, who are far from my eyes

And Moussa would gaze into my eyes and I into his and our eyes would fill with tears and we would sob, and on slips of paper we passed between us we drew small and feeble figures, females, grasping and clinging to one another, large yellow flowers adorning them to the right and left.

9

Once, when we believed we were hidden from view, I held Moussa's hand and he held mine and we regarded one another, drawing closer and diving deep into the other's eyes, but the other children noticed us and began to call us names and in no time the rumour that Moussa and Aslan were beloved and congenial with one another like the biblical David and Jonathan spread through the Jewish Quarter, and from that moment on they did not leave us alone or take respite from us, from the morning they would mock our love and pinch our bottoms and throw stones from the River Barada and muddy dirt from the streets at us, and from behind this barrage, this downpour, I am there, at the head of a bare-chested merchant army on its way into blood-drenched battle, a hoisted flag and a lance and dagger in my hands, poised to behead my frightened enemies, to rout them from my patch of desert, their decapitated heads the path I tread on my glorious way.

From my bedroom in our spacious home I hear Maman and Father speaking in low voices of my disgrace, for the rumour about Moussa and me has reached their ears, though this time his thunderous voice is not heard, Father has a different method, and I know nothing but this: that at the end of seven days from the time Moussa held my hand and I held his and we spoke words of goodness and grace, Moussa ceased to appear at the Talmud Torah and even when I asked and investigated I heard no mention of his departure, the only sound was that of children's laughter as they hurled taunts, mud and slander at me.

I had three uncles, Murad, Meir and Joseph, each pot-bellied like Father, their bodies covered in short, frizzy hair, their shoulders broad and thighs fat, their eyebrows arcing from one to the other and their eyes always scheming, their laughter vulgar and their conversation insipid.

On Fridays, when we met in the private synagogue the brothers built near Joseph Farhi's home so as to avoid mingling with the poor and wretched Jews, they would send evil looks my way, eyeing my stooped and crooked back, my long and spindly frame; they denounced me for abstaining from eating meat and other delicacies, for their own children were large and healthy, each one boasting a pair of chins, and Father joined in their laughter and they threatened to blow me down in order to demonstrate just how feeble my grasp on solid ground was, for I was *sabakh balah ravakh*, a shadow devoid of life.

After days such as these I would descend to the cellar of our home, beneath the kitchen, where a large and gloomy pantry stood, teeming with clay pots and glass jars filled with the very best of everything, and I would open lids and stuff apricot marmalades and date jams into my mouth, heedlessly shovelling the sugared fruits between my lips and swallowing them without desire or pleasure in order to add fat to my body like theirs, and from there I would move to the beans and lentils and other legumes, even though they had been neither blanched nor boiled and had stood for months in their cool glass jars, and I would take handfuls of them and chew them and reach the brink of vomiting, but still I would force, compel and will myself to swallow the foul-tasting mixture, and I imagined that I could discern, between the walls of the dim cellar, pairs of snake eyes boring into me, for they were fattening me up in preparation for their early summer feast.

At holiday meals I was compelled to see the faces of my relatives and watch as they occupied themselves in yet another orgy of drinking and eating, swallowing the *ma'udeh* and the *sfikhah* without pausing to chew and, on occasion, in spite of protestations by the Khaham-Bashi, chief rabbi of the Jewish

Quarter, they would invite Jewish women, dancers and singers, to strut and sing before them; but worst of all is the Seder night of the Passover holiday, when I must watch them all for many hours on end and listen to their collective whispering, and I shoot unrequited glances at my beloved mother of the black hair, willing her to hide me between her breasts and save me from the claws of the avaricious women my uncles have taken for themselves, but she turns her face from me, and here is Aunt Khalda, Meir's wife, coarse of flesh and voice, calling to me in the presence of the uncles and the cousins and the brothers and fathers and mothers: Aslan, *Allah yahdek, ta'el hon*! May Allah take you, come over here! And she quizzes me and poses difficult questions and if I answer she is quick to mimic my voice, small and weak, in her sharp and mocking tone, after which all present respond with a chorus of laughter, and I am horrified to see Maman among them, her skin shining and her jewels sparkling, adding her own taunts about my manner of speech, which is dissimilar to that of other boys and not at all in the way of men, but rather as though I were a featherless chick, bald and blind as he emerges from an unfamiliar shell; and the story of the Exodus from Egypt and the preparation of the *matzah*, the bread of affliction, and the words of Rabbi Tarfon and Rabbi Eliezer in Bnei-Brak as recited from the Passover *haggadah* mix with slanderous exaggerations about Aslan, Aslan, Aslan.

What sort of life was this and what was its purpose and towards what was it flowing? I did not have the answers to these questions, and lo, I pictured myself hanged in the large square at the entrance to the Saraya for a crime whose nature I did not know, or plunged into the River Barada to drown in its chilly waters or escaped to the hills of Lebanon, climbing to the summit of Mount Tzalkhaya from which, like the young virgins married off to old men against their will, I would throw myself down, down, pitching my body into the void to bring to an end these days of senselessness.

At the outbreak of a plague in the city I would try to become infected, and when snow covered the streets I would roll about in it in an attempt to fall ill, and when the governor of the city, Ibrahim Pasha, would pass by, I tried to mock him, so that he would find me guilty, but none of this ever came to pass, and Aslan remained alive and his health remained constant.

In the wretched days following the springtime Passover holiday, when a thick, desert dust covered the city and the smell of summer clung to one's nostrils, it was my custom to leave my little room and make my way through the trees of the orchard then in full and glorious bloom and pass through the opening in the wall that encircled our home and continue from there through the narrow alleyways stinking of sewage, skirting the passers-by and donkey-drivers, past the crowded houses and pushing on from there to the main street of the Jews, passing the beet seller and the greengrocer and the butcher hawking their wares, bypassing Teleh Square, which was always teeming with people and merchants and shoppers and hordes of beggars, and from there straight on to the chicken market, where feathers blew in the hot, heavy desert wind and the blood of chickens stained the mud walls, and I would come to the filthiest corner at the edge of the souk, lift the lid on the rubbish bin used by the butchers, and grimace, poised to empty my innards outwards, down, towards Elnahar Alaswad, the Black River, wishing to deposit there vomit and bile and evil smells, might they depart from my body and descend and drain into the sewage canals of Damascus, but these clung to my chest like sinews and would not give in to the convulsions of my throat and gullet, and for a moment, when the sun appears through the haze that comes before the great hot days of summer, I am gripped with terror at the appearance of black figures in the filthy waters swirling beneath me, and I can see the slaughtered chickens screeching at their untimely deaths and the knife that slits their throats without mercy, and a fresh wave of convulsions pushes to expel itself but does not spew into Elnahar Alaswad; all but a single dangling drop of food swallowed but only partly digested falls and drowns in that water; and lo, it travels far away from my father's home and my mother's home and the homes of my uncles and their children and their evil laughter, to the villages of the simple farmers outside the borders of Damascus, to the desert, where the nights are cool and the hills naked and a wild mare is waiting there and I mount her, armed with a sword and lying in ambush for a caravan of heavy-hoofed camels laden with goods, their humps bursting, and I am waiting to plunder their wares and kill their guides with the sword, and from there, with great exultation, to gallop into the clear air; and suddenly a man is holding me from behind, and he raises my chin and wipes clean the remains of saliva, *Ya walad, shu am bitsavei hon*, Child, what are you doing here, and he returns me, feeble and dependent, to my father's home.

2

Flocks of black-winged cranes invaded the house during a storm, wreaking havoc among the pillows and comforters and spreading a spirit of evil among the curve-necked swans woven into the rugs; from there, to the sound of squawks and screeches, they scattered their long, pointed feathers and disappeared into hidden cellars under the tiled floors until that unwelcome time when they would reappear in flocks.

Who was Aslan and what were his intended paths in life and where was he headed and why were his manners and ways so twisted, his customs so crooked and perverse, why had it been necessary for him to suckle from his mother's breasts, don the clothing of children, develop his organs, grow taller; why were his limbs lengthening, his hair sprouting, his wormlike body stretching and growing and filling out, why was his body now covered with gills, his jaws becoming harder, stronger, his mouth producing bile, why was he so loathsome to other creatures, why did he live among them as a blood-sucking louse, devouring their marrow and awakening in them a prickling anger?

My happy friend, behold, not even a single hair has yet sprouted on your delicate skin, and you are a foundling, fatherless and motherless, the essence of sweetness and charm, never a complaint or cry issues from your mouth even when you are troubled with hard physical labour; how different is your path from that of our young friend Aslan, awash in senseless hatred and indulgence! Imagine this Aslan, lathering himself with Nablus soap in the little room at the edge of the orchard and at once comprehending the meaning of the pores covering his skin from head to toe in flocks, since from each pore he can now see a follicle of pale coloured hair joining its many many sister-hairs, and he hastens to examine his arms and legs and, as far as possible, his back, in order to observe the entire surface of his skin covered with sprouting hairs, now waiting in their hiding places, but in just a few months or even weeks they will become a frizzy black fuzz just like the frizzy black fuzz covering the bodies of Father and the uncles, Murad, Meir and Joseph.

From then on I would peek at Father on his return home without exchanging a word with him, I would steal after him like a cat of the dunghills as he dressed or changed clothes or removed his shirt in the overpowering heat, in order to catch sight of his smooth, fleshy feet above whose smoothness there was a line demarcating the start of a hairy fuzz that climbed up his body like moss, beginning in straight black lines on his calves, leaving small bald spots on his rounded knees and continuing to his thighs, where it curled and frizzed and turned a little darker, and then rose and wound itself around the pair of testicles adorned with veins and then became dense and compressed and very dark on Father's genitals, and from there spread out to great, boundless distances on the jellied flesh of his back, on his round belly, on his arms and chest, until it gathered into crowded black dots in the region of his face and stopped its uproar there, leaving his forehead clear and pure apart from the slight pauses where his eyebrows met and sometimes even his ears, where short, black hairs would peek out from time to time.

Were it possible to put a stop to this dance, to strip off this fur coat and the follicles heralding its onset, I would have taken up blades and razors and removed the fuzz from my body, alienating and abusing that hair; but the more I tormented and tortured them the more stubborn they became, and they were fruitful and multiplied, and the servants cast me scolding looks in regards to the hairy remains I left behind, which they sent tumbling into the latrine and onwards to the Black River.

Once again I am crying in my room. Not because of the abuses heaped upon me by my family – I have pushed them all from my thoughts – and not because of the taunts of my classmates in the Talmud Torah, for I am blind to them as they pass before me, and not because of Aunt Khalda's shouts when she spies me in the street, *Ta'el lahon ha khmar*, Come over here, you jackass! but because of my image as it is reflected in the Damascene mirror in my room, a mirror decorated with seashells and stars and five-sided shapes that trick the eye and appear as a large rebel army, and my reflection is quite strange: a light fuzz will soon cover my cheeks which means I must become like all men in shaving daily, just as Father does, and to entrust monthly to Yusuf *alkhalaq*, the barber, the hair on the back of my neck and the hair in my ears and the rebellious hairs that rise from my chest to mingle with the whiskers on my neck.

By the time the hair on my cheeks had become so thick and plentiful that the children were making my life at school an even bigger misery than previously, I began wandering the streets I knew well and despised, and without knowing why, I arrived at the door of Suleiman *alkhalaq*, one of the poorest barbers of our ranks, whose customers included flea-infested Jewish paupers and beggars whose pubic hair had been eaten away by stinging lice; six of these men were gathered just then and were playing a game of cards at Suleiman Negrin's barber's shop, which stood next to the Alifranj Synagogue.

Suleiman Negrin cast a look of great surprise at me as I stood on the threshold of his dark and meagre shop, wondering how it had come to pass that a son of the House of Farhi – men who had their tresses coiffed, their cheeks lathered and the hair on their necks pruned each month in their homes by the noted Muslim Yusuf *alkhalaq* – had descended to the rank and file, stepping daintily over the open sewage that flowed down the street.

Silence fell on the six paupers in Suleiman's shop; as for me, I was filled with blushing embarrassment over the silk clothing on my body and the scent of soap on my skin and the feeble voice that issued from my throat. I was about to depart, prepared to entrust my first shave to Yusuf, a jabberer and gossip who spoke vulgarities to me about the hair on women's heads as well as their private parts, and all sorts of other matters accompanied by laughter wrapped in narghile smoke, but the barber Suleiman, who was older than I by only a few years and like me was pilose and possessed of jet-black hair, banished his pauper guests and motioned for me to sit, and while noting with disgust the eyebrows that met one another in a long, thick arc, I obeyed, my head bowed, and sat on a low wooden stool. From atop the table in front of me Suleiman removed the remains of men's hair and jars filled with leeches used to cure all matter of illnesses, and with a flourish he spread over me a sort of dirty cloth serviette so that no dead hairs from my head would fall on to my body and tangle with the live ones; wordlessly he took in hand a razor and a wood-and-horsehair shaving brush and I was filled with awe at how I was sitting there in the way of men, on a low chair, and the barber was painting my cheeks with the same cream he used on other men and, lo and behold, I could picture them marching each morning by the legions, hundreds and thousands of men from all parts of the city, young men and old in the Jewish Quarter, the Christian Quarter, the Muslim Quarter, and the men in Bedouin tents and the men in merchants' caravans and men on the far side of the sea, all of them sprouting beards and moustaches and whiskers, combing, grooming, trimming their hair, and just like them here was I, for the first time, placing the stubble on my cheeks under Suleiman's blade and promising myself not to cry, not to shed a tear.

The barber passed his blade gently over my skin, occasionally smoothing the hair on my head, exclaiming about my jet-black, shiny locks and complimenting me on my beautiful clothes and cultivated manners, and from the corner of my eye I could discern the six paupers peering through cracks in the walls of Negrin's tiny barber's shop, straining to watch us in the gloom, all of them excited at the scene in front of them, watching us and smiling and laughing, and the touch of Suleiman's hands was very pleasing to me and I wished to linger there a while longer, far from my beautiful home and tidy room and the furnished *liwan* in which I was living out my days, I wished to remain with Suleiman and his crowd, and when the paupers could no longer contain themselves they piled in the shop, filling it with their gibber and jabbing one another with their elbows, telling me *Sahten*, Congratulations on your first shave, you are now *rajoul*, a man, and straight away they asked, Should we take him to a whore too, to carry out the ultimate act of a real man, what do you say? But Suleiman the barber told them, Leave him alone, we're dealing with a real prince here, not one for your cheap and dirty prostitutes, and he continued massaging my temples, and the touch of his fingers was exceedingly pleasing to me.

Before leaving the shop, while I was doling out a few coins to the paupers, who pretended to take offence at my gift, the barber pulled me to a small and dirty corner of his shop and moved his head so close to mine that his arced brow touched my forehead and his breath entered my nose and he asked if I would like to be engaged in friendship with him, because friendship with me seemed lovely to him and he was very interested in knowing everything there was to know about me.

And with the resulting protrusion that stood out from my tunic and the bashful smile this brought on, the barber whispered – a lecherous look in his green eyes – that I should come visit him that evening near Bab Alfouqara, the Paupers' Gate, three hours after the fourth cry of the muezzin. I did not respond, I merely slipped his fee into his hand and made my escape for home, a cloud of sharp-smelling cologne trailing after me which the beggars continued to sniff.

That very evening, when three hours had passed from the time of the muezzin's fourth call, I rose and set my face towards Bab Alfouqara, towards the reckless meeting with the barber, preparing excuses for my parents to explain my odd and hurried departure, in the evening, when the gates to the Jewish Quarter remained shut and the doors to the homes were closed and no one left or entered unless they were returning late from a party or looking for trouble. But then I filled myself with loathing at Suleiman's thick, dark eyebrows which flowed one to the other without charm or splendour, and this was how I managed to quash the excitement inciting the front of my tunic, and I joined my estranged family, to listen to their gossip about the nasty deeds and evil schemes of the Harari family, may their name and memory be blotted from the earth, chewing carrot stalks with them while we sat facing the apricot tree as it shed its leaves at the very heart of the Farhi family estate.

My happy friend, here you are, a foundling with no family, pining throughout your days for the images of your father and your mother whom you never knew, and I believe I discern in your eyes a certain amazement over Aslan, ensconced in a wondrous mansion, surrounded by members of his family, dressed in pleasant clothing and free of all laborious tasks – that in spite of all these he hates his life and hates his parents and hates himself, and I must reveal to your tender ears that there are still many more hates awaiting this lad. But let us not cross those bridges of evil until we reach them.

In the days that followed I was unable to visit the muddy lane that housed the barber's shop of Suleiman *alkhalaq*, but the memory of his green eyes pursued me everywhere, at times sparkling in the light of the morning sun and at times glowing in the darkness of night, and my thoughts kept wandering to the place mentioned by the barber, Bab Alfouqara, a neglected gate to the city sealed off generations earlier, with no way to enter or depart from it through the Jewish Quarter, hence my curiosity about the meaning of his invitation to meet me there at night-time; once again I found myself in turmoil, pining to go there at that very instant, but instead I remained curled up in my bed and did not move from it.

My parents spoke of the woman who in future I would take in marriage, when I had come of age, and they consulted and whispered among themselves and I overheard the names of young ladies, maidens, whom they counted on their fingers, Father's angry voice erupting on occasion: *La, ya khmara*, She is from Aleppo, do you wish to bring thieves into our home? After this he listed the considerations of profit and loss, the benefits, the status. I heard it all as if I had heard nothing at all.

Apart from my mother and sister and wide-hipped aunts, I did not know the female of the species, I had had neither positive nor negative contact with them, was unfamiliar with their ways and manners and with the secrets they kept hidden from men.

My classmates spoke vulgarly of a certain suppressed and hidden organ possessed by females called *khashush*, and the ways one had of reaching that place and ploughing it utterly; they told of demon dreams and the evil inclination that women awakened in men, and I could not understand these words and was not party to their fantasies; instead I was flooded with thoughts of Suleiman, whose fingers in my hair were exceedingly pleasant, so that one evening I returned to the place I had seen him last, determined to confront him, to question him about that place where he had wished to meet me: what was the purpose of his request and at what was he hinting, and these thoughts pursued one another in my head and I increased my pace, failing to notice the haberdashers collecting their wares or the coppersmiths rising from their workbenches; a hammer was pounding at my temples and a dark screen fell across my eyes and my breathing became jagged grunts and gurgles arising from my throat, and the screen grew darker, then black, and it painted my mind in melancholy colours; all at once the force of life ceased its flow in every organ of my body, pursued and hunted by one word: Aslan.

A small crowd of beggars and passers-by assembled around the haggard, unconscious lad, consulting with one another about whether to pour water over him or slap his cheeks, and I was gripped with strange convulsions as if my organs had quarrelled and were no longer connected to one single body, their joints only tenuously attached. Just then the barber, who had only a moment before shut the door to his tiny shop, pushed his way through and, as soon as he recognised the young man in princely garments who exuded an aroma of pampering and delights, he drew near me and gathered me into his arms, my head lolling behind and my legs drooping; he carried me to the paupers' stool in his shop, and so it happened that after a short while I awoke from the fainting spell that visits me from time to time to find Suleiman whispering pleasantries into my ear, his fingers quivering above my head, my forehead, my temples.

I could not manage to come to Bab Alfouqara that evening, I tell the good barber, nor have I been able to fully comprehend your intentions in inviting me to meet you there. The barber chuckled and gently embraced me, and his smell, the scent of a man, was strange and good to me, sweet and sweaty, and I gave myself over to his embrace, and he said, I had no intentions, neither good nor bad, and he placed a warm and caressing hand in my own and led me outside, to the street, and he was protective as an older brother to me, escorting me towards my family home, and when we arrived there he told me, quietly, Go in peace, and he stroked my cheeks with his right hand and played his fingers lightly upon my lips and kissed them gently, with a dab of sweet spittle, and then he took my head into his hands and kissed my lips again, and at the sound of approaching footsteps he fled.

At once I turned my back to him and ran home, imagining Father's shouts at my tardiness and perhaps the lash of his belt on my back, but when I arrived I found my family in slumber; no one asked about Aslan or his actions, no one was interested in him, and I hastened to wash my tongue with many waters, the smell of another mouth strong upon it, the scent of coarse and simple herbs, and I filled a bucket of water and poured it quickly over myself and I drew a cake of soap back and forth across my body, scrubbing with diligence and determination. A strange sensation rose in my throat and a heavy burden settled on my chest, and again I could hear the stifled flapping of the flock of cranes soon to take wing, and with a raging gust of wind they flooded my brain, made me dizzy, rattled me, shook me to and fro, and in their wake there remained, fluttering in a light breeze, a single feather, black and trifling, which oscillated to the left and right until it reached the earth, dormant.

3

In the waning days of autumn of my fifteenth year, my parents informed me that I was to be wed. The name of my intended was Markhaba Antebi, upon whose face I must at one time have laid eyes, for she was the daughter of the Khaham-Bashi Yaacov Antebi, chief rabbi of Damascus, a girl with no dowry but with a good family pedigree. Two months from that very day we were to inhabit the fourth room from the right entrance to our family home.

Father informed me of this development slowly, in an official manner, as if he were reading a guilty verdict handed down by the *Majles*, the Council of Jewish Elders, after which he departed from the room and left Maman and me to stare at one another.

She asked me through the screen of black hair covering her eyes whether I would like to know further details, but I wanted nothing but to sink into the nuptial grief into which I was being forced; after all, how was Aslan to feed and provide for his wife and how was he to cohabitate with her, to engage in intercourse with her the way men did with their wives, for so delicate was he, his voice so feeble, his eyes moist, and a terrible fatigue descended upon my body and a small gurgle began its rumbling in my throat and Maman gathered her hair and shut me up immediately: Now listen, Aslan, and hear me well! It has been decreed that the perfumed days of your childhood and the self-indulgence and the foolish games of mischief and the teasing of your sister and your brother and the beautiful garments in which you were clothed have come to an end, and if you so much as shed a single tear I will tell your father, who has ordered that Aslan be flogged and his body tortured until he behaves like a man, not to mention that he must cease his pampered gait and his teetering footsteps, for Aslan already shaves his cheeks with a razor and sends forth semen from his loins and he must be a man as other men. It is bad enough that no groom has been found for his blue-eyed older sister, an old maid of seventeen years. Now Aslan will be kind enough to comply utterly with and acquiesce absolutely to the wishes of his parents, who have only his best interests at heart, for they love him dearly.

She took hold of my forearm and led me to that fourth room, a small dark apartment, dim and dank, which had been used by the lowliest of the servants in our home as a place to copulate and to relieve themselves, and now it had been cleared of all chattels and rags, its floor had been cleaned, its old furniture removed, and it stood arid in its loneliness like a land of banishment and expulsion. A wicker double bed in all its heaviness had been placed in the centre of the room.

It is to here that the contents of the bedroom of your youth will be moved, Maman said in a different, strange voice, her fingers clamped around her wedding ring. She deflected my attempts at embracing her and closed the door behind me and that gurgle in my throat burst forth in the form of a potent cough followed by choking and retching and once again that darkened screen lowered over my eyes, though this time no one came to my rescue and I fell supine on to the hardened mattress, pricked by the wicker, and wished my parents their share of tears and misery.

At the end of two weeks' time a festive meal was scheduled, at which I would meet my prospective bride, Markhaba, about whose existence I had been ignorant since I had had no dealings with her father, the honourable rabbi, nor with his rabbi-cohorts or his students; in fact, only this I knew: that these Torah scholars were preoccupied night and day with pleading for a messiah that would never come, and to being transported to a land to which they would never return, and to a god who turned them away empty-handed, and that they attempted to prevent all manner of diversions and pleasures like the bottom-wiggling of the dancers that Father and the uncles watched from time to time, and the drinking of wines made in Sidon and Tyre without rabbinical supervision, and the household ornaments created in the image of man, to which Maman was in the habit of speaking secretly before retiring, entreating them to provide assistance and good counsel.

The rumour of my impending marriage spread swiftly through the Jewish Quarter, and at the Talmud Torah the boys looked askance at me, vacillating between a measure of teasing that was always reserved for me and a measure of envy at the new, lower tones in my voice and the bulging Adam's apple in my throat and my new way of walking. Even the teacher ceased his floggings; but in spite of all this I could not quell the fears of calamity at my impending nuptials, since I could not know whether I would succeed in the great mission at hand. In my mind I pictured the women – gossips, the aunts, market hawkers, beggars – pointing at Aslan from the bottom of the lane and laughing their lecherous laugh.

I began to take notice of this species – women – and found that I abhorred their bodies, that organ they possessed, and was repulsed by what one was meant to do with them; I could not comprehend, nor was there a soul to whom I could turn to ask his advice. Not Father, always enraged and preoccupied, not my friend Moussa, who had been forced away from me and had disappeared never to return, not the barber Suleiman Negrin, whose home and shop I was careful not to pass for fear of encountering a pair of shifty eyes or his mouth, which begged for kisses.

In the bedroom of my youth, which granted me the favour of our final hours together, I resumed gazing at my body, now covered by even more hair, and examined my new voice, which leapt between the high-pitched days of my childhood and low tones, sturdy and new, and my hands descended to the organ that had, over the previous days, led my thoughts like an erect compass to its intended mission, and I searched the words of wise men for clues to the act it was expected to perform and which seemed to me beyond the realm of the possible.

I requested an audience with Maman for an urgent discussion but again and again the servants rebuffed me, until I had no choice but to burst forcefully into the bedroom she shared with Father, and she covered her breasts with a piece of black cloth and pushed me away: Aslan, I have no time for you now, but I asked, Who is this Markhaba whom you have arranged for me to marry? I do not wish to be a husband to her, to copulate with her, to bear the burden of her through the long and miserable life that lies ahead of us. I told Maman about my feelings, how the ways of a man towards a woman were incomprehensible to me, and about the beautiful days of my youth, which I wished to exploit to their fullest.

Maman began to repair a garment that needed no repair – something she was wont to do at times such as these – and told me it had been ordained and there was no going back on this arranged marriage, for due to our interminable wars with the Harari family, who were doing everything in their power to remove the Farhi brothers from their commerce and their position of honour in Kharet Elyahud, it was essential for us to marry into a family of great rabbis.

28

And then I poured out the contents of my heart and said that my father was trading me as if I were a promissory note that had come due, and that he never had a single word of affection to impart to me and that he was distant and estranged, and it was as though he had evil designs on me, and that even worse than Father was my mother, my good friend for flirtatious games of costumes and make-up whose true treachery became apparent at times of reckoning.

Maman laughed raucously and said that my punishment would be grave and immense, that it would not come now but later, over time, over the entirety of my life from its beginning to its end, for he who curses his mother and father is destined for the most horrible tortures of hell, and now would I be so kind as to depart from her room before she summoned her husband, my father.

We arrived at the meagre home of the bride on Sunday, that is, *khad vakasal*, the Day of Laziness that follows the Sabbath, and I was fatigued from the curses I had been hurling at Father, wishing all the world's evil on him, such as bankruptcy, poverty and beggary, but then I was plagued with thoughts of sadness at this new week about to commence and the sorrows and suffering and decrees it would bring, and I sent a look of acquiescence at the virile sun, who was illuminating the street with his penetrating rays, while Father marched with a vigorous step to the meeting as though it were a profitable business proposition from which he would earn many piastres, and he opened the rickety gate that led to the narrow house and said, *Sabakh alkhir*, to which came the immediate response, *Sabakh alfil v'alismin*.

Never before had I visited the home of a rabbi of Kharet Elyahud; it seemed to me more of a nest for rats than a home for human beings. Where were the fruit orchards and pools and fountains with carved roses and sayings of wisdom and good luck that adorned our own home? Instead, this hovel sported a small and fetid well, a cage with two screeching chickens, wretched walls of clay devoid of any picture or decoration, yellow mud tamed by wicker mats; and it was occupied by the rabbi, the Khaham-Bashi Yaacov Antebi, and his wife and their five daughters, and I said in my heart, This woman my parents have arranged for me to marry was taken not from the home of a great man but from the home of paupers.

We are welcomed by the Khaham-Bashi, who pays occasional visits to the homes of the wealthy to request assistance and money for the Torah scholars, and he is dressed in his brown mantle with a colourful scarf wrapped about his waist, and as always he is good-humoured, overflowing with Damascene wisdom, his reddish beard curling down from his mouth, always pinching the children and ready with a *melabes* sweet from his pocket; he knows how even to raise a smile on the serious, dejected face of Aslan, who is eyeing his surroundings with suspicion.

When we have settled on to reclining pillows in the *qa'ah*, the upper portion of the parlour which is covered with rugs, and served tea and *ma'amul* pastries, the two fathers begin conversing, my father's face large, his chin thick, his eyebrows harsh and his hands rubbing one against the other; and the Khaham-Bashi is slight and spritely, his reddish beard in constant motion. The conversation moves from meaningless expressions of *politesse* to the telling of the story of the ban that the Harari family has placed on the Khaham-Bashi, how they have refused to pay his salary for the past two years due to a ruling he made against them once, and how now he is compelled to purchase necessities in a roundabout manner, through loans, and forced to accept gifts of flesh and blood with copious shame. As it is said about money,

Vali ala qalitha shu sa'abeh, How difficult it is when lacking, and Father adds a curse on the Hararis for divesting him of his business interests by making agreements to supply caravans from Mecca and Baghdad with merchandise and guards.

Aslan sits upon these simple pillows nibbling vile, stale biscuits and hopes in his heart of hearts for the evil Harari family to succeed, that they might continue to dispossess Father and the uncles and the parade of wives and the descendants of all their interests and profits, that Father's ascendancy fall and that he become their slave, but the Khaham-Bashi cuts short my ruminations when he says, with a smile, What can we do? – *Hiye, hiye, labaniyeh* – Whatever will be will be, and then he arranges the large skullcap on his head, claps his hands and says, *Yallah, bidkum t'shufu elaroussa,* Do you wish to see the *briiiiiide?* He pulls the last syllable even longer than anyone in Damascus would, accentuating it: *elaroussaaaaaah.*

I have no opportunity to answer since the young woman appears before us, accompanied by her mother, her face hidden behind a black and white veil. Father rises to his feet at once and bows foolishly, his movements excited and sharp, and he motions for me to rise as well and approach the bride, her fingers white and her eyes lifeless, and in whose hands I notice a prayer book.

Offered a taste of the refreshments, she pronounces the blessing over the fruit of the trees before taking a bite from an orange, then a second blessing over the *ma'amul,* and the Khaham-Bashi nudges us and winks, for Markhaba is the most devout of the daughters, his partner in devotion and love of God, and more than anything, she shares his yearning for the Messiah from the House of David; she sits evening after evening in a small, dark corner overlooking a bend in the road, focusing her gaze for the moment He will reveal Himself and unify the holy

Israelites, and even now she requests that, after having laid eyes upon her betrothed, whom her saintly parents have chosen for her, she be excused to contemplate the Lord and His ways and offer her prayers.

After all this had come to pass, on our silent way home, I received permission from Father to part from him and spend time alone with my thoughts while walking the streets of Damascus. I exited from the main gate of Kharet Elyahud and entered the street that is called Straight, crossed it, and continued northwards to the Christian Quarter, passing the Terra Sancta Monastery and the spacious homes of the wealthy, like ours, and my feet carried me to another place, past the walls of the city, where I departed through the northern gate to the good river, whose current was swift and whose scent was pleasant as it watered the city's gardens and orchards and provided tranquillity for the soul and the heart, and I allowed the river's current to wash away the tears I shed for my childhood, now dead and gone, since my destiny had been sealed by a father who could not be contested, and I had no consolation but a brief and turbid memory of the kisses of the barber Suleiman Negrin, and I had no life left in me but this longing for the Muslim youths passing before me and for the embraces and kisses I would bestow upon them and for the other things I would do which the Torah denounced, condemning the practitioners to death by stoning.

How magnificent, how beautiful, was my wedding, an affair destined to be talked about many years hence; whenever someone wished to describe opulence, a true banquet, they would say, It was as the *huppah* of Aslan Farhi. Even after the Farhi descendants became destitute paupers due to their greed and the vicissitudes of fate, and nothing remained and nothing was spared from their great fortune but a piece of an ear snatched from the mouth of the lion, and after the residents of Kharet Elyahud had dwindled and dispersed to the four corners of the earth and abandoned the River Barada and the apricot trees and the exceedingly pleasant summer evenings spent on the rooftops of the houses of Damascus, even then the memory of Aslan Farhi's wedding would bring back a honeyed sweetness, and they would tell one another of the *kubeh* meat pastries you bit into only to discover tiny nuggets of gold, and of the precious pearl or lucky gemstone you might encounter between the potatoes and the ground meat of the *kawaj*. As for me, however, I found nothing of this beauty or happiness, and no memory comes to me but that of a burning nausea and a trembling repulsion.

As a stranger I walked among the wedding guests, among the wealthy Muslims, their fingers rolling prayer beads and twirling moustaches, with whom Father and the uncles traded; among the diplomats from the foreign consulates who spoke melodious European languages and stood laughing with wine glasses in their hands; and among the three members of the Harari clan who attended the *huppah*, their faces filled with arrogance as they shook hands coolly with Father.

I shot glances at that Markhaba as she mumbled holy verses of Scripture. The girl was a stranger to me, her ways were foreign to me, her body odd to me, and I avoided Aunt Khalda's shouting singsong as she chased after me to pinch my thighs and laugh her vulgar laugh; even the Khaham-Bashi failed to raise the slightest hint of a smile on my face when he pointed to the nuptial room and chanted in rhyming couplets, *Arisna alzen yit'hana/ Saar lo sinten bistana*: The groom shall enjoy himself at last/ After waiting these two years past.

I glimpsed Markhaba's face for the first time only under the *huppah*, mainly due to her insistence upon remaining covered and modest, since to her way of thinking this had been decreed by the Creator of the Universe in order to make this a coupling that was pure of heart and body and lo, with her short hair and her bulging eyes and her small breasts she looked to me like a young lad, and an impure hope stole into my heart: that during our copulation she would reveal her male organ to me, and not the female version that made my heart sink just to think of it.

The Khaham-Bashi requested that I repeat what he was saying about not forgetting thee O Jerusalem, and after I muttered my feeble mumblings I was presented with the glass I was meant to shatter against the wall behind me, but my tossing hand was limp and weak and so the glass landed on its side and rolled back my way, to the laughter of the guests.

And so I had to pitch the glass a second time, but my body began to tremble mysteriously and my grip on the cup loosened; Father grew impatient, his face enraged even beneath my nuptial canopy, and he grimaced at Aslan the Fickle, grabbed my hand and squeezed it tightly to assist me in shattering the glass. The shards pierced my skin, causing spots of red blood to flow down to my hairy forearm.

I considered plunging into that darkness and pulling down the black screen over my heavy eyes, but Maman in her benevolence hastened to wipe my hands and revive me, and in order not to bring the festivities to a halt she gave a sign to the servants to bring in the singer.

Since the appearance of the singer was a complete and utter surprise, the students of the Khaham-Bashi had no chance to protest at this part of the wedding banquet and so, as soon as the sign had been given, and while Markhaba, horrified, covered her weeping face and fled, a certain prostitute from one of the local taverns – a woman favoured by the Jews – was ushered in, and immediately the sound of a violin and an *oud* could be heard, and the whole crowd, apart from the Torah scholars who covered their faces with their hats, cheered and applauded, for this singer – I soon learned – was one of the best-known and adored in all of Damascus.

My eyes downcast, I thought about the room waiting for me and about the custom of the aunts to wait for the bloodstained sheet to be brought before them and displayed, and I was grateful for my initiative in insisting that this custom be stopped and that they should not wait for me to come to my bride, and I was further grateful that they had agreed to my request, and I sat wondering how I would accomplish this mission, ashamed to be thinking about one organ approaching another organ and how strange this was in my eyes, so that I very nearly raised my voice to sing tearfully with the violin and the *oud*, when suddenly a wondrous voice reached my ears. It was soft and pleasant, the pure voice of a woman the likes of which I had never heard, for the singer called Umm-Jihan had arrived wearing a dress of feathers which emphasised her ample hips and a pair of sturdy breasts, and she trilled her voice at length and with devotion, and how wonderful it was in my eyes that she was singing the very lines from the old, forgotten poems that I would whisper with my friend Moussa about that almond-eyed lover who walked barefoot among the orchards in the shadow of the moon: he was far from sight, would never be found again; it was the soul who sought him out.

After that an even more wonderful and beloved thing happened: the beautiful singer who awakened feelings in me that I had never before felt for a woman began tapping her feet and dancing slowly to muffled drums, and then she descended from the small stage built for her by the servants and walked this way and that among the guests, sometimes doubling back, sometimes moving forward with determination then once again turning around, but ultimately her path was towards none other than the blushing groom himself, his heart beating wildly and his cheeks aflame, and she crept slowly towards him like a snake and put a hand to his narrow waist and touched him with her fingers and her tongue, and Aslan whispered her name, Umm-Jihan, Umm-Jihan, for as a result of the spell she had cast upon him he now understood the secret of women and could follow his forefathers and all other men, from Adam to the present, who had performed as was expected of them, and he was not a whit different from them.

The dance might have lasted much, much longer if it were not for the loud grumbles of complaint and angry shouts and threats of censure issued by the elderly Rabbi Shlomo Harari and his cohort the Khaham Khalfon Attia, good friends of the Khaham-Bashi whom Maman had taken care to send on false pretences to the small synagogue next to the spacious guest room; but now they had returned, complaining loudly and demanding categorically that this abominable dancer be removed. Umm-Jihan swayed her buttocks demonstratively as she moved away from them and her painted eyes smiled secretively behind her mask and beneath her wig, while Father laughed boisterously at the rabbis and said this was intended only to bring joy to the guests and would not happen again; as for me, I filled my lungs in order to preserve the memory of her wonderful scent until the end of time.

4

After the last of the flocks of guests departed, or, as the Khaham-Bashi jested, *Al'aris b'yakhud al'arus, valmada'ai bitla'u m'thil tiyus* – When the groom lays a hand on the bride, like billy goats the guests take their stride – and after they had left behind them the meagre bouquets of flowers they had brought as gifts and the smell of their sweat from joyous dancing and the remains of the banquet, and after the last of the brooms had been returned to its resting place at the end of the hasty clean-up carried out by the servants, only Markhaba and I remained, alone, in the great expanse of the room, utterly and completely silent.

The choking burden in my throat, which had escorted me through the wedding and festivities, grew larger now, and I said to myself, Aslan, although you are alone on the battlefield there is nothing here but your body, you yourself. Recall that marvellous songbird Umm-Jihan and the desire she awakened in you, and rule over that desire as though it were an axe brandished over the nape of one sentenced to die, and commit this act in one fell swoop, for the hour of your manhood is nigh.

Markhaba said nothing, merely following after me like a shadow to the fourth room, where the air stood still and there was as yet the lingering scent of servants' urine, and she uttered some holy words and departed from the room to pass water and empty her bowels. This bug-eyed, pale-faced maiden of the blessings and whisperings seemed less and less a flesh-and-blood mortal to me than the perfect mate for the holy wooden icons that Maman kept hidden in her room.

While Markhaba dallied, I hovered over our wicker nuptial bed, and there I was, before my first time, standing like a condemned man facing the grave of his own digging, and there was nothing to do but trust myself and my own body, and so I waited expectantly to see what Markhaba would do, and which clothes she would remove from her body, and how she would lie upon the wicker bed, and I feared what would be the wanderings of that organ of my own organs, known familiarly as *khanuneh*, which was impossible to rule and knew no master or harness.

All the while my temples throbbed in anticipation of this act, and I began to rouse, in my imagination, the pleasing and attractive image of the dancer Umm-Jihan, and the sound of muted drums and the patter of her catlike feet, and I removed my groom's shoes and the bandage which Maman had wrapped around my hand, bloodied from the glass, and I entered the bed, about to share it for the first time in my life with a strange body, that of a woman who was not mine, and I wished to evade her and dive into a night of peaceful rest, but then, just as I was wishing for my soul to be sent to the world of dreams and slumber, I felt Markhaba's hand touching my puny chest.

Even before I could gather my wits and flee from the room, Markhaba had clutched at my tunic, already demanding that we fulfil the commandment to go forth and multiply, one of the most important commandments decreed upon the Jewish people and, much the same as that Sabbath Queen descending upon the pious as they pray in the synagogue, she uttered blessings over her own body and mine, wishing to bring them together in absolute matrimony and unity, and she desired to remove the tunic from my thin body and conjugate with me, and I was astonished by this rabbi's daughter, whose ways were the ways of a whore, and I pushed her from atop my body and stepped outside the room in order to take in some air, but I was disconcerted to find Maman, who had been positioned outside the room the whole time, her ear cupped to hear whether conjugation had been achieved, whether the couple had coupled or not, and she chided me and sent me back to the nuptial bed and threatened to call Father, who would pummel me with his fists until I would cease my perverse weakness and my rebelliousness and my shameful behaviour.

Rakhet alek, The game is up Aslan, was the sole thought that echoed in my head as I was returned to the execution room, where the rabbi's daughter had already stripped off her clothes under the blanket. She had no male organ, but rather that scarred valley I had expected to find, and she began speaking to me words she had learned from her sisters regarding which actions to perform and which appendages to lift and move about in order to ensure her conception, God willing, and I was frightened by her words and by the deficient, boyish body sprawled next to me and I acquiesced, choiceless, for this was the purpose and the destiny and these were the cause and effect, and there was no escaping them.

My happy friend, while the image of Umm-Jihan flitted before my eyes I leaned over Markhaba, my wife of an hour, who wished to be impregnated by any means possible, and I touched with wonder her tiny breasts as she held fast to my organ, pulling it near that dark and blocked opening, hidden and tangled, of which there was no way of knowing how to enter or depart from it; all at once my soul fled and the blood drained from my body and I was slack and feeble, plunging like a despondent maiden into the depths of her spinsterhood to avoid being wed to some old sheikh, but Markhaba did not despair, rather, she pressed and twisted my organ, attempting to blow life into it, to awaken it from its dormancy, to restore it to pristine splendour, all the while uttering blessings: *Blessed art Thou, Ruler of the Universe, Who firms man's footsteps* and *Blessed art Thou, Who girds Israel with strength and resuscitates the dead with abundant mercy.* And I, too, was praying, conjuring up the memory of Umm-Jihan of the many delights, but Umm-Jihan appears, drenched in sweat and ragged, clothed in filthy, stinking garments, the look on her face altered – empty and evil – and then a new parade of images arrives unbidden, of shrivelled, ancient women who put my desire to flight, and then finally among them stands a black-haired lad of the Islamic faith and behind him four fat men, their large bellies protruding and their organs erect, and they wish to enter me and I flee from them and run and plunge into my cursed nuptial bed and ask Markhaba for permission to sleep.

With the arrival of morning I rise to escape that narrow room and Markhaba's gaze as she recites a blessing over the new day – *Blessed art Thou, O God, who restores souls to dead bodies* – and I am flooded with relief when I see that no one is stationed next to my door to inquire about the events of the previous evening, and I steal away to the bathing room where I submerge myself in a tub and trickle hot water over my body, but the servants have heard my footsteps and have informed the household that I have left my room, and lo, Maman enters and congratulates me on my first night as a groom and she gazes into the pupils of my eyes to discern whether the fact of my manhood has been etched on to them and suddenly a terrible suspicion takes hold of her and she spreads her jewelled fingers into a fan and shouts, Aslan! How much shame and disgrace can one son bring upon his parents and family! And I tell her that the act required of me is not in the realm of the possible since there is no way of bringing my organ to the tangled jungle of the hole belonging to the maiden referred to as my wife, and Maman commands me to stop speaking and she reproaches me, saying this is an act committed by humans and animals and reptiles and insects and such will Aslan do unto his wife, and a dam of tears breaks forth all at once from my throat, as well as grunts and coughs, and my eyes cloud over, for Aslan does not want this marriage and Aslan does not want this wife, and Aslan cannot enter her, and he requests permission to be freed from these demands forced upon him and upon all men so that he might resume playing the games of his youth and sleeping alone in the bedroom he loved, but Maman does not respond to these impassioned requests, rather, she quickly leaves the bathing room, and a vain hope steals into his heart that perhaps she will return with a notice of the annulment of his marriage in hand.

The shouts that arise from the avenue of fruit orchards in the garden of our home foretell of my bitter mistake, and while I am still crouching in the tub of water Maman enters the bathing room and behind her I am petrified to see Father, enraged as a thunderstorm, sparks and flashes leaping from his eyes, and he upends the tub and pours the water over me, and as I lie naked in a puddle of water he punches my nose and he is all rage and wrath. *Ruakh al'an unik hadihi almarah*, he says, Get in there and screw that woman, and I shrink at hearing these vulgar and incisive words that summon their peers, shameful words of debauchery and curses, which arrive quickly, heedless of syntax or rules, shouted one after the other, thundering from Father's vocal chords, kicking and punching their way forward, and I determine neither to hear nor heed them and I stop up my ears and drop a thick screen before my eyes and the figure of Father is uprooted from my heart to the point that it occupies no place or part of my soul.

Whatever it is he says, at the end of Father's discourse I am beaten back to the fourth room to the accompaniment of shouts and pummellings, to where Markhaba is already sitting combing her short hair in preparation for the new day, and she tells me that she is still a virgin and it is incumbent upon me to perform the deed this very day before her father, too, finds out, and that I must impregnate her one way or another, and that we have been commanded to remain in our room until we are successful in our mission.

Thus were we cloistered for two whole days, during which time I spoke to my organ and promised it all manner of promises and stroked it and pampered it and lavished strengthening creams upon it and chewed herbs and swallowed concoctions, but each time it came time to perform the act and I was expected to bring my organ to that place, my might and vitality ebbed away and it drooped, winking with its one eye.

With each passing hour of failure and with each unsuccessful attempt, my hatred waxed towards my evil father, who had planned this scheme, and towards my mother, his traitorous partner in crime, and towards Markhaba, whom they had brought to my room and thrust into my life, and I wished her nothing but foreshortened days and dark diseases and strange accidents, and if not her, then that they might visit me.

My parents took note of these wicked events and a new idea entered their minds, that an evil-eyed curse had been cast upon me by the Harari brothers, who wished to scorn and mock us and hoped to bring about our downfall. There was no other way but to undo this witchcraft.

The Khaham-Bashi Rabbi Antebi, who was privy to the bitter tears of Markhaba over a husband unable to perform his duty properly, was informed, and it was decided that I should be sent to the Cave of Jobar, known for its curative powers, on the left hand of Damascus, so as to receive blessings for fertility and virility and success in all endeavours from the mystic rabbis there.

After being dressed in garments of blue to ward off the evil eye and doused in salt to blind the eyes of the zealous, I was taken in some sort of wagon harnessed to a donkey, the sides of which were covered in a thick cloth so that the Harari brothers and the gossiping women would know nothing of this disgrace, and I was transported with Father, Maman and Rabbi Antebi outside the walls of Damascus to a distance of several *parasangs* through fields of wheat and corn to the small and wretched village from which was meant to sprout my salvation, and our way was accompanied by the singing of a psalm filled with hope: *Ascribe for God, you sons of the powerful; ascribe for God honour and might.*

Roughly am I transported among the Arab farmers ploughing their fields to a pitiful building covered entirely in stinking mould where, according to the gossipmongers, the prophet Elijah anointed Elisha, and so the place was called *Knis Elisha Alnabi,* which people only bother to visit on the Day of Atonement or in times of great distress, and there are women wailing and offering prayers to cure lepers of their leprosy and boils-sufferers from their boils, and Father and Maman and the Khaham-Bashi pray that my organ cease its feebleness and become the progenitor of a great nation.

Father takes hold of me and attaches a small copper bowl, a *tasa*, to my belt, and inside the bowl is a *kandil* – oil with a wick of cotton wool – and a bleary-eyed Jew places in the bowl a large green leaf, and after the cause of my distress is whispered into his ear he nods sadly and begins to versify rhyming prayers that stretch from his mouth like a string of spittle, and he blesses me with all manner of blessings and summons all manner of angels and cautions all manner of Liliths, and from there I am brought

43

to the cave in the cellar of the synagogue and we descend, slipping on the ancient stones, and the odour of mould and incense and spoiled milk accosts us, and the *tasa* with the oil inside rattles against the belt on my tunic, and we reach the depths of the strange and mysterious cave, the floor of which is covered with old and tattered carpets, and once there, Father and the Khaham-Bashi join in the eerie rhyming chants which are peppered with ancient Aramaic expressions, and they encircle me from right to left while beating on leaden beads and raising their hands over my head, and Maman recites a blessing, *Ayn alradiyeh tirtad anak*, May the evil eye depart from you.

No one warns Aslan, so he is filled with astonishment when his tunic is lifted from him, exposing his gaunt, hairy body, and the tunic is tossed into a deep well at the side of the cave and then fished out with a long pole and wrung, then returned, saturated, for him to wear for seven days during which he must remain beside his wife in order to enter and impregnate her. And then, the *pièce de résistance*, Maman dips her snow-white finger, bedecked with gold rings, into a soot-filled trench and smears black soot on my eyelids and nose and cheeks and it is thus, wearing clothing soaked in well-water and crowned with black spots, that I set out on my return from the adventure at the Cave of Jobar to my unloved wife.

When the wagon returns to my parents' home I ask permission of them to walk the streets of Damascus as is my custom during sad times and crises, to take pleasure in the River Barada as it flows through mysterious channels under the houses and alleyways and squares, and they allot me time and extract promises from me that upon my return I will end this shameful chapter of my marriage with an act of virility and manliness, and I agree without knowing how I can succeed in keeping my promise.

This time my feet lead me not to the river as it flows outside the northern walls of the city, nor to the covered spice market, beloved for its myriad sweets and surprises, but rather to the square before the Saraya fortress in the Muslim Quarter, seat of the present Damascus city governor, Ibrahim Pasha, known as Sharif Pasha, where at this very moment, midday, hundreds and thousands of men are engaging in commerce, their hands exchanging money, their feet ensconced in buckled boots, black tarbooshes on their heads, and they are many and awesome, and among them walks Aslan thinking to himself, Lo, as the number of men teeming here such is the number of their organs dangling in front of their bodies, hanging from their loins above a pair of testicles, and they swing as the men walk, some erect, some flaccid, and all these organs belonging to all these men engage in that very same act, slipping in and out, out and in, and not a man among them raises his voice in protest, for this is their task and this is their way, and there is no place for further thoughts or musings in this matter.

And upon my return to the Jewish Quarter by way of its main gate, open at this hour to all comers, I once again lose my way, and instead of continuing towards my family residence with its spacious buildings I walk to Suleiman Negrin, the barber; although my hair has not yet grown sufficiently I arrive at the entrance to his shop, where he is not working, but stands playing with the leeches he keeps in a glass jar.

Negrin opens his arms to embrace me and adds a kiss and then another on my cheek, *Mabruk*, he congratulates me on my marriage and my woman, though straight away he discerns my sad eyes and filthy tunic and soot-blackened face and seats me in his chair and spreads his barber's apron to towel my head and instantly he understands what has befallen me from start to finish, how my evil parents have given me over to marriage before my time and how I have laboured in vain at my task and how they have attempted to undo the witchcraft, and Negrin embraces me ever more boldly and kisses my cheeks and lips and recounts that this terror ambushes the hearts of all males, from the insects to the mammals, from the monkeys to the Harari brothers, and he adds words of comfort and condolences and places in my hand a small cord to be tied at the base of my organ in order to ensure that the life and blood do not seep away, and he instructs me how to slip this cord on and what to do, and he prepares me for this task of copulation, and adds that once I succeed in my mission I should return to him and he will teach me one or two other things.

How happy I was after doing as he instructed me; I led that organ to the stiff, tight passageway and passed through walls of thick and obstinate skin and paved the way through twisted channels, and the cord at the base of my loins sustained my soul in that valley of death, that it should not fear evil or fall silent or retreat, and my emissary made his odd way into Markhaba, astonished at the fuss his confrères make over this dark passage, and when Markhaba let forth with a scream and the wicker bed filled with a red stain and the scent of blood rose in the room, I swore an oath that this visit, which I had undertaken in spite of myself, would be my last to this vale of horror.

On that very same day I found a way to inform my friend the barber that I would meet him at Bab Alfouqara one hour after the muezzin's third call, and the servant boy returned with a spoken message from the barber that my proposal had been accepted and that it was his intention to close the gate of his shop earlier than usual and that at nightfall he would come to meet me there.

Markhaba, who had set out in the company of Maman to visit her sisters in order to ply them with the whole story of her intercourse and hopeful impregnation, left me with an evening utterly free of her presence, and thus I was able to prepare myself for my meeting by shaving my cheeks and clipping the nails of my fingers and toes and washing with copious amounts of hot water that small organ that had known such great hardships and was now plucked and shrunken and which experienced, with the passing of water, a splinter of pain hinting at the origins of the grave illness that would take hold of me in the future and which has burdened you, my happy friend, with difficult labour that you endure in silence.

No man roams the vicinity of Bab Alfouqara at this time of night, for it is none other than a deserted place of commerce where shops stand silent and sacks of tea and coffee lie forsaken and I reach this place anxiously excited about the act soon to take place and I investigate to make certain there are no passers-by or loiterers or momentary visitors and indeed the area is bereft of people, even the figure of Negrin *alkhalaq* has yet to materialise, and Aslan ponders whether the barber is mocking him, whether he should return quickly home.

However, in the end my arc-browed friend the barber does, in fact, arrive, spouting apologies for his beggar clients who never leave him alone and wish to engage him in senseless conversation and gulp glasses of tea at his expense, and his green eyes sparkle and Aslan is excited beyond measure and listens but hears nothing, and he envisions the two of them holding one another and the whole matter seems so distant and implausible.

The barber queries Aslan and asks after his health but Aslan knows not what to respond, and it appears that Negrin is speaking about all manner of preparations and powders that have arrived from the nations of the world, and about his plans to turn his barber's shop into a place favoured by well-heeled Damascenes, certain is he that it is not his lot to search for lice and fleas on the clothes of his beggar clients, nor is it his lot to hold leeches to their bodies to free their blood of diseases, and as he speaks of all these matters Aslan places his hand on the barber's thigh and the barber's fingers entwine with his and Aslan inclines his neck towards the jabbering barber and draws closer to him and holds his fingers and brings him nearer to his lips and to that terrible act punishable by death, and lo, each falls upon the other's neck with deep kisses, and Suleiman's chattering tongue drowns his words in Aslan's moist mouth and suckles the honey and milk under his tongue, and in his turn Aslan sends a wet emissary between the barber's lips and their tongues curl over one another, and now Aslan wraps his arms around the barber and they become one man, whole, their clipped whiskers touching, their noses rubbing, their thick eyebrows blending, their hairy thighs slapping, their wide feet mingling, and they are reflected, increased, changed in one another, and deep gurgles rise from the two of them as from one man and indeed they are as Adam before the rib was taken from him, in that deserted alleyway visited by none, near a gate no man passes through for it is blocked and hidden and leads to no end or hope and is known to all as Bab Alfouqara.

My happy friend, the foundling, I will go so far as to reveal to you without being remiss with a single detail that against my will and quite early I attained a state of ecstasy, and lo, that same figure that reflects and mocks me *ad infinitum* becomes, in a single moment, separate and flaccid, dim, repulsive, and now the potentates of a new regime have come to govern me and their countenance is grave and they are law-abiding, and a great cry arises from them, that I must cease forthwith from any act to which I am drawn, and the barber leaning over me turns acrid, his skin pricks, his fingers are as nettles and his legs as thistles, and he is nothing like that Umm-Jihan, soft and good-hearted, who is all charms and sweetness, and I push *alkhalaq* away from my person, mortified at the pungently aromatic stain spreading across my clothing, and he wishes to continue sucking honey and milk from my tongue and he draws near once again, but from his own garments rises the smell of vomit and beggary, and he is like those large leeches in his jars, and I spit the taste of his limp kisses from my mouth and push him out of my sight, and he asks only another moment, but in the end he is obliged to dive into the empty sacks and satiate himself there in the way of Onan son of Yehuda, and I swear an oath to myself that I will not gaze upon his evil face again nor will I return to his wretched shop, and I will bring my passion to the paths of knowledge and wisdom and I will stand guard over it well, and I race quickly away from Bab Alfouqara, my eyes steadfast on the path ahead.

5

For the next six months I saw nothing of Suleiman *alkhalaq* and I did not visit Bab Alfouqara and I put away from my soul all thoughts of debauchery, and instead I released myself from the vow I had taken not to come to my wife's gates, and from time to time I would fulfil my manly obligation and her conjugal need to become, at last, pregnant, and the matter was sorely difficult for me.

On Father's command I ceased attending the Talmud Torah and instead was required to accompany him throughout the day, releasing goods at the customs office, signing Arab farmers to mortgages and loans at thirty per cent interest, and assisting him in his disputatious dealings with other merchants like him, accumulating piles of silver as dust.

Father and I pass from place to place, a wall of silence between us, and when he speaks to me I seal my ears shut and my answers are short and nasty and he responds with a familiar dose of his wrath, and thus the days pass for me in sadness and misery.

At eventide, when the gates of the Jewish Quarter close and we must not venture abroad, I have no choice but to enter my small room and there awaits me that holy and pious creature, whose sole desire is to suckle from me the little life left in my blood, and she entreats me to come unto to her as a man comes to a maiden for the purpose of being fruitful and multiplying the Jewish people, and each time I am forced to make unique excuses, for example, that the odour from her mouth is that of death itself, or for example that the mole on her back is exceedingly uncomely, and I continue to insult and offend and curse her, and call her *majdubeh* and *khamarah* until she stops entreating me, but when she is returned to me after the days of her monthly bleeding she begins her lament once again, that from the time her virginity was taken from her I have not known her save on several occasions, and I swear to myself that I will send her away and live a life of loneliness, and perhaps I will take upon myself the Christian religion or Islam and I will be excommunicated and I will pass from city to city and village to village until I take up residence in the hills of Lebanon or the desert of Tadmor, and there I will remain alone all my days and none of my fellow Jews will find me.

Sometimes Father brings me to the residence of the governor of Damascus, north of the Jewish Quarter, and after we walk the entire length of Azm Palace, making our way past merchants selling dusty carpets and jewellery of silver and gold, we find ourselves at the entrance to the great square, and Father always scolds me to straighten my robe and brush from it the crumbs of egg and pickled cucumber still upon it from the breakfast meal, and he instructs me how to comport myself among important officials and how to bow deeply should the governor, Sharif Pasha, pass before us, and on our way there we move among many men and I am flooded with wonder at their bodies, that no two are alike, that there are tall men and short men, dark-skinned men and light-skinned men, blue-eyed men and brown-eyed men, porters pulling wagons, muscled Somalis and Ethiopians, fat men and thin men, a riot of aromas, hair, muscles and sweat that is pleasant to my nostrils, and they are powerful and well formed, and it seems there are none among them who are weak or feeble or faint-hearted or pale like the Torah scholars and the rabbis and Aslan of the white hands who is moving among them, astonished, and he yearns for them sorely.

Father conducts business with the rich, important men at Azm Palace and tries to teach me the intricacies of commerce and lending and bargaining and strange calculations according to the Muslim calendar, and he speaks of matters concerning property and merchandise destined to arrive and then depart after being taxed, and commission fees and the greasing of palms with *baqshish*, but Aslan pays no heed and does not listen, for nothing of these matters interests him, only the shapely palace attendants, tall and proud as they pass through the elegant corridors of Azm Palace, which is near to the perfume market, and he knows and reminds himself that the acts he wishes to engage in with them are lawfully and rightfully forbidden to him for as long as he lives among his fellow Jews.

The more Aslan decrees a state of abstinence on himself and swears oaths that he will not visit Suleiman *alkhalaq* or the Bab Alfouqara, and the more he reminds himself of the feeling of repulsion that arose in his body at the conclusion of that act and also the great danger involved for the two of them if some evil eye should spot them, the more his evil and forbidden desire grows and increases; that desire which was noisily expelled from his doorstep returns, stealing inside through slatted windows, and each morning Aslan awakens to an erect, unsheathed rod and the memory of sweet dreams still in his mouth.

Each Sabbath Eve, when Father recites the blessings over the wine, a deep, Aslanish sorrow settles on Aslan as he regards his siblings and uncles and aunts and cousins, and he sighs to himself, for he has not been created in their image, and he grieves for the grey and wretched life he must live among those who are neither friends nor fellows, and with whom discourse is troubling, and they eat *riz b'hamoud* – rice in a sour sauce – and *kibabat alpasha* – meat patties with pine nuts – and they speak, always, of commerce and banking, and of the competition between themselves and the lords Harari, and in his eyes they are as empty as eggshells, and their merriment is foreign to him, and when, on occasion, they scold him – *Ya Aslan*, when will we see a belly on Markhaba already? – he retreats into himself even further, and his organ shrivels between his legs for, truth be told, he has neither the strength for, nor the intention of, copulating with her again.

And sometimes they spend the Sabbath at the home of her father, the Khaham-Bashi Yaacov Antebi, and there, too, Aslan fails to find his place, feeling among them like a non-Jew, their supplications foreign to him, their intense swaying as they pray odd to him, and afterwards they speak of the Messiah yet to come, who will save the Jews from their sorrows; and all these words are insipid in Aslan's eyes, and he mocks them in his heart, asking how this messiah will reach them and who will send him and to what end, and there are times when Aslan amuses himself with the thought that an angel of goodwill will one day appear in the fourth room in his father's house, that he will open the door and jump into the wicker nuptial bed and send Markhaba home to her parents, and then he will face Aslan, and cast upon him his mantle and tell him that the time has come to reveal the great secret, and Aslan will ask, disengaging himself from troubled sleep, which secret the angel is speaking of, and the angel will say, Lo, I hereby anoint you as a prophet, and he will place before him a white ass to ride upon so that Aslan may save the Jews from their distress, and Aslan will mount the horse in his tattered nightclothes and stocking cap, and he will walk and ride among the Jews and they will say, Is that not the Aslan we once knew, and they will bow and prostrate themselves before him, and when the sign is given Aslan will gallop far away from there and they will chase after him and grab hold of the ass's tail and plead for his salvation, but he will turn his back to those whose knees did not bend before him and those whose mouths did not bestow kisses upon him.

Alas, none of these things ever comes to pass, and not only is Aslan never awakened at dawn by an angel, but the first sight he meets upon opening his eyes is a bitter puss, followed by the sound of curses and arguments he did not know Markhaba was capable of, until Aslan is compelled to ask his younger brother to come and sleep in their room, and when his brother Meir refuses, Aslan commands one of the servants to bring his sleeping mattress near the room, to serve as Aslan's protector from the demands of that woman.

And lo, by the end of six months of marriage, Aslan has forgotten the fright he felt at his previous encounter with the barber Suleiman and he begins to desire another meeting with him, to embark with him on a new path, so that late one afternoon, without pausing to reflect, Aslan sets out for the barber's shop with a proposal to pick up where they had left off.

His rod protruding and his nose sniffing the air and his arms wide open, Aslan bounds eagerly for the barber's, whose shop remains dreary, Suleiman engaged not in catering to the wealthy of Damascus but to drawing the blood of his pauper friends, setting leeches on their backs until they well up hugely, engorged with blood.

When the barber takes notice of Aslan gesturing to him from the shop window, Aslan is surprised to see that Suleiman's green eyes do not sparkle with the light of desire, but rather, they smoulder murkily with disgust, and he turns his face away from him and refrains from casting his glance in Aslan's direction, and this matter is very peculiar in Aslan's eyes.

Aslan enters Suleiman's shop and asks for a cut, even though his hair is shorter than usual and his sideburns neatly trimmed. The barber seats him on the chair and begins massaging his head and lo, the same evil and heavy silence that Aslan knows so well from his roamings with his father now stands between Aslan and the barber, and they are as two competitors shooting arrows of derision and hatred at one another.

And yet, the barber's silence merely serves to pique Aslan's curiosity, and Suleiman becomes even more amiable in his eyes, and Aslan desires to comprehend the meaning of his reticence, and he knows not with which words to open, until finally he wishes the barber, belatedly, good tidings, and in the words of the Damascene saying, *Alsalaam bijir calaam*, To wish one good tidings brings on conversation. Aslan begins to interrogate the barber about all manner of preparations the latter wished to bring to Damascus and why he has failed to do so. And the barber explains that the customs duties are so high and the Jewish customs agents – among them Aslan's father – have schemed to deprive him of his livelihood, and he hates them with all his soul, and then Aslan understands why it was that his friend seemed estranged to him, but the barber, as if reading his mind, hastens to correct the impression that he holds any grudge against Aslan, for it is nothing other than concern for his wife, whom he wed only shortly before Aslan's own marriage and who is now carrying his child, and he is of the mind to cease and desist from all that he has done previously, and he hopes that what has transpired between them will be forgotten and that not even a single word will be spoken about it.

Aslan hears these words while his cheeks are still covered in lather, before the blade has passed over them, and they increase his pleasure doubly, for the more reticent the barber becomes, the more Aslan is aroused, and in no time at all Aslan is wishing they would once again taste from each other's body and become one man, strong and sturdy, and to that end Aslan gropes the front of the barber's tunic until Suleiman's organ stands erect and the barber says as if to himself, If we retire to the corner of my shop and close the door behind us no one will have an inkling of this matter; and even though his pregnant wife awaits at home, she takes no interest in the wheelings and dealings in which he engages to provide for his family, her only worry the foetus in her womb, that he emerge into the world healthy and whole and that she may nurse him and that he may grow up to be a Torah scholar, an observant Jew; and lo, the barber carries out the plan by covering the window of his shop with a thick cloth and bolting the door, and in a second the two young men are touching one another's organs, and Aslan strives to reach that sweet aim that has occupied him nightly, and he surprises the barber with his zeal, racing to lower his friend's undergarments to his knees, and with gentle, hovering strokes he caresses the barber's engorged organ and its deep-red cap with the tips of his fingers, in so different a way from Markhaba, who presses upon him like a vice grips a piece of wood; and at the same time and in the same manner Suleiman caresses Aslan so that four hands and two organs are mixed and rolled together, and from there Aslan continues to his true aim, for only one wish, one desire, has filled his soul through six long months of desolation during which he has spent his days with Markhaba, and he extends his tongue – that very same tongue that once wrestled with Suleiman's own choice tongue – to lick the beloved organ, and his curiosity is piqued to know what will be its flavour, and his belly tumbles with delight, and in one quick motion he slips the whole large head with the smile-shaped slit that runs the length of it into his mouth, and begins to suck the marrow of life from his friend the barber, who, for his part, hastens to do the same to Aslan's organ, and suddenly the barber shouts, Careful, your teeth! And Aslan resumes his suckling, but this time he is careful not to expose his teeth, only his thick lips, which rise and fall and suck and suckle, for here is the origin and the goal, the cause and the effect, the tainted and the holy; and the two men fall to the floor, exhausted from holding one another thus, and there they grasp one another, and they do not notice that the corners of the cloth covering the window of his shop have rolled back slightly, exposing them to the street.

My happy friend, upon my return home towards evening with the taste of the barber's body still on my tongue, I feel a stirring among the servants, how they point at me and whisper until that time when one of them shores himself up and announces that Father is seething with anger and waiting in his study, and I grow alarmed, lest my secret has been discovered, and it seems to me as though the servants are besmirching me, perhaps one of the neighbours or even one of the uncles happened by the barber's shop just as events were occurring and witnessed us in the hour of our sin, and great fatigue and panic fall upon Aslan as he stands on the edge of a coughing and fainting spell, and I ask the servant whom I dispatched to secure the barber's willingness to meet, What is the meaning of this matter, and from his evasive answer I know to take a last lingering look of farewell at the setting sun and the cloudless Damascus sky of blue, and the servant answers that he does not know the meaning, only that I have been ordered to visit my father immediately.

There can be no doubt about it: if my actions with Suleiman are known to them I can expect to be ostracised and excommunicated; perhaps they will stone my young, hirsute body, gathering round me in one of the city's deserted squares, encircling me from every direction, the brothers and uncles and relatives and Torah scholars, each holding a thick slab of rock in his hand, and when the signal is given, they will hurl them one by one in order to increase the agony, and the first stones scratch and hurt, though only slightly, while the wave that follows is stronger, and there are stones that strike my face and mash my eyes and teeth, and now the stone-throwers are even more keen, their routine now well established, their salvoes now quicker, denser, more insistent, and I gather myself in, bow my head between my thin arms, which have never been useful for physical labour, and I entreat them to throw larger stones, that they may crush me with boulders to put an end to the torture, and the servant says, This way, Aslan, your father is awaiting your arrival.

I knock upon the door to his study and at the sound of his voice I open it a crack. Father is sitting with his back to me and I approach him slowly and with trepidation, poised to absorb a blow to my head or nose or stomach, but Father does not move or stir.

He turns towards me, expressionless, his eyes hollow, and I anticipate the string of curses to come, but he utters not a single word, and with difficulty I say, You asked to see me, and he says, Yes, but adds no explanation, and I ask, What, then, is this matter, and this causes Father to push some sort of paper in front of me and from this I deduce that it is incumbent upon me to read it, and I laugh silently when it becomes clear that his wrath is directed not against me but against those ignoble villains the Hararis, who, in their cunning, have managed to bribe the minister of the Treasury, Bakri-Bey, that they should serve as the sole customs agents for the entire city of Damascus and thus they deprive us of the mainstay of our income, and the document shows this in clear wording, leaving no opening for dispute or interpretation, the decree being that from the end of the month and for evermore, the Farhi family will be hard-pressed to maintain its ancient profession and it will be the Harari family that will amass the huge fortune accrued by those responsible for freeing from customs merchandise that has traversed the sea or the desert.

Father orders me to fire off letters of alarm to the minister and, if necessary, to Ibrahim Pasha and even Muhammad Ali, the Egyptian ruler over the whole of the land, that this evil decree be cancelled, and I take this mission upon myself with great glee, overjoyed at the stoning that has not and will not take place, and at the many days ahead during which I may meet with the barber again without a soul knowing of our adventures or intruding upon us, and I sit down to write these missives on thick paper, peering occasionally at the large figure of Father as he sits with his hands covering his face, silent and still.

That same day, late at night, the uncles gather too, and Father tells them – I am present as well – that if we do not succeed in quashing this misfortune and crushing the head of the snake, the Farhi dynasty will in future become impoverished, for no treachery is too unsavoury for the Hararis, and they aspire to remove us from every position and rank we maintain, and after having quarrelled with the Khaham-Bashi Yaacov Antebi and ostracising him and preventing him from receiving his salary, they now wish to strip us from our place in the Beth Din, the rabbinical court of the Jewish community, so that ultimately their antics will lead to a command forbidding the Farhi family from loaning with interest and the fortunes and palaces and beautiful clothing that belong to us will become *à fonds perdus*.

I am filled with wonder and sadness: why is it that men cannot love one another more, instead of beating and striking, oppressing and debasing, despoiling and destroying? Why is it that they do not cast their women aside and come to one another in acts of love, their arms accustomed to brawling now stretched

59

towards one another, their tongues accustomed to curses and humiliations now united in wet kisses; why do they not massage one another's backs, lick each other's roughened skin, remove one another's tunics? The uncles' words have caught fire, intensified, and now they have become one clear voice shouting to annihilate the Hararis, to bring about their extinction on the face of the earth, to assassinate them, one after the next, until the danger passes and is no longer.

I request permission to take my leave from these wrathful men and seek consolation *chez* Maman, in our games of yore, and she, sequestered in her quarters, shocked at these grave tidings, welcomes me as in days past, and she takes my face in her hands and plants wet kisses on my cheeks and I press up against her chest and call to her, Maman, Maman, wicked people are trying to render us asunder, I have been sent to marry a strange and evil woman, I am forced to deal with matters of commerce in Azm Palace and the perfume and spice markets, whereas I desire only your company, to which Maman responds with great affection, and I gesture towards her sumptuous gowns, pass my hand over the choice cloth, favour the patterns ornamented with beads and pearls, and she acquiesces, closes the door behind us and spreads across my body the best of her garments, and I take measure of her shoes and select the most comfortable among them for my clumsy, overgrown feet, and I adopt a delicate, swaying gait and add a long, white necklace and a pair of earrings, and for the moment we are as we were in the past, pleasant and loving, and her laughter mixes with mine, and all at once I am startled to wonder what would be if she knew about Suleiman the barber, whether she would still dance and laugh with me, or whether she would join the circle of stone-throwers, even rushing to cast the first stone, and just then one of my feet twists in her white sandals and I fall, women's clothing draped over my body, and

Maman raises me to my feet with difficulty, Stand up, Aslan, go, a woman named Markhaba is waiting for you and perhaps your father will catch sight of your face here any minute, and so I take leave of her with a light kiss, the kind from the days of our infatuation, and I depart from the room, a trace of rouge still upon my cheeks.

6

An important decision was reached by Father and the uncles, according to which six of our seven servants were dismissed, returned to their villages without severance pay or any other recompense, and the costly garments ordered from Europe would no longer be brought into our home, and the gurgle of two fountains toiling to soothe our souls day and night would be halted, for difficult times lay ahead, and even the verses decorating the inner courtyard of our home, bidding the inhabitants an abundance of riches and good health, were powerless to help us: the finances of the Farhi family were dwindling.

Maman spent entire days sequestered in her room with no maid to comb her long, black tresses and no special messenger to deliver a parcel from England or France containing all manner of fine cloth; and who would toil to carry the wood planks brought by camels to the gate of our estate, and who would lug coal from the cellar in the cold days of winter, and who would root out *alkhayaya*, the snakes, before the cleaning of the carpets? The chesty rumbling of phlegm that was my lot now attached itself to Maman, and she sat through long days and nights alone on her bed, spitting her barking coughs in every direction.

Father and the uncles tried to find solutions, for we were living for the time being on monies earned earlier from loans not yet due and mortgaged lands not yet sold, but now that they were no longer permitted to extend their patronage to caravans travelling to Mecca and Baghdad and they no longer had access to commissions from Damascene customs duties, they had no choice but to slash their considerable expenses, bend their backs – which had never known physical labour – and pray for God's benevolence as in bygone days.

At times when I came to offer condolences to Maman in her bedroom I found her proferring prayers and supplications to the lean figure of a youth hanging from and riveted to a piece of wood hidden at the side of her bed. Covertly, she would entreat him and heap praises and compliments upon him and kiss his bare feet and pass a finger over his emaciated arms, which were spread to the side, and when she finished this ceremony she would command me to bow and lower my gaze in the presence of this terrible god, who must be pleased and appeased, otherwise our world has no future, and I cannot deny that on occasion she spread before him a sliver of meat or blew curls of hashish smoke his way or sprinkled drops of milk on his head, hoping with all her soul and all her might that her maids might be reinstated and her days might resume their path.

As for me, however, the more that my parents and siblings and uncles were occupied with the calamity that had befallen them, the freer I was to pursue my own interests, and I resolved to forsake my obligations as husband, son and brother and leave the Jewish Quarter, beyond the gatekeeper, far from the Black River of sewage that flowed beneath our feet, far from the screeching chickens being slaughtered at market, to the underbelly of the city, which, veiled in the blackest night, offered the men of Damascus to me for acts of pleasure and love.

My first guide in these endeavours was Suleiman *alkhalaq*, whom, since the time of our first indulgences together in his shop, I would visit on occasion to engage in similar acts; it was he who first awakened me to that act I had not even dared dream of, the way of men with men, which is complicated and dangerous and involves maladies and pain, but for him who opens that gate it is none other than the path to the haven of pleasure and joy, even though the barber himself refused outright to tread that path, which he claimed was a trap for fools and utterly forbidden.

Instead, he graciously informed me about the Maqha, a café on the border between the Christian and Muslim quarters, near the home of one Eliyahu Nehmad, a place hidden under a veil of secrecy which the sons of Damascus visit every evening for the wine and alcohol prohibited to Muslims, and for the beautiful whores obtainable for a few meagre piastres, in small rooms where the desires of men shatter like waves on rocks.

On the eve of the anticipated labour of his pregnant wife, Suleiman *alkhalaq* refused to accompany me to the Maqha, willing only to instruct me as to the location and the hour, and he further suggested that I buy the silence of *le guardien* of the gates by paying several piastres; in fact, the barber continued to spurn the promises I heaped at his feet, and my pleas and entreaties for an escort, all because it was his wish, each evening at sunset, to sit with his pregnant wife and hold her hand and caress her large belly.

Thus it came to pass that at midnight one evening, while my parents lay in bed, angry, back to back, Maman with dry tears and Father in thunderous silence, and with no servants in the house save one boy lost in deep sleep, snoring copiously, exhausted by Maman's tyranny, I departed from the fourth room which I shared with that foreign woman who clung to my bosom, and I turned towards the north gate of the Jewish Quarter, where the guard, a one-legged Jew, sat dozing, a ring of keys hanging from his wrist.

If the guard was surprised to see Aslan the Delicate, who was always mindful of his parents and who was soft-hearted and prone to tears, placing a small bribe in the palm of his hand to buy his silence and his freedom to follow a forbidden path, his face showed none of this: he did not smile or murmur or utter a single word, merely pocketing the coins and lifting his healthy leg to push open the gate, which was in any event already open, so that Aslan could pass through into the city.

My happy friend, it is incumbent upon you to understand and realise that Aslan had never before set out alone, at night, into the city, not only because it was forbidden for Jews to leave their quarter after sundown but because of the great danger posed by Arab thugs, African slaves and other wild men who roamed freely and pummelled mercilessly all who crossed their paths. Therefore, Aslan took the utmost precaution, following the barber Suleiman's instructions to the letter, which were scribbled on a folded sheet of paper in his pocket, and he was careful to stay close to the walls of the buildings, and if he heard the low rumble of a man's voice or the muted shrieks of drunkards he froze in his tracks so that no evil eye would divine his presence.

The street mentioned and described by the barber where the café-tavern could be found turned out to be long and narrow, with two-storeyed buildings abutting on both sides and the stench of urine reeking from a distance. As he rounded a certain corner it was possible to discern the sounds of music, even a voice singing, and Aslan followed these sounds until he found himself facing a curtain of red beads, and he handed to the dark-skinned youth stationed there the specified amount of piastres and Aslan ducked into the tumult of people suddenly exposed to him, the smoke of narghiles and tobacco mixing with the chink of *araq* glasses and the clack of backgammon pieces, and Aslan desired to set his eyes upon that which the barber had described in hints, a corner of that place, near the latrines, where men capture the glances of other men and stare at one another for a length of time as a sign of agreement, before departing together for a small park, much like so many other small parks scattered along the hidden channels of the River Barada which ornament the length and breadth of Damascus, and in this place there are those willing and ready to engage in the act that even Suleiman will not consider and does not even dare dream of, for it is a sin punishable by death, an abomination absolutely forbidden in the Torah and the Talmud and by the great and sacred rabbis, and terrible punishments are meted out for this crime, and in the shadow of low bushes or small trees they bend over, and there are those who make use of sheep fat or olive oil to lubricate the organ, and Suleiman maintained that this act was not only forbidden and horrible but also unfeasible, due to the smallness of the place, and in any event, stimulating the area was likely to bring on maladies not even mentioned in the Torah, but Aslan was drawn to that corner and he set out to find it, the penetrating gazes of hairy, pot-bellied Arab men marking his progress.

When Aslan's gaze lit upon the *araq* table, under which stealthy glasses were poured and handed to Muslims to be sipped quickly, then he knew he had found what his soul had been searching for, since near to the moustachioed barman, who carried out his task with a swiftness bordering on the sacred, there stood a short but sturdy man, old and wrinkled and clad in a black cloak, but nonetheless unabashedly staring directly, deeply at him, his pupils boring into Aslan's downcast eyes, and now Aslan felt as though two beams had entered his head and penetrated to the lower regions of his body, and he was filled to the brim with the stare of this older man, and Aslan's organs melted one into the other, rounding out, his buttocks rotund, his chest softening, and he became a sweet, round bubble dripping with ripened masculinity.

Aslan drew near the short older man and was repelled by the wrinkles that furrowed his face and the crafty eyes in a coarse shade of brown that skittered over Aslan's body and did not let up even for a moment, and the older man, some fifty years of age, perhaps sixty, not quite Aslan's height and older even than his father and uncles, said nothing; he merely placed a warm hand on Aslan's right thigh and held tight, as if the thigh had belonged to him since time immemorial, and Aslan, against his will, felt the stirring of that organ that does not know satiation, and the organ stretched and flexed and stood erect in spite of his disgust at the sight of this older man, who signalled to Aslan to lean close and then whispered in his ear, Do you wish to have me *now*?

My happy friend, only one small word now stood between me and that union I had heard tell of, and the appearance of this old man became, all at once, that of one beloved and desired, and I noticed the bulging veins of his hands and his scarred fingers and the overflowing sacs under his eyes and I loved these dearly, for what purpose and what aim could a young man have if not to unite with a man older than he, one sated with love and suffering, to learn from him like a maiden, a virgin, about the twisted paths and dead ends that life doles out, to be embraced by arms consumed by wind and sand, which were, as far as I could discern, thick and tanned, just as I like them, to hear the low buzz of his voice offering instruction and advice, full of experience, and to turn a soft cheek to his thick and prickly beard, to be a beloved and loving son to him?

But before I could respond to the proposal of the older man, a herald came to make an announcement I failed to comprehend about the impending arrival of some singing whore come to gladden the hearts of the growing crowd of men in the Maqha, and the herald held a large lantern in his hand which spilled, momentarily, a narrow strip of light on the face of my new friend, the older man, and how great was my astonishment, and how my desire for him doubled and trebled, when it became apparent to me that the man whose warm hand held my thigh was none other than Father Tomaso, known to all as Baba Toma, from a humble monastery in the city's Christian Quarter, a wooden cross dangling from his neck, a broad monk's cap on his head, his black cloak embroidered with red thread, and he was beloved and very well thought of by all and came quite regularly to the homes of the Jews on all manner of business, once to sell second-hand furnishings and once to negotiate the sale of property and once to provide injections and mix potions, something he had taught himself to do with the aid of an ancient book written in the Italian language, and he was even known to me from my youth, when he would come to inoculate me and the other boys at the Talmud Torah against *aljidri*, smallpox, and he would remove our tunics, revealing our buttocks, and prick each one gaily with his sharp needle.

Tomaso, who seemed to notice my look of recognition, laughed broadly and warmly and began massaging my thigh as his fingers climbed towards my testicles, now tight as two nuts in a shell, and Tomaso straightened the cap on his head and muttered the name of one of the Catholic saints and, in the accent of his youth, which he had retained even after thirty years in Damascus, he repeated his proposal, to which I nodded ever so slightly, and Tomaso loved me mightily for that.

From the moment I gave my consent I was overcome with great feebleness and nearly toppled over, my traitorous legs quaking beneath me, and Tomaso goaded me on: Well then, let's be off, and I asked him, To where, the monastery where you reside? And he laughed raucously and said, In the name of Holy

Jesus, that is not right and proper for a monastery, nor are the bushes near to the Maqha suited to the act of love in which we intend to engage; instead, for this purpose, he could provide us with a small, hidden room near the wall of the city, not far from the Jewish Quarter, which he maintained for acts such as these, and he held me tight, his fingers all the while massaging the entrance to my buttocks, and commanded me to accompany him there immediately, for the hour was already quite late and he would need to rise early for morning prayers, and to greet the small but faithful contingent of worshippers who prayed at the chapel of his monastery.

My happy friend, I was poised to leave with the monk, to meet his uncircumcised member and learn all there was to know about it, and had already shed my feebleness and replaced it with a moment's resolve to carry out that forbidden act, when something wondrous occurred: on a small stage in a corner of the café there mounted a woman, stately and ravishing, her shoulders a bit broad but her eyes almond-shaped and her legs doe-like, and at once she gave over her gentle voice to an old song that tells the tale of a lover who departs, never to return, the song I used to sing with my first friend, Moussa:

Min badak ahgor khali
Ya a'aeb an aynya

To you I will depart from myself
You, who are far from my eyes

Aslan knew at once that this was none other than Umm-Jihan from the day of his marriage, and she was radiant with light and her thick lips were painted red, and her face was gently rouged and her black hair was shimmering and wavy, and Aslan knew that neither the indecent act he was about to engage in with this sinner nor the loathsome marriage to the daughter of a rabbi were his destiny; rather, he was meant for love and peace and tranquillity with this tall, clear-voiced woman, and she was the perfect mixture of everything he had ever desired: the delicate features of her face and her wide, assured gait, the high-pitched sounds she produced from her throat and her gentle gaze; she was a woman of valour who surpassed all the daughters of Damascus.

Imbued with a pure, new passion, I remove Tomaso's fingers from my hot thigh and fix my gaze on that woman full of magic, whose eyes lock with mine, and perhaps she recalls my wedding and our brief dance and she shakes her large breasts, awakening in me, much to my surprise, love and infinite longing.

Tomaso tries to coax me one more time but I turn my back to him and draw nearer to her, and he whispers in my ear that one day we shall meet to carry out that act of union and coupling for which we two were destined, perhaps at that same café or perhaps at some other place in the city, even the Jewish Quarter one day soon, and he utters some Christian incantation to ensure it, but I do not heed or listen to any of his words, I merely draw nearer to Umm-Jihan, that most beautiful of women, and join her in singing that old song I loved, about my lover and the orchards and sporting with him barefoot on the roof under the light of the moon.

When the song ends and Umm-Jihan disappears I am filled with desire to see her at once, to tell her of my love and to sail with her on the back of an Arabian mare galloping across the deserts of Arabia, and I ask the moustachioed barman filling glasses of *araq* under the table, Where is this woman whom I love, and the barman smiles the smile of a pimp, a shepherd of women, and nods to a small chamber behind the stage, and then he winks and I fail to understand the meaning of this, but I rush to that place, catching Tomaso – from the corner of my eye – as he departs from the Maqha on the arm of his young and able-bodied servant and there, behind a curtain of red beads, I knock on a small door and am permitted to enter the room, where the songstress is sipping from a cup of anisette to restore her spirits.

Quickly I compliment Umm-Jihan on her singing – which has captured my heart – as well as her appearance and the feminine wisdom so evident in her, and she extends her cheek gracefully, a true lady, and I kiss it lightly, inhaling the touch of her pleasant skin, and I wish to add more, to tell her that she is my succour and my hope, that to her my secret thoughts are devoted, that she staves off waves of ugly desire, but instead I stand there silent and mute, and Umm-Jihan flashes me a smile of purity and says, *Int mahbub*, You are cute, and she asks my name but then begs my forgiveness, she must be alone, she must change her apparel and leave for her abode, and I say quickly, Where can I see you again? Here at the Maqha? Or elsewhere? And Umm-Jihan laughs, jiggling her gold earrings, and spreads her long, pink fingernails like a fan of blooming violets and tells me that in the past she appeared at many private functions throughout Damascus, but now her time is not free for such things, and in the sound of her fading laughter I note one round tear pooling in her eye and making its messy way down her rouged cheeks, and Umm-Jihan steels herself to ensure that this one tear will not drag forth a shower of sobs whose meaning I do not comprehend, and before I, too, can burst out crying in that way Aslan has, and make myself a laughing-stock in the eyes of the only woman I have ever loved, I lift my legs and propel my body away from there into the crowded and smoky Maqha.

Although the hour is quite late and the Jewish guard has undoubtedly fallen asleep, and the members of our household –

if they have noted Aslan's absence – will be exceedingly angry, Aslan chooses to step out into the street to lie in wait at the gate of the café for Umm-Jihan to exit, and until she has finished gathering her elegant dresses and her long, shiny hair, and instructing the porter to carry her belongings to her home, Aslan is forced to watch the parade of men, drunkards and wastrels, departing from the café after a night of entertainment, and there are those whose buttons are undone after coupling with young whores in the small rooms, and there are those who emerge bellowing rude songs, embracing in their drunkenness, and there are those who stand urinating on the wall, the flow strong and acrid, droplets of urine spewing into the clear night, and there is one gang of men poised to strike out against another gang of men over some trifling incident until the young man at the door, who has been collecting admission fees all evening, hushes them, threatening to summon the agents of the Tufekji-Bashi, the chief of police, to toss them all behind bars, and they cease their amiable tussling and button their buttons and return to their wives and children awaiting them in slumber all across the city of Damascus.

Some time later, convulsed with the cold of darkness but determined to cast a last glance at the woman he loves, Aslan hears thin, high shrieks from one of the hidden entrances to the café and immediately understands that his beloved is in need of his help, and he rushes towards the low bushes, now scented with men's semen and urine, and here he spots two gendarmes roughly removing Umm-Jihan from the place where she sang so beautifully that evening, and they kick her and toss aside her purse and pack her on to a mule covered in a patched and tattered blanket, saying, *Harki tizeq*, Move your arse, woman, *Ya mal'ouna*, and Aslan's heart is stirred, for her eyes sparkle with tears, and when they pinch her buttocks she shrieks those small, thin shrieks that drew his attention and Aslan very nearly jumps up to stop the gendarmes, for what injustice and what sin could so pure a woman cause any man on earth, and why are they handling her so roughly and mercilessly, and Aslan wishes to gather her in his arms and take her into his heart, but he knows that the gendarmes are stronger than he and that he, Aslan, has no home or room to which he can lead her, and no horse upon whose back he may escort her, only his first, unique love, now bubbling through him and filling his veins, and so he returns, confused and elated, to the Jewish Quarter, and he cares not when *le guardien* demands more money from him. In love and distracted, he pours all the coins remaining in his pocket into the guard's cash box and departs for home, anxious and distraught.

7

Umm-Jihan and Umm-Jihan and Umm-Jihan, this was the only name Aslan would ponder and utter and chant from morning to evening. Again and again he would resurrect in his imagination her elegant manners and the lovely things she had said to him during their brief meeting, such as, You are cute, and such as, What is your name, and such as, I must be alone, and then he would recall the coarse shouts of the gendarmes and the lurid curses they had hurled at her and that depressing, thick-headed mule toiling, in the small hours of the night, to carry out its contemptible mission, and Aslan would toss and turn in his bed, unwillingly soaking up the scent of sweat from his wife Markhaba, and his sorrow swirled together with longing.

Aslan prised information from a cousin of his – a cunning gossip, unlike other men – about Umm-Jihan, and this cousin told him with a sly smile that that woman, among the most wondrous of women the world over, had been sentenced to long-term imprisonment for some crime whose nature he did not know, so that instead of baths of milk and honey she spent her days in the prison beneath the Saraya. Further, he told Aslan that on occasion she was granted permission to appear and perform in public as she once had, but that only a tiny per cent of the proceeds ever reached her hands, the rest disappearing into the governor's coffers.

Aslan wished to ask his mother and his father and his uncles for all they could tell him of Umm-Jihan – perhaps she had been born to a Jewish mother, but even if she were Christian or Muslim he thought she might consent to convert to the Jewish faith; such things had been occurring for as long as Jews had been residing in Damascus, and in that case he would divorce Markhaba and distance himself from her family of rabbis and cling to Umm-Jihan instead, and together they would know only happiness and love – but if Aslan were too persistent in his pursuit of the information he desired so dearly about the life of his one true love, his interrogee would nip the conversation in the bud, saying, Aslan, remove your thoughts instantly from this person, who is filled with nothing but sorrow and misery, evil and wickedness, malediction and imprecation, she is like a snake whose head must first be bashed.

These constant thoughts about Umm-Jihan awakened a dormant desire for women in Aslan, inflaming and inciting him with dreams of bedding the stunning songstress, and this led to acts of love with his wife Markhaba, for although she caused his organ to fall limp, in her female body there was some trace, some glimmer, some slight hint of that vivacious and beloved singer, so that Aslan banished the servant-boy from the room and visited Markhaba from time to time and for a moment, with the aid of darkest night, was capable of believing that it was Umm-Jihan who was giving herself over to him and jiggling her thighs and caressing his back, and it was that cherished and long-desired name that he whispered in his wife's ear.

Aslan visited the Maqha, on the outskirts of the city's Christian Quarter, several times more, which was no simple matter, for he had to bribe le guardien and pay the admission fee and sit and wait – in vain – for Umm-Jihan, and no one could tell him what had become of her, his beloved, why she did not set foot on that small stage reserved only for her, and why it was that her bell-like voice did not ring out, echoing through the smoky café, which was suffused with men's curses and lecherous looks.

And it happened that each time Aslan came to the Maqha to await the appearance, if even for a moment, of his only love, that same sunburnt older man dressed in the black robe of a priest, a large skullcap covering his head, would seat himself beside Aslan and lay a warm hand on his thigh and whisper debauchery in his ear about how his organ excelled in hardness and thickness, and how from his foreskin there arose a pleasant fragrance, and how the head of his penis bore a double crown, and how for some time now he had lusted to unite with a lad like Aslan, one with a delicate soul and an innocent look, not like the Muslim Arabs whom one could meet at the baths or late at night at the Khan Assad Pasha, young men willing to deliver their organs to his mouth but who covered their buttocks with two layers of cloth and kept them protected and out of view; even his own right-hand man Ibrahim Amara refused, with the stubbornness of a virgin, to open himself up to the monk's sweet organ and enter into a covenant of unity and love with him in the simple bed they shared in the humble monastery.

Tomaso would whisper sweet and beautiful praises in Aslan's ear about his lovely and pleasant body, about the downy hair that covered his skin like vines and leaves of ivy climbing the fortified walls of a city, and he would explain that it was incumbent upon the Jews to atone for the enormous sins they had perpetrated against Christians and against priests and against their lord and saviour Jesus Christ when they surrendered him to his death and informed upon him and spoke libel against him and for that reason are accursed for time immemorial, and how they could atone for this murder and be forgiven by bending over and stretching their backs so that devout Christians could satiate themselves, spraying their holy fluids into their bodies as a sign of absolution and atonement.

But Aslan had fallen under the spell of that maiden who caused his soul to rejoice, and so he offered no response to the monk, nor did he engage in any conversation with old Tomaso and did not pay heed to any of his arguments or pleas; he would merely sit in his place ignoring the glances of rich merchants as they cast their eyes upon him, and those of the waiters curious for the taste of a Jew, waiting like a faithful dog whose owner had abandoned him and for whose return he will wait a very, very long while.

Tomaso repeated his entreaties to Aslan about that secret room he kept near the Jewish Quarter, eager to escort him that short distance in order to know him and love him there in the way of men with men, and he wished to know why it was that Aslan was so estranged from him, for Aslan had been glad and willing to enter a holy covenant with him at the time of their first meeting; but Aslan filled his mouth with water and repeatedly abstained from revealing the reason for his refusal until one day, when he paid a visit to the Maqha and waited in vain for his beloved to appear, Aslan acquiesced, and told Tomaso, Why do you adhere yourself to me instead of your servant Ibrahim? My heart has one purpose only and one love only, and it is directed to that God-fearing woman Umm-Jihan.

The moment Tomaso understood the reason for Aslan's estrangement he spilled the glass of *araq* he had been drinking, spraying it from his mouth as he laughed uproariously, so that the clients of the Maqha stared viciously at him; in any event they secretly cursed him – a man of the cloth – for entering such a place of ill repute without the slightest embarrassment, and they wished the most scabrous of deaths upon this abject Christian and all the other heretics whose purpose in residing in Damascus was none other than converting Muslims from their true and rightful faith.

Tomaso, however, was oblivious to this animosity. He clapped his hand around Aslan's neck and said, My sweet friend, my dear boy, my beloved comrade: banish from your mind at once these vain hallucinations and foolish visions, for the woman you await and yearn for is not a woman at all, but a man like all men, save for the fact that he enjoys donning women's clothing on occasion for the purpose of entertainment.

A resounding slap on Aslan's cheeks. The stab of a knife. The plunge of the lower intestines to the chasms of despair. The tremor of the upper intestines, a state of nausea and vomiting. Could such a thing be true?

If Aslan did not cry or wail or lament for his love, who had been murdered by a mere utterance, it was due only to his hope that these were lies told to him without the bat of an eyelid, and that through the veil of red beads the singer Umm-Jihan would suddenly appear, just as she had before, just as he remembered, when he had known and loved her with every jot of his soul; but not only did Umm-Jihan fail to appear, she continued to be murdered, slain and bleeding, her skin flayed by a butcher's knife of loud and coarse laughter, and Tomaso strengthened the pressure of his embrace so that it became a lover's grip and he continued without mercy the story of the young man who had led Aslan astray, and this young man was a collector of *aljiziya*, the head tax imposed by Sharif Pasha, and the young man went from house to house among the Jews, and evil people informed on him, claiming that he had embezzled government funds, and for that reason he had been placed in the prison beneath the Saraya, and Aslan plugged his ears for this could not be possible – this same merciful and compassionate woman had held his own hands in hers and planted eternal kisses on his cheeks – and he departed from the Maqha to the narrow and winding Damascene street just as a light rain began to fall, and the water trickled and seeped between the paving stones, pooling in long, narrow channels and from there dropped below the passers-by into rivulets leading to a stream, and the water dispersed to a great distance, sweeping along with it muddy yellow earth and bits of rubbish and the beaks of slaughtered chickens, squawks frozen in their slain eyes, and Aslan wished to join the flow of water, to be sucked down to the wild and ancient river, for what was the purpose of Aslan's life in a world that did not – and never had – contain Umm-Jihan, and any desire and delight and love that had awakened in him, and any gains he had made as a male, were none other than a jest, a deceit, and Aslan stood ready to collapse at the entrance to the Maqha but did not do so.

Ibrahim, Tomaso's manservant, a slow, dimwitted Muslim with a clipped moustache who stubbornly refused to follow his master's religion, exited the Maqha at the monk's command in search of Aslan, found him on his knees sobbing silently and informed him, quite simply, in his master's name, that because the hour was late they would have to postpone the act they had planned for that evening to the next; further, Ibrahim told Aslan that Tomaso knew where he lived and would come to collect him from his home on the morrow two hours after the fourth call of the muezzin and then, without awaiting Aslan's answer, he turned his back and re-entered the café.

Aslan heard his words though his heart did not grasp them, for there was so much he had to do: return to Kharet Elyahud, the Jewish Quarter, and bribe le gardien on the way, then lie next to his wife and pretend to sleep soundly, and how would he manage all this when he saw himself scorned and mocked among men, all of them pointing at the groom incapable of impregnating his wife, at the boy bewitched by a woman who was not a woman, a dancer with no breasts, and it was abundantly clear to Aslan that he had no place in this world, that there was no one else like him, no other created in his image who could fathom his heart, and that he was alone in his confused passion, and he recalled the sharp letter-opener in his father's study: Why not go there this very night and open the top drawer, searching among the mortgage deeds and guarantors' notes stored there to torture the farmers until their souls depart from their bodies? Why not take up the knife and point it at the jugular vein in his neck or at his wrists and then draw lines of blood along his body and fall into deep sleep so that when the servant enters the study in the morning he will fail to awaken Aslan? With this new thought Aslan's steps lightened and he rushed to carry out his scheme, but when he arrived home he was drawn unwillingly towards his wife's sweat and joined her in the bed, and he was overcome with the urge to pray to a god in whom he did not believe: that when he awakens it will be clear that the events of the evening were the product of his own imagination, his own visions of dread and empty dreams. On the morrow, however, Aslan knew that he had not been dreaming and that Umm-Jihan's death was a *fait accompli* from which there was no appeal.

By dawn Aslan had made up his mind not to be seen during the approaching hours in the vicinity of the family estate so as not to encounter Tomaso, or his manservant, or his eternally erect organ. Instead, he hastened to his father's office and requested to accompany him in all his endeavours that day, and his father, who was surprised at his son's sudden wish to remain close to him, agreed to his entreaties and together they proceeded to the Court of Damascus, at which Rafael Farhi presided as a judge.

Aslan regarded the line-up of pickpockets, beggars and rogues waiting to stand trial, among them – conspicuously different – a pot-bellied, moustachioed Arab merchant in the grips of deep humiliation, his cheeks ablush, and in the depths of his heart Aslan knew the reason for his appearance in court, for he was touched by the same urge, forbidden by all religions, and when Father read the indictment the facts became clear: how that evening gendarmes were patrolling the Khan Assad Pasha, where the donkey and mule drivers meet, and how they came across the merchant embracing a Turkish youth, the two of them disrobed, and Father cleared his throat when obliged to recite aloud the details of this hideous act, the things they did to one another with their organs and tongues and fingers, and the merchant – portly and pink-cheeked, his hand over his mouth and moustache, his eyes damp – was given the chance to deny the charges, but instead pleaded guilty to every charge and every detail and begged the court and the judges and God to pardon him for this wicked act, saying that he knew the severity of his actions and was aware of the heavy punishment due him, requesting only that the court be merciful on him for the sake of his wife and children and promising that he would not return to the Turkish youth nor to any youth like him nor to any other man the world over, and the judges consulted among themselves on this matter and when Father asked Aslan his opinion he responded that this man should know no absolution or pardon, that this rebel should be punished according to the strictest letter of the law, that he suffer torture and life imprisonment in the prison dungeon of the Saraya, that he be prevented from any contact with his wife and children, his neighbours, or any other human being, to which Father replied, When did you – soft-hearted Aslan – become a man of hatreds and contention? And Aslan glanced once again at the corpulent merchant, his nipples now erect under his clothing, his full buttocks straining at the cloth of his tunic, and Aslan remained certain that his was the rightful verdict.

The panel of judges announced to the merchant that their verdict would be delivered at a later date, and it was after midday when Father and Aslan departed the court for the family estate. By chance they passed, on their way, the shop of Suleiman *alkhalaq*, and Aslan was flooded with a sour desire to flee from there, to turn his back on the barber, guardian of his dark secret, but the devil himself intervened and Father stopped precisely there, next to the entrance to the barber's shop, abreast of the Alifranj Synagogue, to peruse a large notice posted there:

> May it be known in the streets of Damascus that the Christian woman called Terra Nova, of Austrian citizenship, has departed from this world and left behind a large inheritance and many chattels which will be sold at auction at her home in the Street of the Honey-sellers on Wednesday, at the second hour after the second call of the muezzin. All interested parties are welcome.

Aslan pressed his father to move on from there so that he would not encounter the green-eyed gaze of the barber, but the more impatient Aslan became to escape that place, the more serene his father became, and he read the notice again and yet again, calling Aslan's attention to the fact that it was signed by the Capuchin monk Tomaso, who was always on the scent of some new and unseemly business dealing, and upon learning of this coincidence, Aslan's flesh turned prickly, for it was precisely from this Tomaso and his erect organ that Aslan had run away, having no other purpose for accompanying his father than to avoid the pestering monk who wished to enter his body that very night.

After the midday meal everyone dispersed to rest, as expressed in the old Damascene saying, *Tga'ada wa'ithada, Ta'asha itmasha* – After lunch catch a nap, after dinner stroll a lap – while Aslan scanned the area to ensure that the monk, who had been hanging notices that very same day announcing the auction, did not approach the door of their home on some pretext.

My happy friend, from the tears of dread in your eyes I see that you, like young Aslan, have caught a whiff of the calamity about to befall him, and indeed, many a time, on cold winter evenings, you have sat beside me and asked about the meaning of my presence in this monastery, for I am a son of the Jewish people, and each time I have rebuffed you and turned my face away and failed to reveal how it happened that it is to this place I have come to rest.

And lo, in the few hours left before my meeting with Tomaso the feeling of encroaching disaster prevented me from finding any rest or repose, neither with my pious wife, who was busy in the cursed fourth room of our home preparing herself for her monthly purification at the ritual bath that evening, nor in the bathing room where I washed myself for the second and third and fourth time that day, so that I walked from room to room, pitching pebbles, plodding with heavy feet and noisy shoes until Maman stepped out from her room, furious, to scold me, to which I dared respond with impunity, hurling accusations at her, I despise this life you forced upon me, and, Why was your womb not blocked or infertile, but no, you had to follow the path of females and fall pregnant and give birth to foetuses that had no wish to be born, and Maman responded that in the year since my marriage I had become an overgrown and noisy child with no purpose or benefit, and how comely it would be were I to leave this house with my burdensome bride and cease to be an encumbrance upon them all with my perpetually wrathful countenance, unable as I was to coax even a single progeny from my wife's womb.

At the sound of these words I departed with a slam of the door and went to the old fountain in the middle of the courtyard, which had been silenced since the start of our troubles with the Harari family, and the souls of the goldfish that were once there had departed and the pool was covered in lichen and algae, and there I checked the fury vibrating through me and tried to calm the tremor, weaken its strength, and Aslan knew not the source of this fury nor its nature, but with this sharpening of his senses he suddenly understood this panic that had settled upon him, and the source of this internal uproar was none other than that aperture hidden from view, a place of closing but also of opening, narrow but also wide, deep but shallow, like that kingdom of secrecy that women have, though instead of being hidden among frizzy jungles it is eternally guarded by lush hills, and it was to this place, at once cool and burning, familiar and foreign, that the power of his soul was directed, and to that very same place and at that exact moment the monk's organ was also directed as he went about the city posting his notices, accompanied by his manservant Ibrahim of the clipped moustache; and that very same evening he was destined to reach that moist spot, that warm, recalcitrant, stubborn place accustomed only to the shameful view of the Black River, that place spoken ill of by human beings and used for curses and slander, and it would be the focus of that evening, the place which Tomaso would seek to mollify and soften, and massage gently, and pepper with unaccustomed kisses, and enter into as an act of copulation and unity.

Aslan returned to his empty room, pondering these thoughts and forgetting the ugly things he had said to his mother and she had said to him, forgetting the image of his wife, who had stepped out, he knew not where, perhaps to secure cloth for making costumes, as the Purim holiday was nigh upon them, or perhaps to cry to her father of the evil groom who had materialised under her wedding canopy; and so immersed was he in these thoughts of forbidden acts that Aslan was oblivious to the sound of knocking at his door – his whingeing sister of the blue-eyed gaze requesting that he write a letter of persuasion and entreaty to yet another prospective groom – and could anticipate nothing but the second hour after the fourth call of the muezzin, at which time he would take to the street and follow the monk to that secret room, where he would indeed engage in the act.

8

After our evening meal of seared aubergine wallowing in a puddle of goat's cheese – a delicacy known as *medias bjibnah* – accompanied by the bean dish *mufahrket ful*; after Father locked the doors and bolted the latch against the pouring rain that had begun rapping at the doorways and thundering through the city; after Markhaba fell asleep, breathing in heavy grunts on her distant side of the bed; after all this had come to pass, I rose secretly from my bed, preoccupied with thoughts of the ageing, wrinkled, shrivelled monk, whose gaze was hollow and whose hands were coarse and hardened and in spite of all this I was drawn to him and to the touch of his warm fingers on my thigh, and lo, once again Aslan was sneaking away from his bed and his home late at night, though this time not for child's play with the barber and not for the lecherous glances of men passing in the streets or clients of the Maqha, but for the thing itself.

Aslan calmed himself and spoke to his organ so as not to bring on excessive excitement and spill his seed, and to that end he imagined the calamities and distress that have befallen the Jews: the repeated razing of the Temple in Jerusalem and the dispersion of the people to Babylonia and Europe; the blowing of the ram's horn on Yom Kippur – the Day of Atonement – and the parching fast; the heinous deeds of Haman the Wicked and the Pharaoh of Egypt; and with each disaster that entered his mind his organ lost a bit more of its strength and the blood drained away so that it was limp and contorted as the back of a wizened moneylender.

Aslan waited at the gates of his home at the second hour after the fourth call of the muezzin according to Tomaso's instructions, but the street stood in silence in the flood of rain, and no man passed this way or that, and Aslan said to himself, Look at yourself in your wretchedness, running about in a terrible downpour, leaving behind your parents and family and the woman brought unto you, and all this for what? For an act of sin and depravity, evil and stupidity; but in the next moment Aslan recalled the aim of his desire, and he wished to unite with this ripened male whose grapes were juicy, fermented, and from the fruits of whose body arose a pleasant scent like an orchard, and he was none other than the distant lover from the old song sung by his non-existent beloved, Umm-Jihan, and Aslan knew that his feminine walk and his delicate manners and the tainted garments he adorned himself with would all disappear with the embrace of this older man, would dissolve inside his love and vanish with the rainwater as it poured into Elnahar Alaswad, the Black River.

While pondering all these matters he felt a light tap on his shoulder, not administered by squat Tomaso but his dark-skinned, slow-witted manservant Ibrahim, who sputtered from under his clipped moustache that his honourable master had entered the Jewish Quarter at eventide after a long day of exertions that led him throughout the city, toiling to invite people to the auction of Terra Nova's chattels and other business matters that were preoccupying him, and now he requested that Aslan meet him at the eastern edge of the Straight Street and from there they would set out for a safe and secret place beyond the walls of the city.

Aslan wished to protest at being led outside the city on a night of stormy winds, for previously they had spoken of a secret abode kept by the monk in the Jewish Quarter, but Ibrahim crooked his arm tightly around Aslan's neck and the scent of youthful sweat mixed with the misty rain that was growing stronger and stronger drew Aslan after him like a blind man, and after only a few minutes the two found themselves at the appointed rendezvous, though there was neither sign nor evidence of the monk himself, and his manservant Ibrahim grew worried, for Tomaso had many enemies throughout the city, Muslims who did not accept lightly his proselytising for Jesus Christ and Christianity, and a terrible uproar had erupted not long before that at the Khan Assad Pasha when they had demanded an exorbitant fee for hiring a mule to visit the small villages outside the city and Tomaso had cursed them and their prophet Muhammad and they had sworn he would meet a violent death, and the sputtering manservant began pacing to and fro, swinging his muscled arms, for what would he do if his master died and left him? To where could he return? The poor and squalid village of his birth? He spoke sputteringly of his merciful and forgiving master, who was gracious to him and refrained from spraying his holy fluids into Ibrahim's mouth, for their taste was bitter as wormwood and not at all to his liking.

The two young men, Aslan and Ibrahim, waited for Tomaso for nearly an hour, becoming friendly during this meagre time together, confrères to the same strange fate, and the rain poured between them with great force, and Aslan regarded the manservant – his wide lips, slow limbs, thick hands and neck – and he brimmed with potent feelings of affection for him, desired to cover his body with hot kisses, cure him of his loneliness and sorrow and fears, but just then a lumbering, angry figure appeared, careening towards them down the street, and Aslan felt his old repulsion towards himself and towards this friend with whom he was meant to copulate, and at that moment he decided to turn on his heels and make an escape from Tomaso, his rapid skipping soon becoming a light run as he attempted not to slip between the puddles pooling in the streets. His sole desire was to protect himself and his body from the grave consequences which Suleiman the barber, in his great wisdom, had tried to warn him.

Tomaso perceived that his prey was slipping through his talons and shouted luridly, commanding his manservant to chase after Aslan and deliver him as agreed. He complained that from the time the yellow-haired monk Alpino had departed from Damascus a half-year earlier there had been no man prepared to lay bare the slit of his buttocks and open before him a world of wonder and supreme benevolence, and he went about, among the market-places and the baths and the beautiful Arab men, angry, a bundle of nerves, unable to find gratification, and if this Jewish lad were to wriggle free from his grip his testicles were sure to burst open from the pain of it, and his seed, which sought to flow through them, would fill his head all the way to his ears and he would fall prone and his soul would depart his body on the spot.

Aslan heard his crude bellowing and his fear increased, now it was clear that this man lusting for his body wanted nothing but to hurt him, to prick his delicate soul, and he ran faster, panting and sweating in the ceaseless downpour, but heavy-limbed, slow-witted Ibrahim the manservant overtook him and felled him and held him tight and his body touched that of Aslan's, and he held this frightened bird, which had been fleeing for its life, and brought it to the seditious monk, who planted a lover's slap on Aslan's cheek while the manservant covered Aslan's mouth with a slow, heavy, steamy hand and dragged Aslan towards the city gate, and save a few scurrying passers-by there was no one about to take note of them, as the rain poured and the thunder roared and the lightning flashed.

My happy friend, do make certain to write here, and trace the letters over again with a double portion of ink, so that the elders and the wise men will know that at that moment I cursed myself and my ragged, vacuous brain a thousand times for this escapade I had brought upon myself, for I did not know what evil designs these two had on me nor to what sort of place they were leading me, and only the manservant Ibrahim was kind enough to shelter me under the wing of his thick garment to ensure that I would not fall ill or take cold from this heavy rain and that I would be fit for the deed whose nature I knew not save from delusions of benighted desire.

They brought me to a small shack outside the city walls, a wretched hut covered in a loamy thatch that miraculously prevented the raging storm from leaking inside, and once there Tomaso instructed his manservant to wait at the entrance, to guard against unfriendly prying eyes, and the monk planted flaming, stinging slaps on my face and furled his fingers into fists and beat my nose so that it bled, and just as Aslan was about to faint, to slip away to a world of sweet sleep or death, Tomaso revived him and stripped him of his clothing and warmed him with a forceful embrace and told him, Aslan, my dear child, forgive your father for his actions, and he kissed one cheek and then the other, and this new game was more pleasant in Aslan's eyes than the terror of blows that preceded it, and the monk removed his skullcap and his black mantle and revealed his tiny organ wrapped inside its foreskin, and they pressed up against one another and the monk petted Aslan's head and spoke words of praise, not of censure, unto him, of forgiveness and not of insult, of love and not of hate, for they were momentary lovers, and he said, My beloved son, kiss my lips, and they kissed at length, and the narrow, lustful eyes of the monk drew close to those of Aslan's and they were as two brown stains, flickering, and Aslan loved them dearly and his own eyes filled with tears, and he too begged forgiveness for his estrangement and flight, for he had not known of all the goodness and benevolence the monk would bestow upon him.

After that Tomaso cast Aslan prone upon the bed, spread his legs apart and dispatched his tongue to hidden parts, always hoarded from view, and lavished hot, loving saliva on his buttocks and along the deep, miraculous crevice running between them, and Aslan lifted himself, enraptured, to his knees and one sole desire was in his heart: to welcome into his own body the monk's small, uncircumcised member, and he spurred Tomaso on to carry out the deed and the monk, now sprawled the length of Aslan's backside, was perspiring profusely, his heart still pumping madly from the exertions of his sojourn through the city and the pursuit of Aslan and the walk in the rain and now this act of love in a shack, and he thrusts one finger and then another into the enchanted aperture, bringing a rounded burn of pain to Aslan's body, but this pain turns to love and forgiveness and the fingers churn inside that sweet darkness and bring forth an aroma of burnt honey, figs and almonds, an orchard redolent of spring blossoms, and Aslan, wishing to consummate the act, caresses the receding foreskin and makes way for the tip of the erect organ, and outside the storm crests, rain lashing the ramshackle hut, threatening to collapse it from all sides, and Ibrahim, the spectator and listener, releases a sigh of pleasure, and Aslan feels the encroaching intercourse, first light groping around that precious, pain-prone pucker, then in a faster, more determined manner, and Aslan digs his nails into his hands from fear, for suddenly, all at once, without warning, he is filled with a blazing, glorious, sun-like presence, not that of a foreskin, or a penis, or Tomaso, but the essence of masculinity itself, which hurtles through him, spilling and pouring, filling the deepest chasms, healing his coquettish gait and delicate manners and tearfulness and feebleness and foolishness and haughtiness; all these are banished, vanished, dissolved, and Aslan's body threatens to tear asunder, and he emits not one, not two but a string of shrieks, for that force now snaking through him threatens to destroy his intestines and burst through to his stomach and pierce his heart, and Aslan is halved like a man who has fallen on his sword.

Aslan's shrieks melded with Tomaso's repeated sighs, and the two men sprawled across a straw mattress in a ramshackle hut were as one man, one's belly pressed into the other's back, one's organ inside the other's body, their necks entwined, their sweat mingling, and Aslan allowed that organ to slip gently from his body, and he relaxed his rounded muscles and he was shot through with joy and pride over the act he had committed and the fluid now coursing through him and he craved to glance upon the monk and kiss his hands and thank him for the good luck that had brought them together.

Tomaso continued to lie splayed across Aslan's back, apparently wishing to exploit to the fullest the precious moments of pleasure he had not known since his romantic involvement with the yellow-haired monk who had sailed back to Rome, and Aslan, crushed beneath Tomaso's monkish weight, whispered a request that he might slide out from under him and dress himself, for the scalding cold of winter had hit his body all at once; but Tomaso did not respond and Aslan wondered at this odd silence, for he knew well, even from their limited acquaintance, that the monk was loquacious, always moving, never still and never staid, and Aslan extracted himself, wet with perspiration, from under the aged, shrivelled body, only to come face to face with the shock of Tomaso's wide pupils, his minuscule organ, now feebler than ever, and his shrunken and silenced breast. My happy friend, it was none other than Ibrahim, with his slow brain, who comprehended, all at once, what I myself failed to understand, and he took flight and fled for his life, not towards the walls of the city of Damascus, whose gates were shut but for a single, narrow opening kept ajar for the latecomers to return home, but towards the west, to the tiny village from which he had alighted ten years earlier and taken on the performance of a host of duties under the monk's patronage: the preparation of his morning, midday and evening meals, the laborious rubbing of the floors, the master's erect penis in his mouth and on his tongue.

Only Aslan and Tomaso remained in that wretched hut, a powerful stream of water pounding the thatched roof, one standing frozen, his gaze bewildered, the other lying prone in his nakedness, his hand dangling over the side of the bed, his tongue extended, his eyes open wide in reckless abandon, the odour of sweat, semen and a hint of death wafting above him.

O Happy Friend, O Honourable Elders of Damascus, why did Aslan not take hold of the pocket knife concealed in the belt of Tomaso's clothing, why did he not slit the veins of his wrists, why did he not throw himself beside the body to be discovered later, rotting next to the carcass of his momentary lover?

Drums began to beat in his temples: Flee, Aslan, follow after the dimwitted manservant, depart with no intention of returning. For it is enough if they know you were to be found in the company of the monk prior to his demise, enough if they discover remnants of the act of copulation that occurred between you, that same act now sharpening the openings in his body and passing through them a tremor of deep pain, for Aslan will be condemned to death for this crime, perhaps by hanging, perhaps by drowning, perhaps by strangulation.

Aslan emerged from there to return to the city, wanting nothing more than to cleanse his traitorous, loathsome body and lie down upon his double bed, upon the prickly wicker, which seemed to him now a most wonderful miracle, suffused with precious light, and he would like to remove his shoes and dispatch with his sweaty clothing and sleep soundly, sweetly, free of dreams, beside Markhaba, his wife; So flee now, quickly, before some evil eye beholds you.

But his swift return to the city and its walls, the turrets of the governor's fortress and the Umayyad Mosque on the skyline, awakened in Aslan new thoughts of an evil and distressing nature, warning him with drums and cymbals against acting in haste, without consideration or logic, for the emissaries of Sharif Pasha will set search for Tomaso's pleasure cohort, since the friar is distinguished and known throughout the city, his finger in every pie, a junk merchant who buys for a pittance in the villages and sells for exorbitant fees in the city, and who cures illnesses and diseases and expels the evil eye for a reasonable price and a wink, using holy Christian writings as incantations for trifling matters and remedies for nonsense, thus bestowing upon him great status and spreading his fame to all quarters of the city, and when the devoted emissaries find him and discover, through their evil means, the disgraceful path his soul took in departing from his body, they will surely bring Aslan to his deserved demise, and Aslan foresees, with sharp clarity, the oblong grave awaiting him outside the walls of the cemetery, no headstone, no name, no date, no last words of absolution and atonement upon it, only the smear of blasphemous inscriptions.

And with a newfound serenity at the thought of his own demise, which would come about in any case, one way or another, now or after many years to come, Aslan retraced his steps and entered the cursed hut, removed a knife and several small tools he found in the monk's clothing and pouch, among them a soup spoon and ladle, and he took hold of Tomaso's warm, roughened feet and dragged them, along with the weight they pulled behind them, outside the hut, allowing the monk's skull to jounce again and again on the moist, muddy earth, a trickle of rain – remnant of the ceaseless downpour that had continued that whole evening – dancing upon it.

With the aid of the ladle and the blade Aslan proceeded to dig a pit in the damp earth not far from the Damascus-Safed road, and there were no tears in his eyes or drums beating against his temples, only that serenity, which he now thought of as the serenity of the grave; and when he came to understand that digging this grave might require hours and days of toil, whereas it was of the essence that he finish this labour before daybreak, Aslan could see no other way, even after second and third thoughts which only reaffirmed what he already knew to be true, than to dismember the body of this lustful friar into many pieces so that it would never be found, not by Sharif Pasha's soldiers, nor by the gendarmes of the Tufekji-Bashi, nor even by the evil, satanic, destructive angels of the Jewish Quarter.

Your expressive brown eyes are wide and round now, my happy friend, my foundling, though you are aware and understand that it was not evil that coursed through Aslan at that moment but rather his desire to save his own skin; would that Aslan could be pardoned for his heavy sins, for here he is, his helplessness so evident, so plain to the eye, and he takes the blade and brings it to the monk's skin, removes the appendages from the body one after the other and sends each to a different hill, food for the wild dogs and famished jackals, and the knife in his hand is suited beautifully to this new task, and he slashes the feet from the legs, rivulets of blood draining from them, and Aslan stomps on an obstinate bone and quells its opposition until he is finally in possession of the severed feet, each of which he hurls to a separate exile.

It takes Aslan another hour or more, toiling slowly, to work his way up the body of Tomaso, lopping off appendages – sunburned calves, one thigh and then the other – and he dribbles drawings in blood upon the monk's skin and removes, with his hands, the intestines and lungs right up to the juncture of blood and muscles between the shoulders and head, and when Tomaso's skull alone remains in his hand he has finished the job of dismemberment and is free to distribute the organs on the various hills: some he sends along a gushing river to wash them far, far away; others he buries under a thin layer of sand, leaving small mounds, and a strange happiness spreads through him for having brought the task to its necessary completion.

Last of all is the head, its eyes still open, the hair sparse and the tongue swallowed deep inside the mouth, and this head is not only stunned and decapitated but also strangulated, and Aslan kisses Tomaso on his lips, lowers his eyelids, places him on a pointed rock and punts him into the darkness, wishing him a journey of a thousand days to an uncharted place from which he should never return.

PART TWO
MAHMOUD

1

M y happy friend, on the morrow of an eve of dread and tears spent wrapped in the bosom of an unloved wife under a thick quilt, I awakened heavy with nausea to a morning of evil tidings, the persistent pre-dawn call to worship of the muezzin ringing in my ears while Markhaba continued her holy slumber from the previous night and the air was cool and clear, the sun brightening the rain-washed orchard in the wake of the great storm.

An irritating tingle arose from somewhere inside Aslan, from that vague area between the lower back and the thighs, and it was strange and bothersome, slowly spreading and grabbing hold of his body as though it were the cold, strangulating arms of panic itself, and these arms wrapped Aslan in the throes of a deathly, lucid fear, cold and deep blue as the spring sky visible just then through the window.

Markhaba rolled towards him in their nuptial bed and smiled her quashed smile, kissing the phantom phylacteries between his eyes, and Aslan thought at once, See how you beat her with whips and scorpions, abstaining from coming unto her, never bestowing your smile upon her, offering no caresses, no conjugal future, and she smiled again at him and then, for the first time, he looked into the depths of her face, a face on which was engraved that timeless sadness of exile and destruction of the Jewish people, wandering the earth from Salonika and Lisbon to

Damascus and Baghdad, etched on her face in freckles and papules, and from within her weary eyes his own pale face was watching him, and he wished to share a quick confession with her, but then a sharp and incisive thought caused him to hold back: You must watch your tongue, Aslan, that you not incriminate yourself, that you not blurt a word of your whereabouts the previous evening or of your deeds with the monk and his manservant, neither to your wife nor to your parents nor to a single soul in this entire world; may Aslan remain placid, unlike his usual demeanor, may he conquer his tendency to tears, may he disappear into the masses and behave as other men, otherwise they will flay his skin with metal combs until his soul departs in great agony.

Aslan leaves his room, and his home and his father's estate seem more dear to him than ever. He runs his hand along the clay wall of the two-storeyed abode, passes a trembling finger over its cracks, glances at the spacious garden and the rooms adorned with thick and beautiful carpets, and a bitter knowledge strikes him: not for ever will this home stand in its place, not for ever will the Farhi family and its ivory towers endure; nor Kharet Elyahud with all the Jews contained therein, nor the houses of worship nor the fruit stands nor the cobblers fashioning shoes nor the butchers chopping meat nor the stained-aproned slaughterers nor the small, stoop-backed bakers nor the cooks imprisoned in their kitchens; they are all destined for the same ruinous fate: to fall into the flow of the Black River, to merge with the viscid black filth and from there to shut their eyes beneath mounds of earth, forgotten for ever, no poet to sing their praises.

Aslan wishes to scrub his arms and body in a bucket of scalding water, for he reeks of Tomaso, of his scent of sweet and putrid ageing and his odour of death, fresh and pungent, the smell of the monk's genitals strong upon his belly and buttocks, and Aslan squats, his eyes tearing as he is flooded with sadness for having given in to his tortured desire, grimacing as he recalls the monk's stale kisses and filled with self-loathing at the thought of the man's tiny penis and the foreskin rolled up to the tip like a jester's cap, and he steals away to sequester himself in the bathing room so that no one may spy him and read in his expression the distress that has befallen his life.

Aslan stands above the gaping cesspit, and as he aims his organ to relieve himself of water he wishes he could castrate this limp, foreshortened pipe that has brought upon him the nightmare of the previous eve, wishes he could remove the pair of testicles dangling below that they might no longer disturb him with their destructive commands, thus permitting him to return to his days of roses of yore when his body was soft and smooth, his voice thin and pure, and his mind empty of evil thoughts; would that he could take up the blade sitting on the wooden shelf near the cesspit and slice from his body the organ of impurity and hurl it downwards, downwards, then shave the hair from his body and lather himself with creams and unguents, don a woman's dress and live out his life patching and laundering the tattered clothing of men.

From outside the bathing room Aslan imagines he hears the buzz of voices, the sound of horsemen, loud cries, and it seems that his guilt has already been discovered, and he crouches in anticipation of being found and beaten, his brain a jumble of hallucinations: the battle, cries for blood, falling on his sword, shrieks and wails and lamentations, and suddenly a wide-eyed woman is screeching inside Aslan's body, wishing to tear her way through his internal organs where she encounters, among the pathways of veins and arteries, the remains of a shrivelled womb possessed by Jewish men between their ribs, and with eyes wet with blindness and mouth agape and shrieks she demands to be born, to enter the world and destroy Aslan's time-worn and familiar form, and Aslan lowers his undergarments and spreads his legs, terrified to discover the crack of female genitalia beneath his scrotum.

Aslan recalls Moussa, his first love, pure and innocent, with whom he made feeble drawings and leaned upon him and discussed sweet destinies with him, and Aslan knows that since their parting there is no person in this world he can trust and rely upon, and he sheds copious tears of pity for these years of his life passing in suffering and persecution, and the hammers pounding at his temples and the churling cough rising to a bark in his throat prove to him that he must find a living soul upon whose ears he may unburden his nightmare; otherwise, his sanity will shatter.

The barber was sitting, bored, in his shop bereft of customers, and when Aslan entered he did not smile but rather pursed his lips, for anger at himself and the debauched acts they had committed together still stood between them; nevertheless, Aslan fell upon him with embraces and tears and begged the barber to shut the door of his shop and permit him to tell the terrible story that was his lot, and then, while tearing hairs from his head and pacing to and fro, his heels clicking on the drab and filthy floor, he told, breathlessly, the story from beginning to end, how he had not taken the barber's good counsel and had given in to his evil inclination and visited the Maqha, near the home of the Jew Eliyahu Nehmad, and how he had met an older man there, and what the man had told him about his beloved Umm-Jihan, and what he and the man had planned together and what had transpired, and the barber listened without uttering a word, and Aslan unburdened himself of this heavy yoke, shedding tear after tear, telling of his uniting with the monk Tomaso and what had taken place between them, and in choked terror he described the body strewn across his own and how he had dissected it limb by limb that evening, and lo, that screeching woman in his intenstines had returned to her home in the dried-up, shrivelled womb after depositing her heavy baskets, had locked the door behind her and resumed her confinement somewhere within, allowing Aslan at last to accept the barber's welcome offer: Sit, calm down, drink a cup of tea.

The two sat together, Aslan and the barber, and their organs, once erect and pointed one at the other, once thrust into each other's mouth, were now limp and despairing like a slumped washerwoman whose muscles have gone flaccid, her wrinkled dress spread between her exhausted legs, and Elnahar Alaswad continued to flow beneath them, the silence between them heavy and flooded with worry.

The barber said nothing, neither good nor bad; he did not condemn Aslan for this vexatious deed in which he had become involved, did not utter a comment about the dissection of the monk's body and the scattering of his remains outside the city gates, and Aslan was suddenly hard-pressed to understand why he had come to the barber, why he had run to him so breathlessly, why he had forced him to hear every last detail of his crime, for Suleiman alkhalaq was liable, at this very moment, to deliver him to the authorities, and then he would be brought to trial in the presence of the Damascus governor, Sharif Pasha, and the body of Aslan son of Rafael Farhi would be buried outside the cemetery as a mark of disgrace and eternal shame, and in the next moment Aslan showered kisses upon the hands of the barber, swearing him to silence, claiming even that he had merely been jesting, had exaggerated and confabulated, but Suleiman Negrin did not return his laugh, saying instead only that the evil instinct they shared was dragging them to the depths, to an abyss of dung and filth, and Aslan begged him to promise in spite of his anger never to mention a word of this to a single soul, and the barber consented only after considerable pleading on Aslan's part, acquiescing, too, to Aslan's request for a hug, that quick, manly embrace Aslan had desired of his father from his earliest childhood but even a hint of which he had never found.

After these things had come to pass, the barber impressed upon Aslan to understand that if he wished to extricate himself successfully from this distressing situation that had befallen him he would do well to take control of himself and hold his tongue, abstaining from imparting even the tiniest bit of a single word to any living soul, either within the Jewish Quarter or without, to a relative or not, not to any human being or bird or tree, not even to the cockscomb of a slaughtered chicken, for Aslan's life was in grave danger, and it was not merely Aslan's life hanging in the balance, but the lives of the entire Jewish community; if the story of the monk's death were discovered, the Christians, followed by the Muslims, would rise up and riot against every Jewish soul and avenge the pain of his humiliation with acts of rape and pillage and murder and burning, no justice or trial to follow.

The barber Suleiman Negrin held fast to Aslan's shoulders and shook him, his brows drawn together, convulsed in anger and resentment, and said to him, Do you understand what I am saying? He took special care to warn him and make him swear not to enter the Christian Quarter of the city, not to set foot near there, and that he refrain from any suspicious action and from any sudden outburst of tears on his way down the street and from fainting at the entrance to Azm Palace or any other act of ill-considered alarm, and he reiterated: *Khaliha mastourah*, Keep it concealed. And Aslan said, I understand, I do, and he pleaded with the barber never ever to relate a word of this secret to anyone or admit even that they had met one another or of course that this debauched act deserving of the death penalty and the eternal torments of hell had ever taken place, and Aslan asked his advice whether it was best that he escape the city at once without packing a single thing, just take foot and vanish, but he knew the bitter answer himself, that it was incumbent upon him to stay, in the city whose refuse was roiling and bubbling in the Black River beneath the crowded buildings.

After this conversation Aslan turned with a heavy and contemplative heart to the street and sealed his ears so as not to hear the masses shouting of his guilt, and lo, the passers-by were occupied to a man with their usual daily activities: the yeshiva student fixing voracious eyes on veiled Arab women passing through the quarter with sacks of legumes perched on their heads; the barefoot Jewish children, their bellies swollen with hunger, frolicking in mud puddles; every person going about his own business. No eyes take in Aslan as he passes by, not a single person can spare the time to hear his preoccupations or complaints about the irritating tingle gnawing at his internal organs, and Aslan says to himself, Good is the counsel of the barber: guard your tongue, do not speak a word to anyone, allow this wretched affair to perish on its own, perhaps no one will bother with such a trifling matter as the disappearance of a sinful monk.

Aslan paused at a stand offering red beetroot and bought one steaming hot root with a piastre from his coin purse. The beet seller said, *Shoukran jazilan*, Thank you very much, and Aslan asked whether anything new had transpired in the quarter since the previous evening, whether the gossiping women were chattering about any new edict or the proclamation of a fast day or news of any kind, but the beet seller knew nothing, only that the storm had abated and the days of snow were slowly drawing to a close and the beets had harvested nicely and their taste was sweet and beloved, and Aslan nibbled at the dripping vegetable, his clothes filling with stains the washerwomen would toil to remove on washing day, their skin sagging from this coarse work.

For a brief moment Aslan felt sweet relief pass over him, for his fellow Jews were conducting their lives in peace, with no concern for the monk Tomaso or his manservant Ibrahim or the tiny shed they kept outside the city walls or the orifice of Aslan's that had been breached in that very shed; rather, they continued their routines without interruption, here a caravan of camels meandering down the narrow streets, pausing to drink from the gurgling mules' fountain, there stopping by the lemonade seller's stand to drink from a hammered copper goblet, here selecting a fat carrot from the baskets of peasant women come to town early from the villages, there sucking slowly on a narghile, shutting their eyes to enjoy the blend of smoky vapours.

At the next intersection, at the corner of the street leading to the chicken market, stood a gendarme of the Tufekji-Bashi patrol, his green uniform adorned with medals and badges, and Aslan, who noticed him only a few steps before reaching him, wondered whether he was holding an arrest warrant or a search warrant or any such document under his arm, and Aslan was cautious to walk unsuspiciously, but his strides were too long or too short and his toes twisted so that he fell at the gendarme's feet, quite prepared to answer any question the gendarme might ask him and accompany him to the dungeon of the Saraya fortress in the Muslim Quarter, where prisoners were tortured; and the gendarme, like Aslan, was nibbling a beetroot beneath his thick moustache, fully occupied with chewing the hot, red vegetable on this bright and cloudless day, finally casting an astonished glance at the lean, hairy youth strewn on the wet and muddy ground in precious clothing, and when the gendarme extended a hand Aslan jumped to his feet, startling the donkeys, nearly stepping in their dung, and he raced willy-nilly through the narrow passageways unknown to all but residents of the quarter, but the gendarme was preoccupied with polishing off his beetroot and then picking between his large, wide teeth, capping it off with a sigh of pleasure.

Aslan's flight brought him to the far side of the quarter near the ancient cemetery in the south part of Kharet Elyahud, and close by this eternal resting place, with its white worms crawling between pleasant clods of earth, stood the study halls and academies of the Torah scholars, and Aslan listened with half an ear to the prayers of the men crying out as one to the Master of the Universe, pleading for the day in which Our Father in Heaven might forgive them all their sins, that He might embrace His sons, these men standing before Him, a prayer leader at their head, and that He might love their beards, their low, thick voices, their gaunt bodies bent in study of the Torah and accustomed to the weak light of dim rooms, their thin, frail fingers that will never toil like those of gentile men, and Aslan was overcome with great sadness at these lamentations, unanswered for generations, and also that he could not join them, adding his own thin voice to their eternal cries for help.

My happy friend, thus I stood for nearly an hour on the threshold of the Khush Elpasha, the city's main synagogue, with no one to talk to, no one to take an interest in me, until that time when fate deemed it so and down the steps towards me came the Khaham-Bashi in the company of two constant companions, Shlomo Harari and Khalfon Attia, and the Khaham-Bashi is all joy and happiness at the sight of Aslan and he embraces and kisses me as his two friends look on, and says aloud, See how beautiful and sweet is this son-in-law! And he asks after

Markhaba's health, and the friends, as always immersed in their prayer books and biblical exegesis and Talmudic debate, are arguing about the weight of a shoe permitted to a Jew on the Day of Atonement, and about the appropriate punishment for a man who exchanges even a single word with one banned from the community, and they turn to me, words of blessing on their lips, and the Khaham-Bashi is proud to show me off to his companions and mentions nothing of our experiences at the Cave of Jobar, and he wonders whether I might not have the time to join them for a cup of morning tea, and they take hold of my garment and enjoin me to accompany them.

The Khaham-Bashi seats me at a small table with small chairs which precisely suit the diminutive height of his tiny, aged friends, and Aslan cannot help but compare them to his father and uncles, big-bellied and moustachioed, occupied with their epic wars against the Harari family and always ready for some show of strength and enmity, and how they sneer at Aslan and mock him, a chasm of resentment and alienation separating them! The Khaham-Bashi and his cohorts, on the other hand, are sweet-tongued and soft-spoken, feeble and weak, gaunt, taunting one another with riddles about nothing, pulling at one another's beards, and they offer him a doughnut of honey with a touch of khalvah, sesame paste, and they ask Aslan, in a jesting manner, teasing him, where was the young bridegroom during this night of the great storm, did he know how to comfort the Khaham-Bashi's daughter in the uproarious thunder, and did he cover her with a blanket of piastres as could be found, they had been told, in the homes of the richest of men? And Aslan wishes to laugh along with them but suddenly his throat seizes with panic, for had not these very hands, now stirring a cup of tea and dangling leaves of mint in it, had not these very hands caressed the ragged old body of the monk Tomaso that night, and this tongue, now drawing near the rim of the hot glass, had it not licked the lips of the uncircumcised dead man, and was not this body, sitting now in repose under a benelovent winter sun, the very same body with the very same arms and hands and head, eyes, ears, nose, the very same organs that had brought the monk's body to its final resting place, hacking it to pieces and casting each as far as possible in a different direction?

The memory of the bashed skull causes great weakness to descend upon Aslan; his organs plunge, his fingers grow confused and he jiggles the glass of tea, causing it to churn and froth under the gaze of the Khaham-Bashi, who, astonished, gathers Aslan's fingers into his own, kisses them, and says, My son, you are terribly pale, and even the wise old men Shlomo Harari and Khalfon Attia desist from tweaking one another's beards and say to Aslan, Verily, you seem downcast with gloom, and Aslan scolds himself, *Daber khalek*, Come to your senses; if these old men, whose eyes are weak and dim, can detect your panicky pallor, what will Sharif Pasha's investigators say? Will it be possible to withhold anything from their eyes?

Aslan excuses himself from the kind and caring Khaham-Bashi and his two companions and leaves their company, allowing Kharet Elyahud to vomit him out of it, and in spite of the warnings of the barber he exits from the northern gate into the Christian Quarter, and from afar he spies a small gathering and people talking and arguing among themselves, and he recognises the hoods of the Capuchin monks under Tomaso's tutelage, and they are standing alongside the chapel of the monastery and they are perplexed, and Aslan knows it is incumbent upon him to adhere to the barber's counsel and distance himself from the Christian Quarter, but his wicked legs lead him there and he cannot restrain them.

Some twenty Christian men are congregated at the entrance

to the chapel of the Capuchin monastery and they are pounding and beating at the heavy wooden door, shouting, Tomaso! Tomaso! Ibrahim! Ibrahim! And Aslan steals a glance at the open window on the second floor of the tiny monastery, where Tomaso's bedroom stands empty and from where no response is forthcoming, and he feigns innocence, nonchalantly asking one of the men the reason for this assembly, and the man explains that they have been waiting several hours to perform the morning prayers but no one is there, and that now, well nigh midday, they have decided to send for assistance, dispatching one of their members to fetch the French consul, whose patronage all Christian emissaries in the city enjoy. Perhaps he will know something of this matter; after all, they now fear the worst.

Aslan, his voice shaking, comforts the monk, saying that with the help of God in heaven Tomaso will surely be saved from any misfortune that has befallen him, that he must certainly have been detained by an auction or healing the infirm and will return momentarily to his abode to be greeted by all with relieved laughter; and the Capuchin monk is overcome with tears at Aslan's words of encouragement and he kisses the palms of Aslan's hands and wishes him goodness and divine benevolence throughout his days, and Aslan cries along with him, the tears catching in his throat.

Minutes later the French consul arrives, breathless, a stately, be-suited gentleman with bulging eyes and long, thick sideburns that form a threshold of hair for the lines of his severe jaw, and he is in the company of a big-bellied Arab merchant with the look of a charlatan who serves as his *dragoman*, his translator from Arabic to French, and without delay the consul, who shows himself to be a man of action and vigour, orders a tall ladder to be brought from the adjacent sweet shop, and the shopkeeper leaves off cracking pistachio nuts and does the consul's bidding, and then the consul commands that one of the monks ascend the ladder and open the door from within so that they may search for the missing Tomaso and his manservant.

Aslan does not protest when the gathered crowd of the faithful entreats him to provide his feather-light body for this holy mission, and they kiss his hands and ply him with orchid juleps to strengthen his spirit, and Aslan acquiesces with a frozen, artificial smile, and he does not oppose their plans for him to enter through the second-storey window and descend to the first floor to open the door to allow the congregants to enter, and he says nothing about what he knows of the whereabouts of Tomaso and his manservant, he merely grasps the lower rungs of the ladder and climbs up to search the locked monastery in order to discover whether some calamity has befallen the two, and a weeping hope steals into Aslan's heart that the encounter with the monk at the café near the house of the Jew Eliyahu Nehmad and the act of copulation they shared in the shed outside the city walls did not, in fact, take place at all, that they were castles in the air, vanity and a striving after wind, and that Aslan had lain that whole night in his bed, ensconced in his beloved wife's arms and that now he would climb through the window, pull back the curtain and send a smile of relief to the worried gathering of hooded believers, for the monk and his manservant are lying naked, arms entwined, between silk sheets, fatigue-striken after a night of thunder and lightning that banished sleep from their eyes.

My happy friend, at the end of my endless journey to the window, when I reached the flapping curtain, I planted one leg and then the other in what appeared to be the monk's bedroom, and lo, the bed was not dishevelled, the bedclothes clean and pulled taut, and I descended the spiral staircase leading from the living quarters down to the chapel, passing through the aisle between the chairs, highly vexed by the expression on the face of the female icon holding a naked baby in her arms, his gaze condescending, and from inside the chapel I lifted, at the behest of the congregation assembled outside, the bolt from the door and enabled them to stream in, all the while shouting the names of the missing monk and their murdered messiah.

As the crowd continues to surge into the monastery, Aslan hastens to escape before his guilt is revealed. He lowers his gaze and bows his head so as not to encounter the consul or any of his entourage, and he huddles close to one of the walls, waiting for the flow of incomers to cease, and when the last of the faithful has entered the chapel with a sign of the cross and a muttered prayer, Aslan dashes outside as fast as he can, fleeing this den of vipers, so they will not discern his pallid face or read the guilt in his expression; but an old woman stops him at the entrance with loud cries, and from upstairs, peering through the open window, the French consul's advisers summon him to return to the chapel and give testimony of what he has seen, for even his name they do not know.

Aslan curses himself mightily and drags himself back to the chapel as if condemned to death, and they gesture to him to be seated upon one of the benches, facing that female icon who appears to him now to be evil-eyed, and Aslan takes notice of the men's fruitless searches, of their surprise at finding the monk's scorched cooking pot, the embers still glowing under the bean stew that the manservant Ibrahim had prepared the night before. The consul prattles loudly and authoritatively in French and Aslan is afraid: What will become of me if I fall into that one's hands, what terrible fate will befall me then? After an hour-long search that turns up no trace of the monk or his manservant – no letter, no note, not the slightest of hints at the meaning of their disappearance – after all this, Aslan is called to appear before the consul, who introduces himself as the Count Benoit de Ratti-Menton, and his advisers translate the necessary questions to Aslan so as to compile an official report on their findings at the abode of Father Tomaso from Calangianus in Sardinia, what Aslan had witnessed when he entered through the window, whether he had touched anything, perhaps his eyes had caught sight of some object – a letter, some shred of evidence – and they ask what is his name and what is his place of residence and who are his parents and what business does he have at this hour of the day and in this part of the city, and Aslan sputters that he had been perambulating towards the River Barada to feast his eyes and drink coffee at one of the riverbank cafés, and the consul chortles and slaps Aslan's back: Why, we have a real bon-vivant here! To which his sycophantic entourage laughs heartily.

Apart from this laughter, no one is amused, and the consul tries to console the worried crowd: one hundred and fifty thousand piastres in cash have been found on the premises and none of the monk's possessions seem to be missing, which, the consul points out, indicates that no evil has transpired and that the monk has no doubt been detained at the home of one of the rich families of the city, called upon to care for a sick child, to provide some inoculation or exorcise some witchcraft, making use of his God-given talents, and they answer, Would that you be correct; our saviour Jesus Christ will save Tomaso and bring him back to us whole and healthy. And they continue to interrogate Aslan: What business did he have with Tomaso, perhaps they had known one another, perhaps he knew something of the monk's disappearance, and suddenly they recall that Tomaso frequented the homes of the Jews, that he entered and departed and traded with them, that he knew how to manipulate their renowned cunning; and Aslan reproaches himself for his foolhardiness, how it had come to pass that he was now in the presence of these gentiles, and that they know his name and his place of residence and they are on his trail and the trail of all the Jews; Aslan prays they will let him go and that they will pay no heed to the Jews or to Kharet Elyahud and that this interrogation will be erased from their memories.

After he is officially released by the consul, Aslan turns to depart, his eyes averted to avoid being detained yet again, and he refrains from breaking into a run. Behind him the people chatter and opine, and one of them tells another he had seen Tomaso entering the Jewish Quarter the day before in search of someone, and others respond that they had spied Tomaso heading south towards the Jewish gatekeeper, and thus begins a small but persistent rumour that Tomaso has disappeared in connection with some matter concerning the Jews or the Jewish Quarter, and these murmurings threaten to overwhelm Aslan, and he wishes to don a woman's robe and hide his face beneath the veil, sprout breasts and lush buttocks, marry a wild Bedouin and leave the city with him, never to return.

But he does none of these things, and his legs lead him faithfully back to his father's home.

2

For all that Aslan hoped the matter of Tomaso would be forgotten, submerged in the flow of other events in Damascus such as an outbreak of cholera that claimed many victims and the lust-parties hosted by the city's foreign consuls and the strife, quarrels and disputations between merchants, and all other routine affairs, reality rose up and slapped him in the face, for not only was the matter not forgotten, but now Tomaso's disappearance and the question of his presence in the Jewish Quarter on the night he vanished were on everyone's lips.

Everywhere one went – the Jewish souk, the haberdasheries, the Torah academies, the grand salons of the wealthy, the clay-walled homes of the poor – in all of these places the evil rumour whistled and teemed and intensified and inflated, and no one could stifle it; on the contrary, the Jews themselves padded it with new details: how Tomaso had entered the quarter in the morning to hang notices of the auction, how he had left, only to return, unusually, for a second time in the evening; perhaps someone had summoned him, perhaps a rendezvous had been scheduled. He had been spied nodding a greeting to the Khaham-Bashi and cursing an old Jewess, and the pampered son of Rafael Farhi had been spotted the following morning at the entrance to the missing monk's monastery, and what business did a Jew have at the entrance to a chapel? Aslan attempted to seal his ears against the abundance of new information nourishing the gossipers in a slanderous cycle, his only hope that these evil rumours would vanish as they had appeared and that this foolish affair, which had begun with a depraved act and would end he knew not where, would soon be laid to rest.

At home, too, talk was of the sudden disappearance of Tomaso, and Maman imparted to Father some gossip she had heard from friends, that the monk did not follow the path of the straight and narrow, instead sharing his love with the manservant who lived with him; but Father silenced her: What hearsay you women prattle on about among yourselves! He nearly struck her, but reconsidered; then, while sipping luke-warm tea from a jug, the stench of the day emanating from his bare feet, he told her of the Arab merchant he had tried at court, who was found guilty of such acts of love with men – which had become j'nan baladi, the local craze – and Aslan pretended not to listen as his father related the verdict to her, life imprisonment with hard labour, a punishment which very few men succeeded in surviving for even two years. Aslan's parents fell silent until his father shouted at him, What's with that expression on your face!

The more the stories and rumours increased and tongues wagged over the conundrum of the monk's disappearance, the greater was Aslan's temptation to stand before them and tell them, once and for all, in one long, fluid breath, how he had gone to the Maqha upon the counsel of the barber, how he had met the monk there, how the monk had died in his arms, and then his soul would receive their guilty verdict eagerly and with equanimity, as grave as it would be, and he would incline his head towards the slaughtering knife and request their forgiveness, he would behave, for once in his life, as a man; but Aslan was unable, his weak nature got the better of him, his throat clogged and his tongue cleaved to the roof of his mouth, and he decided instead to wait and see how this matter concerning Father Tomaso would play out.

However, aside from the torrent of evil, malicious rumours, nothing came to pass, and it seemed as though the interrogation begun near the monastery had proven inconclusive; perhaps the chief of police had scribbled his signature at the end of his investigation, decreeing that no further measures would be taken in the matter other than awaiting the monk's return, if not today then certainly next week or even a month later, for was it not true that to the west, in the Levant, churches and monasteries were as plentiful as insects and perhaps he had gone there to join forces with them, or perhaps he had grown nostalgic for his homeland, Sardinia. Then the officer would sip from his tea until it had all been consumed, yawn in boredom, and toss the paper aside, onwards.

In preparation for their journey on Friday evening to the Khush Elpasha Synagogue and later for a festive Sabbath meal at her father's home, Markhaba stood silently in their mouldy, stuffy bedroom, arranging her clothing.

That same queer feeling that had stood between Aslan and his father from time immemorial, that same queerness that stood between him and his siblings, his uncles, their children, the children at school, his friend the barber; that same queerness was there in the room with them like a newborn babe lying between them, and he looked at her straggly hair and her pious brown eyes as she adorned herself in preparation for meeting her parents and sisters that evening, muttering the usual Sabbath song – Come let us sing to God/ Let us call out to the rock of our salvation – and Aslan was overcome with hatred and loathing for this mélange of bodily odours and holy mutterings, wondering to himself when she would next try to force him into conjugal relations he did not desire, and whether he would manage to overcome his aversion and acquiesce.

After prayers in the main synagogue of Damascus, where the Khaham-Bashi led the service with great intensity, pleading for salvation and rescue while Aslan trapped hapless flies in flight, they crowded into the Khaham-Bashi's tiny, narrow home, the ragged carpets of which covered simple floors of clay, and the Khaham-Bashi sang together with all the family members and guests the closing verses of the Book of Proverbs, about the woman of valour, then they blessed the wine and passed the wine goblet from person to person, and when it reached Aslan he took great care not to spill even a single red drop of the sweet wine, so that his guilt would not be written upon his clean, white clothing for all to see.

Miraculously, at this table no one spoke of the fate of the missing monk; instead, the hearts of this household were turned to the assurances of the Khaham-Bashi, his eyes sparkling with tears, for according to secret calculations he had conducted, this very Friday, at the beginning of the Jewish month of Adar the First, precisely five thousand, six hundred years since Creation (give or take a few days), the Messiah was due to arrive borne on a white ass, and he would lead them all to the Kingdom of Heaven whose capital was Jerusalem, and the Khaham-Bashi's daughters squealed and giggled, and the diminutive, bearded rabbi sat facing the doorway, never lowering his gaze from that part of the street visible from the small window in the clay wall of his home, and his excitement and hopefulness seized all the members of his household, who, after each mouthful of *shiwa* soup, stopped for an instant to listen to the sounds from the street, only to be answered by the clucking of hens in their tiny pen in the courtyard.

The more certain the Khaham-Bashi became of their impending salvation, and the more the taste of the thick chicken and rice soup settled on Aslan's tongue, so a new feeling welled up in Aslan, a void, as if his soul, the living spirit within him, had been sucked up inside itself, had been emptied into a cesspit and vanished for ever, leaving him hollowed out, rendering him a shell, a vacant wooden puppet, so that while Markhaba laughed with her mother and sisters, something she never did in their own home, Aslan became convinced he was looking at his own worried face, his small, brown eyes and black hair, all of it floating outside his own body, or perhaps he was outside of them, and the profound queerness was seeping into him now, his soul hovering above the dining table and the wine goblet and the braided Sabbath bread and it was as cold and blue as the cloudless night.

Aslan continued his plunge into the depths of that queer feeling and in the infinite obscurity he heard a loud and jarring shriek; who was it shrieking there, who could it be other than that quarrelsome shrew, spreading confusion, and she had taken on the form and shape of Aslan himself, and his own sobbing was nothing in the face of hers, and she tore out her hair and her shoulders convulsed in waves and her entire being was shouts and screams, and Aslan understood that henceforth she was to be his taskmistress, that she would dominate him and enslave him, that she had set up house inside him during his childhood and had burst free today, seeking to gather in all his strength of being, until the people around the table called, Aslan, Aslan, your wife implores you to leave, and only then did he join her so that they could return to their home, as the hour was late.

On the morrow, in the early hours of the great and holy Sabbath day of beloved rest and relaxation, the Farhi family awakens not to the customary call of the *musha'el elnar*, the Arab who comes to light fires in the homes of the Jews, but to loud voices and the whinnying of horses, and Father shouts, Who is making such a racket? And the pious Jews raise their voices against the desecration of the Sabbath, while Markhaba awakens with great excitement in anticipation of the impending arrival of the Messiah, until we see, on the other side of the clay wall surrounding our home, a posse of guardsmen and policemen and soldiers, their progress marked by the trumpeting of horns.

And to Aslan it is clear that these soldiers are there for him, to lob off his head with a polished axe, and he holds only one hope in his heart: that death will fell him in a single, painless swoop, a quick flash beginning with life and ending with – a nothingness. Aslan dresses hurriedly, his hands shaking; come let us meet death erect of posture, come let us bring this chapter of his queer and strange life to an end, and on his Via Dolorosa he will not turn his head towards his estranged family, will not glance at his strict father, nor at his traitorous mother, his evil siblings, his tormenting wife; rather, he will somnambulate towards his jailers, and after his neck has been broken or he has been asphyxiated or stabbed in the heart, all this will end, not to be followed by the rising of his soul or excruciating torments or heavenly delights but an eternal void, a black and silent abyss, and even the evil hag residing among his bones will vanish, buried under clods of earth.

Aslan stands on the tips of his toes to observe, through a crack in the wall, the gendarmes and soldiers spreading out through the streets of Kharet Elyahud, three or four sentries in front of each home, truncheons, muskets and bayonets in hand, and they stand at attention in perfect silence in every square, in every street, facing every synagogue and yeshiva, they wait in front of the fruit and vegetable stands, now closed for the Sabbath and collapsed one on to the other, and they are stationed in the doorways of the small shops, whose windows are bolted with a slightly sour touch of holiness.

Silence pervades the Jewish Quarter, even babies awakening to the Sabbath morning, and women arising in a panic to the sound of shouting; even they hold their breath and keep from shrieking so as not to hasten the end of this mute waiting, and Aslan, standing on the edge of the desolate stone fountain where goldfish no longer bathe and splash, waits along with all the other Jews for the short blast of a trumpet, after which the measured pounding of bayonets and truncheons resounds throughout the Jewish Quarter on this Sabbath day as the soldiers shatter the windows of homes and business establishments and synagogues, and they storm inside accompanied by hounds and specially trained trackers and a few thugs from the Christian Quarter, who mock the Jews and their desecrated Sabbath, raining blows in every direction.

Father commands Aslan to lock the entrances to the house immediately, punching him roundly on the shoulder and shouting, highly agitated, that the soldiers are poised to despoil the remainder of their magnificent possessions, and Aslan is astonished to discern now, for the first time, a spark of terror in his father's eyes; that strange and estranged father known to stun with his blows and shouts, that father whose every decree was honoured and who required absolute silence during hours of repose and absolute obeisance for every whim and whimsy: that father stands gripped with terror at the door to his own home, and Aslan sings songs of mourning and lamentation to himself for his own impending demise.

Soldiers enter the greening orchard of our estate, lances at their belts, and their commander presents Father with an official warrant, signed by Sharif Pasha and approved by his legal adviser, for the purpose of searching Jewish households in order to locate the monk Tomaso, and the soldiers are black-haired and handsome, tall and well formed, their eyes glittering and their hands rough and strong; facing them stands Father in his undergarments, sleep-wrinkled and pot-bellied, his pudgy, soft-skinned fingers that have known no manual labour are clasped together, his knees shaking as if preparing to genuflect before the great army of soldiers.

Aslan regards his father, now greeting these warriors with eloquence, and a strange, distorted laughter takes hold of him suddenly, for this very same tyrant – whose appearance before impoverished Arab farmers, their bills of debt grasped in his hand, causes them to tremble; from whom Maman keeps hidden the mischievous games she plays with Aslan; of whose long and thick shadow Aslan lives in perpetual fear – that very same renowned man of importance is saying, in a voice saturated with obsequiousness, *Tfadlu, tfadlu,* Please, you are welcome, in that singsong Damascene manner, ushering the young men into our home, allowing them to pocket things at random, whatever they find, from Meir's toys to Maman's strings of pearls, and Aslan is overcome with loathing at his father's submissiveness.

All at once it becomes clear to Aslan that he is of no consequence or concern to these soldiers as they overturn blankets and pillows and burrow into the eiderdown filling of comforters scouting for they know not what, and they pass by him in haste, dallying not with Aslan or his hallucinations or his tormented soul, and Aslan shuts his eyes and wills the muscles in his face into a state of apathy and laxity, he settles his breathing – which had been short and irregular – and he quiets the she-demon churning inside him, plying her with gentle caresses, returning her to her cramped and hidden place between his ribs, and she obeys him with reluctance, squeezing herself inside his organs, and Aslan is able to breathe deeply, calmly, since for the moment he is not under the spell of the tyrannical woman, perhaps she will remain imprisoned there for hours and days, and these searches through the homes of the city's Jews will produce nothing and this affair will end right here and Aslan will be left to live out his days.

Aslan has departed from this scene of his family quaking before the manly soldiers and stepped out into the street, where battalions of soldiers armed with bayonets have forced their way into every home, from the grandest to the most meagre, when suddenly he hears someone greeting him and he turns his head to find himself facing the French consul, whose name he has already forgotten, and the man is elegant, stately, his eyes prominent and his moustaches curled and waxed at the tips, and, as always, he reeks of the scents of faraway Europe. The consul recognises Aslan as the young man who agreed most graciously to climb the ladder and open the chapel from within for the Capuchin monks gathered at the monastery, and Aslan returns his greeting warmly, the translator always at the consul's side now interpreting the consul's proud words to Aslan, for Sharif Pasha has appointed him, just the morning before, to head, in the name of the ruling regime, the search for the missing monk who is suspected of having been abducted by the Jews for unknown purposes, and he adds an amiable request to Aslan to reveal at long last where Tomaso is hidden.

Aslan issues a brief and nervous laugh and waits at the side of the consul to see what the soldiers might dredge up and lo, apart from the tears of Jewish women and the shouts of frightened children, apart from the lamentations of the Torah scholars for the holy and sanctified Sabbath queen that has been desecrated by gentiles and Muslims, apart from all this, no other sound can be heard throughout the Jewish Quarter, neither that of the tortured Father Tomaso nor his heroic saviours, and the Count de Ratti-Menton regards the homes of the Jews made of clay, clinging one to the next as if seeking salvation, and he relates to Aslan that he is fearful for the fate of dear Father Tomaso, and he watches the soldiers as they depart from the homes of the Jews clutching copper vessels and jewels and victuals, confiscated at their will, and they wave their hands in front of their noses to rid themselves of the smells from the Jews' homes, the smell of oil lamps and Sabbath stew and gruel left standing on a paraffin stove for long hours, a holy, suffocating stench.

My happy friend, why did I not hasten to take leave of the French consul, why did I not proffer my hand and kiss his cheek and depart from him in peace; why, instead, did I acquiesce to his small, matter-of-fact questions, when he asked who were my friends among the Jews, and behold, my pale pink tongue, the very same tongue wagging now between my gums, that tongue claimed complete freedom to behave as it saw fit and produced the name of the barber Suleiman Negrin as one of my closest friends, describing with precision the location of his shop and adding a morsel of gossip to pique the consul's interest: that alongside the barber's shop was posted a notice hung there by the missing Tomaso with regards to the public auction, and the consul thanked Aslan brightly and sent him on his way.

Aslan returned to his frightened family and to his father, who stood before him and slapped him soundly: Who gave you permission to leave the house, you piece of filth and excrement! Maman chose the moment to reveal that Aslan was in the habit of leaving the house of late and that there were nights when his bed was empty and his wife left alone and abandoned; and this angered Father until he was burning with murderous rage. What business do you have wandering about, you contemptible rogue! And although Aslan was already a married man, his father rained blows upon him one after another as though he were still a *walad zrir*, a small child, and they mocked and scorned Aslan until he fled to his room to sob into his pillows.

My happy friend, that evening the Khaham-Bashi came to our home, crestfallen, and told how the French consul had forced him to go to the small Jewish cemetery, which bordered on the lower part of the Jewish Quarter, where there were ancient tombstones from bygone days, and he had demanded that the freshest graves be dug up to see whether the body of the monk had been concealed there, and although the Khaham-Bashi had explained that it was unthinkable for a gentile to be buried among Jews, for the matter was contrary to the Jewish religion, the consul nonetheless ordered one of the gravediggers to take up a shovel and dig, exhuming two newly buried bodies that had not yet begun to decompose, one of an infant that had died in its cradle, its strangled throat still showing blue, and the other of an older man overcome by a malevolent disease, and the Khaham-Bashi stood next to my father and wept bitterly, and Aslan could not remove his gaze from them; here, before him, was a vision of the end of days, when they would all be thrashing about in the dirt and the blackened waters of Elnahar Alaswad roiling beneath them.

After that Father and the Khaham-Bashi sequestered themselves in one of the rooms and whispered between themselves in low tones, and by bending my ear to catch bits and pieces of their conversation I was able to learn of my calamity, for it became apparent that the barber Suleiman Negrin had been detained on the orders of the French consul and had been taken, bound and beaten, to the Saraya prison, and several Christian thugs had taken shots at his face so that the length and breadth of it was now stippled with blood.

Before falling into a dead faint Aslan wished to extract information and additional details, such as on what grounds Suleiman *alkhalaq* had been detained, and what his interrogators had learned, but Aslan was unable to gather his wits, for just then the evil shrew imprisoned in his womb ballooned up inside him, bursting forth and filling the hollow, empty space between his ears with howls of pain for Aslan's imminent demise, for would not Suleiman Negrin reveal to the Muslims and gentiles the story of his forbidden copulation? And this secret would not only pull down upon him his own death, but also his disgrace, that very same disgrace that Aslan had attempted to flee throughout his childhood and youth, and Aslan turned to his father wishing to look into the depths of his eyes and confess his crime and beg forgiveness; and if his crime warranted death, so be it, he would die in the Saraya Square. But his father was short-tempered and preoccupied and would not listen to him, he merely brushed him aside, preoccupied with matters far more important than those bothering Aslan, and my uncles and cousins and father-in-law marched in and out of Father's study, everyone conferring and weighing options, for a great terror had fallen upon them that perhaps this incarceration was only the first of a larger plot whose end would be a guilty verdict on all the residents of Kharet Elyahud and the evil which had been perpetrated on generation after generation of Jews would be visited upon them as well and would threaten to annihilate them, and once again the Holy One Blessed Be He would fail to save them from calamity.

3

At eventide Aslan lay in his prickly double bed gazing at the candle's flame flickering above its wick, drawing long shadows across the high walls, and he tortured himself with thoughts of his friend the barber at that very moment not far away, in a similar room, also wrapped in shadow, perhaps maintaining a deep, choking silence in the face of the barrage of questions the French consul is asking, perhaps retorting with impertinent responses that will cause the consul to permit a speedy return to his shop and his six pauper clients; or perhaps he accepts with trembling lips the cup of sweet tea served him by the stately French gentleman who adorns his fingers with powders and ointments that please his skin, and the barber provides him with each and every detail of his conversation with his friend Aslan, kisses the consul on one cheek and proffers the other to be kissed in return. It was not long before there was a knock at the bedroom door.

Without thinking, Aslan answered in a quiet, confident voice, Enter, let the soldiers take him and strip the tunic from his body and he will recount the story of his guilt from beginning to end, yet who entered the room but Maman, who had not visited him there from the time of his undesired marriage, and what did Maman want at this time, and what was the strange look in her eyes? After all, from her womb and body had Aslan entered the world, from her lower lips his head had protruded; why was she so estranged to him? Even her rings concealed their splendour. Aslan allowed her to enter and could see, in spite of the thin light of the candle and her long, black hair, the wrinkles covering her forehead and the old furrow of anger running the length of it, and Maman caresses Aslan's cheeks and brings her mouth close to him, that same mouth whose teeth will one day, in her old age, fall out, as the itinerant priests will inform Aslan one day hence, but for now they lean one upon the other, quivering above infected gums, and she says, simply, *Inte biher?* Is everything all right, Aslan dear? And she moves to embrace him and Aslan permits her, hoping to renew their games of yore, perhaps he will don for just a moment the black cape draped over her shoulders; and Aslan knows not what his mother desires, why she has come to his room, why she has buried his head between her breasts, and what is this scrap of paper she is passing into his hands, and as she departs from the room he deciphers the hurried writing, the curled, flowing letters, the rebellious *hamza*, which changes position each time it appears, the dots that connect to form lines that lend the words their meaning and pronunciation as in his own name, here before his eyes, Aslan Farhi, the *tzad* fat-bellied and fleshy, the *nun* deep as a dark well, the *kha* and the *ya* in his surname short and clipped, pursued by shame, and two definitive lines, thick and coarse, drawn under his name.

Thus Maman's visit becomes clear to Aslan, for six names are listed there on that scrap of paper, people whose surnames attest to the fact that they belong to the impoverished members of the Jewish community, those six beggars, friends of his own friend the barber Suleiman Negrin, and beneath their names his own, the seventh, while above the seven names, in bold print, the words WANTED URGENTLY, and Aslan does not understand the meaning of this matter; bitter laughter fills his heart that his name has been included on this list of impoverished Jews, and he envisions them in contrast to him: their beards eaten away by lice and his own neat and shaven face, their tattered garments and his own suits of linen, the foolish look in their eyes and his own intelligent, serious expression; what a band of buffoons was destined to be the chorus accompanying him to the executioner's rope!

Aslan laughs mirthlessly, he has no idea what hour or place has been scheduled for his detainment. A deep suspicion pecks at him, that the barber, his partner in confessions and acts of love, has not hesitated to provide his name to the consul, just as the Jews have been known for their traitorous behaviour from time immemorial, now once again they are informing on one another, slandering one another, and they know not the meaning of brotherly love or a covenant of community or the importance of working the land or engaging in manual labour; rather, their delicate, deficient souls, which are unschooled in warfare and in facing an enemy and beheading him in a single swoop of the blade, would shatter and surrender against a band of gentile men.

Just then Aslan recalls the good counsel that the barber gave him, and the oath he swore, and their naked embraces of yore, and the deep affection they whispered to one another from the dawn of their first meeting at the barber's shop, and their fluttering kisses and the passion they shared, honest and true, and for the next few moments Aslan feels certain of the loyalty of his new friend, with whom he had shared his secret, and he consoles himself with praises of their loving, manly friendship.

The gate of our home swings shut as I depart as one condemned to die for the interrogation at the consulate, and Aslan stands bare-handed against the raging winds as they flail and assail him with their frigid gusts, spinning and swirling into tall, narrow funnels and provoking the shrew hidden inside him, rapping at the door of her hiding place somewhere between the twists and turns of his colon and his caecum, whistling to her, inviting her to come out and join their dance, and Aslan is swept off in a dense maelstrom now bolstered by clouds gathering from the west and heavy drops of rain, and his legs and arms are drained of blood, utterly pale, and he is tossed and battered by the winds and yearning for the hand of a man, an arm covered densely with black hair, that will rub drops of anisette on his lips to revive his soul.

Never before has Aslan been interrogated, nor has he been required to sleep even a single night outside Kharet Elyahud or his parents' home or his own bed, always wrapping himself up in pleasant nightclothes; as he passes by *le guardien* it seems to him, to Aslan, that he will never see this man again, or the simple clay hovels of the impoverished, or the chicken market or Teleh Square or his own home, everyone and everything has become alien, estranged, they are unconcerned with Aslan, nor do they share his fate: Aslan will proceed to the interrogation, then the trials, and finally the executioner's rope, he will fulfil the destiny proscribed for him for his sins and crimes, and his life means nothing to them.

Aslan shuts his eyes in order to silence the winds and, with the help of the shrieks of that old Jewish hag inside him, a shrill-voiced woman orphaned and widowed and afflicted, he considers matters at hand, arriving at the conclusion that the barber has betrayed him, that he has handed over all his secrets to representatives of the Egyptian ruling regime and they are expecting no less than a confession of his copulation with the monk and the dissection of his body; and Aslan will, therefore, confess to his crime and then request a quick and pleasant death in deep, dreamless slumber, his senses dulled, for he is most fearful of the pain inflicted by a chopping blade.

Aslan is admitted to the consulate at the northern tip of the Christian Quarter, not far from the River Barada splashing about in its waters, and he is ushered to the second floor, which is higher than the other buildings in the street, and he is left alone to inhale the air before the interrogation commences and permitted a moment to gaze down at the crowded, dusty city from whose environs Aslan has never departed in his life, and facing him are the turrets of the Umayyad Mosque from which in a very few moments the muezzin's voice will issue forth, and Aslan bids farewell to these beautiful sights, this Garden of Eden in a desert valley, to the streets of Damascus and his days of roses, and to his dear old friend, his Moussa, and when a polite clearing of the throat from inside the room reaches him, Aslan knows that the hour has arrived and he turns to enter.

Shiny, scented leather-bound books stand in order along the shelves of the consul's massive library, the man's eau-de-Cologne wafting through the air. The rosy-cheeked consul is smiling at Aslan, who catches a glimpse of the thick notebook in his hand, the pages filled with dense writing, and this is the book of his destiny, the confessions of the barber surely written therein alongside his own ignoble deeds, and before the consul has a chance to utter a word and before his acquaintances have a chance to translate the consul's questions into the *Shami* Arabic dialect, the final syllables of every sentence drawn comically, farcically long, the churning storm inside Aslan breaks loose in an enormous wave of roiling water, and Aslan knows that the time has come to make a full confession before them.

Aslan is brought before a team of interrogators – the consul, and Beaudin, the consul's roguish-looking chancellor-dragoman, and a court clerk – and following several short, standard enquiries with regards to his name and his surname and the names of his siblings, they hint, their expressions immobile, that the barber has revealed a number of details concerning him and immediately they begin questioning him as to his whereabouts on that fateful day, a Wednesday, the last day Father Tomaso was seen, and Aslan tells them of the time he spent accompanying his father and what transpired at the *Majles*, the Council of Jewish Elders, and the trial he attended, and he tells them of the moment or two he tarried outside the barber's shop to read the notice about the public auction, and when they ask him about events that occurred in the evening, at night, Aslan's throat constricts and he steels himself to continue telling about the dissection he carried out, about the secret trapped inside him and for which he wishes to be punished; and lo, in the moment before a torrent of words gushes forth from his mouth, flooding the entire room and the ink and quills of the interrogators recording the questions and answers on large squares of paper, the door to the room opens and a fourth interrogator enters and comes to stand beside the escritoire upon which all the other men are leaning, then withdraws his own quill and ink and takes a seat.

Tall and stately, blue-eyed and blond-haired, his appearance is that of a European though he is clearly an Arab by the greeting he utters, and from this man's face, this fourth, kind interrogator, Aslan is struck by a white light, thick and bewitching, which blinds him and hammers between his temples, and the eyes of this excellent man resemble the light blue of the fringe on a Jew's prayer shawl, his own fringe clipped short over his forehead, and Aslan's mind is jumbled into confusion, and he is sucked into the shining ray of light, shifting his weight from side to side on the chair, his head spinning and dizzy, for this is the first time in Aslan's life that such an unfamiliar feeling is throbbing inside him, of tears mixed with exultation, and drumbeats of new hope, and the colourful light of eternity pure and clear, and at that very moment he resolves to change his plans; he will not reveal the secret of Tomaso's death, for his life suddenly seems more dear than he had thought it could be and he wishes to spare his days, the numbers of which had just now grown perilously short.

From that moment Aslan's answers grow vague, confused, he cannot recall his actions of that evening, nor the hour at which he lay down in his bed, nor the final words he shared with members of his family, and it seems to Aslan that the new interrogator has slipped him a small smile, and Aslan wishes to learn the meaning of this smile as he hastens to answer the questions that follow, and from there the interrogation wanders to odd and sundry topics with no connection at all to Tomaso or that stormy night that led to his demise; the interrogators are interested in other details, such as what are Aslan's preferred garments and what are his favourite colours and which songs does Aslan know to sing, and questions about the day of his wedding and what has transpired since and what kind of woman is Aslan's wife Markhaba; and Aslan vacillates at first, but in the presence of the new interrogator's smile and his maddening silence, and his pale blue eyes that shine like a naughty fox among the grape vines, Aslan recounts the story of his matchmaking and of the unloved bride with whom he shares his bed, and he tells them of his birth and childhood, of his tetchy sister of the blue gaze, of his brother and his games, and Aslan glances sideways to glimpse whether these matters are not dull to the new interrogator, or repulsive, awakening his loathing and revulsion.

But this interrogator continues to smile his good, compassionate smile and his eyes continue to shine, and the interrogator moves from the edge of the escritoire where he had sat to listen to the unfolding tales of Aslan's life – which no person prior to this day had deigned to hear, not even a single detail of it – and he gently commands Aslan to carry on speaking, his voice lucid as a singer's, and Aslan takes note of the manly, bulging veins of his hands as they transport the inkwell and quill and record the remainder of Aslan's answers about how he had slept the whole of that night in his bed, had not set foot outside his home, had not seen the monk for a very, very long time, perhaps since he had been inoculated against smallpox long hence, in his childhood.

However, the other interrogators were not satisfied with my responses and they dug deep into my activities that evening, desirous of more details, more precise answers, such as what was the exact hour I had lain down upon my bed, and what were the exact words I imparted to my wife, and what did she answer, and Aslan's tongue mocked him and he answered absentmindedly, for he had not shut his eyes that entire night and they were in a rush to reveal why it was that he had not slept that night, and he hastened to correct himself, that he had in fact fallen asleep but that his sleep was troubled, and they wished to know the nature of his nightmares, and Aslan's tongue stuttered and stammered and he could find no suitable response, and he was about to repent all his lies when the handsome interrogator took notice of the gathering storm and appealed to the French consul for permission to interrogate the young man again in private, when he had gathered his wits and refreshed his memory, and the interrogators consulted and whispered among themselves at length, until the Count de Ratti-Menton cast a penetrating gaze in my direction and told me through pursed lips that I was excused for several hours' leave, that my interrogation would continue that very night, two hours past the muezzin's third call, and only because of my family's good name and the assistance I had given to the monks in entering the locked monastery would I not be required to post a bond, and I was free to go on my way.

*

134

Aslan departs from the consulate without comprehending how it is that the course of his life has drifted off to this particular point; one moment precious light is shining on him and another moment he wishes to cast his life aside, and the glorious ray of light from the Good Interrogator appears then hides behind the clouds of his worries, and thus, deep inside his thoughts, he passes through the gate into Kharet Elyahud, and as he walks along the narrow streets, which are covered as always in a layer of putrid yellow sewer water, the gossiping old hags shout at him to hurry to the Khush Elpasha Synagogue where a huge rally is taking place at that very moment, and every Jewish male of bar-mitzvah age is required to attend, and Aslan goes there against his will, for he has no wish other than to escape to a long sleep – in the arms of the Good Interrogator – from which he prefers never to awaken.

Many men have filled the main synagogue, not only the Torah scholars, sweating in their thick clothing and full beards, but also his pot-bellied uncles, and here was his father, too, alien and estranged to him, perpetually tense and angry, standing among them, his fat flesh trembling as a soul trembles for its life, and all the impoverished Jews are there as well, the simple haberdashers and coppersmiths and shoemakers, and Aslan regards them wearily; like them, he, too, is out of breath and heavy of limb, his soul bereft of strength, and their faces blur and become many dark spots that mix together into an ashen batter, lifeless and meaningless, and in juxtaposition Aslan wishes to recall the Good Interrogator – handsome, radiant, his gaze manly and self-assured, his stature proud and erect, and the dazzling light that shines from him and drowns Aslan with its power – but the rustling of the crowd has intensified and is growing louder in Aslan's ears, and he is about to plunge into that Aslanish gloom of his, to swoon and convulse into it for all to see, but just then the blast of a ram's horn splits the air in a manner not heard even on the Day of Atonement, and the eyes of all turn to the reader's pulpit, where Rabbi Antebi, the Khaham-Bashi, is now standing in his brown cloak, a scarf tied at his waist, and he trumpets the strange and ancient ram's horn, dotted with violet spots and stored among the treasures of Khush Elpasha, brought out only rarely, the *shofar* of one of the great rabbis of yore, Yoshayahu Pinto.

Without understanding the meaning of this urgent gathering, the Jews raise their voices in the wailing lamentations reserved for days of fasting, for they are terrified by the *shofar* blasts, and Rabbi Antebi, short of stature and quick to jest, now grows red from the effort of blowing the ram's horn, and he raises his arms like Moses to quiet the people, but the men continue to talk among themselves, snivelling, wiping their noses with cloth handkerchiefs produced from hidden pockets, and Aslan regards them from afar and removes himself from them, and an ancient loathing arises in him; how he despises their submissiveness, their endless supplications to God, for Aslan knows the meaning of this spontaneous gathering: to bemoan the new edicts befallen the Jews.

Aslan wishes to return to the street, his sole desire is to be alone in his room with his longings for that yellow-haired, blue-eyed man, but just then a new mass of Jews – Torah scholars and merchants and peddlers – assembles at the entrance to the main synagogue of Damascus and so, for the moment, there is no way of departing; instead, a thick, sweet mixture of Jewish sweat chokes the air and from within it, trembling and nervous, rises the voice of Rabbi Antebi, his wife's father, who informs the large and holy crowd that God, His name be blessed, is testing all the Jews by placing before them a new edict, and this is none other than the birth pangs of the Messiah, for according to his calculations the Kingdom of Heaven will descend to earth during these very days, five thousand, six hundred years since Creation.

The Khaham-Bashi tells the large and holy crowd how he was summoned that morning to Azm Palace by His Honour the governor, Sharif Pasha, adopted son of the rebel Muhammad Ali, along with his friends Shlomo Harari and Khalfon Attia, and how the governor had shouted at them in language to which they were unaccustomed: Where is his grace, Father Tomaso?! And how Antebi had answered him light-heartedly, Am I Tomaso's keeper? And how Sharif Pasha had hurled his slipper at him and commanded the rabbi to bow down and bare the nape of his neck to his chopping blade and said, Many are the witnesses who saw Father Tomaso enter Kharet Elyahud on the day of his disappearance, to which Rabbi Antebi retorted, Is the Jewish Quarter closed and off-limits? After all, two gates are there in the quarter, and perhaps the monk entered, spent several hours, then departed. But the governor grew more and more angry with each of Antebi's answers until finally he allotted Antebi and his two aged friends and all the Jews of Kharet Elyahud one day, and one day only, to bring the monk before him, dead or alive, to rescue him from his hiding place or the grave in which he had been concealed, and if not he would command the Damascene army of gendarmes and mercenaries to assault the quarter again and kill every male, from infant to child, from young man to old.

All at once the Jewish men begin wailing loudly, and their tumult spreads to the women, who tear at their hair in the women's gallery above, and Aslan casts about to grab on to a banister or chair back, and Rabbi Antebi strives to strengthen the spirits of his congregation in the face of this trial with which God, His name be blessed, is testing them, and after these things come to pass the rabbi removes from behind the embroidered gold curtain of the Ark of the Covenant the Crowns of Damascus, ancient Torah scrolls saved for times of distress, and swaying side to side with the scrolls crowned in hammered gold he sings – Let us repent to God and He will take mercy upon us and bring us into the light; and then he whispers an oath of bygone days, rife with curses one would not dare repeat, that whoever knows anything at all of the disappearance of the monk and does not come forward at once to make his report will be cursed for ever, ostracised unto the seventh generation from the Jewish people, defiled and untouchable; and this person will bear upon his conscience the bizarre, twisted destiny of his Jewish brethren, not only in the Khush Elpasha Synagogue or the Jewish Quarter of Damascus but in Aleppo and Beirut and Cairo and Acre and Tiberius and Jerusalem and Baghdad and the Jews of every city the world over, in their ritual baths and their synagogues; and these strong words he concludes with a direct plea to Our Father the King who sits on high and takes note of His defenceless, persecuted children, who have nothing but their Talmud and their petty, impoverished businesses, and Rabbi Antebi pleads with Him to open the Kingdom of Heaven and listen to their cries and their shouts, so that He might put an end to this distress that has befallen the Jews, for He is their witness that they have caused not a single hair to fall from the head of the Christian, and they desire nothing but to live peacefully in this south-west corner of the walled and ancient city and to go about their business uninterrupted.

This whole affair causes a frozen laughter, trembling and tortured, to arise in Aslan, a story born of a forbidden act of copulation that has evolved into a threat to kill all the Jewish males of Damascus, and he gazes upon the furrowed faces of the frightened Jews and lo, even the babies and infants are silent, ageing all at once, their hair turning white and their shoulders stooped, and Aslan takes note of the gaunt Torah scholars and his pot-bellied uncles and the paupers and the children and infants and babies, and suddenly they are all deceased, piled naked one atop the other in tall heaps, unburied, with no portion in the world, their skin white, inert, their eyes shut, their limbs jumbled, some of them trampled under the soldiers' boots, stabbed by knives and bayonets, and there are those whose heads have been bashed with rocks and stones, and he wishes to flee that place, to banish from before his eyes the piles of naked bodies, and Aslan pushes his way towards the door of the synagogue, imagining himself drowning in deep puddles of blood, but the crowd of congregants blocks his way, and amid cries of Messiah! Messiah! Messiah! they raise their eyes to the entrance of Khush Elpasha to see whether it might not open for them to catch sight of the white ass and its holy rider marching by in a procession.

Aslan fights against them to depart from there and flee to the Good Interrogator, who will save him from his dread, but from every direction lifeless white hands grab at him, their fingers grasping at the cloth of his cloak, and they do not let him pass, and Aslan fights to ward them off, to remove the hands from his clothing, and he strikes at the prodding fingers and tries to prise them free, to crush them, but they are stronger than he, they surround his body by the dozens like an army of spiders, and Aslan slips out of his cloak and stomps on the floor and on the many worshippers, and their fingers hold tight in order to calm him, and they murmur softly to him, crooning, but the touch of their nails sets his flesh aflame as if they were filling him with their poison and trapping him in their many webs to suck the marrow from his bones and put him to death.

My happy friend, forgive me for the nightmarish visions I am pouring into your youthful, innocent soul; from the look in your

139

eyes I can see that I have troubled your soul mightily, and your heart appears to be beating wildly, so let us now step outside this sombre abode in which we mete out our days and lie down upon the sloping hill, for as it is written, Truly the light is sweet and a pleasant thing it is for the eyes to behold the sun; as for this terrible tale you have agreed to hear and record on paper, it is only a story that takes its form from the power of punctuated words and sentences and nothing more, so now take hold of my hand and show me the path to the pleasant air.

Still, I must add that Aslan fled for his life from Khush Elpasha, but before making his escape he heard, from far away, a voice, and it was none other than the Khaham-Bashi calling him, Aslan, this way my child, over here, and Aslan answered his call, and the Khaham-Bashi embraced him heartily, as a man on his way to die, and he laughed through his tears and said, My dear son, these are black days that have befallen us, days good for slumber and nothing more, and Rabbi Antebi showered Aslan with farewell kisses and another embrace, his priestly scarf wrinkling at their touch, and he did not wipe away the torrent of tiny, transparent tears flooding his face, and his wife and daughters, who came to join him, cried copiously along with him.

And Aslan noticed his father, who was standing in the street as well, pretending to search his pockets for some note lost for ever to the world, and Aslan stood facing him, waiting for him to desist from this searching and turn his gaze to him and offer the caress he so desired, but his father continued to stand where he was, at a distance, and after a long while Aslan returned to his home and its thick clay walls to await his meeting that same evening with the Good Interrogator, who would save him from the prodding fingers, and he glances behind him on occasion to learn whether the Khaham-Bashi had been right, that God's disciple had indeed reached Damascus, or that if not the Messiah King then perhaps his father would raise his head, smile at him and call him to join him on his way.

4

Aslan passes the hours in thrall of the evening ahead and the meeting with the Good Interrogator, and he eagerly anticipates the relief and salvation it will bring both for him and for all the Jews from this calamity that has complicated their lives, and he dismisses the touch of those prodding fingers from his skin and steps out into the orchard of his father's estate in order to calm himself among the long, narrow aqueducts that transport the River Barada and to steel himself with fine, invigorating thoughts, just like the waters of the river itself, for in just a matter of hours he will come before the yellow-haired man and make a full confession of his forbidden intercourse and the events that followed, and the Good Interrogator will be amused, will smile his good smile and wipe away Aslan's tears and comfort his troubled soul, and they will go together to reason with the consul and his assistant and his clerk, urging them to call off the interrogation and their accusations against the Jews, and Sharif Pasha will issue an order to annul the edict against the citizens of Kharet Elyahud, and after many days, when the spring arrives and along with it cool gusts of wind and sweet rays of sun, the two of them will sit at one of the Damascene cafés on the banks of the River Barada drinking cup after cup of coffee, their mouths full of gurgling laughter at the unfolding events of this drama.

Aslan is confident and assured that the tall, handsome interrogator will trample underfoot any poisonous, hairy-legged spider that attacks him, will protect him with sweet embraces and save him from all oppressors, and Aslan reflects upon the Good Interrogator's proud and shapely form, his shoulders protruding under his tunic, his manhood visible through the cloth, his muscled heels in their sandals; how magnificent is this man in his eyes, the symbol, the paradigm of his heroic, esteemed people, the tribe of man. His musculature is well formed, his limbs thick and coiled, the look in his eyes intelligent and powerful, his voice deep and full of assurance, for the glory of the entire world and all its beauty were created by none other than those good men who toil to carry beams in their naked arms and erect buildings and pave roads and plant orchards, among them the porters and builders and labourers; and all of Damascus as it stretches out before you, and every chiselled stone in your father's home have been built by virtue of their vigour and strength, their welcome tenacity and their will-power, and the stately turrets of the Umayyad Mosque and the fortified walls encircling the city and the modern, underground river conduits that lap at the gardens that run its length and breadth: all these were created and carried out and brought to life by virtue of their brains and their brawn.

Aslan's eyes fill with tears, for he cannot count himself among them, and he pinches his arms until they bruise, for he is a son of a soft, deposed and forsaken people, a people so despised that the nations of the world banish them from country to country, from realm to realm, from city to city, and their menfolk are not fit for manual labour, they are neither powerfully built nor courageous, and they are not proficient in the ways of war and are incapable of waging battle; and Aslan's only hope and expectation is to unite with this new love who miraculously chanced across his path, this young man who, in addition to his handsome countenance and yellow hair and pale blue eyes and impressive stature, has posed so many questions to Aslan and, thanks to his sly smile and enticing silence and his shining, compassionate eyes, has prompted Aslan to speak freely; and his beloved will fill him with his love and his juices and his sweat, and he will blend with him and pour into his own Aslanish blood the strength and pride of good men.

While strolling in the orchard Aslan becomes aware of a commotion taking place within the house, and it is soon apparent to him that Father and the Khaham-Bashi have returned from the rally at the Khush Elpasha Synagogue and have sequestered themselves in one of the rooms; through a thin crack in one of the windows Aslan catches sight of their eyes rolling in their heads and the Khaham-Bashi's splayed legs, and he hears bits of sentences here and there, for the time that Sharif Pasha has allocated is quickly passing, and the meeting in Aslan's home grows noisier and noisier, new waves of people are joining, and his cousins are coming and going from the house whispering among themselves. Only Aslan knows that there is no need for their efforts and endeavours, for the Good Interrogator will bring about the end of this drama, and an excellent conclusion it shall be.

Aslan proceeds light-heartedly to the consulate in the Christian Quarter, eager for his encounter with the Good Interrogator, lusting to fulfil his desires. His step is lively, and passers-by cast accusatory glances at his swaying, pampered gait, and he is like the man bearing tidings to King David, a man running alone, but Aslan pays them no heed, for the way to the consulate is sweet at this hour of the day, when the disputations of men have abated, their shops closed under lock and key, their market stalls folded up and waiting mutely for the next day, and the wardens and the prisoners and the clerks and the merchants of cloth and vegetables have completed their dusty quotidian of work, and now the hour is ripe for bringing to a close that which needs to be finished.

En route to the consulate Aslan catches sight of a stately woman of beauty wearing a wide-brimmed *chapeau* in the style of European women, and an unruly hope overwhelms Aslan that this is the woman he has laid eyes on only for a few precious minutes but who, nonetheless, he is certain is the only person in the world who can understand the machinations of his heart, created in the fashion of that gentle songstress of trilled notes and frilled tresses, and he is sorely tempted to call after her but she is quick to slip away and he follows after her in haste through alley after alley, lane after lane; but her sprint is skilful as a man's and in seconds she is lost to him, and the wide-brimmed hat is lost, too, along with her statuesque figure and her fresh complexion.

At a bend in the Straight Street Aslan stops to calm his jagged breathing and a small boy leading a mule to the fields tosses an apple from his sack to revive him, and Aslan bows his head slightly, in gratitude, his breath laboured as he takes a bite from the red fruit.

When the attendant opens the gate for him, Aslan requests to see the good, yellow-haired interrogator urgently, but he is informed that the man has gone to anoint his skin with unguents at the Nur Aladdin *hammam*, the baths near the Khan Assad Pasha, and that Aslan should wait for him a bit, and the waiting is long and agonising, and at last the tall, stately figure appears in the threshold of the building and the Good Interrogator, dripping with pleasant scents, beams at Aslan and greets him and compliments him for reporting as planned and for being trustworthy to a fault, and Aslan wishes to make a full, unadorned confession, barely able to contain himself from speaking out at once, but the Good Interrogator instructs him to restrain himself and to follow him to his private quarters in the consulate, and continue his interrogation behind closed doors, for the number of spies and eavesdroppers and slanderers has increased of late.

They enter a side room in the consulate which appears to be a clerk's chamber only recently converted into the Good Interrogator's private residence, containing a canopied single bed abundant with pillows and bolsters and a window facing east to the wide and endless desert that extends all the way to the rivers upon which the city of Baghdad sits, and Aslan imagines showering the Good Interrogator with many wet kisses and sucking from him his beauty and manliness.

The interrogator explains with an apologetic smile that because of the speed of events he has committed a grave error of *politesse* and failed to introduce himself properly. He tells Aslan that his name is Mahmoud Altali and that he is a Christian Arab, and they shake hands informally, with palpable warmth, and Mahmoud prepares *khalib alsaba'a* for them – lioness's milk – which is *araq* diluted with a small quantity of water, and they clink glasses and sip, an embarrassed silence between them.

Mahmoud breaks the silence, expressing a desire to become acquainted with his new friend in a leisurely fashion, and his voice is sweet and pampering; he is some ten years older than Aslan and worldly, and Aslan is overcome by a pleasant warmth, and slowly a twilight conversation develops between them, and there is nothing competitive or derisive or base about their banter, for they discuss matters of the soul and nothing else, matters such as Mahmoud's father, who was an itinerant merchant, and how when Mahmoud was three years old his father left for Cairo never to return, and how his mother raised him alone and oppressed his soul so that he was forced to run away from her and her sorcery, and the songs he loved to sing and how perhaps one day, given the opportunity, he would sing for Aslan.

Aslan asks many questions of this new friend of his, met by chance, as well as advice from his lifetime of experience, and Mahmoud tells Aslan in a flowing prattle, as if some heavy weight has been rolled away from his heart, about the domineering nature of women, how they have no purpose other than placating their odd-looking and hairy sex, so that rather than leaving their fathers and husbands and sons and uncles to set in motion by their own vigour the river of plenty of life itself, they harness their men to slavery and usurp their power through acts of intercourse and cause disputation between them through evil words and burden them with providing for their whining children, and they spread their net over the boy-child when he is still nursing, and when he is a lad, and when he is a youth, and later they force him under the marriage canopy, and thus a mother's ageing tyranny is replaced with a bride's youthful tyranny, and their faces readily turn sour, their expressions wrathful, and they are always prepared to share evil gossip with unbridled glee, and if the husband requests to join his fellow men, his former friends, for a game of cards or to raise a toast, they make his life bitter with reproaches and stand between him and his confrères, and they make alliances with their sisters – the mothers, wives, daughters – so as to keep one man from the other, one beloved from his mate.

Aslan recalls his former friend Moussa and what became of him and tiny tears clog his throat, and he knows that Mahmoud is speaking in truth and good judgment, and Aslan is extremely grateful and listens eagerly, wholeheartedly, not only to how women are domineering but also how they are traitorous, and how they seek out a man's sex with the desire to lop it off, and for this reason it is incumbent upon men to take utmost precaution when lying with them so that they will not lop off their sex or the testicles that quiver beneath in fear, and Aslan is astonished to find this soulmate and he recounts his failures with Markhaba to Mahmoud, and Mahmoud caresses him with his pleasant voice, wrapping him snugly in words of encouragement and consolation.

After another sip of lioness's milk Mahmoud asks me to draw near, his thighs brushing against my loins, and he wishes to return to the subject of his interrogation, the story of the disappearance of Father Tomaso, but I, my happy friend, I am unable to prevent myself from revealing my dark secret to the Good Interrogator, from beginning to end.

Thus, my brown-eyed lad, I begin to recount to Mahmoud, *sotto voce* and with a heavy sigh, my full confession, for it is I who hold the key to the secret drawers that no one else can open, and the Good Interrogator regards me with a mixture of curiosity and astonishment, for I am speaking with great emotion, my breath shallow, my words swallowing one another, and I tell of that stormy night, and of the manservant Ibrahim, and of the hut that threatened to collapse in the raucous wind, and of the act of love with Father Tomaso, and of the excitement that took hold of him and snuffed out his life, and thus I make it known to Mahmoud that the Jews have no guilt upon them, for they have committed no crime against the monk, so it is incumbent upon us to explain to the French consul and the rulers of Damascus that these charges are incorrect and to request that they annul the edicts against the Jews, and I take Mahmoud's hand in mine and entreat him to come with me at that very moment to the governor of Damascus and elucidate for him how this chain of events came to pass; surely one day we shall sit, all of us, at one of the cafés on the banks of the River Barada, doubled over with laughter and gladdening our hearts with the dinner meal, the scent of Damascene jasmine mingling with the waters from the fountains and the chirping of canaries.

Good Mahmoud smiles broadly again, revealing his pearly teeth set one next to the other in a sparkling string, and he calms Aslan with pleasant words, even rises to embrace him a second time and offers him a handkerchief to wipe his tears of great shame, and he says, Aslan, how valiant are your attempts at protecting your people, how true and beloved are your declarations of our mutual friendship in the shade of the flowering jasmine of Damascus, but your pleas and appeals are for naught, for Suleiman Negrin, the barber in our custody, has already confessed to the crime.

And I am astounded and shaken by this news and request that Mahmoud trickle more *araq* into my chalice, for my hands have begun to shake and my teeth are chattering and the pungent taste of aniseed strikes my tongue and descends to my belly to taunt the one-eyed shrew, who at this very moment is seeking to restore the reins of power to her control, and after calming myself as required, Mahmoud begins an account of the full confession of Suleiman *alkhalaq*, who admitted to having summoned Father Tomaso on that stormy night using a pretext, baiting him with a mission to the home of a Jew, and it was there that he, Suleiman, had handed the monk over to these prominent Jews on whose behest he had acted, and for his services had received the promised sum; but who these Jews were, and for what purpose they had abducted the righteous monk, and what had become of Tomaso – all these the interrogators had not succeeded in ferreting out, in spite of their redoubled efforts, and for this reason they wished to interrogate me a second time, for the purpose of confronting me with facts they had learned from the priests of Damascus.

My happy friend, at that time the one-eyed shrew was storming and shrieking about my intestines, warning me a thousand times of the trap being set before me; but what was the nature of this web, and which spiders would attack me, and what venom would they use to poison my taut body, to suck the marrow from me as the leeches in the barber's shop suck blood? None of these could she elucidate for me, she merely repeated her cries about the chasm of my demise that stretched out before me, and I wished to placate this female, and sometimes Mahmoud seemed full of love and emotion and then immediately thereafter composed and pensive, and while I was tossed about between the two, I succumbed to the shrieks of the one-eyed shrew and was about to beg Mahmoud to listen to my story once again lest in my turbulent state I had erred in my description or wording, and I reminded him that the solution to this conundrum as well as people's lives and deaths were all balanced on my tongue, my word, and I had already begun to repeat my description of that night and the forbidden intercourse, and I was keen to tell him that no Jews had spilled this blood.

But Mahmoud again refused, with his white-toothed smile, to hear me out, so that in the end Aslan's muscles relaxed and his voice and tongue fell limp and anyway, who was this Aslan if not a marginal character, a minor player in this grand scripted plot, whose role was none other than to let himself slip between its chapters, bump against its paragraphs, rest among its semicolons and flow through its commas until reaching the end, that end about whose meaning and significance nothing is known, so that when Aslan considers it, it awakens in him great fear.

After all this came to pass there stood between us a long and contemplative silence; when it ended Mahmoud requested that I accompany him to meet his friend Father Alexis, head of the Terra

Sancta Monastery in the Christian Quarter of Damascus, for words of reason and discernment flow from the lips of Damascene priests, and Aslan acquiesced unwillingly to this request, and on their way to Father Alexis he thought to himself that until two weeks earlier he had known nothing of the flavour of a monastery or a monk and now he was encountering them at every turn.

Together they march along, nearly touching, to the eastern corner of the Christian Quarter, only a short distance from the consulate building, and Aslan glances southwards on occasion, to the cradle of his birth in Kharet Elyahud, and he reflects upon his friend the barber and upon his father-in-law the Khaham-Bashi and upon all those Jews, bothered and burdened with their daily matters, and he is overcome with grief for the misfortunes he has brought upon them without intending to, and now all his plans for making right that which requires repair are dashed, and there is nothing to do but to hand himself over to his interrogators and please them in any way possible in the hopes of silencing and subduing the spirits and the angels of destruction that have emerged to take part in his downfall.

On their way to the Terra Sancta Monastery, Mahmoud hints to Aslan about a certain Christian witch in her ninetieth year who has not washed her hands from the day she came of age in order to wallow in refuse and filth so as to draw evil spirits and sorcery nigh, in the way of witches; and this woman stood the previous eve in the streets of the Christian Quarter, and when the spirits of the dead and other demonic creatures visited her, she swore that seven Jews had slaughtered the monk and taken his blood in order to make unleavened bread for the Passover holiday, and she has been crying bitterly since, allowing no man to console her or kiss her hand.

Aslan remains silent in the face of these hints and he asks himself the meaning of Mahmoud's actions, what benefit he could derive from such behaviour, and the one-eyed shrew carries on shrieking her terrible shrieks and tearing clumps of hair from her head, but he pulls a screen of pleasant words between them to comfort himself with sweet whisperings, for he enjoys himself in the company of this fair and handsome man; Mahmoud will rescue him from the evil edict, and perhaps all he need do is let his tongue rattle meaningless words against his teeth according to what these men command of him, to dribble the sweet lies they wish to hear into their ears, and Aslan invites this fellowship of loving men to enfold him from all sides.

And lo, they enter the tall, ornate gate of the Terra Sancta and Aslan exchanges glances with the icon of that same tortured soul of the wounded feet and hands whom he recognises from Tomaso's monastery and from the hiding place in his parents' bedroom, and they pass by all manner of canvases painted in bold colours, such as one of Bethlehem at night, in which a woman with ample breasts receives her guests, her black eyes cast down, sunken in silence.

They come upon Father Alexis, his back to them as he imbibes glass after glass of cherry liqueur, and when he takes note of their arrival he does not rise from his chair to greet them but motions them to sit with him, and his eyes are veiled and dark, heavy sacs consumed by tears hang pendulously below, and Alexis mumbles words of prayer and crosses himself and cries and drinks, for he is deep in mourning for his friend of many years, Tomaso.

Mahmoud seats himself beside Father Alexis and with great eloquence encourages him to rise and take bread and desist from imbibing these intoxicants, for the church under his patronage is so beautiful and praiseworthy, and his flock of worshippers so devoted to him, and Mahmoud holds him in esteem as first among the priests of Damascus, and Father Alexis carries on sobbing, and he kisses Mahmoud's hands and to my surprise kisses mine as well, and I recoil from his touch for fear that he, too, will die, for Aslan's effect on the tribe of monks has been calamitous.

The dejected Father Alexis, who is now gulping down liqueur from the bottle, asks Mahmoud about the interrogation, and whether there is any foundation for his grave suspicion that there is a connection between the monk's disappearance and the approaching holiday of the Jews, and Mahmoud responds that one of the Jews is with them at this moment and he points, to my horror, at me, and Father Alexis casts a saddened glance my way and says, My son, have you ever paid a visit to the Jewish slaughterers in their booths behind the market and witnessed how they carry out the ritual and what they do with the blood? Have you watched as they slowly brandish the blade across the beast's throat and how they allow the blood to drip gradually? And he describes the slaughtered beast, both beheaded and not quite beheaded, and erupts in sobs for its life that is seeping away, and after this he takes hold of my hand, shaking madly, and tells me, *Ya ibni*, O my son, why do you not remove this stone from your heart, why do you not recount to your beloved friends this dark secret that is poisoning your soul, for the priest knew well how to look deep into Aslan's heart at the black rivers roiling in waves of refuse and dung, and he extends his hands to embrace me warmly, and Aslan falls willingly into his bosom, and the smell of old age upon Alexis is familiar and consoles him.

When they break off from their embrace Father Alexis informs him of the well-known treachery of the Jews of Damascus, who in the past had attempted to kill Paul, disciple of Jesus, for as it is written, They plotted to murder him; they watched the gates day and night, to kill him, so that the disciples took him by night and let him down by the walls of the city in a basket; and further, Father Alexis teaches Aslan of the intrigues perpetrated by the kings of Israel upon John the Baptist, cousin to the Christian saviour, who was beheaded, and his severed head is buried to this very day in a cave beneath the Umayyad Mosque, and he relates again, between sobs and tears, his dreaded fear that the treachery of the Jews has once again broken loose and that the Jews sought to murder Tomaso – Tomaso, who had won over not a few souls among them for the good and benevolent Jesus – and to make use of his blood for their holiday.

My happy friend, would that all my Damascene sins were pardoned, for I have abused and I have betrayed; would that my tongue were not so sedulous, so diligent, so energetic in my mouth, spewing wild rumours. But at that moment, my dear, pure, sinless boy, on that day, in that monastery, Aslan's eyes were blinded, covered by a thick film and darkness and gloom, and within this gloom there shone about me a light from heaven, a bright, blinding, brilliant light, and a still, ethereal voice rang out in my ears, and it was as if my twisted, winding, curling path had been made clear to me behind closed eyes, and this scheme lay before me, unfurled and vivid and full of life.

Aslan pulled his hands free from the embrace and from behind his blinkered, blinded eyes answered the drunken priest that indeed there was a boulder, heavy and black and smothering his heart and poisoning his days, and when they asked him the meaning of this matter Aslan responded that the hints dropped by the Good Interrogator were indeed aimed at the true and proper target, which he had been prevented from revealing to them until this time due to an oath and curse of excommunication upon the Jews, that the monk had been abducted for the purpose of slaughtering him, and that the deed had been carried out by a band of Jews for the making of the unleavened bread for the Passover holiday, and Father Alexis grasped his chest in agitation, for lo, all that he had been told during his studies as an acolyte in Rome had been true, and the ancient texts had not lied, and the Good Interrogator blessed Aslan for his brave and determined decision to break his vows and reveal the truth, and all three men trembled with the power of this holy moment, and Mahmoud held fast to my shoulders and pinned his eyes upon me and tears pooled up in them at the cruelty of this terrible death, and I, too, joined in and took up in my former, disgraceful, Aslanish lament, my eyes shut tight, and we three tearful souls leaned one upon the other and cried for the pain of the world and its torments, and the tears were sweet and very good, and the man of God spread his hands over us to protect us, and that disconsolate woman and the shepherds of Bethlehem and her crucified son all hovered above us in rays of shining light.

5

No sooner have I made my fabricated confession in the arms of Father Alexis than Mahmoud hastens to lead me back along the street called Straight to his room at the consulate, and he is blushing and excited, eagerly plying me with kisses and his warm, manly, abundant love, his fox-eyes brightly sparkling, and when we reach Mahmoud's quarters and pour fresh glasses of *araq*, he kisses my fingers one after the other, for my presence is so dear to him, and he smiles and tells me that he feels and knows that we are soulmates, that my person is wondrous in his eyes, that I am all radiant tenderness and sanctity.

Aslan wishes to protest and demur, for Aslan is ugly of body and soul, as is known throughout the city of Damascus, but Mahmoud reiterates his admiration for this young man whose path has crossed his own and he describes my eyes as those of a falcon and an owl, and he extols the red lines of my lips, drawn as though by an artist's paintbrush, and also the bones of my lower jaw, straight and masculine, sharp and true, and my small chin, its cleft a garden of delights, a hidden orchard to which lovers repair in the moonlight; and while he is speaking, Mahmoud plucks an errant hair from my forelocks and squeezes to death a fatty pustule festering on my cheek, and he sings praises to my dark beauty, and Aslan hearkens to his words and his heart blushes.

And now it is the hour for Mahmoud to confess to me that a life of freedom and liberty is spread out before him, and along with them the delights and pleasures he so adores, for Count de Ratti-Menton has assured him that if he solves the mystery of Father Tomaso's disappearance he will be released from the prison in which he has been incarcerated; now, at the peak of his success, Mahmoud has revealed his secret, and Aslan is astonished, for apart from the singer called Umm-Jihan he has never made the acquaintance of a person in custody, but for what reason and why did they see fit to place this charming young man behind bars?

Mahmoud recounts that until two years earlier he had lived the life of a king, reigning terror on the Christians and Jews in his jurisdiction, for he was responsible for collecting *aljiziya*, the head tax, and he would pass through the Christian and Jewish Quarters and they would bow down before him, prostrate themselves and honour him with biscuits and beverages; but evil people had libelled him, saying he had embezzled monies from the head tax, and from there the path to his arrest and interrogation and trial were short, since all attention was diverted by the power of his libellers' riches, and because of these lies he had been imprisoned for several months already in a tiny cell while the libellers continued their lives of rich foods and earthly delights, though their black day would come, it was nigh; and now, with the ritual slaughter of Brother Tomaso, Mahmoud had offered – from his prison cell – to take charge of the investigation, and he had been promised in writing by his eminence Sharif Pasha himself that if he found the solution to this vexing and atrocious riddle he would be instantly pardoned, so that now Mahmoud had but one request of Aslan: that he continue to assist him as he had done until then, that much as he had confessed to the ritual slaughter in Father Alexis' arms, so should he confess all the details of that stormy evening to Mahmoud; and he rose to embrace me and his touch was very comforting.

At that, Mahmoud became even dearer in Aslan's eyes, for not only was this new and precious friend of his a handsome man of song, he was also a righteous man pursued by evildoers. And Aslan allowed himself to be swept away by Mahmoud's singing and his gay demeanour.

The longer I remained in the presence of Mahmoud, the two of us alone, the more I loved this Good Interrogator, and I learned his likes and dislikes, such as his repulsion at acts of violence and destruction, or his haste in cleansing his hands after touching an animal or an imprisoned criminal or anything filthy or contaminated, and of course Aslan knows of his lover's loathing of mothers and women and girls and females of any kind, how he recoils from their touch, and Aslan knows, too, of handsome Mahmoud's love of song and dance; and on occasion the spirit descends upon him and he rises for a jig, his beautiful feet bare as they move in small, delicate steps, now proceeding now receding, the dance of the mamba snakes in the Khan Assad Pasha.

Mahmoud smiles at me and praises me for behaving with great nobility when I revealed the secret of the ritual slaughter of the monk for the Passover holiday, and he wishes to know whether I might be able to expose, too, the identity of those very Jews who carried out the act, and I respond that I have no information with regards to this matter, for I was not among the slaughterers, and with a mischievous glint in his fox-eyes he asks whether Aslan, whose loyalty and love of truth are so apparent, will agree to clarify for him several questions pertaining to the interrogation, information Aslan might garner by trailing secretly behind his father and uncles and father-in-law to discern what the Jews are whispering about Tomaso; also to gather any news concerning Tomaso's disappearance, and perhaps about the approaching Passover holiday as well, and about the bread of affliction eaten according to religious decree, and Aslan is overwhelmed with joy at his new mission, and he responds that he is ready and willing to do Mahmoud's bidding and assents to Mahmoud's request for urgency, agreeing to pass along that very evening everything he has investigated and discovered, and I plant kisses on his face and, for a brief moment, on his lips, and depart from him in peace for my father's home.

And lo, the Aslan who returns home now is a different Aslan, a new Aslan, no longer ashamed or terrified, no longer tense from fear of his father's shout-and-slap welcome; rather, he is drunk with the love that has been imparted to him and with the strength with which it has imbued him, for is it not within the power of his tongue to determine fates – one way or the other? His tongue moves about in the chamber of his mouth, between his teeth, in the internal rivulets of saliva, and these tiny clicks are meant to be the cause and effect for a great and wondrous chain of events whose outcome and end are unknown and unforeseeable to all; and how agreeable is this strength to Aslan, and how sweet the small glint of terror – fear of the gentiles – that gleams in the eyes of his father, who is called *almuallem* by all, and this gleam is brighter even than the shimmering gold of the gilded pages of the Crowns of Damascus scrolls stored in the Khush Elpasha Synagogue.

Thus, from that moment I departed from my custom and, instead of stealthily entering the house – as was my wont, by way of the malodorous rubbish gate, that narrow and crowded place used by the servants to cast off from our home into the street that which is filthy and fetid, such as the remains of tea or the feathers of slaughtered fowl or their red cockscombs and internal organs – I marched erect, unfettered, to the main entrance of our estate, hidden as it was behind wretched walls of clay to avoid attracting the unwanted attention of tax collectors and the envy of impoverished Jews, and I sniggered at the cunning of such ugly gates, poised to topple, which did not attest to the opulence and wealth of what lay behind them, and my chirping whistles echoed from one end of the wall to the other until the sole servant left to attend to the needs of our household pricked his ears to note how Aslan, habitually tortured and tearful, was sauntering into the house, his chest puffed with pride and his shoulders squared.

New thoughts, rare in Aslan's realm of experience, tweaked at his chest, inciting him to take revenge upon his family and deliver them to the executioner's rope, and the dense, overpowering light blinded his eyes again and lit up his mind: who were Tomaso's assassins if not his father and uncles? And in an illuminated vision he could picture them encircling him for the purpose of chaining him with rusted manacles and submerging him in the waters of the River Barada before he could deliver them to the governor of Damascus, and he knew that this pack of vipers could no longer overcome him, so Aslan stood over them laughing copiously, freely, just like the wizened Christian witch standing at the gate of the city, suffused with joy at the demise of her enemies, her hands unwashed since the day she had come of age, the blackened, irremovable filth between her fingers now an element of her sorcery.

My happy friend, when I caught sight of Maman and my wife, who were sprawling about on the second storey of our home, used in the winter for warming oneself in the generous desert sun, I entered with noisy footsteps, soles clacking, and they were somewhat alarmed, and when they grumbled womanishly of this shameful habit of mine I responded sharply and without delay that the control they have exercised over Aslan and the trampling of his life will cease and desist at this very moment, and I demand that she who is known as my wife at once be turned out of our bedroom, that servants' room scented with urine, and restored to the home of her father and many sisters, for I have no interest in her or reason to detain her.

Maman hearkens to my words but instead of responding she rises and approaches, her dark hair dishevelled, to beat me with a golden rod stored in her *sunduq*, the dowry chest she brought from her own father's home many years past, and she curses Aslan as she has never before, that he might drown or be consumed in flames or burn in hell for a thousand years, and his wife Markhaba claps her hands in sorrow to God the Creator, pleading with him to hurry along the arrival of the Messiah, may He arrive at once, and Aslan utters not a word to his mother or his wife, he merely raises his hand and sends flying the sweetened cups of tea and the patterned china saucers and the apricot pastries, a feast for *mesdames* spread before them upon a tea tray.

The rest of the household hears the din and tumult from the second storey and emerges post-haste, sister Rachel and brother Meir and the manservant, and Aslan regrets that his father has not yet arrived to witness this new behaviour, and Aslan is carried away on the flames of his indignation like a flock of cranes careening high above on gusts of hot air, and his mother and wife and siblings appear to him as trivial, inconsequential, ridiculous, like heaps of rubbish and cesspits the cranes would view from their eyrie, and Aslan snatches the golden rod borrowed from the *sunduq* in order to deter him, and he brandishes it wildly, and a thunderous, fiery melody of curses and blasphemy spews forth, and he casts upon them the fierceness of his anger, wrath, and indignation, an embassy of evil messengers, reimbursing them for all their infectious evil, and he wishes for his sister that her crossed blue eyes will frighten away all the men of Damascus for ever and ever, and he threatens Meir that one of these nights he will be strangled by the house snakes that slither through the thick, hollow walls, whispering and hissing their poisonous breaths, and Maman tears at her long black hair as she listens to these terrible words, the likes of which have never sullied my tongue before, and she screams for me to desist at once, that she will tell Father of all my wickedness the very moment he arrives, but Aslan does not heed her threats, he wishes to raise his hand against her, and he grows larger, his hair stands on end and his neck thickens, and he spits venom at her like his friends the cobras, and he pushes her towards the winding staircase that leads to the floor below, and were it not for Markhaba, who faints dead away, sprawled in all her holiness upon the embroidered pillows and carpets, he would have prodded his mother into the abyss and broken her back and neck.

At once, all rush to Markhaba and stand beside her attempting to revive her, each praying to his gods to save her from this evil, and in the meantime Aslan offers his own secret prayer for the appearance of his father, who suddenly today of all days is belated, that he may enter and catch sight of Aslan in his full potency; then Aslan will position himself in front of *almuallem* Rafael Farhi, whose name is pronounced with fear and awe from Beirut unto Baghdad, from the palace of Muhammad Ali unto Istanbul, capital of the empire, and he will admonish him sharply with a rebuke whose details he is rehearsing now quickly in his head, and he will bring about a show trial for his father's act of slaughter and assassination, and, immediately following the announcement of the wise and true verdict, he will oversee his father's flogging and the bending back of his hands and the breaking of his knees and the clogging of his mouth and the plucking out of his eyeballs, and any such punishment that is just and fitting.

However, for some reason this man of esteem does not make his appearance, and Markhaba's eyes have already opened and the members of the household whisper among themselves and cast sidelong glances at him, and Aslan tries to fan the flames of his passion and anger, reminding himself of the mocking songs they sang him, and how they compelled him to marry an arid bride and how they forced upon him an anguishing journey to Jobar, but the current of hot air that had sustained him on high is now diminishing, and gusts of cool, chilled air transport him far away from there, and Aslan is plunging back to his former, loathsome self, and he is alarmed at his actions and wishes to apologise to Maman and all the others for these things he has said, and a clear blue terror sears his skin for the lies he poured into Mahmoud's ears.

By the time the cool winds arrive, displacing the good, hot air, the familiar, repugnant sounds are audible from the first floor, the low murmur of voices, and Aslan, now completely alone in the centre of the room, feels his strength waning and he falls to the thick, soft carpets and awaits the decree of his destiny.

The heavy footsteps heralding Rafael Farhi's corpulence can be heard clearly now as they draw near, and his usual scent, oily and slippery, precedes the arrival of this portly man, and Aslan tells himself, Confess quickly to your father, stand before him and declaim the unfurling of events from beginning to end, for there will be no other occasion on which to save your own skin and the souls of all the Jews from the tempest poised to engulf our skies.

Below him, on the first floor, Maman has recounted to Father a litany of Aslan's wicked deeds, his brazenness, his shouting, his impertinence, and lo, Father is ascending slowly to the second storey, his booming voice silent, and in the expression on his face Aslan reads his own guilt, and Father utters not a word, neither good nor bad, does not even clear his throat or grumble; instead, he takes hold of Aslan and leads him outside, to the street, through that same gate on either side of which are heaped piles of rubbish, and they move along in tandem and turn into the alley separating their own house from that of the Stambouli family, and from there Father pulls him along to the right as a lamb to the slaughter, still clutching his arm, hurting him like the blade of a knife, perhaps he is bringing him to the Christian Quarter or to the River Barada where they will stop for a father-son chat, the first and only of their lives, instead of clinging to the thicket of their hatred, and at the Tayyek Altalaj, the Alley of the Ice Sellers, they pause for a moment, and Aslan lifts up his eyes and lo, his father seems hesitant, as if considering two options, and in another moment he will enclose Aslan in the embrace of a progenitor with his progeny, for great love prevails between generations, why should such great love not visit them as well?

But his father does not kiss Aslan, does not embrace him, but brings him instead, in mute silence, to the home of his uncle Meir, this, too, a grand estate with mosaic tile floors and, upon its ceilings, tendrils of stone and sacred verses for blessings; however, his father does not lead him to the orchard or the fountain, but to a small and hideous room left unfinished, the floor of which lies uncovered and is full of dust and dirt, and Aslan, despite his occasional visits to his uncle's home, has never known of the existence of this hovel, and placed therein is a pile of wood and several extinguished, besooted candles alongside which lies a sort of long wooden beam bound with thick ropes, and Father throws me down without an explanation and without a word and presses my body against the beam, and before I can protest even ever so slightly my dreaded uncles emerge: Meir, the owner of this house, and Uncle Murad and Uncle Joseph, and it becomes clear to Aslan that they have spoken to one another and planned this in advance, apparently even before my evil actions of this evening, but for what purpose and what aim I do not even dare conjecture.

In silence, Father and the uncles toil, and they rivet Aslan's body, stiff from cold, to the beam of his crucifixion, knotting and tightening the ropes, and suddenly I, Aslan, become aware that they wish to interrogate me and not I them, they wish to prise from Aslan a confession to all manner of evil deeds that he has committed, so that when his father begins slowly reading aloud from a page of paper of these weighty matters, Aslan already comprehends its wretched contents, for this description, these facts, these accusations are nothing but an exact recounting, astonishing in its details, of the acts he carried out with the barber Suleiman Negrin so long ago at his shop, whence they transgressed grave sins forbidden in the Torah and the Talmud, and his father, in a loud and steady voice, describes in detail the act of love Aslan demanded to give and receive, and the organs that were shoved into this and that, and the tongues that licked and the embraces embraced, and all this his father and uncles had gleaned from the mouth of an informant, an old and righteous woman who spied Aslan and the barber through a parting in the curtain flapping in the window of the barber's shop, and at the conclusion of the long and detailed list of claims that shout Aslan's guilt, his sins of adultery and engaging in abominations, his father lifts his head from the page, allows the fatty flesh of his neck to wobble and settle into place, and tenderly asks Aslan, his tongue steeped in their silence, to utter one word: truth or falsehood.

Tears threaten to overflow Aslan's throat and eyes, for *he* is the interrogator and not the interrogee, the accuser and not the accused, the libeller and not the libelled, and he pricks once again the sweet, addictive, invigorating hatred inside him, and the waves of hot air carry him on high, and he enflames himself with words of wrath about his family, his parents, and he looks his father and his uncles in the eyes and condemns them for their evil deeds, and in his mind's eye he envisions how they toiled over Tomaso's body to siphon the blood, how they cut patches from his skin, how they allowed him to writhe in agony until his soul departed, and there was no mercy in them, just as the hearts of their ancestors sealed shut when Jesus was crucified, just as the hearts of the Jewish butchers were coarse with the suffering of beasts beheaded by their blades, and Aslan surges with strength and he denies all these accusations, for he did not carry out these acts attributed to him, such as the sucking of the barber's tongue or the cramming of his organ into his mouth or the licking of his testicles, of which the mere thought repulses him, and he swears thus to them upon the lives of his mother and father.

Upon hearing these words his father rises and slaps his cheeks again and again, turning Aslan's face red and blue, but these slaps do not cease, for Aslan continues to shout his innocence, and when Father tires the uncles approach and slap him as well, and some of them ball their hands into fists and beat his nose, and they kick his testicles and they land terrible blows upon his belly, and they shut his mouth to stifle his screams, and they demand he confess by raising the thumb of his right hand, but Aslan does not acquiesce, and he allows them to punch his head to and fro and smack him with planks of wood, and his only hope is for the dark screen to fall over his eyes and spare him this torture, and he hears his father cursing his own seed, from which this sorcery emerged.

And Aslan understands and recognises that this weak and diminutive worm – which wends its way among the creatures of the world, awakening loathing in them, some of whom trample it underfoot or slice off its tail – will, with the aid of the pincers concealed behind its mollusc legs, put a stop to these fat and ill-tempered men now threatening to extinguish it, and Aslan swears that this act being perpetrated upon him at this moment, in his smallness and helplessness, will be perpetrated upon them, and he resolves in his heart to find Mahmoud that very evening and to reveal to him the identities of the wicked murderers, the suckers of the blood of that good and holy monk.

6

My happy friend, these nights you spend at my side, listening to my story and applying compresses to my feverish brow – these nights alleviate somewhat the shame of old age and the dismay of far off and powerful memories that tweak my brain hour after hour, and I cannot but offer a cornucopia of thanks to you for standing by this beleaguered, bedridden old man, and for never, ever being deterred, even from the contemptible, the uncontrollable leaks from my body, and if it pleases you I will continue to unravel for you all that which is true and frank.

I have already recounted to you, my happy friend, that I had made up my mind to carry out this deed, and so, after being returned to my bedroom – the former servants' quarters – my cheeks still aflame from the painful slaps and my bones still in agony from the pummelling, I slip away from my father's house, making my way quickly with a determined limp to the consulate, for the purpose of serving my father and uncles to them, for I have reached the decision that this is their due, and I fabricate many details in my mind, morbid ones, libellous and scheming, and they fan the flames of my wrath and blind my eyes with their radiant light.

Aslan encounters Mahmoud in the foyer of the consulate, his fox-eyes shining and smiling at him, and Aslan is choking with the desire to share the results of his investigations into the matter of the monk at the hands of his father and uncles, and he is careful to provide the name of each and every one of them, *almuallem* Rafael Farhi and Murad Farhi and Joseph Farhi and Meir Farhi, and he tells how the four of them had dragged Tomaso that stormy evening to a small and hideous room left unfinished, the floor of which is covered with dust and dirt, and how they bound him to a crucifix of wooden beams and how they tore his flesh asunder so as to remove the blood, and Mahmoud says, Slowly, Aslan; have you seen these things with your own eyes or merely heard them as rumours passed on by others? I inform him that these matters have been made known to me in a roundabout manner by virtue of the investigation I have conducted, for I myself was not among them when they committed the act, nor did I set eyes upon this, I merely awakened in the wee hours of that stormy night to the sounds of my father's footsteps and the passing of his water into an open cesspit of the Black River, and thus rose from my bed to follow after him, observing my father surrounded by my uncles; and from somewhere among the clay-walled houses closing in on the neighbouring street I heard a short whistle, and the lot of them hastened in that direction, and Aslan caught sight of the barber motioning to them, and their lanterns blew out in the howling storm, and together the group of men proceeded to the home of Uncle Meir to carry out their evil intent.

Mahmoud continues to praise and extol me for having opened my eyes to the evil acts of these Jewish lords and for having girded myself with the courage to stand up to them, and while I float above the blackened, putrid branches of my father's house like a delicate songbird, Mahmoud adds that the crime was not perpetrated by these four alone, but also by the barber, without whose eyewitness testimony at the slaughter itself the four could not be detained, so it was now necessary to extricate this truth from Suleiman *alkhalaq*, barber and witness, for the purpose of meteing out the punishment due the wicked gentlemen.

Before I can change my mind, Mahmoud grasps my hand and leads me to the cellar of the consulate down a winding staircase, and as we open a dark and heavy door Mahmoud clasps Aslan around his neck and embraces him. There, in the pit of the building, lies a living, breathing human carcass bound in chains and shackles, his body stripped bare, his buttocks and testicles exposed, and Aslan is shocked to discover that this is the barber, insensible from the frequent lashings, exhausted and famished and parched, and Mahmoud whispers into my ear that in spite of the starvation and torture, in spite of the hourly lashings of the whip, and in spite of the threats to tear off his limbs and chop up his body, they have been unable to extract from him the names of the murderers.

Suddenly a rancid, blood-filled gurgling issues from Suleiman's throat and he awakens from the faint induced by the beatings and his eyes are blurry and his lips cracked, but he does not plead for anything but a drop of water to moisten his lips, and Aslan, incredulous, slips down into a long and eternal void, but his screams do not escape beyond his gaping mouth.

Just then the creature spies him, recognises his face, and begs him in a shattered voice to dribble a thin stream of water on to his lips from a clay jug standing nearby, otherwise he will hand his soul back to the creator of the world that very moment, and Aslan is nonplussed in the face of these whisperings, which pin the guilt on him, and he casts alarmed and perplexed glances at his new friend Mahmoud, the Good Interrogator, but the barber rattles his chains and calls Aslan by name and entreats him to perform this good deed and to provide him with a little water in the name of their religion, their people, and Aslan is about to grant the barber's request when he notices the way Mahmoud is staring at him, his expression critical, measuring Aslan up as friend or foe.

My happy friend, at that very moment Aslan – young and rash – could have offered his own hairy back to the lashings of the *kurbach* for was not the destiny of his brother Suleiman Negrin, a member of the same tribe, his very own destiny? Instead I followed the radiant light that I imagined to be shining from Mahmoud Altali and I disregarded all obligations to my friend, my family, my people, and that is when I committed the injustice, perhaps my gravest crime in this drama being recorded by your industrious fingers, and if I requested several weeks ago that you listen and hearken to these deeds of mine *min sint jidi* – from days of yore – it was, after all, for the purpose of confessing my evil deeds, so that even if the task weighs heavily upon your ears we cannot desist from the telling of this tale, nor may we allow this story to be forgotten unto the end of days, for this tale must be told and sealed and bound.

So it was, my happy friend, that I took up the *kurbach*, hanging from a metal hook in the wall, and it was fashioned from horsehair and still warm to the touch from the latest round of lashings, and I asked my former lover whether he would not hastily surrender the assassins' names, and when *alkhalaq* remained steadfast in his silence I had no recourse but to brandish the whip in the air, which trilled in the tiny, narrow, stifling room, before I landed it squarely on Suleiman's back, and the blow was so forceful and resolute that the barber did not even shriek, the jolt had stunned his limbs, and I administered blow after blow, as if threshing him like Gilead with instruments of iron, calling to him to give up the names of Tomaso's murderers, and the barber shouted my name with a power that caused the walls of the dungeon to tremble, Aslan, Aslan, Aslan, and he raised his hand to plead with me to desist.

Then, at my request, I am permitted to relieve Suleiman of his torment, and I revive his soul with refreshing water and massage his shoulders and replace the patches of skin torn from his body, and I kiss him upon the lips as in those wonderful bygone days, and Suleiman's body is weak and his eyes are wide open, the lashes thinned like the teeth of a comb, and I embrace him for a long moment and his arced brows once again flow together as they did on that evening of ancient memory at Bab Alfouqara, and Suleiman is fatigued from sobbing, and I instruct him to cease his foolish obstinacy and forthwith provide the names of the lords of the House of Farhi, and Suleiman responds to my outstretched hand and I summon Mahmoud to record the confession.

And Suleiman unravels the chain of events of which he had until that time, in his disgrace, denied any knowledge, and he begs the pardon of the faithful Christians for these terrible matters he kept concealed in his heart, and we gather round him to hear the story of four members of the Farhi family who dispatched him to coax the monk, who was making his way through Kharet Elyahud, to come with him, and he delivered the monk and his manservant for a meagre sum, two hundred piastres, perhaps three hundred, enough to provide for the needs of his household – his wife and their small son – and all this for the purpose of a ritual slaughter to extract blood for the Passover holiday, and the barber confirms Mahmoud's questions with regards to other events of that evening, that the monk was murdered and his body dissected, that the purpose was without question a religious one, and Suleiman even responds to Mahmoud's explicit request for the names of each of the men responsible for the crime: Meir, Murad, Joseph, Rafael, all of the Farhi clan, and he adds, upon the advice of the Good Interrogator, that the Khaham-Bashi, Rabbi Yaacov Antebi, was also among them, to instruct them in the meaning of the commandments and their implementation.

And lo, the barber's confession, from the moment it is given, takes action as hastily as that of prunes on the intestines, and it is expressed to the palace of Sharif Pasha and from there, as a result, urgent orders of detention are issued and sent with runners and dispatchers, and gendarmes pound on doors and ropes are wound around sluggish veins and feet are dragged along on a clear night, and on that very same night, the eve of the Jews' holy Sabbath, all are assembled in the qa'ah of the palace, Rafael Farhi and Murad Farhi and Meir Farhi and Joseph Farhi, and Rabbi Yaacov Antebi is summoned there as well, and between all these men stands the barber Suleiman alkhalaq, scarred and dishevelled, and Aslan and the Good Interrogator watch the gang of suspects from a narrow chink in the black curtains at the end of the room, behind which they hide so that the Jews will not know who is the spy among them.

The uncles stand whispering among themselves, as yet oblivious to the meaning of this absurd scene, and after an hour of being made to wait they thunder and complain to the aides of the Egyptian, Sharif Pasha, who has not yet made his appearance, about the panicked and sudden detention of important personages like themselves, known for their contribution to the commerce and welfare of the city of Damascus, and if they are to be interrogated, why so late on a Friday eve, no time provided even to change their robes, and why has the good rabbi been snatched from prayers in the Khush Elpasha Synagogue?

From the moment Sharif Pasha enters the room dressed in a black smoking jacket with gold pleats in the manner of the Europeans, but still in his slippers, made from golden cloth, he hastens to subdue the voices of protest and grumbling, and suggests that the Jews be seated and calm themselves, and he offers them cups of tea with baklava, and they drink greedily, consoling themselves with the momentary warmth of the heavily sweetened brew.

After their cups of tea have been sipped and the men's cheeks have reddened a bit and tight, forced smiles have risen on their lips, Father appeals to Sharif Pasha, imploring him to release them to their homes, for they do not comprehend the purpose of their urgent summons to the palace, and they do not comprehend why they should be in this position, what such important Jewish personages could have to do with Father Tomaso and the barber, and *almuallem* Rafael Farhi draws near Sharif Pasha and kisses his cheeks and his fingers as if to appease him for treating these men of good intentions in such an indecorous manner.

Sharif Pasha does not answer him, instead informing them as to the reason for their urgent night-time detention by reading to them a brief summary of the confession made by the barber, now standing in the same room with them, about how a group of wealthy Jews had summoned him several days earlier, how he had delivered Father Tomaso to them for the purpose of taking his blood for the baking of unleavened bread for the Passover holiday, how the monk had met his bitter end, how they had siphoned the blood into a glass bottle in order to blend it in with the batter used to prepare the bread of affliction, and how this matter was in any event known and familiar to all before him.

Upon hearing these accusations Father and the uncles and the rabbi spread their arms in astonishment, crying *La samakh Allah!* Heaven forfend! And they ask the barber to look them in the eyes and swear to this matter in which he has charged them, for this is the first time they have encountered this man, who

174

appears to be an ignoramus, one of the impoverished of the Jewish people, and it must be that he desires to take revenge upon them for their wealth, and they encircle Suleiman *alkhalaq*, nearly slapping his cheeks, asking how he dared to defame them thus, and they press upon him to withdraw his statement and tell which of them it was that summoned him and on what day and for what purpose, for each one of them could prove beyond all doubt that he had been in some other location on that fateful evening, one at a party in the Christian Quarter, another in the arms of his wife, and Suleiman *alkhalaq* cannot answer them, his silence long and ponderous, and his foes stand poised to celebrate their victory by returning to their soft feather beds.

Sharif Pasha instructs the barber to repeat before all assembled the accusations he had made less than an hour earlier under interrogation, but the barber's gaze is one of terror, as if all at once he understands the enormity of his crime, and he stammers a response to Sharif Pasha that he does not recall who summoned him and he is neither assured nor lucid enough with regards to the events of that evening, and while he did in fact state that the monk had been murdered he had not seen this with his own eyes, he had only learned of the matter from others, and when Sharif Pasha concludes this round of pointed questioning the barber bursts into shattered tears, for he has no wish other than to be reunited with his wife and first-born son, now seated at a sombre Sabbath table bereft of husband and father, no meat or rice on their table, only lentil soup, a few beans, and a pair of silent oil candles flickering faintly.

Then Sharif Pasha motions to one of his adjutants to bring something hither, and a bright white pallor floods the barber's face when the adjutant produces a horsehair whip of medium length, that *kurbach* with which he was tormented in the dungeon of the consulate, and before Suleiman is able to protest or cry out or flee for his life, his shirt is stripped from him and his back exposed, the skin already flayed from lashings, and the sound of the whip, like a pack of vipers, spikes the air, preceding by an eternity the sidelong, slashing blow as it lands on his flesh.

Immediately, the barber is ordered to stand and repeat his confession or the whip will be applied again, and the barber rises laboriously to his feet, teetering, and he is required to provide a simple answer to Sharif Pasha's question: Were these pillars of the Jewish community of Damascus now present in the room the same men who slaughtered the monk? The barber mutters several incomprehensible syllables, the blood still snaking across his body, and the details of the incident mix riotously on his tongue.

When Sharif Pasha discerns that there is no purpose or benefit in pursuing the questioning of the barber he orders the second witness who confirmed the barber's story to be called, and at once several servants approach and draw back the curtain behind which I am hiding, and I am revealed to my father and the uncles and the Khaham-Bashi, and when they perceive my small and haggard figure – that of a pampered child easily provoked to tears – they burst out in uninhibited laughter, their anger evaporated, for it is not possible that this overgrown baby, who does not come unto his wife, afraid even to remain alone in her presence, could stand up to them, and when their great, cackling laughter ceases they slap their thighs as if to signal that the time has come to depart, and they rise to their feet; but when they are prevented from opening the door in order to return to Kharet Elyahud they comprehend, all at once, from Aslan's frozen stance and the silence of the governor of Damascus, that these accusations have, in fact, been levelled at them, and – deeply shocked and affronted – they return to their places and say to Aslan, Surely you jest, some Purim hoax this must be, and Sharif Pasha asks Aslan in a loud, clear voice whether the matters previously confessed by the barber are indeed true, that the members of the Farhi clan gathered before him joined together to put an end to the life of the monk, may he rest in peace, for the purpose of removing his blood as ordered by Rabbi Antebi for use in preparing the unleavened bread for the Passover holiday. All eyes turn to Aslan to learn his answer.

My happy friend, my brown-eyed foundling of gentle expression, many years have passed and often the memory of those events tosses about in my mind and becomes mixed with hallucinations and sorcery and the evil touch of pallid, prodding fingers upon my skin, and I do not know for certain what precisely were Aslan's actions at that time, whether my memories are clear and correct or whether they are the product of my imagination, the foolish chatter of an old man tormented by a past that was not his, for then Aslan stands before the gathered crowd and states the following: The Right Honourable Sharif Pasha, beloved soldiers of Damascus, indeed the barber has spoken the truth, from his own mouth have I heard that this gang of men who face you now banded together in premeditated fashion and by ruse seduced the Christian to the home of Meir Farhi, though not to the fountain or the orchards or the rooms adorned with mosaics did they lead him, but to a small and hideous room left unfinished, the floor of which is covered with dust and dirt, and there did they bind the monk to a crucifix of wooden beams and wind ropes round his body, tightening them, and with the instruments of slaughter they had prepared, they combed his flesh, catching at the veins, and wielded a cleaver to bleed him alive, and the monk pleaded for his life as it seeped away into the glass bottle held by Rabbi Antebi.

Father and the uncles and the Khaham-Bashi take in my words, stunned and terrified, their laughter turned to sobs, and Aslan watches his father to see whether he will beg for his life, but Rafael *almuallem* Farhi stands apart from the rest, a grimace of scorn upon his face, and he remains hateful to Aslan, and estranged from him.

A deep and empty silence follows, and Rabbi Antebi asks permission of the governor to approach the witness, and he draws near Aslan, his reddish beard glowing in the light of the candles and torches, and he embraces Aslan valiantly and says to him, My son, whom I loved, you are as one with me, my own flesh, you are married to my daughter, and with God's help a great nation will burst forth from your loins and you will raise a large family. Why should you remove yourself from your people and make a covenant of lies with these gentiles, and he whispers to me that if my father has wronged me I will one day be avenged, and if my uncles have angered me their retribution will surely come; but words such as those issued from my mouth are liable to bring down a holocaust upon the entire Kharet Elyahud.

And the shrewish witch in Aslan's intestines blinks her eyes and growls and snarls like the belly of the earth before a quake, and Aslan awaits some small sign, some unnoticed hint from his father – clasping his fingers or tugging at his earlobe or curling his lower lip as it trembles – for if he gives him even the slightest hint, Aslan will retract the entire story immediately, will fall to his knees and cry bitterly and confess his many sins, from the first of them to the last, and his father will gather him in his arms and embrace him boldly, forgivingly, and his body will press up against his father's, thighs, groins, bellies rubbing against one another, their warm fingers spread wide across the other's back, and the scent of men, like the aroma of myrrh and persimmon, will waft above them. But his father remains estranged and hostile.

Aslan is overwhelmed by the wailing of that hag, and she stomps her bare feet and tears at her hair, and I grow dizzy when the Khaham-Bashi turns away from me, his shoulders stooped, and these Jewish lords are made to stand in a row, their bellies cascading, their brows furrowed, and a tempest brews in my intestines when they are instructed to cross their hands behind their backs and cuffs are snapped into place in anticipation of their arrest that very evening.

My happy friend, once again nimble spider's legs have come to dance upon my skin and I thank you for the cold compresses you apply to my feverish brow; would that we had some of Suleiman Negrin's leeches to place upon my veins and arteries to suck away the blood and blackened pus that has not yet departed from my body, and would that I could dive in among the pages of the book you are now writing, to plunge between its lines, to grab hold of young Aslan by the lapels or by the hair on his head and rescue him from this turn of events, which he has concocted with his own two hands, but there is no rectifying that which has been, and the imprisonment of my father and uncles thanks to my lies is fated to be written and sealed in this book as eternal witness to my evil deeds.

The first to be imprisoned are my father and my uncles Murad and Meir, in one low-ceilinged cell with a cesspit in the corner, and later Uncle Joseph Farhi and the Khaham-Bashi are stuffed into an adjacent cell, and all of the men loudly broadcast their innocence until there is no choice but to shut their mouths and make each one stand on a single leg, the other leg raised in the air and cuffed to a hand forced behind the back like those waterfowl who bathe in their own excrement, and their muscles are ruined and their bones break and Joseph Farhi, oldest of the four, shouts in grunts and no one relieves him of his agony.

When the last of the candles burns out and thick, heavy smoke swirls above them towards the cool night and the guards return to their posts at the end of the dungeon, I approach in stealth the cell where my father is incarcerated and I peer through the bars to see what is happening to him, and I glimpse his large pot-bellied figure, limbs distorted, one foot trembling from the weight of his enormous body, the hair on his neck and arms slightly raised, his flesh pressed close to that of his brothers as they attempt to keep warm, and Aslan wishes with all his heart for his father to turn his head for a moment towards the hall and notice him, he sorely wishes that his progenitor and provider will stare directly into his eyes so that Aslan can catch, in the split of a second, the most trivial plea or request or wink of any kind, and lo, his father is turning his glance to the darkened hall and Aslan stands facing him, levelling his gaze; perhaps he will take the few steps necessary to reach the door of the cell, perhaps they will exchange a few words, for they are, after all, father and son, not two strangers. But Aslan remains rooted in place and his father does not see him, does not even sigh despairingly or mash his face in his hands, he merely closes his eyes as he stands on one leg beside his brothers and dozes like they do.

Aslan closes this chapter of the grief that has befallen him, his father and uncles housed together in two cells, grunting as they stand in the awkward positions thrust upon them without warning, the lamb and fish from their Sabbath meal mixing inside their stomachs with the fried rice and noodles, vomit frothing upon their lips, and the eldest among them, Uncle

Joseph, floats in and out of consciousness, and as Aslan slowly ascends the staircase, immersed in sadness, a tune of yore catches his ear, that melody of his long-distant childhood:

Min badak ahgor khali
Ya a'aeb an aynya

To you I will depart from myself
You, who are far from my eyes

And Aslan is once again a beloved babe in the arms of his mother and father, and the melody is false and deceiving, seeming at first to rise from an upper floor of the palace, then to issue from the night-abandoned square, or from one of the cells, as though the Jews are singing their pain, and Aslan's astonishment increases when he realises that the voice behind the pleasant song is that of the only woman to have aroused true desire in him, and that she is incarcerated in this very dungeon, prey to the sodomites in her cell, and Aslan races back down the stairs, perspiring with anticipation, but the song fades as though he has drawn away from her, so Aslan ascends once more, glancing around with half-closed, roving eyes, and the melody dims slowly until nothing is left of it but a distorted delusion, trilling in a clear, feminine voice, swallowed by the night sounds of grunting Jews and the groans of prisoners coupling one with the other.

7

My happy friend, what was my lot in this unfolding of events if not heart-grief and a flow of tears? As for the night when I delivered my father and uncles to stand on one leg in a prison cell, well, after that I was released by Sharif Pasha's adjutants to return to my father's home, and told not to leave there until I was called to give testimony a second time in the trial that would begin when the suspects had been interrogated, and I was warned firmly against violating these terms and then sent, unescorted, on my way.

Aslan returns with dawn's first light to Kharet Elyahud, all the while his friend the shrew tamps faintly on his wickedness and sniggers at his various evil deeds and prophesies that the hour of his retribution is nigh, and Aslan consigns her to the murky abysses, chokes her until her blood runs, and she falls silent for the moment, jammed in between his third and fourth ribs, wedged among his intestines, and Aslan calms his soul by walking slowly, rhythmically, wishing to hold on to the familiar sight of the buildings in order to placate the shrew, and the Jewish Quarter stands hushed as death this early morn, its edifices silenced and mute, bereft of its men, for many are the Jewish males who have escaped Damascus with their lives, some gone north to Aleppo, others south to Safed or to the village of Jobar, where they rent clay huts, and the only males left in Kharet Elyahud are the children and babies, and their mothers stand beside their beds to soothe them in the wake of nightmares that terrorise their sleep, and at the sound of marching in the street they rush to hide them in their cradles or between old and dusty feather pillows or in niches in the walls of their homes, for they are in great fear of the strong arm of the ruling élite of Egyptian rebels.

Aslan enters his father's home and finds it empty of the man, husband and father who, in normal times, rules it despotically; his frequent quarrels with Maman have fallen silent, his heavy footfalls are mute, the thick scent of him is evaporating from the rooms, and Aslan tours the spacious courtyard and ascends the wide staircase, the rapping of his shrewish friend upon his ribs all the while resounding behind his tired eyes, and he walks as if sonambulating until he chances upon his younger brother Meir crumpled like a newborn babe in his room near the abandoned fountain, his sleeping mother lying beside him, her arms embracing him, and Meir sucks his thumb in sleep and his eyes roll in their sockets as he dreams of his father and the games they played together, and his warm and loving voice.

In the tiny, repugnant room transformed from servants' quarters to the bedroom he shares with his wife, he finds said woman, whose name is Markhaba, and she has risen early, her hair dishevelled, a book of psalms in her hands, and she is using it to murmur a string of verses and blessings as long as eternity and does not take notice of her husband who has returned to his home from who-knows-where, for she bends and sways her body in prayer to God, that He may spare her father at once from these rioters and that He may visit the Messiah upon them swiftly and soon, and let us say: Amen.

And Aslan stands inside the walls of his home, now alight with the first rays of the day's sunshine, and he is immersed in his loneliness like a swamp fowl slogging through ankle-deep waters, and Aslan fails to comprehend how it is that the parade of people who loved him has grown so terribly thin, for was it not that when he came into the world so many years earlier he was the first-born son of his parents' children, their joy, the apple of their eye? And how is it that his fortunes have changed so very rapidly, how has their love turned to blazing hatred so that even the abandoned dogs that roam the streets of Damascus and the weeds that grow along the roadside and the insects and worms and reptiles all seem full of wrath and reproach for Aslan, wishing to ostracise him for his many acts of treachery?

With daybreak Aslan rushes to his parents' bedroom and seizes several of his mother's garments, long dark scarves and thick cloth skirts, and he steps into a pair of her shoes and makes haste to depart from there on a fast mule to find refuge and shelter in one of the villages surrounding Damascus, or perhaps as far as Aleppo or further north, he will leave this scene behind him before all the Jews find him out and snuff his soul for his heavy guilt.

Aslan hastens to dress himself in a hidden corner of the estate behind the orange and lemon trees, and the fine clothing is drenched with Maman's sweet scent, a faraway aroma of infancy and childhood, and he tucks his curls under a woman's head-scarf and minces along in tiny shoes that pinch his over-large feet, and Aslan flees with a coin purse of piastres saved for a moment of crisis, and he will not leave behind any note or letter; the conundrum of Aslan's disappearance will waft above the Jews of Damascus for generations, no solution at hand, and he jiggles his head in order to arrange the lock of hair on his forehead and thus, dressed as a woman, he wobbles his way along to find a young mule driver willing to rise early in order to lead him to the western gate of the city from which they will proceed to one of the villages, and there he will bide his time until their wrath has subsided, supporting himself with his hoard of piastres and he will work anonymously writing letters for others, just as he has done many a time for his father's business interests.

And lo, the first passers-by stare, astonished, at this strange woman waddling alone through Kharet Elyahud, and it is not long before hooligans begin to harass Aslan, calling the woman blasphemous names, and Aslan attempts to ward them off, all those who wish to bring about his demise, begs them to leave him be, and when they tug at his dress and very nearly reveal a hairy arm, he flees, running awkwardly, tears flowing, and an image comes to him of a woman he has laid eyes on only for a few precious minutes but who, nonetheless, he is certain is the only person in the world who can understand the machinations of his heart, that gentle songstress of trilled notes and frilled tresses, and he recreates in his mind her chiselled shoulders and her fresh complexion.

In a bend of the Straight Street he comes upon a young mule driver with a sharp, direct gaze who agrees to lead him, in spite of the strangeness of the hour, to the estuary of Elnahar Alaswad and the fields of the Arab farmers west of the city, and Aslan opens his purse of piastres and slips the lad two coins, and it appears that his hasty plan, to whose details he has given no forethought, might very well succeed.

No one seems to stare at the woman riding the ass, covered as she is from head to toe, the lad with the black expression on his face seated in front of her, and when Aslan passes by a group of soldiers assessing the vicinity of the Jewish Quarter for suspicious signs on command of Sharif Pasha, he bows his head so that they will not catch sight of him, so he might be vomited out to the river that slakes the farmers' fields.

A large wagon loaded full with copper vessels stands sideways before the western gate, blocking the path of the camels and mules, and Aslan begins to perspire under the heavy clothing he has pilfered from his mother, garments unsuitable for long journeys or outdoor perambulating, and he wishes to remove the head-scarf to allow his sweat to evaporate in the cool early spring Damascus air, and while the soldiers and gendarmes are preoccupied with the hammered copper narghiles, handiwork of the Quarter's Jews, Aslan takes advantage of the momentary distraction and removes the head-scarf to breathe.

When he replaces the head-scarf over his hair the one-eyed shrew imprisoned between his intestines thunders, What foolishness you have committed, Aslan of the pea-brain! For when these soldiers catch you trying to smuggle yourself out at daybreak they will surely bring you straight to the torture chamber at the Saraya prison, and what then will you tell your inquisitors? What lies and fabrications will you invent for them? Better you should order the mule driver to retrace his steps and stealthily drop your mother's sweat-drenched and dusty clothing into the wicker clothes hamper for the washerwomen to clean in the waters of that river in which you wish to splash.

So Aslan orders the mule-driving lad to return half his piastres since the journey outside the city has been cancelled, but the youth with the sharp, direct gaze answers impudently that he will not return any piastres to this coquettish woman with the croaky voice, and when Aslan snatches the two piastres with the strong grip of a man, the lad wails and sobs; just then the wagon loaded with narghiles moves forward to the villages, the open hills, the cool desert, and the soldiers guarding the western gate cannot but help notice the bony woman, alone, shaking to and fro the young mule driver who has requested to be paid his wages.

And when they draw near, amused, to watch this strange sight, they discover it is a man disguised as a maiden and their suspicion is aroused, and they order him to dismount from the ass and deposit his coin purse in their care and identify himself, and at once they understand this is a Jew, and Aslan attempts to jest with them, for on this day has fallen Purim, a holiday when the Children of Israel are commanded to don guises, and the soldiers are overcome with fury at these strange Jewish holidays, for is it not because of this Passover season and their Seder night and the eating of unleavened bread that they slaughter the good citizens of Damascus? And so they summon reinforcements, including soldiers bearing bayonets and lances, and a throng of men congregates around Aslan, surrounding him from every side, and they lead him, manacled, to the Saraya dungeon prison, and Aslan can hear only the thin, high shrieks of his shrewish escort, and he plugs his ears against the din but cannot overcome her.

Aslan is led to the Saraya prison, where his uncles and father and the Khaham-Bashi are already incarcerated and it transpires that from the day before, when they were detained, they have refused to confirm even a single detail of the barber's confession: neither that they had assembled that evening, nor that they had joined forces to extract the monk's blood, nor that they had risen up to slaughter him; rather, they are adamant in their protestations and have provided contrasting testimony as to the events of that stormy evening, for one among them had been revelling at a party in the Christian Quarter and could provide witnesses to testify to his presence there, and another had battened down the windows and sunk into deep sleep with the members of his household, and another was travelling abroad on matters of business, as a number of clerks and customs officers could affirm, and their denials only served to provoke the anger of the consular officials and Sharif Pasha against this Jewish cunning that sought to mock and scorn them all.

Aslan sees them imprisoned in their cells and they are right fatigued and wish to die, for they have been subjected to strange tortures, the first of which was being made to stand on one leg, and then being submerged in barrels of cold water, where they rebound against the sides and then surface, and many other such terrible persecutions, and in spite of all these they do not confess to their cruel crime, nor do they supply new information with regards to the location of the dead monk's body, so necessary to the success of the investigation.

My happy friend, at the same time as I was being escorted by soldiers to the prison dungeon of the Saraya, many others Jews were streaming in, stooped and parched and manacled, all of them new detainees brought in with the hope of spurring on the interrogation, which for the time being was not achieving any results due to the obstinacy of the Farhi brothers, and I see alongside me the Jewish gravediggers, who have been arrested and are filing in, three gravediggers and four assistants and three sub-assistants, all of them former Talmud scholars who had abandoned their studies, and their bodies are heavy-limbed and cumbersome, their hands coarse from labouring to dig graves and from brandishing shovels, and their eyes, which have seen so many Jewish bodies shrivelled with age, withered with disease or blue with crib death, those eyes brim with fear at this valley of the shadow of death, a dark and narrow chamber around the edges of which are cells and in the middle of which are whips and ropes and all manner of strange machines meant for bending and smashing, and the gravediggers pass by one after the other, heads bowed and stooped, and they are taken at once to be interrogated jointly and severally and questioned as to whether they have assisted the suspect Jewish magnates in any manner, whether they have concealed the monk's body, whether they have buried it in this place or that, and if not, whether they lent their shovels or pickaxes or any other tools good for digging, and afterwards they are forced into the centre of the airless room where they must stand, without food or water, until it can be decided what is to be done with them.

The next to be incarcerated are two feuding bands of Jewish butchers, one the Fakhima family and the other the Nawamehs. Under normal circumstances their time is occupied with dishonest commerce and the dissemination of deceitful rumours against their competitors – that their meat is not kosher and their heifers tainted and their lamb meat full of worms, and he who eats from them endangers his life and soul and the lives and souls of his family unto the seventh generation – and now they are being led in as one group, their hands stained with the blood of chickens, feathers stuck to their sleeves and the odour of slaughtered beasts fresh upon their skin, and they are suspected of having donated their equipment for use in preparing the holiday and are asked to state whether cleavers or carving knives or any other blades have been taken from them, and they are made to list all the tools in their possession and explain their methods for slaughtering cattle and sheep and bleeding them, and the butchers hasten to cast blame upon each other, that a member of the rival family must surely have assisted in this abominable act, for they would certainly not hesitate to rent out their tools even for slaughtering an unkosher beast or for committing a murder in order to satiate their greed, and the soldiers interrogating them rise to pull them apart as they try to strangle one another with blackened fingers covered with congealed blood and everlasting sweat.

And lo, the tumult increases as the soldiers of Sharif Pasha lead the children of the Talmud Torah school into the overflowing interrogation room, for the purpose of – as the proverb goes – *Khudu siracom min tzia'arcom*, Extracting the

189

secrets from the mouths of babes, and Aslan regards them from a hiding place he has found for himself in the bowels of the dungeon, watching these children so like all those who used to tease and mock him, and now they enter the teeming, airless dungeon sobbing, ruined, their noses running, each holding the shoulder of the one before him, and there is no purpose for their incarceration other than to cause their fathers and mothers to grieve, so as to bring about the end of the interrogation and reveal the awful truth.

And the mothers, thick-armed, strong-voiced women, call after their children loudly and the soldiers stop them at the entrance to the prison, and so they find slits in the floorboards to scour the dungeon for their loved ones, each woman crying the name of her son through these tiny apertures until one of the prison guards has an idea and he covers the eyes of the children with strips of black cloth and places copper basins like hats on the crowns of their heads, and the children collide one against the other and they fall, bruised, and the basins resound noisily, thunderously, and, against his will, Aslan hears this copper-bashing orchestra and the wails of the children and the mothers' shrieks and the agony of tortured men, and he stares, eyes wide as can be, at the huge crowd assembled there and he is overwhelmed with desolation at himself, for this is all his doing, he has mixed this filthy batter with his own two hands, and he wishes to find his friend the Good Interrogator, Mahmoud, and take hold of his lapels and plead with him to issue an order confirming the lies of his confession and sending the Jews back to their homes, for his Uncle Joseph is having convulsions and might return his soul to his Creator at any moment, but Mahmoud is nowhere to be found, only the hard pinches of the prison guards on Aslan's scrawny arms.

*

My happy friend, at that moment I yearned to be brought to a hidden cell in that dismal dungeon where I could wait, head bowed, for Mahmoud to save me from this distress, for the Jews knew it was I who had informed on them and turned them in, and they were liable to rise up against me and slay me, and indeed they had never been known for their love towards this worm who gnawed and slithered his way around them.

Aslan proceeds, hunched and stooped, his limbs gathered inwards to deflect attention, and he is thankful for the prevailing gloom and the tumult at every juncture, for in addition to his fear of revenge on the part of his clansmen there arises in him, in the form of reddened cheeks and the buds of a flame in his breast, the first signs of shame for his evil actions, and Aslan wishes to receive their pardon but he knows not to whom to turn, nor what to say.

So Aslan continues to walk with bowed head and gathered limbs and he is being ushered into one of the detention cells when suddenly he notices, between the butchers and the gravediggers and the children crashing and clanging into one another, that he is being stared at, and in spite of the grave warnings issued by his friend the shrew to avert his eyes, to proceed hunched and stooped, Aslan cranes his neck like Lot's wife and another moment passes before he recognises, among the Jewish prisoners, the face of the Khaham-Bashi Rabbi Yaacov Antebi, incarcerated along with the rest of them, his customary garb replaced by a striped prisoner's uniform, his ginger beard faded in the dim light but his eyes skittering like burning coals as if they are about to burn and consume Aslan's limbs in their flames.

From the diminutive body of the rabbi, which contains too little virility to sire sons, and he is small and insignificant and always good-humoured – from this body now rips forth a huge shout that silences at once the prisoners and guards alike, for the Khaham-Bashi is pointing at me, my happy friend, and bellows, Here he is, here is the traitor!

In an instant all eyes and the lanterns of the curious prison guards have been raised towards me, and Rabbi Antebi steps on to a stool tossed to him from somewhere and in a clear, booming voice he tells the crowd of my evil deeds, that in spite of my loving parents – their exertions and toil in changing my soiled clothing and educating me and feeding me and sustaining me – I had not hesitated in blaming them for naught, and two soldiers stepped forward to remove Rabbi Antebi by force, but his tiny body withstood them, a new power surged through him as he warned the great and holy crowd against exchanging even a single word with the Jewish traitor, the wicked son who has turned his back and exempted himself from his people, and the rabbi concludes with a plea to the God of Abraham, Isaac and Jacob to speed along the arrival of He who is hoped for and to annihilate the wicked and the informers, may they be dispatched to hell and perdition.

And now all knew of Aslan's guilt and they denounced him and cursed him in secret, and the Khaham-Bashi took care to remind them hour after hour of my loathsome actions, and as for me, my happy friend, I was sequestered in my cell, rejected and ostracised from my people, and what did I have left but to beg for my own death, for Aslan's prosecutors were correct in their plaints, and Aslan stands before the rancid, mouldy wall, its bricks black with filth, and beats his head to expel the malevolent thoughts, and his friend the shrew affirms that he should behave thus, but in spite of the heavy blows and the terrible pounding pain in his forehead and the cracks he imagines have cleaved his skull, Aslan's breath continues, regular and obstinate, to inflate his lungs, and his sealed, petrified heart continues to beat, and the Aslanish darkness that descends upon him from time to time refuses to redeem him now so that, on the contrary, Aslan is wide awake and alert in order to watch his sins like a father watches his bastard children.

8

My happy friend, the strength I need for telling this perplexing, long-ago story is ebbing, though it still throbs in my veins; these words force my ill and worn-out member to raise its ancient head unwillingly and now the tormenting pains that plague it when I pass water grow more intense and I must ask to pause in order to step out and calm myself with gloomy thoughts about my final days as they draw to a close, and you, my friend, you must continue to enjoy these carefree days of your youth: leave aside your plan to record this epic and set yourself free, take your meagre belongings and leave this monastery in which we dwell, for I am overcome with fatigue and wish to shut my eyes and join the everlasting, persistent journey of the Black River; just remember, please, to empty the bedpans, for they are overflowing.

But if the will to hear more of this tale is strong in you, then I will tell you only this, that after the Khaham-Bashi's curse I remained alone in my cell day and night listening to nothing but the profanities hurled my way by the Jews, and I am forlorn and abandoned, despised by the members of my family, disowned by the entire community, my head bashed and battered, and that witch, the shrew, is flitting about inside me without mercy, and Aslan pictures himself an empty vessel lying lifelessly on the ground, no knowledge or insight in his brain, and again he yearns for death to overtake him at last, to rescue him from these torments of hell, and then, in the deep gloom of the Saraya dungeon I notice the group of gravediggers assembled by one of the cells and they are removing the body of a Jew who could not withstand the tortures, and Aslan regards the shape of the body in order to discern whether it is his father who has expired, but in fact the man is Uncle Joseph, and the Jews are mumbling *Ma bidun illa Allah*, Only God is eternal, and they say the *Kaddish* prayer over him before the prison guards order them to lie down on the cold stone floor for their fitful sleep.

And lo, as Aslan gazes in bewilderment at the bars facing him, and blue and purple shadows stretch out from him on either side and he is sunken and feeble and detests life, suddenly a scorching yellow ray of light strikes him, and a trickle of warm, sky-blue water, and a melody of the purest joy, and his eyes do not deceive him, for between the shrivelled body and the butchers and the gravediggers he catches sight, to his amazement, of the profile of a seated woman, her back to him, and she is wearing a long gown that stretches the length of her and is bedecked in gems and jewels that sparkle in the dark of the Saraya dungeon, and her serene presence there in that valley of the shadow of death late in the evening seems not strange to him, but quite fitting, and Aslan already knows this is the songstress, that very same singer who has captured his heart, and in spite of what the dead and dissected monk told him she is not the creation of his imagination nor the fruit of his hallucinations, but a flesh and blood woman, curvaceous, and Aslan knows that she is waiting for his kisses alone, his love.

Wordlessly, he approaches the bars of his cell and beckons to her with the words of the secret song the two share, and with every note that floats from his throat he is firmer in the knowledge that this noble woman has come to the Saraya prison to confess her love for him and that she anticipates the touch of his fingers on her shoulders, and he utters not a word, merely blows tiny, unseen kisses aimed at her white and dainty back through the bars that separate them, and she sighs in affirmation, and he sends kisses from afar that pass over her narrow, feminine shoulders, over the long, light-green sleeves of her gown so soft to the touch, and without turning her face to him she joins him in singing their song, that ancient song from his wedding, which she tapped with her feet and danced slowly to muffled drums for the gathered guests, and now she hums the familiar tune, *Min badak ahgor khali*, To you I will depart from myself, *Ya a'aeb an aynya*, You, who are far from my eyes, and her small chest rises a bit with each breath and her stuffed breasts sway and the words of the song form in their mouths and they tell of the love between a man and a maiden, and the song is more right and fitting than any other, and after Aslan has stared deeply at her for a long time, her back all the while towards him, she turns her face in his direction, and her head tilts slightly and she wears a shy smile, and she draws near his cell at a leisurely pace, and when she reaches him she kisses him chastely, gently, slipping her tiny tongue into his mouth, and they continue to sing as they kiss, and he rubs against her breasts and presses his nose between them, as far as the bars of his cell will allow him, and his member stands quite erect, ready for the act, but it is not lust-drenched debauchery or release followed by self-loathing and repugnance that he craves, but rather to join and unite with this soulmate of his, whose secret is already known to him, a secret which only serves to increase his excitement and his love.

Then the songstress takes hold of a small key dangling on a chain around her neck and opens the door to his cell and slips inside, and Aslan well knows the true nature of this pure maiden and understands the delays that have kept her from him until now, and in the dim light from the lanterns in the dungeon her dress appears to him as a wedding gown and the hat on her head as a veil and the small red purse in her hands as a bridal bouquet, and he wishes to transport her in his arms to the ratty, narrow divan in his cell, but too tall is she, and so instead she sits regally on the divan, which seems to Aslan as if it were glowing in the light of betrothal, and Umm-Jihan sees none of this, for her sky-blue eyes are lowered in modesty and bashfulness, and Aslan speaks to her softly, telling her not to cry, for even one of her tears is more precious to him than the great wealth of his family, and Umm-Jihan smiles shyly, and her neck is as that of a swan's, her breasts ample and full, and Aslan whispers to her, *Khabibti*, My love, and he refrains from sullying her sanctity with his caresses, but only moments later he desires to pump life and passion into her blood, and again he kisses her, voluptuously, and removes the hat from her head and pulls her dress low, to her breasts, and he encounters her muscled chest and her pointed nipples and he kisses the short, white hairs on her thighs and he exposes her sex and sports amorously with it and smiles to himself at her attempts at concealing her true nature, and from inside her clothing Umm-Jihan writhes and twists and frees himself and lo, he is Aslan's beloved, eyes smiling and sweet to the touch.

My happy friend, I could no longer control my impulses and so I stripped her clothing from her body, and with skills acquired from my former lover, the barber, I stuffed her member into my mouth, and its taste was sweeter than any delicacy, and from there, in the same manner that the dearly departed Tomaso had taught me, I turned to the task of awakening her sexual heat, her passion, and Umm-Jihan's organ swelled and stood very erect, and she was not deterred from releasing loud moans and feeble cries on that betrothal divan, and Umm-Jihan's thin sighs turned into Mahmoud's pleasant voice, and Aslan finds himself concurrently making love to both lovers, and they mingle and transform one into the other before his eyes, at times the soft, hairless curve of her white buttocks, at times the strong, jutting shoulder blades of his manly back, and Aslan covers both with many kisses, and he has no aim and no desire beyond pleasing this maiden and this youth until their bodies drip with sweat and love.

And while Aslan kisses his lovers, Umm-Jihan resumes her frightened, fragile expression, and she tells him in a worried chant, high and thin, that their mutual friend, the arc-browed barber, has retracted the true confession he made and sworn his statement was false and deceitful, that he had begun to blubber like a terrified woman about his conscience and his sins, and Sharif Pasha had summoned her and instructed her to find new evidence or he would set the Jewish magnates free at once, and she does not know what to do, for now, because of the traitorous barber's blunders there would be no solution to the puzzling matter of Tomaso, and this meant she would be returned to the prison and, like an ill-treated wife, would not receive her fine clothes, her raiment, her conjugal rights.

And this fear causes Umm-Jihan to sit upright and ask that they cease this act of love and she buries her head of golden hair between her arms and her eyes search for her gown, and the sweat of men upon her body chills quickly and her skin turns cold and frozen, and Aslan hastens to embrace her from behind and he wraps his hairy arms around her manly, muscled chest and he promises to do anything he can to help her, for her sorrow is his, and they are together in the same cauldron, and she relaxes her muscles upon hearing his fine words and she thanks him for the goodness and benevolence he has imparted to her from the very day the paths of their lives first crossed, but she does not believe that the power of his love and his excellent words can condemn their enemies and set her free from prison, and she sobs from the depths of her heart at the nightmare of having to return to her cell, where procurers are waiting to stifle the song of her life.

Aslan knows the only escape from this grief and is well aware of its urgency, and he kisses the nape of his sobbing lover's neck and promises to pen a full confession to the act perpetrated upon the person of the monk Tomaso in which he will admit to having taken part in the deed about which he will, at last, reveal every detail, but Umm-Jihan requests that he desist from these oaths, that he should not confess for her sake to matters in which he bears no guilt, nor bring upon himself unnecessary danger, but Aslan quashes her words with a smile and a wave, prepared to undertake any action required to help her, and he tells her there is nothing protective or false about his confession, that in fact it is pure and true, for he was in the presence of his uncles and father when they murdered the life-loving monk, and it was only his wish to honour his father and his mother that prevented Aslan from making this final admission of his guilt until now, this confession that is essential to condemning the assassins, and a letter of this nature will be enough, a few lines in his own hand which they will write in haste, negligently, without forethought, and which will bring about the desired conviction of his enemies, and in exchange she will most likely be granted clemency, and Umm-Jihan is grateful for his promise and she hops up and down exuberantly in the low-ceilinged cell and bestows embraces and kisses upon him, and they return to their lovemaking, and Aslan takes up arousing her orifices once again, inflaming her passion for him and bringing them to the act of becoming one.

His lover asks that he use utmost precaution, for there are those who carry out this act roughly and rashly and bring terrible pain to his body, and Aslan swears he will treat him with delicacy and love, and he rolls his lover on to his stomach to rest comfortably and stimulates him by rubbing gently, preparing him, until Aslan feels the great heat that has gripped his body and he knows the gates have been breached and the paths cleared and the way opened, and still he is gentle, making his way inward with caution, and he kisses Mahmoud's ear lobes and helps him to relax, consoling him, and he helps his lover overcome the small, desired pains of their coupling, for they are giving birth together to their act of love with a new and faster rhythm, and they are as a rider on a wild horse, a cruel Bedouin warrior leading an army of bare-chested mercenaries to rout his enemies from my patch of desert, until I stain my glowing path with drops of my love, and only a few seconds more are needed for my lover to pour forth her treasures as well.

The very next day, when one of the guards entered my cell, I asked him for an inkwell and a sheet of paper and I wrote my *ard khall*, my request for clemency, and I placed this letter in the hands of a courier for immediate delivery to Sharif Pasha, and all the while that ancient song was singing in my heart.

My happy friend, I place now in your trustworthy hands, which tremble at this august occasion, the original copy of that infamous *ard khall*, preserved among my possessions for many long years in spite of my endless wanderings from place to place, for it is fit and becoming to append this missive to our expanding work, but know, my happy friend, what young Aslan did not, and that is that written words, imprinted with ink on paper, are more resilient and more terrible than those of a wagging tongue, which are heard and then forgotten, for even after all those involved have passed away, and after our epic tale has been resolved, and after the storm and the terror of it all have ceased to exist in the minds of men, the written words persist in clinging to the page, and they serve as an eternal memorial to all that was evil and foolish. Here then, my happy, beloved, friend, are the words I committed to paper:

To His Eminence Sharif Pasha
From Aslan, son of Rafael Farhi (*almuallem*)

Lord Governor Sharif Pasha, by this letter I present you with my confession in the matter of the murder of Father Tomaso, *requiescat in pace*, in exchange for my being granted clemency and being protected from any edict or sentence issued by any court of law, though as for God's court I will pray each and every morning until my dying day that He have mercy on me from on high, for the cup of my guilt hath runneth over.

As I have already testified before you, on the fourth day of the first week of the month of Adar the First in the year five thousand, six hundred, according to the reckoning of the Jews, my father and my uncles and the Khaham-Bashi gathered in a room of the home of Meir Farhi, to which the barber Suleiman Negrin had brought Father Tomaso; now, however, I must add to my testimony, revealing that which I have heretofore kept secret, matters I have observed with my own eyes.

I, too, was among those gathered to ensnare Father Tomaso; under orders of my father I accompanied him and my uncles to the home of Meir Farhi to carry out the terrible act, and once assembled in this unfinished room I watched as my father unsheathed a sharp and shiny carving knife, the mere touch of whose thin blade would slice a finger into rivers of blood, and he assigned me the task of holding the monk's right leg and pinning it down firmly on the plank, for they were planning to draw the blade over his jugular vein, to slaughter him for the purpose of extracting his blood, and the Khaham-Bashi produced a glass and copper gathering jar for the purpose of saving the monk's crimson blood. To my frightened questions I received the response that this was essential for the baking of the unleavened bread for the Passover holiday.

At once I asked to be allowed to leave there for I was sore afraid to watch this act of murder, but my father forbade me absolutely to depart from the room, and thus I was forced to hold the right leg while my friend the barber held the left leg, Uncles Joseph and Meir procured his arms while Uncle Murad held fast to his shoulders. My father made slits in the wretched monk's neck and the Khaham-Bashi stood alongside him, collecting the blood, and Tomaso's life seeped away, and he tried to cry out in protest but could not overcome these men pinning him fast, I, my Lord Governor, among them.

While Father was thrusting the blade deeper into his neck and the monk was still clinging to life, a sharp, deafening scream escaped his mouth, and Father hastened to cut the thread of his life with one final plunge of the knife, and the monk's eyes spun in their sockets, turning inside out and swelling until his groaning ceased and only his blood continued to flow copiously from the exposed veins into the glass and copper vessel that the Khaham-Bashi held.

Upon observing the river of blood and the swollen eyeballs I was visited at long last by a much-awaited redemption and I fell into an unconscious darkness. When I awakened I found myself ensconced in my parents' bed, my dear mother standing over me with smelling salts to revive my soul, and she rubbed my fingertips to remove the bloodstains from them.

From that day forth I was ordered never to speak about or even mention this event and I possess no knowledge of what became of the monk's body or what was done with his blood, only that from the Khaham-Bashi I learned that this act is carried out for the purpose of baking unleavened bread as is required from generation to generation on the eve of the Passover holiday.

My Honourable Lord Governor Sharif Pasha, I have penned this statement on my own accord and from what I have witnessed with my own eyes in the matter of Father Tomaso, *requiescat in pace*, and I have not refrained from including any detail in my account and ask only to receive His Lord's clemency, that I will not be maltreated in any manner nor that any sorrow should befall me, for I am greatly afraid of my uncles and father and of the vengeance of my fellow Jews.

Signed,

Aslan, son of Rafael Farhi

PART THREE
MOUSSA

1

My happy friend, as an empty glass bottle left to stand for years in some dark corner away from the eyes of all beings, barren and despised, into which all at once a sweet and holy wine *de bonne qualité* is poured, so was I now filled with Mahmoud's sudden love, flooding and frothing, and I wished nothing other than to forget the wicked missive I had penned and all the other creeping, crawling creatures slithering in the dark box of my soul, and immerse myself instead in the holy, red, syrupy liquid coursing through me and raising a smile of joy to my lips.

Mahmoud and Mahmoud and Mahmoud: this was the only name I would pronounce and express from morn until evening, and when the young attendant came, the day after I made my confession, to release me from my cell on the order of Sharif Pasha, I did not even tarry to exult at the joy of freedom, for a single passion engulfed me, that is, the powerful desire to meet my lover again, to inhale the scent of his body, to taste his kisses and live out my days to the very last of them with him.

The imprisoned Jews, the Khaham-Bashi at their head, watch as Aslan gains his freedom, and they hurl curses at him, and prayers for his demise, but as for me, my happy friend, I turn my back on my father and uncles and all those acquaintances of mine incarcerated there, requesting only that the young attendant escort me not to my parents' home nor to the gate of Kharet

Elyahud, nor to the Quarter itself, but to my sweet lover's chambers, for I am keen to smother him with embraces and stroke the hair of his head and dribble words of love and affection into his ears and kiss his mouth for all to see, and to permit the waters from that dam to gush forth and rage before all the world, for my love of that man is so vast and abiding.

The young attendant grants my request and leads me to Mahmoud's quarters, but my lover is not to be found; his belongings, however, stand as he left them, and they carry his pleasant fragrance, the seal of his blessings and love, and Aslan dances and prances among them, and begs to remain in Mahmoud's chambers to await his arrival, and when permission is bestowed he seats himself, with an aura of holiness, on the nicely made bed, and he caresses the sheets, whipping them about and crafting them into the shape of his love.

Aslan is preoccupied with rearranging the folds of the sheets when Mahmoud enters the room silently behind him and closes the door, and Mahmoud lavishes many unexpected kisses upon him, on his ear lobes and his neck, and Aslan gushes and giggles and turns his face to observe his beloved, and he drowns in the tears of Mahmoud's sky-blue eyes and suckles his fine white teeth as if they were the full and ample breasts of Umm-Jihan, and they embrace at length, then sit discussing events of the ensuing day, for from the moment that Umm-Jihan departed from his prison cell, Aslan has awaited their next meeting, and Mahmoud croons in Umm-Jihan's voice and wriggles his fingers in dance, and Aslan's laughter is loud and boisterous.

And lo, my happy friend, all my sorrows were forgotten, just as they were whenever I was in the company of my beloved, dropping like filth into Elnahar Alaswad, disappearing, vanishing, like smoke from a narghile in the wind, and my eyes were engorged with the features of Mahmoud's face and his beauty increased tremendously and I shaded myself from its shining brightness.

After these things come to pass Mahmoud presses me to his body and he whispers in my ear that it is now time for us to celebrate, and he expresses a wish to take me to a far remove from this land of cells for tortured prisoners and dunghills of hatred among the people of my faith, to a new land, both near and far, a realm of golden scarves and *masbakha* beads and snaking narghiles, a place where no Jew has ever trod, behind hidden passageways and twisting byways that none but the initiated, the holders of the secret, would ever guess exists, and my beloved takes my hand in his own warm hand that sports a ring of gold and *sharshar* pearls, the aromas of his foreign perfumes heavy in my nostrils, and he opens before me the door to Damascus the whore, roiling and gurgling, and she is as an enchanted city suspended above everyday Damascus that no man may reach but by ascending a magic ladder hidden from view or by mounting a bewitched ass or by putting his fingers in the hand of his one true love.

Mahmoud leads me into the Muslim Quarter late on an evening crowned by a full moon to a hidden wooden door pressed close between two filthy shops, closed at this hour, and the door swings on its hinges as quick-footed men slip past it, and Mahmoud brings to my attention that this is the entrance to the Nur Aladdin *hammam*, a meeting place for men in search of that pure, true friendship of men beloved to one another, and I do not protest when he pays the price of my admission, and a young bath-attendant hastens to place towels in our hands, leading us down a long, dark, narrow corridor, and my beloved plants a stealthy kiss on my neck, and after three or four doors have been opened and closed behind us we are presented with the key to a *cabine*, where we undress, and Aslan slouches for his body is woolly, unattractive, as it emerges from his clothes limb by limb, from his flaccid, hairy thighs to his chest dotted with curly black hairs, and Mahmoud, a captivating smile on his face, allows his own member to dangle freely like a stray arrow from the wheel of fortune, and he resumes kissing Aslan, and Mahmoud loves Aslan deeply.

We quickly find the *hammam* itself, a large bathing room thick with scented steam and abuzz with life, many men lounging about at this late hour stark naked, and nearby, broad-muscled youths, and in the mouths of all are pearly teeth and laughter, and not one expresses surprise at the excited kisses Mahmoud and Aslan exchange; rather, they encourage the two and affirm their beauty, and several approach Mahmoud and place double kisses on each cheek and embrace him, asking after his health and congratulating him upon returning to the land of the living, for they well know of the hell to which he has been sent because of the libellous declarations of slanderers.

Aslan proceeds, arms interlocked with his beloved, and he knows that they have reached a place of fraternity and friendship, that these are men in love, imbibing to the fullest – drinking, immersing themselves in the baths, smoking hashish – and they delight in one another's bodies, washing their comrades' backs, supplying kisses and embraces, and as one moustachioed man passes by Aslan and Mahmoud, a ripe and pungent aroma rising from under his arms and from his genitals, they pass their hands nonchalantly over his nipples, and Aslan is giddy with the freedom he has been granted and his temples flood with joy, and he knows and feels in every limb that for the first time in his life he is experiencing life at its truest, that he is living with utmost vitality, that he is being fashioned anew all at once, and his blood flows wildly and surges, his pupils are wide and his eyes sharp, and all his limbs are aflame and alive, and he shares kisses more precious than gold with everyone generously, without recompense or fear, and these kisses sparkle through his teeth in spite of the dense darkness of the *hammam*, and his laughter refuses to pass from his face.

My happy friend, at that very hour Mahmoud broke away suddenly from Aslan's grip and informed him they would meet up again after twenty minutes, without saying where their meeting would take place, and Aslan did not comprehend the meaning of this hasty parting and wished to protest, to plead for a reprieve for these precious moments during which he must endure the forced celibacy of being separated from his beloved, but he was compelled to continue alone on his journey, satisfying his increasingly zealous curiosity.

Aslan inspects the damp wooden stools upon which lounge men of a certain age, their faces furrowed with wrinkles, and they stare broodingly, lecherously, after him, and on occasion they motion for him to sit near them or they send sweet kisses through the thick, steamy air, and Aslan, dizzy and delirious, approaches them for a light kiss, an oblique embrace, and he declines with a smile when they pat his buttocks and offer him a suck on their water pipes, and they expose their penises to him and he passes a caressing hand over them like that of the Bedouin for his horse, and sometimes he tastes drops of their seed that have smeared at the tip in thick and shiny beads.

From there he arrives at a small pool of water, hidden behind the wooden stools, in which young men are massaging one another's backs, and he dips his toes into the tepid water then enters the pool gingerly, removing the cloth draped over his loins and joining the group in the water, and at once he is inundated with fingers that knead his body and seductive whispers and petting and kisses as sweet as nectar, and Aslan weeps at the days of his youth and childhood that have vanished, borne away by the wind, ground to nothing, without his ever knowing about this place of love and lovemaking, and the Arab lads bathing alongside him in the tepid pool ask his name and they praise the thick, dark hair of his body, but he does not tarry long with them for he is overcome by a great and burning desire to reunite with his beloved.

It is then that I begin retracing my steps to find Mahmoud, passing by the wading youths, but Mahmoud is not among them, and my search for him lengthens, for my yellow-haired friend is nowhere to be found among the entwined men, nor do his limbs appear beneath the water of the tepid pool, and a light, nagging fear that perhaps Mahmoud has returned alone to his chambers grips Aslan's breast, and he reviews all that transpired between them with regards to their appointed meeting place and time, and the details of his beloved's hasty parting fill him with worry: Why did he disappear so suddenly, and why does he not reappear, and as Aslan toddles along in the darkness, his legs threaten to give way on the slippery surface of a stair overgrown with mould.

He makes his way back along the same route he took before, but now the men seem dark and threatening to him, their very appearance debauched and sinful, and they are ugly and repulsive to behold, and his insides throb: How could I have let my beloved slip away and vanish into the darkness of Nur Aladdin? Aslan questions men who cross his path: Have they seen Mahmoud, that stately man of blue eyes and yellow hair, and they point in opposite directions or shrug their shoulders or snigger, and the shrewish hag mocks him with poisoned whisperings, that his beloved has departed and deserted him for ever, and Aslan threatens to drown her in the sweat-soaked waters of the pool, but the shrew is undaunted and carries on deriding him, saying that Mahmoud is now entangled in the arms of another man, more handsome than Aslan, taller and more masculine, for Mahmoud has no interest in the ugly young Jew's arced eyebrows or the hair sprouting from every pore on his body.

And as she continues to shriek her lies, Mahmoud's fair body covered in sweet, blond fur comes into view, and Aslan is aghast to find him deep in conversation with a curly-haired youth, and they are taking sweet counsel together and grazing their hands over each other's muscles, and a short, sharp, feminine cry escapes from inside Aslan and Mahmoud turns, amused, towards him, but he does not desist from standing too close to the Arab boy and they continue their pleasant conversation, rubbing each other's members all the while, and Aslan observes all this and cannot help but come between them, and he dispatches the Arab youth with evil looks and silent curses, and he plants his kisses upon Mahmoud's lips, and Mahmoud responds with his laughter, pure and benevolent, and he acquiesces to Aslan's stubborn pleas to depart forthwith from that den of vipers, and Aslan grips his lover's hand so tightly as to leave an imprint, and he sucks the heat of his body from him like the leeches in the jar at the barber's shop, and he vows a thousand oaths to himself never to let Mahmoud stray from him for even a moment, so vast and abiding is his love for that man.

Thus, my happy friend, we walk through the night-dark streets of Damascus, our organs still warm from the steam and the hair on our heads damp and thick, and I am attentive and alert to grant every wish of my lover; when he coughs, I proffer my handkerchief, when he jests I gush with boisterous laughter, and when he indicates that I should leave him in peace, for he desires to breathe the clear air or sink into his own thoughts, then I become a shadow at his side, silent and sombre, and I hold my breath until he crooks his little finger at me, signalling that I should return to the land of the living, and this tiny gesture causes the blood to course through me once again.

A gripping fear begins to buzz in Aslan's breast lest his lover forsake him on this very night, lest he not invite him back to his chambers, and Aslan waves his hands to expel this buzz of meaningless fear, and he is careful to laugh with Mahmoud and he puts forth his pleasant nature and pure smile, yet beneath it all, in the walls of the tunnel that house her, the one-eyed shrew disturbs his peace, whispering that Mahmoud holds no love for him, for one thing is known of the character of males, and that is, in the wake of lovemaking, a man's affections turn to loathing and his yearning flows to another object, one he has not yet known, and Aslan recalls the curly-headed Arab youth who wooed his beloved and he knows that just as he dissected the limbs of Father Tomaso atop the bald mountains outside the city, so too could he pass the blade across the throat of that son of a whore.

All the while Mahmoud whistles and remains utterly complacent, and when we reach a fork in the road, one path leading to the Jewish Quarter and the other to Azm Palace, Mahmoud stops walking, approaches Aslan, takes his hands in his own, levels his gaze at him and requests, in a festive whisper, to speak his mind.

I am aware, my happy friend, of your meagre years and your innocence and your scant experience in matters of love; indeed, it is upon my command that you are imprisoned in this house of God every day of the year so that you not fall prey to the temptations men will offer you, and still, my young companion, in the depth of your eyes I do believe I can see that you understand Aslan's soul, how my heart sank at that moment to an abyss of desolation and despair, and how in my mind I could hear the very words I dreaded more than any others, that Mahmoud would toss me aside as men do with their former loves.

Mahmoud gathers himself for a long moment before speaking, and he leans upon an adjacent building, sheltering me with his body, and Aslan wishes to hasten the end of his torment and he appeals to his beloved, saying, What is the matter? And Mahmoud laughs uncomfortably and grasps Aslan's fingers, and they are cold and limp, fidgeting like the spindly legs of a stray spider, and Mahmoud thanks me for my help and assistance from the day of my first confession in the arms of Father Alexis with regards to the slaughter perpetrated by the Jews, and for the confession I extracted from the barber and for my stance against my father and uncles, and for the listing of criminal actions in my affidavit to Sharif Pasha, and he is aware that it was I who purchased his freedom, and that he owes his very life to me, and then Mahmoud stutters as if attempting to speak but unable to do so, and he falls silent for several moments, and the terror ascends noisily from Aslan's neck into his ears, his temples, and the shrieks of the hag pound their wings, and Aslan fears the two will cease to walk together, that he will fall as a stray bird, confused, in a snare upon the earth, and Aslan mourns their lovely days together now doomed to die with no chance of a stay or pardon, until at last Mahmoud takes hold of his shoulders with two sturdy hands, leans towards him and quickly, briefly states, in the gentlest, simplest of words, I love you.

Aslan wishes to run shouting his love through the streets of Damascus, to plunder the homes of the Jewish Quarter, to stand its men and women in a procession to witness his great love, to free the prisoners from their incarceration and the weary from their fatigue and the infirm from their illnesses and the buried from their graves, to march them all on the abundant, fruitful, springtime earth, to infect them with his tempestuous love, for his love is patient and generous and immortal, and Aslan now comprehends that he has been endowed with magic powers, and it is his wish to restore the Jews to their rightful land, to make the mountains skip like rams and the little hills like young sheep, and perhaps the holy year five thousand, six hundred has arrived for no other purpose than that of raising him up to greatness, and the pain and distress that the Jews have endured were nothing but the birth pangs of his arrival, and he has lived among them the entire time, hidden from sight, silent, shamed, and he himself did not even know until this very day the power of his sanctity.

Mahmoud gathers me into his embrace and praises me for my beauty and wisdom, and adds that he can reveal to me that in this matter of the Damascus Blood Libel, as it will come to be known, a place of honour and greatness will be reserved for me, not as some marginal character, mentioned in the drama only in passing, a character sketched haphazardly in the coarse outline of hearsay, but as one filled with life, an essential being whose desire conquers all and whose lust spills on to the words and letters of its design, and this character shall be nourished by abundant descriptions of its thoughts and moods, by words it speaks and expresses, by depictions of its body and soul; and all the beings in its orb have been created for the sole purpose of glorifying, praising and causing the life energy of this person to flourish, for he will make love over the course of many pages.

And when they retire to their bed Aslan hears the scantest of rumours of the trial poised to commence in the wake of his written confession, and of his father and uncles, accused of murder, and of the verdict that awaits them, whether by hanging or strangulation or beating, but these images slip from his mind, flickering and shattering into tiny, forgotten shards; their story will be told in a different book, the cover as thick and fattened as their skin and bodies: let Aslan and Mahmoud seal their tale with this great love, and Aslan is full of smiles and laughter, and he asks Mahmoud not to mention the fate of the Jews or the envisioned verdict against his father and father-in-law again, nor any of these old and distant sorrows, nor should he mention the cold draughts undermining the currents of hot air of their love; instead, he begs Mahmoud to don a wide-brimmed purple hat and sing the songs of Umm-Jihan, and they recall the story of their first meeting on the day of Aslan's wedding and each enjoys hearing the other describe how their gazes met, and how they danced together without knowing of the other's desire, and Mahmoud does not withhold any of the knowledge he has accrued in pleasures and delights, and they make love and sport for many hours all through the night, and he recounts and confesses the love coursing through his heart, and Aslan does not restrain his own heart from any joy, rather, he reciprocates with a confession of his love, even stronger, and he hastens to learn studiously the secrets of pleasing a man, and together they write their epic love in the minutest of details and they roll it about in every direction and learn its secrets and its sighs, and at its apex they return to the start, to renew the story of an act whose end never comes.

2

How sweet it is to slumber with my beloved, his naked loins pressed to my body, his sturdy arms encircling my chest, his wide, pink bare feet entwined with my own, his belly exposed, vulnerable, above his genitals, and how lovely his breath, how lovely his eyes shut fast under long, pale lashes, and the smooth bronzed skin, and the blond fuzz of his head, and the tough, chiselled lines of his jaw, and Aslan is never sated from this vision of the body of a man deep in sleep, and the beauty of his musculature and his courage and his decisiveness and his pure intentions, all these sequestered for a few short hours from the world, and Mahmoud lies beside him as a dead man, bereft of strength, his faith and his fate entrusted to Aslan's loyal custody, the slow and steady rhythm of his breathing visible in the rise and fall of his chest, and these are the only clues to the life locked inside and the soul that has not yet left his being, and I stroke his yellow hair and whisper words of love to him until at last it is decreed that I, too, shall be exiled to the realm of slumber, and I draw close to his bosom and join him in the depths of princely sleep.

Aslan is immersed in the sweetest of dreams when his beloved awakens him with the rustling of his belongings, knocking his inkwell to the floor, searching frantically through his papers and documents, and Aslan stretches his neck to receive a belated morning kiss, and he purses his lips and smacks them and makes all manner of kissing and sucking noises to remind Mahmoud to indulge him, but Mahmoud responds only with a low grumble, and Aslan sits up abruptly on the bed, an expression of concern on his face, prepared to carry out any request Mahmoud might make of him: to be his slave, his manservant, his maidservant, whatever it will take to ensure his continued presence with this prince of virtues, and Aslan rises to dance attendance on Mahmoud and offer whatever assistance he may need, though he does not yet know what that might be, for his beloved seems increasingly anxious, and estranged from his kisses and his love, until slowly the matter is revealed to Aslan, that Sharif Pasha has ordered the postponement of the trial of the heinous murderers until such time as he is presented with some tangible evidence and not another affidavit or confession or other tongue-wagging, the veracity of which may never be proved.

And I swear to Mahmoud that tangible evidence will in fact be found, perhaps a piece of cloth from the monk's cloak or a chip of bone or the vessel that contained his blood, but Mahmoud is agitated and nonplussed, for my wicked father and uncles have refused to utter a single word, in spite of their being dunked in freezing water, stretched on racks and subjected to other methods of torture, they have made no confession in the matter of the monk's murder and have provided no details, and I comprehend the machinations of my lover's heart and gather him into my arms and press him to my breast, for it is the fear of being returned to prison that makes him troubled and distraught; instead of the soft kisses of young men at the pool of the Nur Aladdin *hammam* he will be treated to flagellations at the hands of the men in his prison cell, who will come unto him one after the other without any feeling or compassion or lubrication.

Mahmoud wriggles free of my grasp and continues to rustle papers as if hoping to find some lead that might save him, and he turns to me and demands to know what was done with the body of the monk, where it was buried, to where it was removed, and he pinches me hard with his fingernails and shakes me to and fro to make me confess at once the details of the ancient and mysterious ceremony conducted by the Jews, and presses me to rescind my claim that I fell into a deep faint in that half-built room in which the murder was committed, for did I not witness with my own eyes all that had come to pass in disposing of the monk? And with the onset of tears I request that he stop shaking me, for I am prepared to recount to him all that he wishes to hear.

After a long moment of silence between us, Mahmoud relaxes his muscles and begs my forgiveness, for he knows I am his true and everlasting friend who will always succour him in every matter, and again I cover his face with many kisses and assure him that we will find a way of extricating us from this *cul-de-sac*, and without knowing why I suggest that we return to that highly intelligent and resourceful priest, Father Alexis, to receive his good counsel in this matter.

Every last bottle from Alexis' secret cellar at the Terra Sancta Monastery has been exhumed and consumed, so that the priest is on the prowl for new ones, and because he is completely given over to his desire for wines and liqueurs, so difficult to come by in Damascus, he has entreated his congregants to provide him with these libations essential for prayer and in uniting with God, and without them he sits despondent and slack at the edge of the altar in the chapel, his lower lip trembling.

And lo, in spite of his great weakness, when he takes notice of our sudden appearance at the door Alexis rises to his feet and greets us warmly, and he surprises Aslan by remembering his name, and their earlier embrace remains fresh in his memory, and after receiving us with a bright countenance he turns, suddenly outraged, his hands grasping a chair in his path, and asks Mahmoud why those men accused of Tomaso's murder have not yet been hanged, why they are still contaminating this beautiful God-given earth with their tainted breath, for indeed their disgraceful, evil holiday is nigh upon them and their unleavened bread has been baked in preparation for the Seder night, drops of the murdered Tomaso's blood concealed between its rows to satisfy their savage cravings, and he pounds the chair with a trembling hand, loses his balance and tumbles to the centre of the holy room, and now he pummels the chapel floor so that Jesus and Mary, sculpted into the wall above him, can witness his fury and the war he is waging.

Mahmoud explains to Alexis that this is precisely the purpose of our visit, for Sharif Pasha has demanded decisive proof in the matter of this murder, in order for there to be no further doubt as to its veracity, and Alexis, standing now but terribly wobbly from drink, removes his lips from the mouth of a bottle he has found discarded on the floor and says to Mahmoud, Ask the Jew, he will tell you everything, and he gestures grandly with his left hand in my direction, and when I remain silent he motions for me to draw near and he places a fleshy hand on my neck, and I remind him that I have no memory of the rest of the story of the Blood Libel for I was in a dead faint from the moment Tomaso was murdered and I have no knowledge of what Jews do with the body of a Christian after extracting his blood for the unleavened Passover bread.

Burping and hiccoughing, Alexis tells me with heavy breath all that he knows from ancient stories of ritual murders such as these, whereby Jews of every generation are in need of the blood of Christians, and not merely for the baking of unleavened bread but also for mixing with an egg to be given to a bride and groom before their nuptials, and for diluting in holy wine for the circumcision ceremony, and for curing all manner of illnesses and diseases brought on by the devil, and Aslan recalls the leeches that Suleiman *alkhalaq* stored in jars, and they were plump and swollen from fresh blood and were never, ever satiated.

Aslan presses the venerable priest with questions about what, from generation to generation, is customary for the Jews to do with the body of a murdered Christian, for the matter is well known and quite familiar in the faraway lands of Europe, and Alexis is prepared to divulge this terrible secret for the price of a libation which I must present him, and when Mahmoud and Aslan have pooled all the drops of liquid remaining in all the bottles scattered about the chapel floor he reveals, in a whisper, that after the murder and the slaughter the Jews dissect the body piece by piece, breaking, crushing, pulverising the bones, and they lower them into the latrines so that no man may ever discover them. This is similar, he says to me, to what you did with Tomaso, is that not true? And his face is red from exertion.

I free myself from Alexis' grip and recount, to Mahmoud, the rest of what transpired, for it is true that I fainted upon seeing the copious flow of blood and Tomaso's upturned eyes; however, I lied in my affidavit when I wrote that I did not awaken in that room, for at once my uncles slapped my cheeks and revived me and ordered me to steel myself as a man in order to assist them wholly in the work needed to gut the body drained of blood.

It was then that my uncles and father removed various odd chopping implements from their bags and before my astonished eyes dissected the body piece by piece, limb by limb, and they explained their intention was to wrap these pieces in discarded coffee sacks they had collected and deposit them in the latrines so that Elnahar Aslawad would whisk them outside the city along with the excrement and filth, and they would become prey for the wild dogs and famished jackals, and they snarled at me to desist from my womanly weakness and join them in this hasty work, for they feared some unwanted guest might suddenly appear at that secret room and catch them in their shameful deed.

Unwillingly I took part in this horrible, bloody mission, and they placed a sharp cleaver in my hand and ordered me to hew the feet from the legs, and I did as I was commanded and I placed the flesh in the grey and crumpled sacks littered about, and next to me Suleiman *alkhalaq*, too, was hard at work dissecting Tomaso's body, trampling the thighs and adding the torn flesh to his sacks, and when we were told to do so the two of us collected the many sacks that had accrued, in one of which were Tomaso's tongue and ears and nose, while in Uncle Murad's sacks were the internal organs, and when the Khaham-Bashi noticed this he hastened to remove the liver and the heart and he wiped away the blood, deep red and congealed, and placed them in the copper vessel in which he had collected the precious liquid.

Then the barber and I were instructed to empty the sacks into the Black River and so we departed, one after the other, in stealth, with hurried steps, each in turn skipping to the end of the alley outside the home of Meir Farhi to the place leading to the river, just next to the home of the rabbi Moses Abulafia, and there we heaved the contents of the sacks into the river and returned to the room, our sacks empty, and we refilled them with pieces of the murdered monk.

And I tell him that from this confession, which at long last completes the affidavit I wrote to the governor, the resting place of the dissected body is finally known to be that pit leading to the Black River, near to the home of Meir Farhi, and that is where we must search for remains of the body and bring them to Sharif Pasha as final and decisive proof of the guilt of my family.

After all this has come to pass I turn my gaze to Mahmoud,

my most beloved, and he seems shaken, though a little encouraged, and he rumples my black hair affectionately and pats my buttocks and calls me his small and hairy monkey, and from there we return to Azm Palace, our mouths full of news for the team of investigators and judges, the head of which is his eminence Sharif Pasha, governor of the city of Damascus, that we have a lead in finding the body of Tomaso, may Allah have mercy upon him.

The rumour that the whereabouts of the bones of the deceased monk had been discovered took wing and circulated around the entire city, and at once an order was issued by Sharif Pasha that the bones be removed from their burial place by their gravediggers, Aslan and Suleiman, and put on display for all to see, after which they would be interred in a religious ceremony to be conducted by the priests of the city and attended by the entire Christian congregation of Damascus, as well as priests and monks and Christian faithful and other holy men from other cities, for Father Tomaso was well known and dearly beloved among his fellow sons of man.

Thus, the next day, Suleiman *alkhalaq* was brought forth from the place of his enchainment in one of the cells of the Saraya prison with me at his side, and we were transported as one man in a cart to the Jewish Quarter, where gangs of hooligans whooped and shouted at us along the way, and Suleiman, his face swollen from many lashings, unable to sit or stand, lay on the floor of the speeding cart and did not understand the meaning of this hasty journey, nor did Aslan explain this tumultuous turn of events, only hinting that he should trust him.

Aslan shows the young cart-driver where to turn, three soldiers guarding him, and all eyes are upon me, impatient and curious to see where I will direct the careening cart, and Sharif

Pasha's horsemen and a regiment of gendarmes careen along with us in order to find the pulverised bones of that dear and beloved man the Jews rose up against and murdered in a manner that makes the ears ring and the heart thunder merely upon hearing.

Dressed in a red tunic and a flapping apron, and riding at the head of a battalion of horsemen in the black carriage of the Damascus governor, Aslan arrives at Kharet Elyahud and slowly takes in the familiar buildings, Teleh Square, the chicken market and the Khush Elpasha Synagogue, and at this point the cart slows to a crawl because of the narrow and winding streets, and Aslan directs the cart-driver to the environs of his father's home, which stands stooped in its place, its wretched walls casting an ashen and disheartening shadow, and from there the cart turns right and left until it reaches the estate of Aslan's uncle Meir Farhi, the site of the loathsome ritual, and there, next door to the Eljuma'a Market, open on Fridays only, adjacent to the home of Rabbi Moses Abulafia, Aslan instructs the young cart-driver to come to a halt, and Aslan descends from the cart escorted by three soldiers, his red tunic billowing in the cool winter wind, and he proceeds to search out the *balua*, the cover to the hidden aperture whence the maidservants dispose of all that is filthy and polluted, such as the cloths used by women during the days of their menstruation and for wounds and papules, and whirlpools of vomit and congealed, blackened blood, and in the meantime battalions of soldiers arrive and they encircle the place, their bayonets poised and ready, and residents of the Christian Quarter are in evidence as well, and all pay heed to Aslan's actions.

At that moment I become overwhelmed with fear that my lies will be exposed, for I cannot locate any place from which refuse is dispatched to the Black River that winds about under the buildings of Damascus and into which flow all the lavatories and sewers, and I overturn the paving stones with no success, and at those moments when I regard the mob, tense and anxious, I catch sight of the Good Interrogator, his pure smile beaming, his yellow hair glistening in the winter sunshine, and he is my sweet beloved, and as I gaze at him I stumble at the edge of the opening and I pull aside several paving stones and discover the aperture, calling out in a loud voice, Here is the place, and the Good Interrogator joins the shouts of the crowd, and one of the gendarmes asks me whether it was to this place we dispatched the remains of the monk's body on that cursed night, and Aslan answers that indeed it is the very place of Tomaso's burial, here are interred his bones and flesh.

The barber is lowered from the cart but he is incapable of moving his legs for his knees are broken from beatings and floggings, and a stretcher of sorts is procured and upon it he is placed, and the battalions of soldiers make way for the arrival of one lofty man, head and shoulders above the rest, approaching in ardent strides, and lo, it is the noble consul, Count de Ratti-Menton, come to supervise the exhuming of the slain monk's bones, and he draws near Aslan, his face glowing though stern in accordance with the gravity of the situation, and he shakes Aslan's hand and pinches the cheek of the barber lying semi-conscious on the stretcher, and then we are commanded to descend to the Black River along that same dark path and resurrect from there what was inside the coffee sacks – the broken bones, the dissected limbs – while the mob, gripped with horror and curiosity, observes us, myriad eyes upon us.

Aslan descends into the pit with the aid of a small ladder brought from somewhere, and the broken-limbed and battered barber is lowered down after him, and there the former lovers find themselves together within the reeking abyss of a darkened valley, only their black eyes blinking one to the other in the gloom, and Aslan coughs and retches from the stench of a donkey's carcass among bits of flesh tossed there by the butchers of the Eljuma'a Market, and Suleiman of the shattered jaw and ruined teeth glares at Aslan and curses him, and curses his father and his mother, and he curses the day he and Aslan first met, and his voice is hoarse, exhausted, low, and he wishes upon Aslan all manner of strange deaths and diseases and tortures, and with his last bit of strength he attempts to rise from the stretcher to which he is strapped and strangle Aslan with his hands, but they are weak and to Aslan it feels like a lover's caress, and he is overcome with laughter and returns Suleiman to his stretcher and tightens the ropes that bind him so that he will not fall and break his body.

A few minutes later they ascend from there, Suleiman dragged, semi-conscious, on his stretcher, his lips still uttering weak curses, and behind him, his arms laden with goodies, emerges Aslan son of Rafael Farhi, who hastens to present the loot he plucked from the belly of the dead donkey to the consul Ratti-Menton and to the huge gathered crowd, and Ratti-Menton burrows into the mounds of filth in Aslan's hands until he produces a patch of black cloth and calls out, See before you, a torn piece of cloth from slain Father Tomaso's cloak! And the crowd responds with a lamenting cry, Ahhhhhh! And Ratti-Menton continues his search until he comes across tiny bones from the donkey that Aslan had gathered quickly, nearly collapsing and retching from the stench, and the French consul extends his arm into the air and cries out to them, Here are the bones of the holy monk, who has been murdered!

At once, a huge commotion breaks out, accompanied by the din of lamenting cries from female mourners and the shouts of men calling for revenge, and in the hands of the Christians are sticks and clubs, and they go forth and encircle the Farhi estate as well as that of the Stambouli family, and the homes of the poor, and they demolish beams and they twist the arms of Jewish passers-by and they smash the heads of the Torah scholars who happen by on the narrow lanes of the Jewish Quarter, and in the midst of the shouts and the brouhaha Aslan catches sight of that feathery yellow hair and that stately posture, but Mahmoud's gaze is distant and altered and he averts his eyes from Aslan and does not look upon him, and a great terror befalls Aslan and the paving stones upon which he stands begin to rattle one against the other and he is about to fall down between them, to the place where the carcasses of beasts of burden and impure animals lie, and he wishes to grasp for one short moment more that wisp of a smile, that ray of light, that tiny spark from the face of his beloved, but a wave of Christian faithful pass between them and he can no longer see Mahmoud, who has vanished in the wake of their uproar like a light and summery feather-cloud, and Aslan is anxious and terribly burdened with worry.

My happy friend, two days were necessary for Sharif Pasha's physicians to determine whether the bones placed before them were those of man or beast, and during these two days Mahmoud disappeared and reappeared again and again from Aslan's side; at times he would meet Aslan in his chambers and he was all pleasantry and niceties and at times he would abstain from sharing his dear, beloved presence, and Aslan was overcome with silent tears and plunged into an abyss of worry, and Mahmoud teased him with his dazzling smile, assuring him he would visit him during the night but then failing to appear, and sometimes he surprised Aslan as he lay dormant on the bed and awakened him with clever prattle, and Aslan did his best to respond with smiles and confections, never to utter a bad word or grumble, never to display the slightest sadness, for even the tiniest convulsion of anger that flashed for a fraction of a second at the corner of Aslan's lips would enrage Mahmoud and then he would depart from Aslan and remain estranged from him for many long hours and would not so much as glance at him.

Tomaso's funeral was set for the afternoon and Mahmoud informed Aslan that he would meet him there, then he departed, leaving Aslan to arrive alone at the Capuchin monastery, where he found a huge crowd assembled. At the head stood Sharif Pasha and the French consul and many priests who had arrived from near and far and Christian men, women and children, all gathered round a magnificent oak casket lined with black velvet in the middle of which lay, among huge funereal bouquets, splendid and beautiful, those tiny bones found by Aslan and now lined up one next to the other, clean and scented with perfume after having been washed diligently by the women of the Christian burial society and sprinkled with holy water by Father Alexis.

Aslan walks among the hordes of mourning Christians as they cry profusely, scouting for Mahmoud and cursing him in his heart for keeping his distance, and against his will he joins in the festive burial procession proceeding slowly in mourning black from the church of the Capuchin monastery to the altar of Saint Elijah in the Terra Sancta Church, and there are those in the crowd who recognise Aslan and cast sidelong glances at him, though it is unclear whether they denounce him for participating in the murder or whether they bless him for his full and atoning confession, and Aslan is infected by their grief and he joins in their tears, and he recalls his sin, how he dissected the monk and left his flesh for the desert foxes and jackals, and he pushes his way towards the faithful monks as they cross themselves again and again and carry, with their white hands, the small wooden casket, and all the while his eyes roam in search of his yellow-haired friend.

The enormous crowd of the faithful gathers at the entrance to Terra Sancta and several priests who have come from afar stand over the open casket and they praise the deceased monk before them for his good deeds and his deep faith, and they praise the Creator, upon whose deeds one may not cast doubt or wonder, and who chose for Tomaso so cruel a demise, and suddenly Aslan catches sight of Mahmoud and he wishes to wave gaily in his direction in spite of the mournful nature of the occasion, but Mahmoud's face is grave, only his eyes express a pure, smiling blue, and next to him, Aslan is horrified to discover, stands the curly-haired youth from the Nur Aladdin *hammam*, and the two of them stand together while Father Modesto Donano, one of the priests who has come specially from the Vatican, eulogises Tomaso in a broken voice and kisses the casket lined in black, and he calls out to the bones, The voice of Tomaso's blood cries to me from the earth.

My happy friend, at that moment a great calamity befell me and Aslan wished to make haste to reach the pair and come between them as Father Modesto asked the Creator of the Universe to avenge Tomaso's death, and the priest took his leave of the monk and the remains of his bones with a grand prayer to the almighty God in heaven and once again he kissed the casket with closed eyes and deep conviction, but as for Aslan, he hears nothing of the deeply emotional and venerable eulogies, nor does he perceive the profound and heavy mourning of the huge crowd, nor even the tremors of his fellow Jews who are preparing all manner of hiding places for themselves in fear of the gentiles, for his entire being is given over to the sob that is shaking his soul as his true, first, life-giving love drifts away and leaves him, before his very eyes.

And when the last of the eulogies has been delivered, voices rise in a requiem while ten pallbearers dressed in black place the casket of bones in a sumptuous grave, its headstone inscribed in Arabic and Italian, and a long procession of mourners, a black wave of the faithful, trudges by the fresh grave, among them many Capuchin monks who cling to one another in consolation and friendship, and Aslan is among them, his sobbing deeper now, and he passes by the donkey bones buried under the headstone and he bursts into copious tears for lives doomed to death, for buildings doomed to destruction, for health doomed to disease, for blossoms doomed to wither, and for the great, precious, glittering love stolen from before his eyes, and he wishes to rescue it but does not know how, and through his tears the writing inscribed in Arabic on the monk's headstone cries out to him, words never effaced and, to the best of my knowledge, my happy friend, words still engraved on that headstone in that church graveyard in faraway Damascus to this very day:

> Here, in this place, are buried the scant remains of Father Tomaso of the Order of Capuchin Franciscan Friars.
>
> May it be written in the Chronicles that he was slaughtered by Jews, who left nothing of him behind.
>
> Our Father who art in Heaven, to You our souls will depart from us; You, who are far from our eyes.

3

L ast evening I recounted to you, my happy friend, that the donkey bones were interred in a splendid burial and I stood over the headstone reading the inscription dedicated to their memory and I was mournful over the estrangement to which my beloved was subjecting me, my soul as ragged and withered as that of a ninety-year-old woman.

Aslan departs from there, his head drooping and his cheeks hollow, and he meanders without purpose through the alleyways of Damascus as hoarse, goading cries rise from the Christian Quarter and the gentile women curse and revile the Jews, inciting their husbands to new, more violent, acts of vengeance upon the traitorous, murderous Jewish people, and Aslan quickens his pace in flight, but where will he go if not to his parents' stifling, noxious home, and when he returns to Kharet Elyahud the place of his childhood and lifelong residence appears to him as a silent city of spirits, still and empty but for the ghosts, the inhabitants locked into their homes in cellars and other hiding places, the market stalls collapsed one on to the other, and even the beet vendor always stationed outside the Khush Elpasha Synagogue is not at his usual corner, his sweet, hot beets missing as well.

Aslan hesitates, unsure whether to pass through the walls of his father's home to reach that servants' room with its lingering scent of urine, for he does not wish to encounter Markhaba or his mother or his siblings and endure their curses, and while standing there, uncertain as to what to do and not yet burdened by the one-eyed shrew who is sure to come and cast over him her twisted, tyrannical power, he hears a nightingale calling to him, the sound echoing rhythmically from afar, and Aslan turns his gaze and is filled with happy surprise to see Mahmoud bounding towards him, and Mahmoud pats Aslan's shoulder and smiles radiantly at him and showers him with many kisses in the manner of Damascene men, and he relates breathlessly that he has been searching for Aslan throughout the city in order to beg his pardon and forgiveness, and he hastens to apologise to his beloved, the Jew, for the estrangement to which he has subjected him and explains that he was so distraught at Tomaso's interment that his good judgment was confounded and the entire world slipped from his mind and he was only barely aware, through a veil of mourning tears, that his beloved Aslan was waving to him, and this was the reason he did not return his smile or gaze; and upon seeing the sombre expression in Aslan's eyes, Mahmoud embraces him boldly and swears that the youth in his company at the funeral was none other than an old chum, their friendship pure, and he reassures Aslan that there is no passion between the two, no acts of lust or fornication, only companionship and pure manly affection, for it is preferable for men to love one another and protect one another from the poisoned arrows of women, instead of gorging themselves on competitiveness and hatred, and Aslan affirms his words and slackens the tension in his arms and presses himself into Mahmoud's chest.

At that moment, my happy friend, I was overwhelmed by that sweet and soothing melody of clemency and absolution, for my beloved, to whom I would depart from myself, was not, at long last, far from my eyes, and this consoling, healing song flowed warmly, steaming through my veins and swallowing any grudges and resentments in its path so that my former pure love returned to me and I forgave Mahmoud wholly for all his caprices, and I made him swear not to turn away from me again, nor deprive me of his presence for long hours.

And Mahmoud levelled his sky-blue eyes at me and swore to me that our love was holy and eternal and that he would never, ever abandon me or cause me any harm, for the tip of the curly black hair growing from my little finger was more precious to him than all the treasure of Araby, and Mahmoud and Aslan linked fingers and rubbed noses; and yet a doubt, sharp in its obscurity, pecked at Aslan's ribs, and it was the beak of the one-eyed shrew come to warn him in her shrill and wicked voice not to fall into the snare of this comely man, for his lies and fabrications were well apparent to her, and she cautioned Aslan that in the end he would be stuffed full with these lies, gorged too on large doses of heart-grief and worry, and he would suffer protracted and numerous torments in hell for having informed against his father and progenitor and his wife's father and the entire community of Jews, and for having beaten his friend Suleiman the barber with a whip, and for the falsehoods that danced so gaily across his tongue; all these he had committed for the sake of his handsome lover. But Aslan silenced the evil witch, suppressing her with a light laugh that squeezed her back to her place between the third and fourth ribs, for what were worries and suspicions to him now that the man loved him utterly and he was protected by his embraces like a harbour, safe from the torrents and tumult of stormy seas?

And thus, my happy friend, we remained, mired in our happiness for many days, and Aslan did not heed the news that reached him of the start of the murder trial, nor did he torment his soul with stories of his father and uncles and father-in-law, charged with having slaughtered Tomaso and interrogated daily by the court clerks in the *qa'ah* of Azm Palace, as they attempted to dispel all the groundless accusations with the voice of reason and refined wisdom, but they were subjected, again and again, to Sharif Pasha's derision as he repeatedly presented them with the evidence of the bones that had been found from a body slain and dissected, and Sharif Pasha was as swollen with arrogance and self-importance as is the cock crowing like a king from atop his dunghill, as in the Damascene proverb: *kul dik alla mizbalto sayakh.*

And Aslan was content with lying in Mahmoud's arms for long nights, he had no *raison d'être* beyond the naughty games he played with his beloved and with the wondrous organ dangling between Mahmoud's legs, and he pleasured it till Mahmoud groaned with pain, and he worshipped it, became its slave, studied it from tip to base, tickled it with his fingers and tasted it with his tongue and learned the secret of its thickening and lengthening, and afterwards of its shrinking, and he spoke to it words of pleasure and perversity and extracted from it all its juices and watched its downpours, its storms, but he observed, too, its long, peaceful flow and rubbed it indulgently with all manner of unguents, and also when it closed into itself, the head and glans hidden away in slumber, then, too, Aslan carried on loving it in its puniness, its helplessness, and there were yet countless other acts he planned to carry out upon it.

And if Aslan ever recalled the trial for the murder of Tomaso that was taking place in the *qa'ah* of Azm Palace, and if many poisonous spiders skittered back and forth across his skin, and if fingers grasped his lapels to make him stop his dance, then he banished all thought of them from his mind, for he had no need for that trial, nor interest in it, not for that Tomaso or those spiders or those fingers: he wished that Sharif Pasha would pass whatever judgment he would and then leave Aslan to indulge in his games.

When Mahmoud disappeared without explanation to his increasing preoccupations, leaving Aslan alone with his enormous longing, Aslan would be overcome with restlessness and he would open and shut many drawers in Mahmoud's chambers and slam doors on their hinges until one day he shifted one of the many pillows, orange and afloat in Mahmoud's scent, and discovered a small mirror – the handiwork of Damascene Jews – its frame curved and its edges patterned with triangles and diamonds so as to tease the eye with its deceptive lines, its handle studded with chips of shiny, sparkling seashells.

Aslan pities, slightly, the weedy creature staring back at him, trapped in its disappointing love, and the two of them are small and feeble figures grasping and clinging to one another, and it seems to Aslan that he can see large yellow flowers adorning them to the right and left, and he wishes to console his cohort, for she shows many signs of exhaustion – the wrinkled sacs that have formed under her eyes, the lifeless yellow tinge to her skin – and his cohort is consoled and even consoles him in return, sending her hand to caress his breast, and she points a finger at him and his own finger points back and they touch through the veil of the mirror and Aslan smiles at his cohort and encourages her during these difficult days, and she is encouraged and her lips form a small smile, revealing her tiny teeth.

And Mahmoud returns late each evening to his chambers and enters our common bed and tells me of the murder trial, that it is progressing nicely and the verdict is well nigh, and now they have reached the eve of a decisive session during which it is important that Aslan speak his piece, and so Sharif Pasha demands my presence.

But Aslan has no desire to attend, he is content with lying in Mahmoud's arms, and Mahmoud strokes my head to placate and pacify me with his pleasant words, and he sings his wishes to me in lullabies ringing with Umm-Jihan's voice, her light humming, her swinging breasts and slightly swaying hips, and Aslan pleads with Mahmoud not to grant Sharif Pasha's request.

But when the trial resumes the next day Aslan appears in the *qa'ah* as commanded by Sharif Pasha and follows the cues of the court attendant Abu Shihab Tufankaji and takes a seat among the witnesses for the prosecution to await the arrival of the defendants, and he catches sight of them from afar, his broad-bodied father plods in heavily, dragging a ball and chain behind him, and he is weary and weakened, and the Khaham-Bashi marches alongside him, silent and downcast, hobbling on thick, olive-wood crutches, at times leaning upon Father like a wife in the throes of calamity, and they are holding hands, their breathing laboured as they sit upon the pillowless yellow bench, and they are as parents on trial for all the sins they have committed against their children, from abuse to maltreatment, and next to them the accused uncles, shuffled along like a herd of beasts to the slaughter, and all of them maintain their refusal to confess to the act of murder and dismemberment.

Aslan casts a brief glance at his father's face, and it is as if he is looking into the deceptive glass of a Damascene mirror: he has never before noticed the colour of his father's eyes, and they are green and here and there stippled lightly with yellow, his pupils large, and there is none of that familiar evil present, no rebuke or reproach, only fatigue and sadness and a thin layer of a father's disappointment with his offspring.

A deep sense of shame settles on Aslan for all his evil deeds, and for his ingratitude, and for his many lies, and the knowledge that he has erred gravely descends upon him in a flash, that malevolent, contagious maladies have taken hold of him and poisoned his blood, and his sins are compounded because he has led countless others astray and contaminated countless others with his poisoned soul, and now he cannot but observe, powerless, the scene unfolding before him; and now you, my happy friend, are charged with continuing to unravel the plot to its end.

Aslan's father averts his eyes from him and Aslan is left alone and lost once more, and he knows not to whom to turn with a request for advice that would put him on the right path, for among all his relatives and acquaintances there is not a one whose trust and affection he has won, only his beloved; but this Mahmoud appears for a short while then vanishes to attend to his various preoccupations, and he is as reliable as a house built on sand.

At this time Sharif Pasha calls an important witness to the murder trial, after which the doors open and a Muslim gentleman wearing an elaborate white turban that extends to cover his face enters the *qa'ah* and Sharif Pasha introduces him as Muhammad Effendi, and it is his plan that the Muslim will engage in a religious disputation against Rabbi Antebi and provide crucial evidence from Jewish writings that the slaughter of Christians is a cornerstone of the Mosaic faith and of the Jewish people, thereby engendering the full confession that will lead to the death penalty that my father and uncles deserve.

When Yaacov Antebi learns of the religious disputation awaiting him he is flooded with self-confidence, the priestly adornments on the scarf tied round his waist grow more colourful, and he extricates himself from Father's embrace and stands firm on his own legs to confront this boorish, uncultivated Muslim, Muhammad Effendi *elmuslemani*, to strike down with a victorious blow the lies and fabrications and exaggerations and slander and calumny and nonsense and ill will that he has been forced to listen to throughout this trial from the mouths of

Christians and Muslims, along with their groundless accusations, and the blood is coursing once again through his veins and his voice has regained its power, and by raising his finger he indicates that he wishes to speak first, and he sets out to prove their enormous mistake to all present in the *qa'ah*, for it is entirely inconceivable that Jews are commanded to slaughter Christians and take their blood, and to make certain his message is perfectly clear he wishes to remind them of several sayings from the Jewish canon, and indeed, the Holy One Blessed be He, Father of Abraham, Isaac and Jacob, had bestowed the Ten Commandments on the Israelites and among the commandments it was stated quite explicitly, Thou shalt not murder, and in His Holy Bible, in the Book of Genesis, he warned that Whoso sheds man's blood by man shall his own blood be shed, For in the image of God made He man; thus, is it utterly impossible and unfeasible that Jews have been commanded to take the lives of others in the name of religion.

After a brief pause for gulping water down his parched throat, the Khaham-Bashi adds words of reproach and fury, namely that in addition to the prohibition against murder in the Bible of Moses and Israel, Jews are also explicitly forbidden from eating the blood of beasts, as it is written, You shall eat the blood of no manner of flesh, and if the blood of the beast is forbidden then all the more so that of humans; and further he quotes, You shall not make yourselves abominable, and again, *You shall not make yourselves abominable*, and this verse he repeats several times before returning to Father's arms like a submissive wife, casting a bold and taunting look at Sharif Pasha over his success in providing resounding proof to the boorish Muslim, as if he has won the disputation even before the Muslim has had a chance to open his mouth, and my uncles regard the Khaham-Bashi with encouraging expressions on their faces.

Muhammad Effendi clears his throat and begins to talk in a low, deep voice, his eyes covered by the turban, and he says, in a near whisper, that indeed it is known that the Jews have been commanded by Allah to refrain from committing murder, but that it is equally well known that the Jews are woefully neglectful in upholding the Ten Commandments, and as proof he mentions the Book of Judges, in which the Jews constantly do evil in the eyes of the Lord, and the Jewish canon is rife with stories of the rebelliousness and treachery and hard-heartedness of the Jews, and their wretched manner of turning their backs on Allah the good and beneficent.

Before the Khaham-Bashi even has a chance to counter this claim, the esteemed Muslim adds in a whisper that the books of the Jews contain explicit commandments about the consuming of blood, many of them part of Scriptures themselves, and he picks up the book he has brought with him and quotes – his finger pointed accusatorily – from the prophet Ezekiel: Assemble yourselves on every side to my festive meal that I prepare for you . . . that you may eat meat and drink blood. You shall eat the flesh of the mighty, and drink the blood of the princes of the earth; and from elsewhere he quotes, None devoted of men, which shall be doomed to death, shall be redeemed, but shall surely be put to death; and, he continues, there is a general rule among the Jews, as it is written, For it is the blood that makes an atonement for the soul; and even if this were not Allah's intention, the Jews in their blind hatred found in this passage justification for their many crimes.

In fact, he expounds, it is not only the Holy Bible that the Jews have become adept at distorting but also the Talmud, for in the unabridged version – one which no crafty Jew has tampered with to remove offending passages – the Jews are unambiguously commanded in this matter, for is it not Rabbi Simon bar Yochai himself who says, Even the best of gentiles should be put to death, for the gentiles are not considered human? And Rabbi Moses ben Maimon wrote, It is forbidden to rescue them if they are about to die, for example when a gentile falls into the sea do not lift him out; and it is also said, Pour out thy wrath upon the nations and peoples who know thee not, and upon the kingdoms that do not call upon thy name; and it is a holy obligation upon the Jews to make use of every ploy and artifice available for the murder of Christians, and if a Jew sees a gentile at the precipice of an abyss he is obligated to push him over the edge, and these matters are clear and obvious to all; and upon concluding, Muhammad Effendi takes his seat, straightens his turban and bows his head.

All await the response of the Khaham-Bashi Rabbi Yaacov Antebi, who himself is astonished at the proficiency of the Muslim with regards to Jewish texts, and a deep suspicion arises in him that this man is an apostate Jew, one of the many converted by Muslims, as has been the case in Damascus since time immemorial; there were those caught in the nets of the Muslims, and those caught in the nets of the Christians, and those caught in the nets of the Karaites, and indeed countless snares and stumbling blocks lie in ambush for the Jews in every generation and in every period, for the nations of the world are envious of this beloved and desirable people, and when the Khaham-Bashi rises to his feet he commands his partner in the debate, Cast aside your turban and reveal your face, so that we may know who you are!

And the great Muslim cleric hides his face no longer, pulling the turban from his head in one swoop. Here am I! he declares, and how great is our dismay; the Khaham-Bashi would collapse and slip to the ground were it not for Father, who has collected him into his warm and able arms, and a cry of astonishment escapes the lips of the uncles, for that zealous Muslim cleric who wears his turban in the manner of the Damascene Muslim elders and calls himself Muhammad Effendi is none other than Moses Abulafia, a great rabbi of Damascus, son of the grand rabbi of Tiberius, Haim Nissim Abulafia, and Moses had been among the many prisoners incarcerated as a result of the Tomaso affair, and he had accepted the Islamic faith and converted by reciting the *Shehadeh*, and now he has confronted the Jews in their own language, with an eye to bringing about their demise and extermination.

My happy friend, many were the times my family had pondered whether to walk about in the streets of Kharet Elyahud lest they be accosted by Moses Abulafia, for they knew his hot temper and his predilection for outbursts and his extreme adherence to the commandments and his impassioned hatred for those who imbibed and were raucous and those who invited dancers to please them, and more than once did he rage against my father and curse him unto the seventh generation for partaking of the food of unclean animals and for obsequious, sycophantic behaviour towards the Muslims and Christians, and he had raged, too, against the Khaham-Bashi, whose laxity with leaders of the Jewish community and failure to castigate them vehemently in the Beth Din irked him, and now he was standing before them, restrained, his teeth clenched, his eyes flashing with wrath.

The Khaham-Bashi laughed and cried in turn, and called out to Rabbi Abulafia by his nickname, Mouchon, Mouchon, for together they had toiled to ensure a supply of kosher meat for the Jews of Damascus and to train ritual circumcisers and to purify in boiling water utensils needed for the Passover holiday and to adhere to all six hundred and thirteen commandments, from the simplest to the gravest, and to rent buildings for study halls and yeshivas for the leading scholars in the Jewish Quarter, and they had prayed with deep intent for the Holy One Blessed be He to bring about the long-awaited days of the Messiah; but alas, the rabbi was refusing to answer to his former name, his Jewish name, for henceforth he was to be called Muhammad Effendi *elmuslemani*, and he had changed the course of his life and become an adversary to Israel and now he was attacking the Khaham-Bashi with increasing effrontery, determination and zeal, as if trying to lift from his heart his heavy guilt, for after converting to the Muslim faith and declaring that the prophet Muhammad is *rasoul Allah*, God's envoy, and taking upon himself the custom of bowing in the direction of Mecca and joining the prayer service five times each day, it had become easier for him to reveal the secrets of his former and erroneous faith, and he baited Antebi, saying they possessed a joint secret in their role as leaders of the Jewish community, a secret passed only from mouth to ear, from the great rabbi of each generation to his successor, and this secret was that it was necessary to place the blood of a slain gentile inside the unleavened bread baked after midnight on the eve of Passover, and there were some who mixed the blood of Christians into love potions and others who threw it upon the copper trays used in burnt offerings.

The Khaham-Bashi broke free of his astonishment and came to his senses, and he turned to Sharif Pasha and said, Your Eminence, the governor of Damascus, I am a man getting on in years, and it will not be much longer until the day of my reckoning before the celestial court, before the God of Israel, who declared on Mount Sinai, Thou shalt not murder, nor shalt thou take the name of the Lord thy God in vain; and upon uttering these words he removed the Holy Bible from the hands of the newly converted Saracen and swore upon it before all present: If my tongue speaks not the truth in these matters may

I be visited by all the curses mentioned in the books of Leviticus and Deuteronomy, including the worst of them – excommunication and divine punishment by premature death – and may I fail to witness the restoration of Israel and its blessings, nor be on hand for the coming of the Messiah and the resurrection of the dead, and my name will be obliterated and effaced from the earth; and he fell, weak and drained, upon the yellow bench, and Aslan knew he wished to die.

But Muhammad Effendi was not unduly affected by Yaacov Antebi's grave oaths, and he remarked – his voice dry and scornful – that nothing stood behind Jews' oaths and vows, for was it not in the *Kol Nidrei* prayer, recited on the Day of Atonement, that they annulled all vows and oaths? And the language of their prayer, declared publicly, without fear, was: All vows, prohibitions, oaths and consecrations from the last Day of Atonement and until this Day of Atonement are hereby null and void.

And all of these matters were recorded by the court secretary and this full confession of Jewish crimes was brought by the court clerk for signing by the man who made it, the Islamised Jewish rabbi Moses Abulafia, and he appended his signature in Arabic under the name Muhammad Effendi, without reading its contents, and from there his confession was brought by ship to the people of Europe.

After Sharif Pasha had summarised the confession of this crucial witness he thanked him profusely and bestowed two kisses upon each of his cheeks, and Muhammad Effendi apologised for having little time, for he was in a rush to attend the prayer service at the Umayyad Mosque in order to pray to Allah and thank him for his great benelovence in showing him the straight and true and good and just path, would that all Jews were to follow his example, for they were greatly misguided, not

244

merely with their customs of murder and slaughter, not just for drinking blood and mixing it into baked goods and libations, but for their customs of vengeance and envy in which they are so well versed, their wish to annihilate the Muslims and make them perish, and it was not enough merely to despise them.

And when Muhammad Effendi turned his back on the *qa'ah* and walked in his slow, arrogant, self-assured manner from the room, a profound sadness befell Aslan for this spiteful rabbi who had turned his back on his people, and the buds of Aslan's shame returned to him and covered his face and caused his cheeks to redden deeply, and Rabbi Antebi sat in the courtroom mumbling to himself over and over again, You shall not make yourselves abominable, You shall not make yourselves abominable, You shall not make yourselves abominable, and his father sat mute alongside Rabbi Antebi, his head swivelling, slow and heavy, his gaze unfocused, and for a brief moment our glances crossed paths, mine and my father's, my progenitor's, that man from whose loins I emerged and who had raised me and educated me and in whose image I was created, this father for whom I had no love and who had no love for me, and the two of us had no love for one another, and in his father's weakness Aslan recognised the evil of his own deeds, in this man of great wealth before him, with his protruding lips and stooped shoulders and ill, pale flesh, and in a flicker of memory Aslan longed for his father's swarthy, expressive feet which he would cross, one over the other, on the small stool in the courtyard, and this memory filled Aslan's nostrils.

Later, hunched in Mahmoud's chambers, Aslan came to understand that his mark upon this story appeared and was reflected not only in his father but in Muhammad Effendi and Yaacov Antebi and in his two remaining uncles and all the other male figures, and they splintered in the Damascene mirror he was holding in his hand now, a small mirror, the handiwork of Jews, its frame curved, its edges patterned with many shapes to tease the eye with its deceptive lines and its handle studded with chips of seashells and mothers-of-pearl mourning for their daughters swept away in the strong currents and lost for ever on the shore, chips of those shells inlaid in the mirror itself, their tears alternately sparkling and shining.

4

My happy friend, the trial of the Jews accused of murder dragged on and on, branching out and widening to include witnesses, and witnesses' witnesses, and witnesses for the defence, and Sharif Pasha interrogated the accused backwards and forwards, and not only them but their servants and their guests and even their washerwomen, and he wished to know every person who came into their homes, and what each of them did on that day of the great storm, and they answered him again and again that they had not gathered to slay Tomaso, they had not stood over him to slit his throat in that unfinished room, but there were those witnesses who, under the power of the iron torture machines in the Saraya prison dungeon, confessed to the crime, then later rescinded their confessions and denied their involvement, and Sharif Pasha's patience was coming to an end, and indeed, there could be no fitting conclusion to the trial other than a full confession by the accused so that they might cleanse their sins before Allah and make penance for their cruel error and their perverse ways.

On the Friday eve following the confession of Moses Abulafia for the sins of the Jews, Sharif Pasha endeavoured to bring the trial to a final conclusion and hand down a verdict in the matter, so that when the four defendants were seated on the cushionless yellow bench allotted them, and after the court attendant, Abu Shihab Tufankaji, had declared the session open, Sharif Pasha appeared in his black smoking jacket with its gold pleats, took his place on the governor's throne and extricated his feet from his gold cloth slippers for their pleasure, then began reading summaries of the testimonies and the grave accusations of Father Tomaso's slaughter, and he noted that two witnesses were here *in situ* and would affirm all that was written there, and these were Aslan son of Rafael Farhi and the barber Suleiman Negrin, and he pointed in the direction of the barber lying supine on his stretcher, the blood gurgling in his throat, and then at Aslan, in his beautiful attire, and Sharif Pasha added that even true and tangible proof had been found – the monk's bones and a piece of cloth from his robe – and he reminded them of the lucid religious argument of Rabbi Moses Abulafia, and now he urged them to confess to their wrongdoing in order to purify themselves before Allah so that He could pardon their sinning souls in their deaths.

Uncles Murad and Meir cleared their throats to signify their wish to respond to Sharif Pasha's incisive questioning, but lo, even before they had been given the floor to offer a rejoinder, Sharif Pasha called for a brief intermission in the trial and at once his attendants hastened to provide him with a cup of sweetened tea and several biscuits glazed with honey, and he perused an urgent letter sent to him by his father-in-law and adopted father Muhammad Ali, then requested a quill and inkwell in order to craft an immediate reply that would be posted from Beirut in an Alexandria-bound vessel, and he jested with several of his attendants as they covered him with a colourful patched quilt against the cool Damascus air wafting into the *qa'ah*; and after all these things had come to pass he removed a pressing missive from inside an envelope and his face grew serious as he read its contents, and at once he dispatched his servants with an urgent command to summon new witnesses with the greatest speed.

The uncles tried a second time to request an audience before Sharif Pasha, but he did not even bother to silence them with a wave of his hand, merely continuing with the everyday matters occupying his realm, his servants all the while plying him with all manner of *hors d'oeuvres* and delicacies, and Sharif Pasha cracks open choice pistachio nuts from Aleppo and snacks on apricot pastries and guzzles lemonade scented with rosewater, and he banters with his assistants and kisses the lads and Aslan notices that his uncles are standing apart from his father, attempting without success to catch the esteemed governor's eye, their jaws sagging each time they swallow the juices in their salivating mouths.

And before any of the defendants has the opportunity to respond to Sharif Pasha in the matter of their guilt, a short trumpet blast resounds in the courtroom and five members of the Harari family enter the *qa'ah* dressed in white, with blue shawls draped over their shoulders against the winter chill, their skin well oiled and emanating pleasant fragrances, and Aslan does not know the meaning of their presence until Sharif Pasha questions them for all to hear as to whether the matters about which they wrote in their urgent letter are true, on this, the eve of the handing down of the verdict, and they answer in a cacophony of voices, Every word is true, it is inscribed in stone, to which Sharif Pasha replies, In that case, repeat these words aloud, and David Harari, the eldest among them, takes the floor, and in a voice trembling with the intensity of what he is about to reveal to the courtroom dotted with plain yellow benches, he informs them that in writing the letter he has sent to Sharif Pasha he has resolved to remove a boulder that has weighed heavily on his heart for many, many years and that now he wishes to confess his sins.

And when those present ask him to what sins he refers, David Harari answers that it is the sin he has committed by failing to inform the authorities for thirty years about the activities of the Khaham-Bashi Rabbi Yaacov Antebi and his partners-in-crime the Farhi brothers, for the act of taking the blood of a Christian – which they carry out in their wickedness just before the Passover holiday each year – is a known and open secret among the Jews, and they abduct Christian passers-by, among them babes in arms and innocent children and choice young men in their prime, and they slaughter them precisely in the manner described by the murderers' offspring Aslan son of Rafael Farhi, for all that he wrote in his affidavit is true, and now it behoves the court, as is only right and fitting, to impose the death penalty on these man-killers and free the residents of Damascus from this scum that has settled upon them and sullied them with their sins.

David Harari has not yet shot all the poisoned-lie arrows in his bow when his brothers rise to their feet, each one telling a different tale of the misdeeds committed by the Farhi family, embellishing many details according to the fertility of their imaginations, such as how the Farhis store Christian blood in glass jars in the pantry of their home, nourishing the vipers living in the walls of the house with it; and how the Khaham-Bashi incites them to perpetrate ever more wicked crimes in order to increase the supply of Christian children, to bring him ever younger children whose blood is redder and more pleasant; how they stow blindfolded victims between the wicker baskets stacked atop the camels' backs on caravans returning from Baghdad and Mecca, their prisoners barely conscious from the severe desert heat, reviving them on occasion with just enough water to keep them from expiring, until such time as they relieve them of their souls and their blood in one of the cellars of their homes.

My happy friend, I was overcome with astonishment and wonder to see that this Aslanish affliction had spread and infected all the other Jews, for they betrayed one another and did not abhor the telling of blatant, brazen lies and falsehoods, even the magnates among them, and I was dizzy from hearing confession after confession, and I scrutinised my arms and my tongue to discern how it was that they had released into the air their foul, evil temperament, and Aslan felt overwhelming contempt as he looked upon the Hararis wagging their tongues in slander and fabrications, and with his fingernails he scratched his anus and he rubbed his skin raw and lashed it, and lo, his back and his belly and his underarms and his hands and his legs tingled and reddened at the touch of his pallid, groping fingers, and Aslan resumed his scratching so as to drive the pain from his flesh, but the tingling and redness covered his skin once again and his hands would not obey him and they cast about, seeking out hidden organs and picking at the dead skin, removing it from this living body of his, which was saturated with the venom of snakes and scorpions.

And the Khaham-Bashi is no longer capable of containing himself and he screeches at the Hararis in his high-pitched voice that his eyes have never before witnessed an act of such imprecation, and he curses them for their wickedness and their excessive perfidy, and he mutters verses in Hebrew and Aramaic to drive out this apostasy, and although the uncles urge him under their breath to desist from this raging torrent before they are all put to death, he does not cease his shouting; rather, he rolls his eyes heavenwards and pleads with He who sits on high to destroy this evil kingdom and rout it from the world and cause His salvation to sprout and bring His Messiah near; and it is only for the sake of the last bit of honour accorded him that the guards of Sharif Pasha do not bludgeon his head with their clubs.

The face of the Damascus governor turns grave and terribly cross, and he orders his attendants to remove the raisins and dried dates placed in front of him; still, he does not turn to Father or the Khaham-Bashi or the uncles, whose backs are turned to him, but his cheeks rouge like angry roses, and he briefly thanks the Harari family and praises them for their courage, and on the spot he signs a writ of clemency to pardon them for their sin of failing to inform upon my family, and a celebratory feeling descends upon all those present in the qa'ah, for these Jewish magnates themselves had come forth to admit and confirm the deed and now it is clear that this is no libellous or false accusation, but rather the absolute truth, and the French consul Ratti-Menton shakes the hands of all the members of the Harari family, and the men's fingers intertwine in an act of both strength and caress, and the scent of their sweat is pleasant and sweet.

After these things come to pass Sharif Pasha announces that the day's session has come to an end and they will reconvene on the morrow, and the gendarmes rise from their seats to escort the defendants back to their cells and their tortures, and Father stands first to leave along with the Khaham-Bashi, while the two surviving brothers, Meir and Murad, remain seated, and all present see that their throats are clogged with tears, their brows are furrowed, and they are soaked in their own urine.

Sharif Pasha commands Meir and Murad to rise and leave the qa'ah instantly, for they have polluted the room by passing their water, but Meir and Murad remain seated and do not budge, their heads hidden between their arms and their shoulders convulsing from their copious flow of tears, and Sharif Pasha asks them the meaning of these tears, is it because they, too, wish to confess to the deed, and they answer as one, Yes, and he asks whether Aslan indeed spoke the truth of their crime and their sins, and they answer, Yes, he spoke the truth, and they add through their blubbering that they would not have taken part in this murderous deed or been dragged into it were it not for the bullying and wheedling of their older brother, Rafael *almuallem*, standing beside them, for from an early age he had pressed them again and again to follow his lead, and in spite of their resolve to oppose him and their countless pleas, he forced them to enter this demonic, blood-soaked covenant with him; it was thirty years and more since he had introduced them to that rabbi who calls himself the Khaham-Bashi, and it was he who induced them and instructed them on this Jewish path of blood, he who made them swear never to relate to another soul this ritual that passes from generation to generation in the greatest secrecy, and they added through a stream of tears that flowed from the bottom of their hearts that they had tried over and over to pull themselves free from this curse, that they had sought to estrange themselves from their brother's bloodthirsty whims, that they had confronted him and proven to him that his was a path of evil and they had reminded him of the Jewish prohibition against taking a life and consuming blood, but their brother, with the aid of that puny, innocent-faced rabbi with his sharp mind and slippery tongue, knew just how to manipulate them towards the path of murder and crime, until against their will they became experts in the slaughter of human beings, and with their bare hands they had ripped apart the flesh of Christians under the watchful eyes of their brother and the rabbi and had siphoned their blood into the unleavened bread of Passover from year to year.

And at the conclusion of their fluid, poignant speech, which burbled from their throats in two voices but as a single song, the pair of brothers is presented with new yellow tunics to replace those soiled with warm, sour urine, and they are served hot water to revive them, and they smile at one another, for they have escaped the death sentence, and Sharif Pasha praises them for their courage and with his signature consigns them to life imprisonment with hard labour, for he who chooses the path of truth and honesty cannot be condemned to the same fate as those who remain stiff-necked and steadfast in their insubordination, refusing to make full confession of their weighty sins.

Father stands beside his corrupt brothers, and he has no love from his brothers and no love from his son, no love from his fellow Jews and no love from gentiles, no parents to console him in his misery, nor is his wife present at his side, only the burning hatred of his neighbours and his family, and Aslan is amazed to see in his father, for the tiniest sliver of a second, his own distant image, and this feminine image is faintly reflected in his facial features, in the curve of his eyes, his nose, and down around his lips and chin, and for a brief moment an echo of my own, tormented female grimace is there between the arced brows and the wrinkles that grace my father's mouth, and and now it seems as though there are tiny transparent tears twinkling in Father's eyes; but then, in an instant, Rafael Farhi has returned to his customary, angry countenance, and he turns his wide back to us and plods his way towards the Saraya prison dungeon, the Khaham-Bashi at his side, his small footsteps tapping like a woman's.

My happy friend, since those events I have pondered many a time why I have been made to endure the blind, blocked life that fate forced upon me, a long and tortured life written in the Book of Bitterness, and its binding is tattered, its pages in dispute with one another, its lines of print unkempt, its stories muddled, and this Book is one of many like it among my people, the pages torn and stained and burned, carried by the wind, and all share a common fate: to be snapped shut and thrown unceremoniously on to a shaky heap and forgotten to the end of days.

Bewilderment has taken hold of my heart, at God, who has lengthened my days on earth in spite of the blundering path I have followed, and when I look upon you, my happy friend, at the beauty of your youthful days and your gracious, pleasant manners, and as I inhale the breath from your mouth, fresh and pure, I can see in your face, if only for a moment, the shadow of my own image, Aslan as a youth, in the days before the Blood Libel, and my tears flow for this life of his, diverted as it was to the path of the evil, the betrayers, for Aslan erred greatly on his way, while you, you are constant in your silence.

5

It seems to Aslan that a terrible infirmity has befallen him.

His legs quiver, there is a pounding at his temples, nausea begins to bark in his throat, contaminated blood floods his veins, but his body is healthy and whole and every organ in it is carrying out its silent task in flawless fashion, and yet he is plagued and tormented by his deepest suspicions, and the fear that his shaky health will lead him to his deathbed gnaws at Aslan.

Mahmoud places a hand on Aslan's head and with a single gesture dismisses all his complaints, and he urges Aslan to rise from the bed in his chambers for the purpose of attending this last session of the murder trial, for today is the handing down of the verdict; but Aslan is weak, fragile as a driven leaf, and to Mahmoud's questions he answers: No, he has no ache in his throat, nor fever on his brow, nor trouble passing his bowels; still, a deep feebleness resounds in his head and he holds Mahmoud's hands and tells him his days are short, for a terrible infirmity has befallen him to which he shall surely succumb.

Mahmoud purses his lips for he is in a rush to attend to his many secret affairs, whose nature and purpose he never discloses, and Aslan knows in his heart that Mahmoud is unravelling their love stitch by stitch, for nothing but tatters and shreds remain of this magnificent garment made of the finest Damascene cloth and embroidered with their love and desire, the edges now curled and fraying.

This grave and terrible infirmity weakens Aslan and confines him to his bed, and he welcomes the shivers it brings him and the quivering muscles and the cold that sears his bones and the prickles upon his skin, and Mahmoud wishes to take his leave of Aslan shortly, mirthlessly, for it is clear that Mahmoud is displeased with Aslan as he cowers in his chambers and sullies the bedclothes with his thin and sickly spittle, and Aslan is aware that Mahmoud no longer loves him and perhaps never loved him, and he grieves at this knowledge but comes to terms with it as well, is appeased, and he lovingly accepts this fate that has been decreed upon his frail body.

Aslan has but one request, which he places before his estranged lover of the pursed lips and sealed heart: before Mahmoud turns his back upon him and departs from his chambers, Aslan wishes that he might grant him, one last time, just a glimpse of that merciful, righteous woman Umm-Jihan, and Aslan swears that afterwards he will leave this place and set forth for Kharet Elyahud, never to return, but for this moment he requests nothing other than that this excellent and beloved personage sing him a short song, contained and fragile, and that its measured notes be the last melody to accompany him down into the silent pit.

Umm-Jihan acquiesces with that former look of love, and her face forms itself upon that of Mahmoud's, and her countenance, delicate and noble, settles on to his sharp and rigid bones, and she takes my hands with such gentleness, and while stroking my fingers she sings to me one last time our old, shared song, which has been present with us right from the beginning and all the way to the end of this affair, now fast approaching: *To you I will depart from myself / Ya a'aeb an aynya.* And Aslan is aware that these moments, during which he lies dying upon his bed from a mysterious ailment, are their final shared hours, and he swallows her expression so as to recall every line of her face, her bright eyes with the pleasingly feminine streaks of gold, her clear skin as soft as velvet, her sweet breath, her tiny teeth, her long, tapered fingers, the crease between her round and ample breasts, her nipples, constantly erect in his presence and ready for mischief and lovemaking, and they envelop their last song in kisses and elaborate embraces.

Aslan knows, too, that he will for ever long for her soft, engulfing caresses and for the childlike serenity with which she imbues him, and now, when he is sure and certain that his days have tapered to mere hours, he releases her from her vow of love and sets free this bird, this dove of love, to other realms, far from view, and he thanks her for this true love which she imparted to him, and because he does not wish to grieve her with the sight of his sickly, languishing body destined soon to rot until the soul flees, he declines her pleas and commands her to leave his side post-haste so that upon her return to these chambers he will no longer be lying there in repose, for the banks of Elnahar Alaswad will have claimed his body and transported it far from there, and Umm-Jihan presses her palms to him for one last, brief embrace from which Aslan will distil her essence to the end of his days, and when she slips away from there, letting the door shut behind her, she hastens to fall into the arms of Mahmoud, who awaits her, teary-eyed, and Aslan knows that this final chapter of his love for her has come to an end and he wishes to plunge into his mourning.

Several hours later Aslan quits Mahmoud's chambers and he does not tarry even to take his leave of the beautiful views, he simply walks towards his death, to receive the fatal decree proffered by Sulini Elkhakim, the Farhi family doctor these many years, perhaps Aslan will even request that the doctor ease his torment and hasten a painless demise, and as he rambles through the streets of Damascus towards the Christian Quarter he notices on every doorstep and at every turn the malady that has spread through the city, and anguish and sorrows have seized upon Damascus as a woman in labour; the passers-by are jaundiced one and all, sorely fatigued, saliva frothing upon their lips, and the thousands upon thousands of leeches preserved in thousands upon thousands of jars in Damascus will not suffice to put an end to this plague, and these leeches suck the contaminated blood from the veins of the infirm and they swell up greatly as leeches have done from time immemorial, and they die from the poison and are sent down to Elnahar Alaswad, and Aslan imagines row upon row of the carcasses of Damascene citizens piled high on wagons and in trenches, and when he reaches the clinic of Sulini Elkhakim he collapses as if dead upon the doctor's oak desk, and waits to receive the toxin that will hasten his death.

My happy friend, when our family doctor took note that it was I in his surgery he quickly drew the curtains and ordered his manservant to bolt the door, and he examined Aslan at length, taking his pulse and his temperature, and he stripped him of his garments and inspected his orifices, each and every one, and he noted all manner of numbers and letters to himself in the Latinate alphabet, and Aslan was prepared to take his leave of this world and this meaningless saga, and he answered the doctor's questions: No, he has no pains and no ailments, but he is exhausted to his core, his life strength has been sapped and is no longer extant, his blood has changed colour and is not red any more but yellow – sickly and sluggish – defeated as if that of a ninety-year-old woman.

And Sulini Elkhakim's face grows grave and angry furrows form at either side of his mouth, and he tells Aslan of the terrible plague that has erupted recently in Damascus, and this plague has been felling the aged and the infants; already the Maristan Nur Aladdin Hospital is flooded with dead bodies, and this plague affects the blood and is passed from the blood of the beast to the blood of man and from neighbour to neighbour and from beloved to beloved, and it seeps into the body, teeming and gaining strength in secret, hiding in the deepest veins where it works its black magic and sorcery until it attacks the healthy bodily fluids in one fell swoop, befouling them with black and filthy pus, and this pus spreads through the internal organs, to the heart and the liver and the lungs until it overwhelms them, all of them, with its contamination, and the blood transports it to all the organs of the body and immerses them in its poison.

In fact, Sulini Elkhakim cannot determine what malady has visited me, whether I too have fallen into the clutches of this terrible plague; however, upon taking note of my jaundiced visage he fears that this illness has taken up residence in my body and so he orders me to lie in my bed and take a mélange of many herbs he has concocted so that I may gather my strength, and he instructs me to receive the much-needed love I crave, for without it the body shrivels and the spirit perishes and the soul desires to die.

But to where can Aslan return if not to his parents' home, whose windows have been criss-crossed with planks and where thick, choking dust is destroying the rugs, and Aslan, his head covered, rushes mournfully to his house, and in his parents' bedroom he knocks at the door of the closet to scare away the house snakes and he removes from there a thick blanket and he wraps himself up in it in the deserted bed of his progenitors, for his mother and his siblings have long since escaped, and he falls into a feverish sleep and his head throbs with pain and his body is exhausted, and he knows for certain, without the slightest of doubts, that he too has fallen prey to this plague of the contaminated blood, and from the depths of his heart he condemns himself for having been among the first to engender it, and he is willing and ready to welcome its torments and to die there alone as a dog whose day has come, in this manner so suited and fitting to him.

My happy friend, at that selfsame moment the prison guards of Sharif Pasha were leading the defendants into the *qa'ah*, the brothers Meir and Murad whose sentence had already been determined and who were dressed in prison uniforms, many scars slashed across their skin; and the Khaham-Bashi Yaacov Antebi, who was leaning heavily in his weakness upon my father, drawing his last strength from him, and they have been summoned to stand for the final session of their trial, at which their sentence will be handed down.

While Sharif Pasha continues partaking of thick *atayif* pancakes in a sweet syrup, and many types of dried fruit whose pips he spits into a hammered copper tray – the pride of Damascene handicrafts – he announces the outcome of the trial, but first he provides the courtroom with the rational and simple reasoning that led him to this conclusion.

The governor of Damascus points out that if only the decomposing body found in a cesspit near the Farhi home had been placed in front of him, he would not have found the defendants guilty; and if in addition to the body, only their rivals of bygone days had accused them, he would not have found them guilty; and if in addition to the body and the rivals, only the stark and unambiguous confession of Muhammad Effendi had been sounded, he would not have found them guilty; and if in addition to the body and the rivals and the confession of Muhammad Effendi, he had only been presented with the testimony of

Suleiman *alkhalaq*, he would not have found them guilty; and if in addition to the body and the rivals and the confession of Muhammad Effendi and the testimony of Suleiman *alkhalaq*, he had only been made to witness the tears and passing of water of the Farhi brothers, he would not have found them guilty; but since this trial rested on the sturdy, trustworthy foundation of Aslan Farhi's affidavit, the first-born son and product of the loins of Rafael Farhi himself, and since this confession was chock full of details, all of which had been verified through repeated and ongoing investigation and by other confessions and by findings, well, he – Sharif Pasha – found the decision regarding their sentence to be clear and simple, and he had no doubt with regards to its truth and its sincerity, for if the first-born son found them guilty how could the governor himself set them free?

Many years hence people will still be speaking, as they sit on the rooftops of Damascus on pleasant autumn evenings, of how Sharif Pasha sentenced Father and the Khaham-Bashi at once, and they will still be clucking their tongues at how the two consoled one another in each other's arms; and in their lives and their deaths they would never be parted, for Sharif Pasha decreed that they should be hanged seven days hence, at the end of the Passover holiday, in the Saraya Square, and the Harari brothers standing alongside them in the *qa'ah* and Moses Abulafia and the Christians and converted Jews and Muslims could not contain themselves, and they burst out in boisterous shouting, for the time had come for the city of Damascus to burn away the evil in its midst, and indeed there were many dead as a result of this sudden plague that had broken loose and rampaged through the city's quarters, and this was the finger of God, his wrath pointed at his sinning children for slaughter and for sucking and licking the blood of the victims, and if Sharif Pasha had not handed down a sentence of death by hanging then the earth would have opened up and swallowed them alive.

Father and the Khaham-Bashi are placed in a cell designated for those condemned to die and Sharif Pasha signs their sentence with an official seal, and with this it is clear that the affair has come to a close, that this is the last word in the trial, and Sharif Pasha dispatches the Christians to celebrate the Easter holiday beginning the next day and curses the Jewish people, for were it not for their religion, perverted and sinful, and were it not for the act of murder in which they were involved, they could at that moment have been partaking of those stale perforated wafers, so odd of appearance, eaten during the Passover holiday in the company of friends and relations under the trees and arbors of Damascus in all her blessings.

Aslan is burning with fever just then in his parents' bed, and in spite of his absence from the legal proceedings in which the sentence was handed down, he knows full well the fate of this pair of fathers, and the illness courses through him with increasing vigour, sloshing noisily between his ribs until his friend the one-eyed shrew hangs on to them so as not to drown in the riotous waves of disease-ridden blood, and Aslan wishes to assist her, that witch who is now his sole companion in the world, and he rolls on to his side so as to allow her to breathe a little in the cavern of his stomach and his intestines, and his illness throbs violently inside him and gnaws at his internal organs and he imagines himself dead, yet he lives on.

And it is clear to Aslan that he has erred greatly, and his friend the one-eyed shrew, now battling for her life, affirms this with a silent nod of the head, and in a break in the waves, which are beginning to abate, she embraces him, an internal embrace that consoles him, and she encourages his stubborn thoughts that follow, one after the other, that he must atone for all his sins by taking his own life, for Aslan hates life and hates all the labour he has toiled under the sun, for no person will be remorseful over the departing of his soul; on the contrary, all the birds and plants and even the lizards and all the other reptiles on the face of the earth will feel less burdened when Aslan is removed from the world and leaves it behind, and how beautiful will be the world and how wondrous God's creation without Aslan; would that it were possible to eradicate every trace of his jaundiced bones and the foul flesh that will remain after his death, for that way humankind will be spared every memory, every shred of evidence, and his name will be effaced for ever from the earth.

Aslan rouses himself with difficulty from his parents' bed but is incapable of smothering his own life, and his gaze falls upon the crucified statue kept in a niche on Maman's side of the bed, and Aslan grabs hold of this lonely messiah, his house companion, and lo, he looks at the sunken eyes painted brown but faded with age, and they do not condemn him for his sins, in fact they are full of forgiveness and pardon, for many are the sinners observed by the eyes of Jesus, and in his greatness he has made it his custom to atone for all of their iniquities.

And Aslan is overcome with a new vigour and the torrent of blood washing through him grows calmer and Aslan enters the kitchen to bring the holy icon an offering of fresh water, scented herbs and incense, and he knows well how right the saviour of the Christians was when he offered to pardon completely even the whore, and he recalls things told to him by the priests visiting Damascus, that Jesus was abandoned repeatedly by his Father, who would leave him alone in the desert faced with evil, and allowed him to be crucified at Golgotha alongside two common thieves, and who did not reveal Himself even when Jesus called to Him in the heavens above Jerusalem, and in spite of all this his love for his Father was great, and he returned to his Father's fold, for it is pleasant and good for a father to shield his son under his wing, and it seems to Aslan that beneath its drooping nose the figure of crucified Jesus is smiling his first, wan smile.

Although Aslan recalls the severe warnings issued by the Jewish elders of Damascus not to take heed of the gentiles' creeds, nor to be drawn to them or fall prey to their false enchantments – their pork-filled pots, their sculptors' sins, the deceit of their graven images – and although it had been told to him what the Christians had perpetrated upon the Jews, how they had slaughtered them in the lands of Europe and other countries, he nonetheless was drawn to this dreamy and tormented youth, for Jesus' only intent was to improve the lot of humankind and win the love of his fathers, both the carpenter, who had abandoned him from infancy, and the One in Heaven, who had abandoned him in his adolescence, and in his abundant benevolence he would gather Aslan in his arms and forgive his wickedness.

How sad, how wretched was that Passover holiday of the year five thousand; six hundred, when all awaited the coming of the Messiah and lo, there came no messiah, no king, no resurrection, no redemption of the Children of Israel, only shame and disgrace and heart-grief and low spirits and dejection.

My happy friend, the Seder night of Passover fell that very evening, but in the whole of Kharet Elyahud not a peep was heard: not the sound of the reading of the Haggadah, not the sound of the hard and fragile unleavened bread crunching between the jaws of the Jews, only a deathly silence reigned, and if there was a tiny band of Torah scholars in some hidden corner of a yeshiva somewhere in the Jewish Quarter, well, they carried out the Seder meal in whispers, in tears, spewing their fury for the gentiles while at the same time quivering in fear of their lives, and in our home and its many rooms there was not a soul but Aslan and the crucified one, and they wished to help one another, Aslan by bringing many offerings to him where he remained nailed to planks of wood and by allowing him to rest upon costly pillows placed on his parents' bed; and the icon of Jesus by the light of reason and assurance that he beamed upon Aslan, this light the final refuge in the face of agony – gruelling, excruciating – and they embraced one another, the statue's fingers resting upon Aslan's eyelids, and they consoled one another on the bed of his mother and father, and his friend the shrew added her blessings, for the thing was very good in her eyes.

And in the Saraya prison the prisoners are carrying out their Seder night in disputation and conflict; the butchers and the gravediggers curse one another and feuding families blame one another and all the Jews wish upon their brethren the plagues that were visited upon the Egyptians, rivers flowing with blood, and an onslaught of lice, and the death of the first-born sons, and there are still children incarcerated there, more tearful even than usual, and they recite from memory the promises of the God of Israel to deliver the Jews from slavery to freedom, from darkness to light, and the Saraya guards oppress them and do not permit them to remove the copper bowls from their heads.

And in the tiny cell of those condemned to die the Khaham-Bashi Yaacov Antebi is filling up with new life at the prospect of his holy death, and he recites to my father from the Torah and he searches with a candle for any last crumbs of the leavened bread forbidden during the Passover holiday, and he burns them thoroughly and declaims from the Haggadah from beginning to end, recalling the deeds of Rabbi Elazar and Rabbi Tarfon, and in the highest of spirits, wondrously joyful, he passes Father an imaginary Seder plate, and he laughs his familiar laugh of former days as he savours the invisible bitter herbs and makes a blessing over the hard-boiled egg of his imagination and drinks the four cups of wine and samples the Passover cake and eats from the sweet *kharoset*, and their taste is true and sincere on his tongue, and he lays a piece of cloth on his shoulder and recites from the Passover ceremony, Their kneading troughs are bound up in their clothes upon their shoulders; but Father does not give in to this game and does not respond to his questions, *Min wein jai ulawein rayekh*, From where do you come and to where goeth you; instead, a heavy Aslanish feebleness befalls him, and his large body and its well-known portliness plunge down, down, to the floor of the cell that is blacker than black, and he no longer pays heed to Rabbi Antebi, who is tempting him to take a bite from the leg of lamb he has conjured with the power of his words, nor does Father bother to refuse the many pots of multi-hued rice placed before him in silence, yellow rice coloured by saffron and grey rice coloured by beans and red rice coloured by tomatoes, and he does not taste the *kusa makhshi* or the *riz ubamyeh*, the stuffed marrows and the rice with okra; and Aslan and the crucified one, splayed across the parental bed, feel a light stabbing, a tiny incision, and they can picture Rafael and Yaacov at the bottom of the pit that is the Saraya prison dungeon, and at each incision, my happy friend, we would pray for some solution to this saga that had became so unnecessarily tangled, and if it were possible we would have rolled it backwards, rescued it from its snarls, disengaged it from its knots and cut it short in its infancy, at its inception, at the point of the original sin of bringing into the world a bleating, breathing overgrown baby whose body would one day sprout copious hair and who would be known by the name of Aslan son of Rafael Farhi.

6

nd when a spirit of desperation and nullity settles on
Aslan, and when the cords of death surround him and
the pains of the underworld seize him, he consoles
himself with the organ that brought upon him all his troubles
and ruin, and while massaging it he conjures visions to please and
comfort his pining soul, but the organ does not lift its head, does
not stand erect in its glory as in bygone days, even when incited
by thoughts of Umm-Jihan or Mahmoud; it remains flaccid, lazy
and feeble like Aslan himself, and Aslan yearns to deliver his soul
from death and his eyes from tears, so that he may extract this
final pleasure from the enfeebled organ, return to his original,
childish, love, to the first step on his path to hell and delight,
namely the Jewish boy whose name is Moussa, and though his
image is faded a trace of the memory of his scent remains in
Aslan's nostrils, and he is visited by the sounds of their play, and
Aslan is catapulted to those distant, other years before he became
entangled with all manner of troubles, and once again he is that
boy sharing a secret with a friend, surrounded by other children
who mock them.

Other images from his life pass before his eyes faster even than
the rubbing and massaging motions he is applying to his organ, and
he wishes to suck the marrow of life from these memories, imbibe
the blood of his infancy, and now he is a chubby-kneed babe or a
pampered boy clinging to his mother's skirts, acquiescing to her

traitorous affections and draping himself with her soft scarves, and Aslan finds himself nostalgic for the scent and the touch of that woman and her fine breasts, for many days have passed since he has seen her last, and he recalls the love she would give him, and the lyrical voice with which she sang him lullabies whose words he did not comprehend, and he wishes to hold fast to these slivers and fragments that revive his soul, but his illness returns and grows stronger, quashing his manhood risen ever so briefly, and the contaminated black pus fatigues and weakens his body and he ceases his onanism and gathers unto himself the statue of the saviour so that he may cry upon its wooden shoulders.

When his friend the one-eyed shrew hears the bitter sobs of his lamentations as Aslan mourns his life, she hastens to press his ribs to find out how he is, and Aslan responds to the questions of his intestinal resident and lo, her words are consolatory and pleasant, not capricious or evil-minded, and she encourages him to gird his loins as a man and combat this wicked illness frothing in his veins, and the one-eyed shrew seems now to him sincere and full of goodwill, her voice no longer shrieks as it did in the past, but is quiet and mothering, and Aslan wonders whether the shrew is truly one-eyed or whether the dusky gloom of her cave-like residence has covered her eyelids with a thick and delusive layer of filmy blackness and her damaged eye is as sharp and well-honed as her healthy one.

And this intestinal resident, who ekes out her days among the ribs of all Jewish men, goads him to form a connection with his new friend – a Jew, and afflicted just like Aslan – for Jesus is a good and loyal friend, and if Aslan truly and wholly joins forces with Jesus perhaps his new, true friend will agree to relieve him of his heavy sacks of guilt and evil deeds and sink them in pure and many waters, thereby restoring Aslan to bygone days when he was clean of sin and iniquity.

Her words are good and pleasant in Aslan's ears and he strings one hesitant word of his own to the next without knowing what will follow, but the words interlace and for the first time in his life Aslan finds himself uttering words of prayer, and his prayers are sincere and true, not a prescribed formula from the worn-out books thrust into his hands by the synagogue beadle, nor a recitation in the style of perspiring Torah scholars, but deep prayer full of intent, which cleaves to his tongue, and Aslan confesses to his good friend Jesus the sins he has committed and the path of sinners and evildoers which he has followed, and he adds a supplication to his friend that he might petition their Father to set right what may be righted and perform some miracle like the ones he has performed in the Land of Israel, such as healing the lepers from their leprosy or resuscitating the dead, and this is precisely what he would be doing for Aslan were he to pluck him from the entanglements of this affair, like a seamstress parting threads that cling together, and he will remove lie from truth and evil from justice and guilt from innocence, and Aslan's first, hesitant prayer gains strength and continues, and Aslan appends to it all manner of promises and oaths and vows, that if his entreaties for a miracle and a solution are answered he will shed the slough of Judaism from himself like a slippery snake and he will assume the mantle of Christian doctrine in all three hundred and sixty-five sinews of his body, and he hearkens to the heavenly voice echoing inside the statue of Jesus, and it praises him for his supplications and affirms that it will indeed bring about this miracle that will put an extraordinary end to the affair of the Blood Libel, and upon the command of that heavenly voice he rises from his sickbed, descends to the pantry in the cellar and removes from there every kind of cake and confection he can find, stuffing them into his body in order to strengthen his soul.

New hope fills Aslan, for Jesus will speak to the hearts of his followers and will make it pleasant for them to rescind the Blood Libel, and he will bring much love to the priests and the consul and all the other Christians of Damascus, and he will rescue Aslan's father and his father-in-law from the executioner's rope and their deaths, and he will absolve Aslan of his terrible guilt, and Aslan repeats his vow, with increased intensity and intent, that if this grand miracle comes to pass – this miracle that seems too remote, too implausible – if somehow this grand miracle comes to pass, if Jesus releases the confined and annuls the edicts and saves the Jews, then Aslan will offer up his own life to him, will devote the rest of his days to worshipping him and praying to him and loving him munificently.

Aslan lies on his parents' bed passing between sleep and wakefulness and back again, and lo, the inkling of a sweet faith overwhelms him, for the Christian saviour will indeed draw from his soul the eddying pus, blacker than black, and he will remove from his blood the frothing eruptions, the disease; and if Jesus does not come to his rescue Aslan will fade to his own death, his limbs withered and weak, and with these thoughts in mind he falls into a long, feverish slumber of nightmares.

A week passes, then another, then a month, and the wooden statue in the image of Jesus lies upon the headrest of Aslan's sickbed, his deathbed, and not only have the heavens failed to answer his prayers but a new evil, worse than its predecessors, has visited the city of Damascus.

As if the trial of the pair of accused murderers, whose public hanging in the Saraya Square has been inexplicably postponed time and again, were not enough, and as if the outbreak of the terrible plague that descended upon all quarters of the city and claimed many victims were not enough, now people were agog and aghast over an impending war whose war-drums were already resounding in the pale grey skies that were dawning after the difficult winter.

The reason for this war, my happy friend, was that the rebel Muhammad Ali had rent asunder the yoke of authority of the Turkish sultan and had broken the bar of Damascus and conquered many other great lands, and now the wrath of the Europeans was upon him, and they exhorted the Turkish Sultan Ibd Almajid Khan, a thin and haggard youth of sixteen prone to fainting spells, to stand up to the ageing Egyptian rebel and reclaim the severed pieces of his empire, and with their assistance he had assembled his forces and was threatening to recapture his plundered lands and put to death Sharif Pasha and his aides, leaving none among them alive.

And a terrible dread descended upon the Christians, for they had enjoyed the flattering protection of Muhammad Ali and his governors, who permitted them to wear white turbans and chime the bells in their churches, and now this awful darkness was engulfing the city and Sharif Pasha's clerks were recruiting young men and forcibly conscripting them into service for the purpose of fighting the young sultan's armies that were now gathering in the north.

Aslan does not bother to conceal himself from those wishing to ensnare men for battle and slaughter, he does not spirit himself away to his secret hiding place between the walls of the cellar, in the company of the house snakes; instead he repeats to himself, again and again, with great purpose and deep suppli-cation, the prayerful chant he composed, and he is filled with dread at the thought that perhaps not only are his prayers not being answered, but that the invisible, ethereal angels swarming round him seek to prevent them from reaching a heedful ear, for they despise and detest Aslan and wish him great suffering at the hands of this malady that has no cure, and that he may bear witness to the results of his many, many sins.

And lo, my happy friend, it became known to me only many years hence that at that very same period in time, when it seemed the death by hanging of the two accused prisoners was imminent and the world was blacker than black, that many strange events and deeds were taking place in foreign lands, for word of the incident that began with an act of copulation with the monk Tomaso that stormy night had reached the Houses of Parliament in Paris, Vienna and London, and many were those discussing the trial – some denouncing the Jews, others defending them – and in all manner of journals and daily presses throughout distant Europe long, detailed articles were being written about the crimes of Rafael Farhi and about a small glass bottle in which blood had been collected, and even the name of the informant was provided, Aslan Yehudah son of Rafael Farhi, and massive riots erupted across Europe in the wake of this trial and this Blood Libel, and writers and journalists from far and near descended upon Damascus in order to relate all that had taken place in this ordeal of blood and slaughter.

Furthermore, as I was to learn much later, urgent missives were dispatched to kings and sovereign rulers asking them to plead with the Egyptian governor Muhammad Ali to commute the sentence, and among those who came to the aid of Damascus Jewry were members of the hugely wealthy Rothschild family, who appointed a fiery French lawyer by the name of Adolphe Crémieux, and a portly hook-nosed English gentleman by the name of Moses Montefiore, and they sailed to Alexandria with the greatest of speed for a tête-à-tête with Muhammad Ali.

My happy friend, wondrous are the ways of our lord Jesus, at times revealed and at times concealed, and he always stands ready to aid his believers and does not abandon them and is prepared to embrace them with welcoming arms.

For indeed, in a manner whose details are a mystery to me to this very day, Aslan's prayers were answered and a great miracle befell the Jewish people: a sealed envelope was sent in tremendous haste by Muhammad Ali in Alexandria to Sharif Pasha in Damascus, and it contained orders to liberate forthwith and unconditionally all of the incarcerated.

The first to be set free from prison were the children, sixty-three of them in number, the copper basins removed from their heads, their runny noses wiped clean of yellow snot, black blindfolds lowered from their eyes, their gait unsteady and troubled, for throughout their imprisonment they had been allotted a mere twenty *drahim* of bread and a tiny portion of water each day to keep them alive.

The children walk in single file, holding hands, as they emerge from the prison to their mothers waiting in the Saraya Square, but there are no exuberant cries of joy as at the end of a day of studies at the Talmud Torah, nor shrieks of happiness or calls for open-air games, rather, their heads are bent and their noses snuffling, for their souls are scarred and cleft and a deep, adult grief has taken seed in their eyes, and when they reach Azm Palace Aslan catches sight of them and it is then that he learns that his prayers have been answered and the end and conclusion of this affair are drawing near.

Once the liberation of the children has been completed an order is given to open the prison gates to release all the other prisoners who did not stand trial, and these are the butchers and the gravediggers and the hapless passers-by who fell unwitting prey to ambushes set by Sharif Pasha or the French consul and were consigned to the dungeons for this extended period, and their beards have grown exceedingly long and their shoulders are hunched and their voices hoarse and their fingers withered, and the Jewish expression on their faces – of grief, and wandering, and exile – is more apparent than ever, and Aslan understands that like him they, too, have a one-eyed shrew for a friend, and these shrews wave a greeting to him from between the men's ribs and express their deepest gratitude for his prayers that have been answered, and Aslan returns their greetings with a smile though it delights no one other than the shrews to see him; rather, these mournful, exhausted men emerging single file from the Saraya prison remain silent as they take the hands of the spouses and children awaiting them, and if one among them catches Aslan's gaze he turns his head and mutters a curse, for great is the sin of this traitor.

The doors of the homes of Kharet Elyahud are open to welcome the return of its fatigued population of males, yet there is none among them who celebrates this unexpected salvation, for once the surprise command had been issued by Muhammad Ali and transported by a swift caravan of camels from Alexandria to Beirut and on to Damascus, and once the missive had been presented to the disbelieving Sharif Pasha instructing him that he must grant a sweeping clemency to all the Jews, then the fate of these Jews was transformed and they emerged from slavery to freedom, from darkness to light, from death to life; and yet, as they arrive at the gates to the Jewish Quarter, they remain distraught and reserved, greatly frightened by the arbitrariness of the sovereign ruler.

And from his place in the mosque next door to the prison, the Islamised Jew Muhammad Effendi gazes at the lengthy procession of his Jewish brethren and he hastens, though fearful, to learn whether the rumour is true, that the pathways have opened and the gates have been breached and the way paved, for this is the hand of God, the God of the Jews, and he casts off his white turban and goes out to them and they receive him, silent, allowing him to join their ranks homeward-bound to Kharet Elyahud, whose gates are thrown wide open.

As the procession marches on, the bars of the cell holding the Khaham-Bashi are opened, and his body is crushed, his eyebrows shaven as a sign of humiliation and from his ears grow long, white, lifeless hairs, and his glory has become thin and his flesh lean, and he emerges from the prison dejected, stooped like an alms gatherer in a city of ghosts, not as one cleared of blame but as one granted a clemency of benevolence, and two young Jews hasten to support him, and in no time his daughters come to join him from their strange and scattered hiding places, and as he watches the long, silent procession of people with slashed hands and cracked kneecaps and carrying no belongings, Aslan discerns that Moses Abulafia has slowed his pace so that his dear old friend will catch up to him, and now they are marching together, side by side, Abulafia still in his Muslim robe and the Khaham-Bashi in his filthy tatters, and for a brief moment Aslan can see how their shoulders touch and the impurity upon Moses Abulafia falls away, along with every hint of the confrontation and the lies and the abuse that were hurled like muck, all of it is swept down to Elnahar Alaswad and washed away to a place far distant, and Aslan, too, wishes to join the procession, but how deep is the chasm that gapes between him and the marchers, and how could he ever hope to cross it?

The last to emerge from the prison are the Farhi family, and they walk as one, the brothers weaving and blending among themselves so that Aslan does not know which is his father, and it is as if he has already forgotten the contours of his father's face and his gait and the timbre of his voice, and a deep shame arises in Aslan for all his deeds, and the quiet of the silent procession shouts out his guilt as though these many feet and these stooped backs have only one purpose, and that is to point out, for all to see, this stubborn and rebellious son, this traitor and betrayer, and their clemency is his sentence, their liberation the seal of his fate in death.

And when the doors are opened and the house fills with the old familiar noises and his mother and his sister and his brother and even the manservant return, battered and beaten but alive and healthy, Aslan sequesters himself in the servants' room and does not go out to greet them, but he hears their communal tears and their bereavement for Uncle Joseph, and they remove the criss-crossed planks from the windows and they rinse the fountains with new, fresh water and they rake the leaves from the orchards that have clogged the courtyard, and each and every one does his part, not a one shirks from labour, and quite slowly, shards of laughter steal their way back into their lives and they resume their pleasure in one another, and Aslan's parents embrace and kiss, and his younger brother, whom he has not seen for so long, regards them with knowing, mature eyes, and it is as if his older sister's infamous fury has dimmed, and the manservant prepares a light evening meal for them to partake under the apricot tree now beginning to blossom, and Aslan shuts himself inside the servants' room and with tremendous strength attempts to squeeze out of himself his tears, to let them flow to the water from the latrines and the evil depths, but he is unable to extract anything from his body but a single, dry cough and a throttled gurgle from his throat.

7

The war anticipated by all broke out a short time later and was brief and blood-splattered, and the young Turkish Sultan Ibd Almajid Khan, so prone to fainting spells, dispatched his many forces to engage in battle with Muhammad Ali, and the nations of the world supported him and offered assistance in the task of restoring freedom and his courtiers encouraged his fighting spirit, and the greedy Egyptian rebel sent many of his sons to defend the lands he had plundered, and these were faced with tens and hundreds of thousands of the Turkish sultan's troops reinforced by garrisons from England and Austria and Russia and Prussia; thus the men were squared off against one another in long lines, and when the sign was given they approached each other at a gallop and clouds of dust filled the arenas of battle near Beirut and Damascus, and their skirmishes ensued for many long hours and they beat one another brutally and showed no pity for these precious manly bodies – not for their stubble-studded cheeks, nor their low and pleasant vocal chords hidden deep in their throats, not even for that sweet organ always ready for acts of pleasure and love – trampling all these into a single colourless mash, first with shots and the firing of artillery shells and finally, sleeves rolled back, uniforms in shreds, exchanging powerful bare-handed blows, each man grabbing hold of his comrade and roaring in his ears until both fell dead, some by strangulation, some bleeding to death, some through sheer exhaustion.

And when the dust clouds of this brief war dissipated, the young sultan's grand victory was known to all, and the massive armies of Ibrahim Pasha, from among the regiments of Muhammad Ali, fled southwards to Egypt and all the young men fell in the streets, and all the men of war were cut down, and they abandoned Aleppo and Damascus and Tiberius and Acre and Jaffa and Jerusalem to their former owners, rightful and desired, and Sharif Pasha, governor of Damascus for the seven years of Muhammad Ali's reign, gathered his aides urgently and ordered them to spirit him secretly out of the fire-rampaged palace, but Muhammad Ali's emissaries beat him to it and forced him to follow them into a side room in the palace where they fell upon him at once, and after binding his body with thick ropes and gagging him with a black handkerchief they smuggled him away to Egypt where he would be tried by Muhammad Ali, who was sorely suspicious that his subordinate had betrayed him.

Several days later the armed forces of the Great Powers entered the city of Damascus with pomp and circumstance, among them troops of the Turkish sultan and many English soldiers, and the Muslims welcomed them and their commander, Augustus von Jochmus, with sweets and rice and cheers, and great was their joy at the end of Egyptian rule, for the Egyptians had debased themselves before the Christians, had allowed the infidels to raise their heads high and sound their church bells and ride through the city on horseback, and now, at last, order would be restored.

The first order issued by the new Turkish governor of Damascus, Yusuf Ahmed, with the blessings of the young sultan, was to cleanse the city of its diseases, for the plague had claimed so very many victims, and he authorised the temporary diversion of the River Barada to flow into the numerous sewage canals linking the buildings throughout the length and breadth of the besieged city, and masses of men strained their muscles to the limits in order to erect provisional dams that would force the water to wind its way to the valleys and the streams flowing underground, and Aslan peered through a crack in the wall of his father's home into the street, where a great horde of beggars and curious onlookers had assembled to watch this wondrous display after so many years of neglect, and the water rose suddenly from afar and the River Barada roared in upon them with great speed, sweeping through and overflowing, reaching as high as a man's neck, wings of water outstretched, and the flow of the river is strong and abundant and it fills the channels and gushes over the banks, and the waters are clear and blue and fresh and in one thunderous swoop they cascade through fetid Elnahar Alaswad, and with the meeting of the two rivers, the debris and the bones and the rats in residence for such a very long time are swept away, uprooted from their filthy abodes and transported downriver with the force of a cleansing volcano outside the city gates, to the poor farmers whose lands are mortgaged and whose herds are enslaved, and in their turn these poor farmers laud the many waters come to irrigate their wretched plots of land, enabling them to grow the most sumptuous tomatoes and aubergines.

And the river descends upon the Farhi household and the fountain sprays its waters once again and the manservant irrigates the jasmine bushes and the lemon trees, and at eventide, when Father returns home after a long day of commerce, he removes his cloak and shows his family the wounds that have not healed, the snaking scars from the *kurbach* lashings and the raw, seared skin left exposed from toenails torn from the toes, and Maman hastens to massage the damaged skin, spreading upon it unguents that she had used, in better days, for her own grooming, and Father sighs deeply, and slowly his body mends and his shorn nails grow back to cover the raw skin and his blue bruises lighten and disappear, and if Father awakens in the small hours of the night, his heart pounding and his eyes dark and black and his muscles tense and his sweat dripping, then Maman covers him with a blanket and reassures him in a light whisper that he is back in his own home, his magnificent family estate, and she flutters lemon blossoms under his nostrils and smears his lips with anisette.

And it seems to Aslan that his family is learning the pleasure of their great wealth and their spacious home, and it is as if a new-found spark of wisdom lights their faces, even that of his sister, whose blue gaze bemoans her lack of a groom, and she seems more clever, more reasoned, more beloved to him now, intelligence emanating from her visage, and his younger brother Meir has ceased playing his childhood games and is now a quiet, pensive youth, and when a sad spirit settles upon Aslan, and he takes to his room and sobs, he knows not why, and he seeks to comfort himself with words of consolation and encouragement, for Egyptian rule has ended and its evil representatives have been heaved from the city, and now the Jews can expect times of peace and pleasantness for endless generations to come.

Aslan overhears his parents whispering to one another and he pricks his ears to discern the meaning, and he learns that they wish to uncover the root of the evil that befell them and the acts of envy and evil that plagued them, and Father tells Maman of the matters that the Khaham-Bashi preached to him during their long weeks of imprisonment, how they have neglected their religion and their tradition, and with Maman's agreement he removes the crucifix hidden under her many pillows and snaps it in half, and with his own hands he sweeps up all manner of incense and burnt offerings meant for the statuette and dumps the lot of it down that cesspit from which the bones of the donkey were exhumed, and they descend to the good and winding river as it perseveres in running its course under the city streets, and the eddying water whips the broken statue to and fro and submerges it to the depths, and lo, that very same messiah that had provided so much aid to Aslan and was his true love and the first friend not to abandon him was plummeting down the slopes of refuse and sewage just like Aslan himself, to the absolute bottom, to the ebb, to the hush and stillness, but Aslan knows that the tiny wooden hands and the tiny wooden head of the statue will float to the surface of the water and the daughters of the poor farmers will mend his broken parts and place him in the wall of their home.

And after three days and three nights during which the cold waters of the River Barada flowed through every quarter of Damascus and left them clean, the new governor ordered that the river be restored to its natural course, and the city's doctors announced that the plague had abated, that it was dissipating and disappearing, and the health of Aslan's own family improved immensely and they grew round and fleshy, their cheeks rosy, their appetites aroused, and it was clear that they enjoyed the company of one another.

However, the exception to all this, my friend, was, as always, Aslan, and he is not a partner to their laughter nor recipient of their pleasures, the members of the household are united in their treatment of him and they do not exchange words with him – neither good words nor bad – and they do not lay a place for him at the table at dinnertime, and if they hear him sneeze they do not bless his health, and if they cross paths with him they turn their heads, and he lives among them like a leech in its jar, and he shares eye contact with no one, shares conversation with no one, and Aslan's head droops and he accepts all these torments with love and goodwill and his soul is debased and dejected.

My foundling, my happy friend, one evening at the onset of summer and very near to the end of the affair about which you have written with your very own hand, I was sitting in the servants' room when I discerned through a peephole all the love and happiness with which my family had been blessed, and there was Father embracing my brother and planting a kiss on Maman's neck, and with every caress a butcher's knife plunged deeper into my own neck, for I understood all at once from the swift and cruel thrusts of the knife that it was I who was the evil one and not my family, and it was they who had been my victims and not I theirs, and already I can see by your widening eyes that that which I comprehended only then, after many episodes, at the end of many long paragraphs and sentences, you yourself understood the very first time you drew your quill across the page as you wrote the first paragraph, the first sentence, of this story.

So then I arose, greatly dismayed, and exposed my body at once, my skin, to discern whether my evil were inscribed there, and lo, my flesh was healthy and shiny, free of congealed blood and lacerated skin, and there were no snaking scars from *kurbach* lashings nor bluish bruises nor shattered limbs, yet my blood still pulsed its impurity and my weakness was still great, and even greater was the movement of black pus through my body, not only to the organs hidden deep within me, but also to my very essence, to the root of my soul, that Aslanish spirit – flawed, conflicted – and I can feel it contaminating everything, drowning even my friend the one-eyed shrew in my intestines in filth and muck, and I go out into the street to vomit, but I do not vomit.

I had yet to fathom what I would do with this new-found wisdom and sadness when my fine, blameless parents who expressed their love in kisses announced that they would be hosting a festive banquet in our home for their friends and acquaintances, as a way of marking the month that had passed since their sorrow had turned to joy and their days of mourning had turned to days of celebration, and they wished to make them days of feasting and revelry, and of sending choice portions to one another, and gifts to the poor, and they had already ordered the slaughter of many lambs and sheep, had invited cantors to sing praises to God and to offer prayers of thanksgiving, and Maman, whose eye I was now careful to avoid, was reviewing the guest list and she had pardoned and forgiven all her former enemies, and was prepared to invite her traitorous, lying brothers-in-law and their wives and children, and Father approved it all with a nod and a murmur, and she added the courageous Khaham-Bashi, who was still heralding at every occasion in the Jewish Quarter the imminent arrival of the Messiah, his many followers cheering loudly and kissing and embracing one another, for relief and deliverance were on the rise in that period, and when Father mentioned the names of the Harari family and the Islamised rabbi Moses Abulafia they fell briefly silent, then decided as one to invite them as well, that they would throw off the last vestiges of muck and filth that had sullied their clean garments, would sit and share bread with them in irrational, groundless love, for in the end they were Jews one and all.

On the eve of the festivities, my happy friend, all the invited guests arrive at my father's home, their faces glowing with gratitude, and the many servants hired by my parents serve them wine and liquor and all the best Damascene delicacies, and their laughter blends and mingles in the air like curls of hashish smoke and I spy, among them, my former friend the barber, and he is still using crutches but his face looks healthy, invigorated, and there is Moses Abulafia, a prayer book tucked under his arm, and

I exchange no words, good or bad, with a soul, nor do I approach the mounds of rice heaped on enormous trays or sample the roasted lamb's meat, for I am in the grips of a terrible fear lest I taint these good guests – by my hand or by my tongue or by the breath that wafts from my lungs – with an impurity they will fail to remove from their skin for all eternity.

In my evilness I step away from the throng of guests, better to watch them from a corner, and from my hidden perch they appear glowing and beautiful, attired one and all in their finest raiments, and the Khaham-Bashi, whose thin bones have acquired some flesh in the meantime, embraces the members of my family, and after hesitating briefly he allows his nemeses, these men who withheld his salary – the Hararis – to enfold him in their arms, and the six pauper friends of Suleiman Negrin are there as well, stuffing their mouths, their cheeks swollen with effort.

I sit on the ground like a mad dog, for my body is betraying me: the din of a storm is raging inside me, my heart is racing and I cannot make sense of this uproar, it is as though my illness has finally claimed victory and wishes to shatter my life, this divine punishment descending upon me now for all my heinous sins; and so it seems that my death will not come about by hanging at the city gates or by stoning or by slashing my throat or by strangulation, rather, by this whirlpool of pains and tremors, and I lean against the wall of the building, taking note that this is the wall of the servants' room, its only tiny window locked and bolted shut.

A large group of people gathers round the fountain in the courtyard to listen to the speech of a young British officer, a Major Churchill, who is among the liberators of the city, and he is a handsome man, and tall, his uniform pressed and spotless and spangled with medals and decorations, and the crowd cheers him and applauds with rapture, and the affable officer delivers a speech that is translated by one of the Jews, and he points out that in the course of this affair England has proven that she is a loyal friend to the Jews and that England and her queen have brought this evil to its knees and rescued the oppressed from their oppressors and banished the French consul – that instigator and inciter – and young Major Churchill goes so far as to venture a prediction that one day the English nation will assist the Jewish people in reclaiming its place among the nations of the world by renewing its existence in the Holy Land of Israel, and the many guests, their hearts gladdened with wine, brim with laughter at his exaggerations.

Good tidings lead to more good tidings, for during the sumptuous thanksgiving feast at my father's home a courier arrives in great haste bearing a sealed missive from Istanbul, capital of the empire, and Father opens it with trembling excitement and reads aloud to the assembled guests the contents of this firman signed by the young Sultan Ibd Almajid Khan in which he proclaims that in the wake of an appeal by Moses Montefiore and after having weighed the matters of the affair with great seriousness he has issued an order to all his subjects in the many lands over which he reigns to the effect that blood libels against the Jews are henceforth in breach of the law and strictly prohibited, and the Jews are beside themselves with joy and they swamp Father with hugs and kisses.

While the cantors fill the house with their sweet voices and praises to God, and aromas of fried *kubeh* and roasting meat scent the air, waves of nausea take hold of me, and they sear me, harass me, snipe at me from within, and my throat constricts and my colour drains away so that I am pallid, and I understand that now, with the affair over and done, my turn has come to receive my due punishment, namely a swift death at the hands of my roiling, poisonous blood, and I whisper to my friend the one-eyed shrew that my time has come to die.

I have not yet finished uttering these difficult words, their acid taste still in my mouth, when a whiff of impending disaster, the smell of undigested food, rises from my belly, and I attempt to put a stop to this vileness which I detest more than anything, but the flimsy floodgates have been breached and a thick swill ascends with great speed, foaming upwards in my throat until it spews forth like gushing waters in an unnatural fashion, past my tongue that has grown accustomed to spouting odious lies, past my mouth that cultivates such pearls of wisdom, and it sprays upon tiny flowers placed there to adorn the window boxes, a row of bright roses which I douse with turbid liquid, and when I gulp down a quantity of air in order to mitigate the sour odour of my intestines I am attacked by another acrid wave, and another and another and many more, each one worse than the last, and I rise to escape from that place to mingle into the throng of celebrants, to stand between the two cantors singing praises to God, but the waves are stronger than I, pushing out from inside me, and the stench of vomit mixes with the purity of the cantors' voices.

In an instant several thugs hired by my father to guard our estate take hold of me – on Father's orders – in their sturdy arms, not for purposes of cuddling or lovemaking but to remove me to the far side of the outer wall, into the street, so that I will not sabotage my family's happiness.

From the moment I am expelled from the house it becomes clear to me that I was never on the verge of dying, it was my many sins that strangled my soul, and now, when the suffering of the Jews has been resolved, my health is slowly restored and my breathing grows regular; still, the impurity does not ebb from my feeble, evil-ridden body.

I can still hear the sounds of merrymaking from the feast as I walk away from it, slightly scratched and bruised, and in my heart there is a buoyant feeling of relief at being expelled, and now that the entire city has been washed clean and its diseases have been exiled and its oppressors have fled for their lives, there is nothing left but this final step, that is, to purify Damascus of all the bitterness and blackened pus in my body, and I am overcome with longing for that wooden statue that was hurled into the water and I wish to follow in its path, and my first, original prayer returns to me and I thank the Messiah of the Christians for his help in saving the good Jews from my evilness, and I desire to fulfil my part of the agreement by cleansing the Jews of my repulsive presence and accepting upon myself the benevolent faith of Jesus the Nazarene, and I approach the gate-keeper in the alley that divides the Jewish and Christian quarters and I leave Kharet Elyahud, but I know not where I am headed nor what I will do.

From there I walk northwards, beyond the city walls, and in spite of the grave danger of being attacked by marauding Bedouins I have no fear at all for my life, and I place my trust in the Messiah, the Jew, that he will show me the right way, and I remove my outer clothing and proceed, half-naked, while a spring breeze carries the pollen of many flowers, and my path becomes clear: I will immerse myself in the good, translucent river and wash away my sins to the last of them.

Here the current of the River Barada is swift and frothing and I remove my shoes and my undergarments and enter the water barefoot, prepared to place myself naked and unencumbered before the celestial court, and I await a sign to show me that I have taken the proper action in seeking divine forgiveness and that the terrible evil will be washed away.

I am emerged to the loins in the roiling water but still firm in my stance when a band of priests passes by on its way into the city, and they take note of this young man immersing himself and they wonder at the late hour and at the act itself, for the lad's face is bearded and his eyes have known torment, and they rush towards him, agitated, to fathom whether this is their Messiah come to earth, as it is written in the Holy Scriptures, after soaring through the highest turret of the Umayyad Mosque, and bringing with him the kingdom of heaven and the end of evil and stupidity and bestowing his kingship on his flock of faithful.

The priests remove their sandals and enter the water clothed, and they question the tormented youth, asking him to explain himself, and so I tell them that I wish to be baptised there at this very hour of the night in order to remove my grievous sins, and they proffer threefold blessings and place a warm and loving hand on my head and they bend my upper body and immerse my head in the pleasant, night-darkened water three times so that I may enter the Christian faith, and after that they draw me away from there, with loving arms, to one of the city's monasteries, and I emerge dripping from the water, ready to follow wherever they will lead me.

8

M y happy friend, I have told you of my immersion in the river and my baptism into the faith of Jesus at the hands of the priests, after which I accompanied them to one of the monasteries of Damascus, a proselytising monastery whose few monks were timid and kept to themselves, and they lived together in harmony, tending a pleasant garden of vegetables and red and white roses.

They offered me a bed of snowy linen and placed a soft pillow under my head and instructed me to rest and sleep well, for my wanderings had been many that evening and they were sore afraid that my body had caught a chill from being immersed in the icy river, and they dried my skin and my hair and made pleasant quips about the abundance of fur covering my body, and they asked no further questions, merely wishing me a good night and pleasant dreams.

On the morrow, my happy friend, they placed before me a breakfast of newly picked cucumbers from their garden and homemade yoghurt and fresh baked bread from their oven, and I told them how I had spoken with their Messiah, pleading for relief and deliverance, and that he had come to my assistance and brought about a solution to the nightmarish entanglements of this affair that I had caused to rain down upon the good Jews in my foolishness and vice, and that when my prayers had been answered I had hastened to fulfil my part of the bargain with

Jesus the Nazarene and went to immerse myself in the waters of the River Barada and take upon myself his teachings.

The kind monks praised me for this deed, adding that Jesus son of Mary is prepared to shoulder the burden of all the sins in the world and had done so in the past, for his doctrine was none other than that of forgiveness and atonement, and it was he who had removed my onerous guilt, and after my baptism I am pure and cleansed and on my way to a new life, the life of a believer atoning for his villainy.

I responded by telling them that my sins were black and burdensome, and that a lifetime of purification and atonement and supplication lay ahead but that I could not pursue this path there, nor could I remain a Jew or remain in Kharet Elyahud or in Damascus for that matter, that I must roam to a distant place, and I requested their help in leaving the city, that they might bring me to some faraway monastery, solitary and remote, of their order, and I pressed upon them to hasten with these plans to remove me from Damascus so that I might not come face to face with a member of my family or tribe, whom I would be unable to look in the eye even one more time, and they agreed even without understanding my meaning, and they packed a small bundle for me and placed it in my hands, then they hired a mule driver in the Khan Assad Pasha to lead us away, and we left in the afternoon on several dark and sturdy mules, and I sat among them wearing their clothing, a golden cross glittering on my chest, and when we departed from the city gates we were subjected to a dust storm that blew many grains of sand into our eyes, and I gazed upon that place, that city, and I knew it was the last time I would see Damascus, never to return to it, and I thought about those persons and characters I was leaving behind, and they are now buried in the pages of this book, alive one minute and frozen the next, trapped inside a short description, a fistful of words, their fate bound and sealed until a reader brings them to life, only to be forgotten, after that, by one and all.

Moreover, I know their story has not been told as it should be, my happy and industrious friend, for the evilness of the teller has seeped into the descriptions and into the words by which the characters were created, and all their beauty and innocence has receded, so that it is incumbent upon you, my young foundling, and incumbent upon all who read these pages after you, to rescue the truths from among the lies and injustices committed by the teller in the grip of his story.

My original, impromptu prayer returned to me then and settled in my heart, and I spoke with God and asked His forgiveness for estranging myself from my father and my entire family for the whole of my life, and I condemned my foolhardy blindness in failing to recognise within myself the spirit of love, and now that my mind had settled at last, I was filled with hope of being pardoned and purified, and of realising a long and continuous life of faith.

My happy friend, from that day forth I have indeed devoted my life to the study of Christianity and the priesthood, first in several monasteries in Lebanon as a novice and then later, as a result of my diligence, I was sent to the Vatican in Rome, where I spent seven full years learning the Holy Order until I confessed to my teacher-priests my burning desire to live out the rest of my days in a small monastery where I could pray to our Father in heaven that He might blanch my sins white as snow and send them tumbling down the banks of the river to be carried off to the sea and swallowed up.

After many hardships I arrived hither, at this desolate, windswept monastery on Mount Lebanon where the seedlings and flower bulbs do not survive and the trees are blighted, and from the summit of this hill I gaze eastward day after day at the city I left behind, and I pray for peace for Damascus and all her inhabitants.

Whenever some Damascus-bound traveller happens upon our monastery I am in the habit of asking if he would be kind enough to make inquiries with regards to my family, and it is in this manner that slivers of rumours of their lives following the time of the affair and in the ensuing years have reached my ears.

Thus I was informed by an itinerant priest who heard it from a benevolent woman that on the day I took leave of my Jewish heritage my parents rent their clothes and mourned me as is customary for seven days, and from that moment forth did not mention my name even once until their deaths; they removed my belongings from the servants' room and destroyed or conveyed from the house all traces of Aslan in order to render my existence in the world null and void.

Upon learning the news of my conversion to Christianity, the Khaham-Bashi hastened to extract from the Beth Din a writ of divorce which was presented to Markhaba so that she was thus divorced by law, and within several weeks he married her off to one of the poor Torah scholars, a tall young man of weak eyes and white skin who was as thin as a palm branch but who was faithful to her and loved her deeply, and she bore a great number of children to him and presented him with an abundance of descendants, many of whom grew to be Torah scholars themselves who in turn gave birth to more Torah scholars, and I was pleased to know that at last she had found joy.

Other voyagers have informed me about my sister, who migrated to Baghdad to marry a wealthy widower who fancied her, and about the wedding of my younger brother, Meir, and the five children he raised strictly and lovingly according to the laws and precepts of Judaism, and I would recite their names and light votive candles for them and pray to Jesus to keep them safe under his wings, free from any harm.

With trepidation and anxiety I received news of my family's finances as they progressed from bad to worse, first on account of the ubiquitous Harari family, who had resumed their rough and cruel business practices as before and wore down the Farhis with underhandedness and unfair competition, and later, some thirty years after the Blood Libel, on account of the digging of a deep canal through Egypt designed to accommodate fast ships, and this canal put an end to the livelihoods earned by both families, since the caravans of camels that had transported goods from Damascus to the Indian subcontinent and the Far East and Egypt and Africa were now replaced with ships as fast as fire that passed through the canal and sprinted the distance in a matter of days, and then, to add insult to injury, the mortgage bonds they had loaned to Istanbul were annulled due to the bankruptcy of the Turkish rulers so that the assets of the Farhi and Harari families plummeted.

Late one afternoon while I was perusing the Holy Scriptures, the bitter news of my parents' deaths was brought to me by an itinerant priest covered in dust on his way back from Damascus, and the angel of death had visited them with speedy stealth, taking first the soul of my mother, who was wrapped up in the finest cloth of the gowns she loved so well, and then the next morning, in a flash, that of my father as he lay slumped upon the lounging pillows in his plundered, decaying mansion, already an old man, his strength long since sapped.

I took it upon myself to fast but I was not overwhelmed with sadness, for our king Jesus had informed me of his second kingdom, in which all of our dead will return to live with us, so that perhaps the next life we live will be wiser than the present, and all humans, with Aslan at their head, will be more loyal, more loving, more forgiving, and I will reunite in perfect faith with all those who cherished or despised me in this life and with my family, from whom I parted and remained distant.

And I learned that I was not alone in awaiting the kingdom of heaven, that the Khaham-Bashi Rabbi Yaacov Antebi – who had not lost faith in spite of having been disappointed in the decision of the Messiah King not to bring about his reign in the year five thousand, six hundred – stood ready for his arrival as well, and chose to live out his remaining days in the holy city of Jerusalem, quitting Damascus just two years after the conclusion of the Blood Libel and moving there on his own, his many daughters and their husbands and children left behind, and the Jews in Jerusalem bestowed considerable honour upon him for they knew of the martyrdom he had endured in the Saraya prison and of his firm stance in the face of the devil's temptations.

The Khaham-Bashi met his demise only a few years after the affair and his bones were interred on the Mount of Olives overlooking the walled-up Gate of Mercy, through which, according to their tradition, the Jewish Messiah will re-enter Jerusalem and magically raise up all those sleeping beneath their ancient headstones on that holy hill, and when I learned of his death I shed copious tears for I recalled his light-hearted humour and the way he would rumple my hair, and of all the men of Damascus he was the kindliest, tickling the palms of the children with his ginger beard and making them giggle.

One other character doomed to depart Damascus never to return was the powder-cheeked French consul, the Count de Ratti-Menton, who was called back urgently to the Foreign Office in Paris and dispatched on to new postings in faraway countries and I never again heard of him, or, for that matter, of my old friend the barber, Suleiman *alkhalaq*, all trace of whom seems to have vanished.

Many days have passed since that affair, my happy friend, and when I come to speak with you of Mahmoud Altali my heart still fills with emotion, for that man was the only one to have touched my soul, and in my memory he mixes and blends with another, the woman I loved, and there are times, on spring evenings, when a bewitching scent of blossoms thickens the air and the moon is at its fullest and all the creatures that buzz and slither and float overflow with life and come together in acts of desire and love, and I am flooded anew with longing for her, and her image is true and clear in my nostrils, and I offer many prayers of thanksgiving to our God in heaven for making our paths cross and for His generosity in granting me that taste of the goodness of her love, for numerous are those who live their long lives in boredom and vapidity without ever sampling the juiciness of that apple, while I, thanks to the benevolence of our God and our saviour, did just that.

Countless and contradictory rumours have reached my ears concerning Mahmoud Altali, some of them heinous, causing me no end of worry, some of them soothing and consoling, and there are those who claim Mahmoud Altali succeeded in escaping to Egypt, where he entertained the men of Alexandria with his prodigious talents, while others swear he was captured by Turkish and English soldiers and hanged in an abandoned field on a dark night, his body left as prey for the jackals and foxes, and I vacillate between the conflicting tales about my beloved of yore, and in my long conversations with my friend Jesus I add a special request that, whatever Mahmoud Altali's fate is or was, I plead before the Creator of the World to spare the essence and the honour and the person of that revered and righteous woman Umm-Jihan, for what sin was it of hers to have found herself inside the body of Mahmoud Altali? She was a woman whose every path was of peace and whose cheeks blossomed in roses and whose voice was pure and clean and lucid as the soul itself, so what possible reason and purpose could God have for destroying and smiting with His own hands so exemplary a specimen that He Himself had created and brought into this world?

As for that woman who made her home in my intestines and chided and cursed me without mercy, well, her shrieks and moans gave way to good counsel that she would dribble into my ears, and she always took good care from her perch between my ribs to look after my health, catching sight and informing me of any growth or illness about to wreak havoc upon my innards, and instructing me on which medicines to consume, and even now, in her great old age, she is ever wise, her skin furrowed with wrinkles, her advice still advantageous.

And as for me, my happy friend, through all these many winters I have aged considerably, and I am no longer a lad prone to tears cringing behind his mother's skirts, for the fifty years that have passed have taken quite a toll on me, as you can see by the belly that sags before me and the wrinkles spattered across my face, and when the doctor-priest arrives once every few months to check my health I see clearly in his expression that the remainder of my life may be counted in months, even weeks, for many diseases are gnawing away at my body, the first of which is this illness in my privates that makes passing water so terribly painful since it passes devoid of might or strength; still, these torments I accept with love, for they are but the tiniest taste of the punishment I deserve for my wicked deeds, and indeed, their offspring and descendants – the tortures and clubs and whips and scorpions – will all come to afflict me in the eternal hell that awaits me after my death.

At times, my happy friend, as I lie upon my bed in this small monastery in which we tarry, or when I gaze upon the image of the Holy Mother Mary etched in the coloured stained-glass windows here, I am pestered and plagued by questions: to what purpose was that Blood Libel, and what did its perpetrators have in mind, and why was it that I laboured in such wickedness – so generously, so diligently – to ensure it would come to what it did, and what could possibly have been my justification for hurling such muck at my father and father-in-law, and I think of the lives that were cut short because of me and the tortures endured because of my actions, and all this in a year which should have seen, according to the calculations of the Khaham-Bashi, the arrival of their Messiah.

At such times, when I discuss all of this with Jesus and with God, our shrewish old friend the innards dweller chimes in to remind me of reports we hear from time to time from itinerant priests who inform us of the tempest that broke loose among the Jews of the world in the wake of this affair, for news of it reached Vienna, London, Paris and Amsterdam and it was discussed by all, and they bellowed about the impotence of the Jews, how they had no land and no army, how they were made to bend to the tyrannical whims of those who ruled over them, and lo, a new idea began slowly to take root in the hearts of the Jews, and it was as that English Major Churchill had stated at the festive gathering in my father's home: why should the Jews not set themselves up in the home of their forefathers and become a nation like all the nations of the world? And several wealthy Jews had already pricked up their ears at this strange suggestion and established a handful of settlements for Jews in the Holy Land, where they could leave behind their contemptible professions as tanners and dyers and coppersmiths and the never-ending study of the Torah, and go out into the scorching sun to till the good earth and take up arms to defend their bodies from ill-willed enemies, and I would laugh at the words of the one-eyed shrew, for what could my coupling with Tomaso possibly have to do with the history of the Jews?

Now nothing more remains, my happy friend, but to thank you for the long days during which you have sat beside this aged, wizened priest and listened to all his stories and written down with silent diligence his every utterance and filled many long pages, and never once did you complain of weary bones after endless hours of sitting, nor of my long-windedness, nor of these frequent interruptions during which I was obliged to pass water and then pass water again only several minutes later.

On your face, my happy friend Moussa, the face of a fifteen-year-old youth of intelligence, I see for a brief moment the face of young Aslan, whose Hebrew name is Yehuda, and his face is smooth and glowing, free of wrinkle or wrath, and possessing a purity of youthfulness that is so beauteous to me, and my soul mourns the withering of my youthful visage and the death of the roses that kept me company at the outset, for with my own hands I choked their natural goodness and turned my back on those who loved me, and lo, my wickedness has spread, infecting even you.

Yet even in these final days of my life I have believed that the beds of roses on your cheeks might infect me with their blossoms, and I have been on the verge of soliciting an embrace and a kiss for this old man full of experience and suffering, for you are a soft-hearted lad who has taken not the path of love and who knows not the bed of a woman; you are wholly pristine and virginal, and I wished to whisper in your ear that God has no wrath for the love that exists between His creatures, for this love which Jesus commanded us to celebrate does not differentiate between believers of one religion or another, between one lover and another, between one man and another.

And lo, during these many days you have sat beside me and seen to my every need without so much as taking the respite I ordered you to take, my soul has bonded with yours and I have discovered a great deal of love welling inside me, the beautiful kind of love I felt for Umm-Jihan and Mahmoud Altali, and now, my happy child, that I have laid myself bare before you and exposed the ancient blackness of my soul and presented to you the one-eyed shrew who threatened to bring me to insanity and confessed to you my lies and offences, now I must complete the very last paragraph of this story of the Damascus Blood Libel and entreat you to finish the writing of this story, then take your leave of me for ever and depart from that door and this monastery upon this hill never to return, with only my love locked in your heart.

How salty are the tears sprinkled upon your cheeks, dear boy, for it is the time for us to part, the time to gather our bones and descend to the bitter clumps of earth, and how lovely are the kisses you plant on my lips, and your breath is soft and fresh and your muscles tender and pliant, ready, my foundling, for my embraces like a babe in its parent's bosom, but I must plead with you again and again to leave me here lest I die before your very eyes, before I breathe my last in your arms, for I have vowed to die alone atop this arid mountain visited by none save the doctor-priest who will come in several months' time, and when he does he will cross the threshold and lower my eyelids and cover me with a blanket and chime the church bells to summon the gravediggers from a nearby village.

My happy friend, in your graciousness you submit to my request and agree to leave me alone with my prayers and supplications for forgiveness, and now, with these last kisses, perform please this one final deed which I entreat you to take upon yourself, namely, to carry with you this story of the black-tempered, baptised betrayer still bathed in bad blood and bring it to my brethren, the Jews of Damascus, or what descendants among them remain alive, and tell it to them from beginning to end and beg of them their sincerest, overflowing forgiveness, time and again, so that they will know that Aslan has repented for his terrible wickedness.

And now with these parting kisses, my happy friend, with our bodies pressed to one another for a short moment – one aged and putrid and decayed, one flowering, budding, splendid – with this final act of intimacy, my dearly beloved, happy Moussa, we have reached the end and the conclusion of the Damascus Blood Libel and its telling.

– Signed and sealed by Moussa Abd-Elazzziz in the presence of the Elders of Kharet Elyahud and their descendants, Damascus, 1899

POSTSCRIPT

The writing of this book is based on research carried out on the Damascus Blood Libel – or the Damascus Affair as it is sometimes called – an historical event that took place in Damascus, Syria, in 1840 in which Christians falsely accused the Jews of Damascus of having murdered a monk and his manservant for ritual purposes. All the central characters in this book – Aslan Farhi and his family, Yaacov Antebi, Suleiman Negrin, the monk Tomaso, Mahmoud Altali, Sharif Pasha, the French consul Count de Ratti-Menton – were real people.

The Damascus Blood Libel commenced on 5 February 1840 with the disappearance of the Capuchin monk Tomaso, a resident of Damascus, and his Muslim manservant Ibrahim Amara. This is how Yaacov Antebi described it subsequently in a letter to Sir Moses Montefiore:

> And on Thursday morning a shout went up in the city: Padre Toma and his manservant had left their abode at the onset of evening but did not return there, and the place was opened and a pot was found cooking on a flame and the food was burnt, and no man was present. At once the gentiles commenced with a cry that surely

the Jews had murdered him in order to take his blood for baking *matzah*.[1]

With regards to the central issues of the plot of this book, I tried to remain true to historical events by basing my descriptions on those of Antebi (e.g., the above quote) and on the many historical essays written since then about the affair. The following is a partial list of events that appear in the book by virtue of the fact that they played an actual role in the Blood Libel: the break-in to the monastery – at the instigation of the French consul Ratti-Menton – on the day following the monk's disappearance (albeit without the participation of Aslan Farhi); the rumours that spread through Damascus that the Jews were connected to the disappearance of the monk and his manservant; the search of the Jewish Quarter on the following Sabbath; the exhuming of bodies from graves in the Jewish cemetery; the remand of Suleiman *alkhalaq* as the first suspect in the affair; the recruiting of Mahmoud Altali to investigate the matter; the arrest of Aslan Farhi; the ultimatum handed down by Sharif Pasha to Yaacov Antebi and the two Jewish elders, and the subsequent urgent rally held at Khush Elpasha Synagogue; the falsified confession of the barber under extreme torture that the monk had been slaughtered for the purpose of using his blood in the baking of unleavened bread for Passover; the Sabbath Eve arrest of the men of the Farhi family.

The historical chain of events also includes facts that in hindsight would appear to be fictional, even phantasmagoric, but they are in fact part and parcel of the factual historical record. Thus, the report of the ninety-year-old witch who accused the

[1] This and other quotes from the letter written by Rabbi Yaacov Antebi were taken from A. Elkhalil, 'An Important Original Document Regarding the Damascus Blood Libel', in *East and West*, No.3 (Spring 1929), pages 34–49 (Hebrew).

Jews of carrying out a ritual murder; the colourful character of Mahmoud Altali, known for his songs full of sexual innuendo and his prankish nature, who was placed in detention for having 'made off with a few thousand', in the words of Antebi; the mass incarceration of the Jewish children and the copper basins fastened to their heads; the burial of the bones (suspected to be those of an animal) and the funeral performed on them; the conversion to Islam of Rabbi Moses Abulafia, who co-operated with the libellers; the terrible plague that broke out in Damascus in the middle of the affair; the sweeping clemency – nearly miraculous – attained by the intervention of Moses Montefiore and Adolphe Crémieux; all these were not made up for the purposes of this book but are part of the historical record.

The description of Aslan Farhi in the book is also based on true historical testimonies. A priest by the name of Pieritz, one of the first to report on the Blood Libel, wrote about '[Aslan's] notorious childhood timidity, which he carries so far as actually to refuse to be alone with his wife, and some of the household are required to sleep in the same room.' Muhammad Ali, conquering sovereign of Egypt, noted that Aslan 'is yet young . . . he has not imbibed the Jewish tricks.' Professor Jonathan Frankel, an historian at the Hebrew University of Jerusalem who has researched the Damascus Blood Libel, writes that 'Aslan was around twenty, already married – to the daughter of the chief rabbi, Yaacov Antebi – and clearly did not see himself as made in the same unflinching mould as his father-in-law.'[2]

At the same time, while adhering to the general outline of the Damascus Affair, even to the point of including small anecdotal details – such as the number of children imprisoned (sixty-

[2] Frankel, Jonathan, *The Damascus Affair: Ritual Murder, Politics and the Jews in 1840*, London: Cambridge University Press, 1997.

three), and the speech made by Major Churchill at the close of the affair, and the Nur Aladdin baths, which were an active *hammam* in the city – I have intentionally inserted changes and exceptions into the historical truth.

The subtext of homosexuality in the book is the result of my own decision, in spite of the lack of any concrete evidence in the historical record, the 'source' being the description of Aslan's character as cited above; neither is the conjecture that Father Tomaso met his death while engaging in homoerotic intercourse supported by any historical evidence, even though the accepted explanations for his disappearance are no more plausible. On occasion, rumours of Tomaso's assassination by Jews for ritual purposes still surface in the Arab world, and on anti-Semitic websites it is still possible to find 'proof' of the truth of the affair. Others have hypothesised that he was murdered by Muslims for having insulted their prophet during a brawl that erupted in the Khan Assad Pasha. In fact, nothing is known about the true fate of the monk and his manservant to this very day.

I omitted a large number of factual historical details in order to make the story told here cohere. For example, both the monk and his manservant were known to have disappeared, but for the sake of simplicity and brevity I have left out the investigation into the disappearance of the manservant, Ibrahim Amara.

According to the facts it was actually members of the Harari family (Joseph, Aharon, David and Yitzhak) who were charged with the murder of Father Tomaso, supposedly aided and abetted by Joseph Laniado, Moshe Bechor-Yehuda Saloniki and Moshe Abulafia, while another seven men (the Farhis – Aslan, Murad, Meir and Joseph – along with Yaacov Abulafia, Yitzhak Fijuto and Aharon Stambouli) were accused of having slain the manservant. For the purposes of this book I omitted the accusations against the first group and made the Farhi family the defendants in the monk's murder trial. To them I added Rafael Farhi, Aslan's father, who was not among the direct defendants though he was still considered a suspect, as all the Jews of Damascus were considered to be involved in the affair, as well as Yaacov Antebi, who was deemed responsible in the eyes of the libellers in his position as chief rabbi of the Jewish community.

Aslan Farhi's false affidavit that appears in this book is based on the language of the affidavit that appears in *The Matzah of Zion*, by Mustafa Talas.[3] Talas presents the affidavit and the affair without mentioning that this was a blood libel; thus, I would question his motives. However, it seems that his book is based on authentic documentation, including original protocols of the interrogations carried out on the defendants. That notwithstanding, I altered the contents of the affidavit to make it suit other changes to the plot, as mentioned above.

Supplementary reading on the Damascus Blood Libel (numerous books and essays have been published on the topic) provides additional information, especially about the Great-Power politics of the era, the international aspect of the affair, and its influence on Jewish solidarity and the rise of Zionism.[4] Further, there is no lack of anti-Semitic essays questioning the validity of the libel against the Jews, citing as evidence the fact

[3] Talas, Mustafa, *Fatir Zahyon*, Damascus, 1986, page 91 (Arabic).
[4] For an example of the effect of the Damascus Blood Libel on the rise of Zionism, see *The Revival of Israel: Rome and Jerusalem, the Last National Question* by Moses Hess. Translated by Meyer Waxman. Lincoln and London: University of Nebraska Press, 1995.

that the affair ended in a general pardon and not with a comprehensive clarification of the facts.

Those interested in the Damascus Blood Libel and that period are advised to read the detailed letter penned by Yaacov Antebi to Moses Montefiore in which he summarises the affair, as well as two books recently published: that of Jonathan Frankel (*The Damascus Affair: Ritual Murder, Politics and the Jews in 1840*) and that of Yaron Harel (*By Ships of Fire to the West: Changes in Syrian Jewry during the Period of the Ottoman Reform, 1840–1880*).[5] The latter two offer detailed references to numerous other essays and perspectives on the affair.

I would like to take this opportunity to thank all those who helped in the writing, research and editing of this book. Thanks to Prof. Jonathan Frankel of the Hebrew University and Dr Yaron Harel of Bar Ilan University for their useful advice; to Dr Yaron Ben-Na'eh of the Hebrew University for his instructive suggestions with regards to the background of the period; to Elioz Hefer for his comprehensive research on the topic, which provided me with enormous assistance; to playwright Yehoshua Sobol for helping me set my path; and to Alain Farhi, scion of the Farhi family, for providing useful information. The responsibility for any errors of historical accuracy rests solely with me.

Above all, my deepest gratitude goes to Eli Hirsch for being an editor par excellence – wise, encouraging, sensitive; to my English translator Evan Fallenberg and my agent Deborah Harris for their vital input; to my wife Shari for her encouragement and

[5] Harel, Yaron, *By Ships of Fire to the West: Changes in Syrian Jewry during the Period of the Ottoman Reform (1840–1880)*. Jerusalem: The Zalman Shazar Center for Jewish History, 2003.

support; and to my Damascus-born parents, Rachel and Nathan, for sharing pithy Damascene aphorisms with me, as well as the stories and memories of their childhoods in Kharet Elyahud, which was once part of Damascus and is no longer.

Alon Hilu
Tel Aviv, February 2004

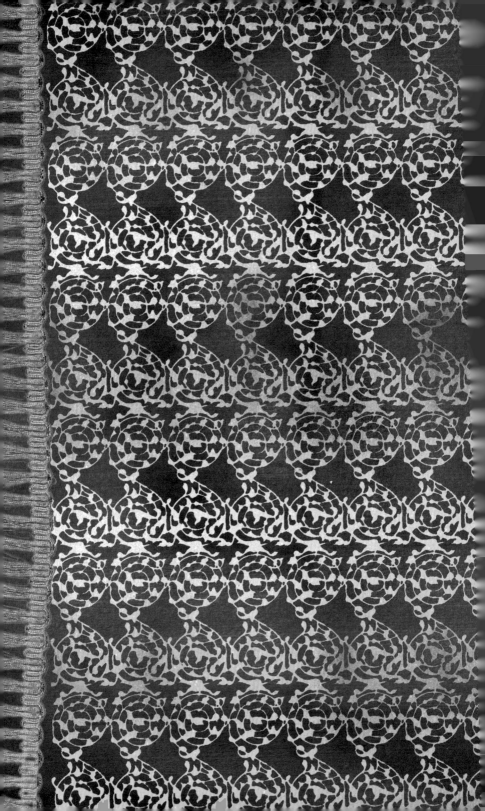